# ALPHA'S CLAIM - BOX SET ONE

Born to be Bound (Book One)
Born to be Broken (Book Two)
Reborn (Book Three)

Cover art by Raven Designs and Zakuga

# BORN TO BE BOUND

---

ALPHA'S CLAIM, BOOK ONE

**ADDISON CAIN**

*Praise for*

***Born to be Bound***

*Alpha's Claim, Book One*

Alpha males and Omega women clash in this fantasy novel about the power dynamics of sex and gender. There's no shortage of drama as alliances form and surprising betrayals are revealed. ~ Kirkus Reviews

The violence, emotional trauma, and complete subjugation were hard to process at times, but at the same time, I couldn't put it down. I wanted to know more. This book is dark, suspenseful, rife with emotional turmoil, and the sex is dark ~ The Romance Reviews

Well, I'm not sure what the hell I just read, but I do know that it's on my Best of 2016 list and I f**king loved it. ~ Summer's Eve Reads

Born to be Bound is one of my favorite books of 2016! I read it four times in as many days. The writing is addictive. ~ SRR

# 1

She had made it this far... wide eyes peered through the narrow slit between wool cap and layer upon layer of dingy muffler wrapped around the lower half of her face. No one seemed to be paying much attention as she passed, ignoring the creature in the stinking, oversized coat when it hesitated at the bottom of broad stairs and looked up at Thólos Citadel. Clutching tighter to the bottle of pills in her pocket, madly gripping her life-line, she took the first step.

For two days, she had taken one of those priceless pills every four hours like clockwork. Walking into what had once been a restricted area, she should have been saturated in the medication, her metabolism and hormones deceived into complacency. A week's worth of food had been traded so she could make the climb up those steps without being torn to pieces.

She was still mortally afraid.

The roar of the monsters inside—the cheers and heckling as her people were stripped of their dignity, then stripped of their lives—turned her stomach, though the acid feeling may have been a side-effect of the drugs. Already sweating, grateful others had covered her in so many layers to hide what she was, Claire took the smallest of breaths, tried not to gag from the stink of rotting corpse that had seasoned her clothes, and walked into madness.

Crossing the entrance was almost too easy. There was no hand gripping her shoulder to cease her movement, no barking Follower demanding she state her business. In fact, the black hole seemed only too willing to suck her in. Over the threshold, the air was ripe with the scent of men; a pungent mixture of aggressive Alpha and some of the more violent Betas who had come to snarl and yip at whoever was that day's entertainment.

Birth titles littered the ground, parchment showing tread marks where uncaring boots had trampled what had once signified a life. A tally of names that had been stricken from the books. The scraps of paper were tossed away to mix with discarded flyers, wanted signs, and garbage.

The deeper she went, the more packed each chamber grew, filled by a horde borne of citizens and the castoff Undercroft scum set free the day terror breached Thólos. They were thugs who had taken up the banner of the Dome's conqueror, men with the power to do as they pleased. Men *encouraged* to do whatever they pleased. Evil men.

She had to be quick, knowing that if the jostling mob discovered what she was under the stinking filth wrapped around her, she'd die horribly, and all the others would be left to starve. One foot after another, back pressed against the wall, eyes darting to and fro, Claire skirted the crowd and prayed to remain unnoticed.

The male Claire sought had a reputation for standing where any could reach him. Where all could see who held power, so challengers could be killed—if rumors held true—with his bare hands.

One could not have missed him if they tried.

The villain who had the audacity to call himself *'The Shepherd'* was massive, the largest Alpha she had ever seen. And not only that… the Da'rin markings. Whatever they were, they swirled over sun-darkened skin as if an extension of his wrongness—animalistic, unnatural. The intricacy of the patterns drew the eye straight to muscled arms, warning all who looked that the bearer was treacherous—not to be trusted.

Before her city had fallen, to bear those shifting black marks above ground had been highly illegal—the punishment: execution. He was a convict of the Undercroft, the one who'd liberated the castoffs, and he was the monster responsible for the suffering of her people and for the corpses piling in the streets of Thólos.

Claire swallowed, creeping nearer, choosing to look instead at the armored Follower Shepherd nodded at; a Da'rin marked Beta, from the look of him. It was that man whose sharp blue eyes caught her creeping nearer. Though diminutive was a gentle way to describe Claire, from his expression, the Beta found her to be nothing... less than nothing. He looked away, dismissing her approach.

Gripping those pills, her talisman against evil, Claire walked straight up to the two conversing conquerors. Seeking the giant Alpha's attention, she fought for the words. "I need to speak with you, please."

Shepherd didn't even look at her, blatantly ignoring the swathed female in her stinking clothes.

"It's very important," she tried a little louder, the sincerity in her eyes, the desperation and overwhelming fear apparent.

How many times had this happened in her life? The total disregard, the blatant rejection...

Claire released a frustrated sigh and clutched her pills even tighter. Standing like a tree, a small sapling in a forest of redwoods, she waited and watched him. There was no way she was leaving until she'd spoken with the only person who might be able to save them. He wanted to be a leader, he wanted to rule... well, they needed food. Pride had only lasted so long. Deep down she knew it would not keep them alive, so she'd come to Shepherd to ask for help.

Eyes trained on the man, on the largest in the room—maybe in the world—she waited for hours. It was hard to ignore what was taking place around her. The weeping of the once mighty reduced to sniveling wretches, dragged in to be *held accountable*. Claire was unsure what they were being held accountable for. All she knew was that everyone unfortunate enough to be hauled to the Citadel was executed, regardless of begging, bribery, bloodlines... nothing mattered to the mob. Not even guilt.

It grew dark. Claire remained, drawing in those same tiny breaths, holding her ground when all she wanted was to run screaming. Pretend she had not just heard a stranger be sentenced to have his skin peeled off *so the world could see what he was made of underneath*. It had grown so late, her sad bravery seemed pointless. Not once had those silver eyes turned towards her. Not once.

Claire had hoped her determination would draw Shepherd to at least glance her way as his follower had, giving her a chance to plead her case. Yet the longer she waited, the more her heart began to beat erratically. For a moment, she felt she might vomit from the smell—not just of her clothes, but of all the Alphas raging in the room—and drew out her pills. With the quickest speed she could manage, she opened the lid of the bottle and pinched a little blue tablet between her forefinger and thumb. Her gloved pinky hooked the dirty muffler, pulling it down just enough to get that pill between her lips. Once it hit her tongue, Claire fought to create enough saliva to swallow.

It was jagged passing down her esophagus, made her cringe, then groan when the feeling of it hitting a hollow stomach almost made the precious pharmaceutical come right back up. Her fingers quickly readjusted the wool to cover as much of her skin as possible, pulling the reeking smell back over her nose and mouth... but then everything went wrong.

The very air altered and a shot of instinctual fear was the precursor of her greatest nightmare. It was Shepherd, suddenly unnaturally still. She could hear the bones crack in his neck as he turned his skull a few more degrees in her direction.

Sweating profusely, feeling so ill, Claire spoke the instant she felt his attention. "I must speak to you."

He had killed so many people. Even through the fabric around her face, she could smell him; more potent than the others, for certain. But the look in his eyes was far more frightening than the Da'rin marking. Hard, unforgiving mercury seemed to see right through her, shredding away her disguise. Shoulders drooping, Claire felt a rush, a burning scratch in her stomach that turned into painful cramping, total terror left in its wake.

Everything had been for nothing.

Sucking in a ragged breath, swaying as if her legs could not decide which way to run, Claire whispered under her breath, "No... no, no, this can't be happening."

Somehow, all the preparations, the pills, had not been enough. There were too many Alphas, too much of their scent in the air, and she had gone directly into heat. Already she could feel the slick gathering between her legs, the smell of it, of something so laced with pheromones that it would not be masked by the horrid stench she'd purposely dressed in. All those hours she'd thought it had been lack of food, the stink of rotting things, and the weight of the cloak… she'd stood there in the wolves' den like an idiot while the signs had been building: nausea, racing heart, fever... and the biggest wolf of all was staring straight at her.

Claire finally had his attention, and now it was worthless.

She was already becoming delirious, panicked, her voice

cracking and accusing all at once. "I just needed to speak with you. I only needed a minute."

That urge—the one she had fought her whole life—was making her tremble and prepare to flee, but there was already a commotion all around. She tried to hold her breath as Alphas sniffed the air like bloodhounds. Shepherd countered her mincing retreat, facing her full on, staring at her with the wide, focused eyes of a predator.

It was his attention—the attention she had needed to save her kind—that drew other eyes in the room. More of that damn fluid began to drip down her legs, saturating the fabric of her clothing, signaling that a rare Omega had appeared out of the blue, and that she was broadcasting a heat cycle.

There would be a riot, a bloodbath as they pulled at her... probably mounting her right there on that dirty marble floor.

Another cramping wave and she doubled over, her pupils slowly eating up green irises until only black with an emerald ring remained. A roar came from behind, tight grasping hands clutched at her arm. She screamed, and the frenzy began.

Alphas were dominant. They had an animal need to mate an Omega in heat. Self-control, they possessed that, too... but not the monsters who were in the room. Not the kind of men who were attracted to Shepherd's cause. Not what the men in Thólos had become since that bastard descended upon them. She would be raped to death, could already feel someone tearing at her clothes.

Her body's response, Claire could not prevent. The snarls and barks only drew out more slick, made her crave to be mounted... but not by anything that was crawling in that chamber.

A howl so deafening she covered her ears, shook her to the bone. There was the sound of a struggle, gunfire, Claire instinctively curling in on herself.

Fighting her response, forcing her body to straighten so she could do more than yank away from clutching hands, she opened her eyes, exposed blown pupils, and prepared to run. They would chase her, she knew that. Alphas were stronger, fast, and being that she was surrounded, one would catch her. But at least she would have tried.

Claire was unprepared to see the amount of bodies already littering the ground. The sight of so many broken men made her freeze, and that was all he needed. In an instant, an arm as thick as a tree trunk came around her middle, and she was carted off, hanging doubled over, by the swaggering pace of a man staking claim... of the victor of the battle. The room still echoed with snarls and shouting, but more so, the pained moans of the few on the ground who were lucky enough to be alive.

Combat boots and familiar armor, all looking as if they'd been cobbled together from scraps, encased thick thighs. Shepherd. Praising Nona for the horrible stinking scarf she'd prepared, Claire fought herself—fought her instinct to smell him—and did her best to repeat the mantra that had gotten her through this nightmare before. *"Only instincts."*

She had to speak to him, had to fight her baser urges.

*Do you think he will fight his?*

The thought made her sag, an action he no doubt took as submission, and not its counterpart, despair. Claire lost track of the distance or direction he had taken her, only noticing the dimness and the strange feeling of being underground. Over and over in her head she prepared what must be said, promising herself she would say it. Even if he was rutting, she would say it.

Even if he would kill her, she would say it.

A door was pulled open on thick metal hinges, whining the way she imagined the doors would in the old-world submarines she'd read about in books, and they entered a room.

Every inhalation, even through the reeking muffler, was saturated in him—in the heady musk of the prime Alpha. Pressing her hand to her mouth and nose, she felt her body writhe against her will, and focused again on the small shallow breaths of control.

Lowered to the floor, her body convulsed in another cramp, drawing out the female's pained groan. She wanted—no, *needed*—to press her hands between her legs. But the smell of rotting flesh was turning her stomach, just as much as the delicious smell of the Alpha's den was driving her mad.

With words made bleary by craving, sentences broken up by little grunts, she fought past the overwhelming desire to spread her legs and grind. "We are starving. The Omegas need food. I have been sent to ask you to arrange a safe place where we can procure our portion before we all die."

She watched him bolt the door with a rod so thick it dwarfed her ankle, trapping her, cornering the Omega for mating. Unsure if Shepherd had heard, she used her feet to scoot away from the male until her back hit the wall, and tried again. "Food… we can't go out... hunted, forced. They're killing us." Her blown pupils looked up at the intimidating male and pleaded for him to understand. "You are *the* Alpha in Thólos, you hold control... we have no one else to ask."

"So you foolishly walked into a room full of feral males to ask for food?" He was mocking her, his eyes mean, even as he grinned.

The horror of the day, the sexual frustration of her heat, made Claire belligerently raise her head and meet his eyes. "If we don't get food, I'm dead anyway."

Seeing the female grimace through another cramping wave, Shepherd growled, an instinctual reaction to a breeding Omega. The noise shot right between her legs, full of the promise of everything she needed. His second, louder grumbled noise sang inside her, and a wave of warm slick drenched the floor below her swollen sex, saturating the air to entice him.

She could not take it. "Please don't make that noise."

"You are fighting your cycle," he grunted low and abrasive, beginning to pace, watching her all the while.

Shaking her head back and forth, Claire began to murmur, "I've lived a life of celibacy."

Celibacy? That was unheard of... a rumored story. Omegas could not fight the urge to mate. That was why the Alphas fought for them and forced a pair-bond to keep them for themselves. The smell alone drove any Alpha into a rut.

He growled again and the muscles of her sex clenched so hard she whined and curled up on the floor.

It was hard enough to make it through estrous locked in a room alone until the cycle broke, but his damn noise and the smell invading past the rotting stickiness of her clothing was breaking her insides apart.

The degrading way he spoke made her open her eyes to see the beast standing still, his massive erection apparent despite layers of clothing. "How long does your heat typically last, Omega?"

Shivering, suddenly loving the sound of that lyrical rasp, she clenched her fists at her sides instead of beckoning him nearer. "Four days, sometimes a week."

"And you have been through them all in seclusion instead of submitting to an Alpha to break them?"

"Yes."

He was making her angry, furious even, with his stupid questions. Every part of her was screaming out that he should be stroking her and easing the need. *That it was his job*! With her hand still pressed over her nose and mouth, her muffled, broken explanation came as a jumbled, angry rant, Claire hissing, "I choose."

He just laughed, a cruel, coarse sound.

Omegas had become exceptionally rare since the plagues and the following Reformation Wars a century prior. That made them a valuable commodity which Alphas in power took as if it was their due. And in a city brimming with aggressive Alphas like Thólos, she'd been trapped in a life of feigning existence as a Beta just to live unmolested, spent a small fortune on heat-suppressants, and locked herself away with the other few celibates she knew when estrous came. Hidden in plain sight before Shepherd's army sprung out of the Undercroft and the government was slaughtered, their corpses left strung up from the Citadel like trophies.

Claire had been forced into hiding the very next day, when the unrest inspired the lower echelons of population to challenge for dominance. Where there had been order, suddenly all Thólos knew was anarchy. Those awful men just took any Omega they could find, killing mates and children in order to keep the women—to breed them or fuck until they died.

"What is your name?"

She opened her eyes, elated he was listening. "Claire."

"How many of you are there, little one?"

Trying to focus on a spot on the wall instead of the large male and where his beautiful engorged dick was challenging the zipper of his trousers, she turned her head to where her body craved to nest, staring with hunger at the collection of colorful blankets, pillows—a bed where everything must be saturated by his scent.

An extended growl warned, "You are losing your impressive focus, little one. How many?"

Her voice broke. "Less than a hundred... We lose more every day."

"You have not eaten. You're hungry." It was not a question, but spoken with such a low vibration that his hunger for *her* was apparent.

"Yesss." It was almost a whine. She was so near to pleading, and it wasn't going to be for food.

The prolonged answering growl of the beast compelled a gush of slick to wet her so badly, she was left sitting in a slippery puddle.

Doubling over, frustrated and needy, she sobbed, "Please don't make that noise," and immediately the growl changed pitch. Shepherd began to purr for her.

There was something so infinitely soothing in that low rumble that she sighed audibly and did not bolt at his slow, measured approach. She watched him with such attention, her huge, dilated pupils a clear mark that she was so very close to falling completely into estrous.

Even when Shepherd crouched down low, he towered over her, all bulging muscle and musky sweat. She tried to say the words, "*Only instincts...*" but jumbled them so badly their meaning was lost.

Starting with the scarf, he unwound the items that tainted her beautiful pheromones, purring and stroking every time she whimpered or shifted nervously. When he pulled her forward to take away the reeking cloak, her eyes drew level with his confined erection. Claire's uncovered nose sniffed automatically at the place where his trousers bulged. In that moment all she wanted, all that she had ever wanted, was to be fucked, knotted, and bred by that male.

*Only instincts...*

Shepherd pressed his face to her neck and sucked in a long breath, groaning as his cock jumped and began to leak to please her. He had gone into the rut, there was no changing that fact, and with it came a powerful need to see the female filled with seed, to soothe what was driving her to rub against her hand in such a frenzy.

The words were almost lost in her breath, "You need to lock me in a room for a few days..."

A feral grin spread. "You are locked in a room, little one, with the Alpha who killed ten men and two of his sworn Followers to bring you here." He stroked her hair, petting her because something inside told him his hands could calm her. "It's too late now. Your defiant celibacy is over. Either you submit willingly to me where I will rut you through your heat, or you may leave out that door where my men will, no doubt, mount you in the halls once they smell you."

A knock came. Shepherd rose up tall before her, staring down with open demand that she submit and obey. Dominance established, he went to the door and pulled back the lock. Claire saw the same soldier, the smaller Beta with the far too vibrant blue eyes, and found him sniffing the air in her direction, growing openly excited at the intoxicating blend of pheromones her slick and sweat were pumping into the air.

Shepherd was right. He had taken her from what would have been a mass rape, saved her from damage and most likely death. He'd listened, though he had not answered her, and men were already salivating in the hall. The understanding of the situation passed openly across her face. Claire nodded, estrous clouding her judgment.

Something was muttered between the men, ending in, "...only Betas on guard."

A tray was handed over, laden with food, another armful piled with bedding and pillows, and she went white. They had already known Shepherd would have her, and had prepared accordingly. The little chat had no purpose but to make her think she had a choice. He saw her expression and the rumble of his purring returned.

She had to eat... he had to feed her before it began. The tray was set on the floor where she crouched, his order loud enough to grab her attention away from where his pants bulged. "Eat."

As she picked at the unseen food, he began to undress. All armor, every under-layer, was carefully removed and organized, the man having no shame about the state of his Da'rin marked body or the jutting cock proudly on display. But more than the visual, it was the smell—the scent of a rutting Alpha, aroused and swollen for her—that made reason completely flee her mind. Everything hummed in that incessant purr, reminding her that he was what her body needed, and she was salivating for it... even if she was scared.

Shepherd began to pace, naked, rolling his shoulders as he prowled, all the while watching her and sniffing the air over and over. "Eat more... drink the water."

Voice downright nasty, threatening, Claire hissed as if he should have known Omegas could not eat during estrous, "I don't want food!"

No, she wanted the thing that was supposed to happen. He was supposed to be fucking her. Why was he waiting? She came to her feet and he was there, the dominant male growling so loud her eyes rolled back in her skull.

A rending of fabric preceded cool air over fevered skin.

He was all around her, tugging away unnecessary things like clothing. The smell of him, the raw sweat, sent her cunt to seeping. Sucking in great panting breaths of the fertile Omega, Shepherd sought out to stroke uncovered flesh, a bit surprised all her body hair had been permanently removed—recognizing the precaution the Omega had taken to help mask her scent.

She was so far gone, her little tongue already licking at his skin, completely high on the taste and smell, that when his finger swiped drops of his leaking pre-come to run over her lips, she moaned loudly and sucked it deep into her mouth.

Claire was so small compared to his mass, easy to move where he wanted. Her back hit the bed, Shepherd standing between her slender spread legs, staring down with wide, hungry eyes at the river of slick that came forth. Little pink lips were spread, the swollen glans of his cock lined up where she seemed far too small to accept an organ so large. With one hand on her chest, petting the twisting thing, Shepherd pressed forward, breaching her slippery womb, and gave a full body shudder at the sound of her desperate cry.

The woman had not lied... she was so tight it made his cock pulsate more fluid to aid her. He only got halfway before she began to whine and squirm. Alphas were big and Shepherd was huge, his girth massive, and there was only so much space inside her body.

"Open for me, little one," Shepherd growled, using his thumbs to stretch her lower lips further apart, thrusting forward, gaining hard earned inch by inch while the female watched a cock as thick as her forearm slowly disappear between her legs.

When the expanding thrust bottomed out, when all her tightness enveloped that hard length... utter bliss. She needed it, was moaning and arching, grinding her sex against his pubic bone. The stretch was divine, the vibration from his purrs, the *smell.* When he began to pull out, she showed her teeth and snarled at a man many times her size. Shepherd seemed amused, and then snapped his hips, burying that massive cock to the hilt, knowing she would squeal.

Claire learned quickly that he liked her little spurts of temper, but it was Shepherd who dominated the exchange. He rutted with the vigor she needed, hard and fast, building up that furious pulse in her core. When she began to roll her hips, eyes closed and lost in the insatiable need to mate, he took her by the scruff of the neck and barked at her to open, to look at the male fucking her, to recognize his prowess.

Those harshly snarled words sent her over the edge. Perfect fulfillment exploded. Claire felt every single muscle in her pussy jump to life, saw his eyes grow vicious and feral, felt his knot expand as he ground in, hooking behind her pelvic bone, locking them as deep as he could go. Jerking under the intensity of the orgasm, she felt that first hot gush of semen, heard him roar like a beast while she screamed. Shepherd came again, more of that copious fluid, her body's need finally met, and with his third liquid surge, she blacked out.

It could not have been long before she woke, as his knot was still binding their bodies together. He lay below her, her body sprawled on top, Claire's ear to his heart. The serenity from the mating was fading and the impulse to fuck was back again. The urge, the only thing that defined her at that moment, grew beyond her when her tongue darted out to lick the salt of sweat from his chest, to entice the tattooed male to begin again.

The instant the knot began to diminish, she registered the loss of precious fluid, felt his seed leaking out of her, and whined. As if knowing her thoughts, Shepherd dragged his fingers in the little river and brought his ejaculate to her mouth. The smell alone drove her wild, the taste a thousand times more.

"They would have broken an Omega so small." Shepherd watched, fascinated, as she greedily sucked his fingers, explaining quietly as if educating a female who should have known better. "Not shown restraint at a scent so overpowering."

She didn't want him to talk. She wanted him to fuck her again. A large hand came to her hair, rubbing at the scalp of the female, soothing her with pets and purrs while the knot slowly abated so he could thrust against her jerking hips.

The second mating was much less frantic, far more fulfilling, and when he had filled her again, Claire began to lose the edge that was making her so ferocious. It was his hands, maybe, lifting and lowering her at the tempo that made her cunt sing, or the look in his eyes, the unabashed lustful pleasure.

*So that's what it was like to mate an Alpha.*

He seemed to know her thoughts, and by the crinkles at the corner of Shepherd's eyes, she could tell he was amused with her. He cupped her face, tender and gentle, and she didn't feel overpowered or forced... She felt mistakenly safe in the delirium.

It was not until a day later, when he took her from behind at the peak of estrous, his full weight on her back, that she sensed trouble. The high had not faded, the slow building fervor of her heat nowhere near breaking... but he roared, began to squeeze and bruise; to restrain her. Fighting the hold, writhing, Claire had a sobering fear the tyrant might bite her so savagely it would scar—that he intended to leave claiming marks.

Worst of all, instinctively, she wanted him to. Her estrous-high mind wanted to bond to the monster that had destroyed Thólos and made her life hell, simply because he was the one who was fucking her.

"And you will!" he growled in her ear.

She told him no, panting it over the sound of his skin slapping against the fleshy mounds of her ass. Sharp teeth came to her shoulder, Shepherd's knot growing bulbous until the Alpha could no longer thrust and she could not squirm away. She screamed in pain and pleasure, sobbing as his teeth ripped into her skin, Shepherd growling long and low with her flesh torn from his bite.

She climaxed from the claiming, rhythmically squeezing, drawing the jets of fluid from his dick while he crooned at her and lapped up the blood.

Claire cried even as he purred and petted, wept from the hazy recognition of the total loss of control she'd so carefully cultivated in her life. When ten minutes later her body sent out signals it was time for Shepherd to fuck her again, he pulled her beneath him and was gentle, caressing the woman he'd stolen even though her tears fell throughout the whole coupling.

When it was over, when he had wrung out another explosion that chased away the urge of chemical madness, a calm descended on them both. Claire briefly slept against a man she did not know, pressing as close as she could, in the exact place the brute expected her to rest.

In the end, it took three days to break the starving Omega's heat. She was sleeping, nesting deep into the blankets covered in his semen and her slick—blissed out. Toying with a strand of her sooty black hair, Shepherd mulled over just what to do with what was now his possession, impressed that the little female was plucky enough to dress in a corpse's clothing and parade into a pack of Alphas just to speak to him. She would have died if he had not found her scent worth killing for.

Claire would also be sore now that estrous had ended, and her mind was not clouded with the insatiable drive to mate. He was certain she would also be resentful of the binding he'd forced. But that was the lot for Omegas, the way of nature. He wanted her, he took. End of story.

Silver eyes ran over the lithe dancer's body she possessed, the Alpha growling at the obvious fact his Omega was underfed. It was getting him into such a mood that, when a knock came to the door, he covetously grabbed what was his and roared.

The commotion—being jerked against a mountain of heat—woke Claire, and she hissed in discomfort. Everything felt sticky, a male pawing over bruises that did not appreciate the attention. The words he spat were in another language—an outskirts' lost tongue, she assumed. Remembering who he was and what he'd done to her, she pushed away from Shepherd's chest, only to feel his arms grow impossibly constrictive. The conversation between the Follower on the other side of the door and her captor stretched on, Shepherd tightening his grip each time she squirmed.

When it was over, Shepherd swung his skull her way, barking, "You need to sleep more." It was not a suggestion, and she could clearly sense he was provoked.

"The Omegas." That was the reason she had come to him... not to have him knot her for three full days.

Mercurial eyes diminished between narrowed lids. Shepherd sniffed her once, then he growled, "Your assumption it would be plausible to have a private distribution of provisions is flawed. It would only draw attention to your group. All Omegas will be delivered into my care and segregated from the population in the Undercroft. Should any come into heat, an Alpha will be chosen from amongst my Followers. Most will be bonded at their next estrous."

"What? No!" Claire's voice was pure horror. "That's not what we want. They need food, not to be made into slaves."

"This is best. You are Omegas, fragile, and it is not your place to decide such things."

Everything about the male was suddenly repulsive. Claire wanted him off of her and tried to scoot away. "I won't tell you where they are."

As he smirked, a scar across his lips made the expression sinister. "Then they will starve and be picked off one by one. That is your decision, little one. If given to me, they would be protected."

"From whom? The very men who are raping and knotting girls who have not reached maturity are the same you surround yourself with."

Shepherd was petting her, touching her hair as if she were not upset, as if she didn't loathe him in that moment, and it was setting her into a temper. When she tried to bat his hand away, he snarled and pinned her beneath him. His teeth went to the crook of her neck and he smelled, growling at the sweetness while using his thigh to pry her legs apart.

Claire felt his cock pulsing against her belly and grew frightened. There was no estrous, no abundant slick, and she was sore. Shepherd didn't care. He reminded her who was dominant in one sharp thrust, taking his Omega with no purrs or caresses, knotting without her climax to urge his seed forth. When the powerful spurts bathed her womb, there was no settling peace, only frustration and tears.

When he seemed to have caught his breath, the unwelcome press of his mouth came to her ear. "You will sleep more."

His fingers went back to toying with her hair while Claire cried herself beyond exhaustion, embraced by a man who lived up to his reputation as a monster.

# 2

It was dark the next time she woke. Though Shepherd was not physically there, he was still humming inside her. The new bond stuck like a greasy string to her ribcage, burrowing steadily. Claire had only heard descriptions of the pair-bond and read about it in the Archives. Each Omega experienced the link differently. Some compared it to a wellspring—an endless offering of cool water—others to a knife wound that tore and twisted their insides. Hers felt like a worm, writhing and going deeper. A subjugation and a leash. She already hated it. It was unwelcome, invasive, and something she could not ignore.

At that moment, it hummed in an off-putting, out of tune twang. Like a bad note on a violin.

Feeling her way around the walls in search of a switch, Claire stumbled into unfamiliar furniture and cursed. The feeling of the bathroom door came under her fingers. She went inside and flicked on the light.

Her reflection stared back at her.

Naked and so covered in Shepherd's semen it was caked in her hair, she looked shattered. In the hazy, blissful high of their frenzy, he'd fed it to her, rubbed it into her skin—saturated her inside and out with that viscous liquid. If he had not spent so much time running his fingers through her hair, she was certain it would have been a matted mess.

Disgusted, Claire approached the stranger in the mirror. In the months since she'd last seen her body reflected back at her, she had become so thin. Her ribs protruded, the bones of her hips stuck out. She'd grown skeletal. But it was not the emaciation that won her attention. It was the inflamed bite mark on her shoulder, the swollen red scabs throbbing.

Shepherd had bitten her so deeply she would carry the scar of his claiming forever.

Tracing a finger over the two crescent wounds, Claire felt shame in her ignorance. She didn't fully understand how the bond was formed. A lifetime of concealing her nature had made it dangerous to ask too many questions. All she'd known was that it involved marking and an Alpha's initiation of the act.

Maybe it was just instincts.

*Only instincts...*

A sinking despair grew in her belly, made worse by the still thrumming string her body was trying to reject. Claire pulled in a deep breath and scanned the rest of the simple lavatory. Either the man was fastidiously tidy or he had an underling clean for him. The sink was gleaming white, the mirror polished, not even a speck of toothpaste on it.

Opening the medicine cabinet, it was almost bizarre to find ordinary things such as a toothbrush and mouthwash. It was the Da'rin markings maybe, the fact he had lived long enough in the Undercroft to garner so many. She'd been taught they were all unwashed savages, less than human.

Wavering between using his toothbrush to get the fuzzy feeling out of her mouth and disgusted because it was *his* toothbrush, she finally just reached for the damn thing. A few minutes later, her mouth no longer tasted like... things she didn't want to think about. Setting it on the shelf in the exact position she'd found it in, Claire turned towards the shower and cranked it on.

Stepping under a scalding spray, she invited the burn, wanting everything Shepherd off of her. Eyes closed, hair under the stream, she let water pour like lava over her body. The puncture wounds at her shoulder started to ooze, the scabs softening from the moisture.

There was only a basic bar of soap.

Every possible inch was scrubbed until her skin grew raw, every trace of that man and his smell stripped away. She soaped up her hair, dreaming of the days she'd had access to such simple things as shampoo. When it was done, she stepped out of the steam, looking at the man's towel, and chose not to use anything of his that might re-apply his scent to her body.

Skin bumped from the cold, she air-dried, wrung out her hair over the sink, trying her best to finger comb the black mess into order. Paranoid about punishment, she wiped down all traces of her time in that room, leaving it as close to how she'd found it as she could.

With the light from the bathroom streaming into the cell of Shepherd's den, Claire found a table lamp and switched it on. In estrous, her mind had not focused on such paltry things as furniture placement and decoration. All she'd seen was where she wanted to nest and the male waiting to mount her.

After all the years of careful seclusion, all the tortured heat cycles spent locked away to prevent such a thing, it felt like she'd lost a part of herself knowing she had been mated... and not by an Alpha she'd chosen.

Now, she was somehow less. A failure.

That humming little cord in her chest pulsed as if to suggest that she was more... that there was *more* now. It whispered that Shepherd had only done what was supposed to be done.

The plaguing vibration made her angry. Desperate, she grasped for any potential relief. The pair-bond was still new, it was fragile. Maybe she could break it?

How often had every other forcefully bonded Omega wished for the same thing?

It was almost laughable how quickly the little cord in her chest hummed, tempting her to accept her position, to submit to such a strong Alpha.

The feeling made her want to vomit.

It was unsettling. The change in Shepherd from the coercive beginning to the unquestioned authoritarian frightened her. He had forced a pair-bond, made a choice that would impact the rest of her life. Alphas and Omegas only bonded once, except for extreme cases when mates died. It was Betas who lived without the bond. It was Betas Claire had always envied. They had no estrous and could still bear children. Betas got to choose. They mated at will, some even with the same partner for a lifetime, not from some device of nature that forced a permanent pairing. To make the sting that much greater, unlike Omegas, Beta females were treated with the same respect as Beta males.

Betas were also second in the hierarchy of the three human dynamics. They had freedom to do as they pleased with their lives. Omegas, so rare and highly desired, had been relegated to a prestige of prized pet—a status symbol for powerful Alphas to claim. They were smaller, no less intelligent, but as their numbers were decreasing, it was an easy minority for the rest of the colonies to force into some archaic ideal. The Alphas ruled the last bastions of civilization, were supreme in every Bio-Dome, every regulated quadrant, every powerful business, and there were a lot more of them than there were Omegas.

Looking over the dim room, ignoring the nest she'd built between sessions of being fucked, Claire wondered about the man. Spartan was not exactly the right word for what she saw... maybe utilitarian was better. Only the basics existed: a bed, desk, small table, and a few other useful pieces of furniture; all mismatching, none chosen for anything other than practicality.

Then there was the bookcase.

Stepping barefoot over a concrete floor, she looked at the titles, several of which were in different languages, and found his collection of literature... surprising. These were the books of an intellectual, many clearly having been read more than once. She recognized several of the authors, Nietzsche and Machiavelli to name a few, only because books penned by those men had been banned from the Archives. The penalty for possessing such literature was so severe, even knowing her government had fallen, Claire was nervous to touch them.

Then again, who but Shepherd was going to punish her now?

Limbs shaky from the toll taken on her body during estrous, Claire reached out and traced her finger over the spines. It was cold in that subterranean, windowless space—a reminder that he had dragged her down into the Undercroft. She abandoned her exploration and sought out her clothes... only to find that every last shredded piece was gone.

She would rather face Shepherd's wrath for wearing his clothing without permission than wait around naked like an odalisque. Digging through the room's modest dresser, Claire found a sweater that would pass for a dress on her much smaller frame. Pulling the grey thing over her head, she was relieved to find it clean, the garment holding only the faintest trace of his scent.

Stomach rumbling, she began to pace, her eyes inadvertently looking toward the part of the room saturated in the dried reek of their combined estrous emissions: her nest. Claire had built them before in seclusion—it was an obsessive part of the heat-cycle, everything arranged just so. Blankets, pillows, all forming the shape that best suited the Omega. That made the females, or in the extraordinary exception the Omega was male, feel safe. The idea of nests had always fascinated her, the way she knew exactly where every piece should fit, the comfort she took in lying in the finished product; even though the ones she'd created in seclusion had never been used to mate.

Betas didn't nest. And base Alphas, or so she'd heard, would mount any Omega without allowing the nest, in a frenzy to begin the seeding. Proper Alphas understood the necessity. Shepherd had let her build it, had supplied extra blankets and materials aside from the usual things already on his bed. He'd even tried to help, crouched naked at her side, tugging fabric and fluffing pillows to hand to her. When he'd become too involved, she'd snarled and pushed his hands away. The nest was her job. He was an Alpha; his only job was to fuck her in it.

Her first mated nest was supposed to be something beyond special, a cherished memory, and not a thing that made her eyes well each time she foolishly glanced in its direction.

There was nothing special about the fluid crusted, sticky arrangement she had woken up in.

Frowning, Claire looked away before she screamed. The door was in her line of sight, one metal blockade between her and air that did not stink of sex. Pacing again, she tried to steady the wave of horror in her gut. The lack of windows, not knowing if it was day or night, feeling trapped underground, was itching uncomfortably under her skin. She didn't even know where she was in relation to the Dome.

The longer she walked the length of the room, the more she wanted out of it.

She ran to the door and tried the knob, knowing it would be

locked but needing to feel the immovable metal with her own fingers. The cry she made was unavoidable. A sad whimper of someone who'd hoped. Someone on the verge of panic. She was a prisoner bound to a man she did not know, hungry, scared, and suffering an unwelcome thread that would not stop existing no matter how hard she willed it away.

By the time her captor returned, Claire was stretched out on the floor, staring at the ceiling with glassy eyes.

"You have been distressed," Shepherd grunted, sniffing the air. "Because you are hungry?"

Blinking at the ceiling, wondering if he could feel just what she was thinking at that moment, Claire glanced past his massive legs to the door that was now unlocked, and imagined she might make a run for it, that freedom was hers.

"I see," he growled, eyes narrowed to slits.

As the breath left her lungs, she admitted, "I am very hungry."

Crouching over her, he found her green eyes had shifted under her scowl. "You woke sooner than I anticipated."

There were a million things she wanted to shout. Instead, all she did was give a forlorn sigh. "I don't know what time of day it is."

"It is the midday hour. Food will arrive shortly."

"Grand." Claire's attention went back to the cement ceiling.

The male went so far as to run his fingers over her pouting lips. "Do you have any desire to mate?"

"I do not," she answered quickly, still frightened from the last painful coupling. It was all Claire could do to fight the urge to scoot away, certain it would only entice him to chase and do it again.

Small crinkles formed at the corner of Shepherd's eyes, the bastard smug. The softest of purrs began, and in answer, her scowl somewhat lessened. The unconscious reaction annoyed her, even more so when his hand burrowed into her hair, pulling gently at the roots, and her eyes mechanically closed with the wave of contentment that came with each little tug.

By the time a sharp knock came to the door, she was a puddle on the floor.

Shepherd called for the familiar Beta to enter, continuing to pet his female while his Follower set out a tray. Claire wondered if he did it just to make a point to another nearby male, to be possessive, or simply because it seemed to appease her. Probably all three.

They were alone again. The giant gave her a nudge to open her eyes, cocking his head toward the table. "Eat."

He insisted on helping her stand, making her touch him more than she wanted. Glancing at the delicious smelling tray, Claire found that there was only food for her. Throughout the meal, he watched her as one watches prey, noting the minutiae of her movements. She didn't like canned green beans, but she ate what was given. She hummed at the taste of ham. The glass of milk made her lips curl just a little.

There was a pill on the side of the tray, a thing she had seen, then forgotten—too caught up in an actual warm meal. Shepherd's large fingers pinched it and held it out for her to take.

"What is that?" Claire asked, covering her mouth as she spoke.

"You are deficient in many nutrients from starvation and recent estrous."

There was no point in arguing. Whether it was a vitamin or poison, if he wanted her to take it, it would be a simple thing for him to force.

As she swallowed the tablet, Shepherd said, "The blue pills I found in your coat pocket. Do you know what they were?"

Disgust was clear in her expression. "They were supposed to be heat-suppressants—cost me a week's worth of food. I had been taking them for days before I came to the Citadel to beg for your help. Clearly, they didn't work, and you didn't help, either. So... as far as I see it, they were a bad joke."

Reaching across the table for her free hand, Shepherd wrapped his great paw around her wrist. All he need do was squeeze and her bones would be crushed and broken. She took it as a subtle warning to watch her tongue.

Tracing his thumb over her pulse, he explained, "I had a lab analyze your pills. They were quite the opposite, little one—designed to prompt your heat-cycle."

Opposite? Fertility drugs... Other girls in hiding had been taking those pills. Dozens of the Omegas could have gone into heat unexpectedly, exposed, just as she had been. That was exactly the point he was trying to make.

With her head in her hand, she heard him outline precisely what she was already thinking. "Someone clever is using your needs to hunt down the Omegas. They know the females taking those pills believe in their effectiveness and don't anticipate they'll go into heat out in the open. And like you, they will be mobbed, hunted down, or taken."

"That's barbaric. You men are so fucking evil..."

Shepherd knew it was a generalized collective of males she was referring to, not him specifically, and did not allow more than a hint of anger to come through his voice. "Where did you get them?"

After a deep breath, she admitted, "From the same men peddling drugs on the causeways. Anyone has access to them. I approached as a Beta, covered in the smell of another."

"The smell of another?"

"Those who are strong enough to leave our hiding place steal the clothes from the dead rotting on the streets. We use their scent to hide our own, as you must have noticed when I came to you. It is unpleasant, but we need supplies, we need food. We do what we have to, to survive."

"Why was a young female chosen to approach the Citadel and not someone older, with less chance of entering estrous or attracting attention?" Shepherd demanded.

"I volunteered."

"Why?"

"I am healthier than most of the others, have lived for years passing myself off as a Beta, and am trusted to think objectively for the collective as I have no mate or children."

"You have a mate," he reminded her, releasing her wrist to brush the sore bite mark he'd left on her shoulder. "I claimed you. You belong to me now."

Her stomach churned and she worried her lip. Looking up into his steady silver eyes, she whispered, "You could change your mind."

For a split second, Shepherd seemed a little disappointed. An instant later, he grew viciously determined. "I am not an impulsive man. I made a decision. What was done is done. I claimed you. You are mine now. That is all."

"But you don't even know me," Claire tried to explain, realizing the male couldn't care less about something as inconsequential as the personality of a female who would be compelled by the bond to be his mate. Her wishes no longer mattered.

In a low, enticing purr he explained, "It's amazing the things you learn about the female writhing on your cock for three days."

Blushing up to her roots, Claire hid her face back in her hand.

Shepherd hooked a finger under her chin and brought her flushed expression up to examine. Tracing the pink on her cheeks, he said, "For example, you were pure... had not wasted yourself on the first Alpha to cross you in a heat. You also have a strong will for a member of a submissive collective."

"It's not submission if you're forced!"

"If you had behaved, I would not have punished you."

The way he spoke, the low rasped words, brought back all her fear. "I didn't want you to touch me—"

With eyes still dangerously narrowed, Shepherd leaned across the table until they were nose to nose. "I will touch you when I wish, any way I wish."

All the accumulating stress, the horror, the rage, just made her snap. "I do not want to be tied to a brute, to be pawed at and raped by a stranger—especially a male who wants me to sell my kind into sexual slavery!" Claire could hardly believe she had screamed out her feelings, and instantly pressed her hand over her mouth, staring at the seething male with frightened eyes.

There was no question of what was coming next. Shepherd stood and plucked her from her seat, returning to the nest they had created in her heat. He ripped the stolen shirt from over her head and already began to peel out of his clothing.

It was unfair how easily he could subdue her. Claire was pressed naked into the cold, sticky fabric, trembling, but too proud to apologize or beg. It would have been pointless anyway. Shepherd's naked weight came upon her, his hand cupping one swollen breast, tweaking her nipple until she squirmed.

Shepherd growled, his voice monstrous, "Raped? You screamed and begged, little one. You scratched and snarled if I did not fuck you when you wanted to be mounted. Have you forgotten? Shall I remind you?"

His hand dipped between the trembling legs his thick thighs spread open. She was dry as a desert until he pressed his chest to hers, put his scarred lips at her ear, and let out the slow animal growl that caused her to gush. Her folds grew slick, her body instinctively answering the call of her Alpha. He tugged and teased her labia, spreading her secretions, circling the nub of nerves at the apex of her sex while the Omega wriggled pointlessly in an attempt to get away. She was twitching each time he pinched her little bud, so frustrated and outraged that, when his cock was jammed inside her, she screamed. Her cry was far more than aggravated anger. It was positively dripping with the unwanted hunger the growls and touches her paired Alpha forced on her.

Holding her hands pinned by her head, Shepherd began to pump his hips, his silver eyes locked on hers. He made that growl again, felt her juices around his cock, and grinned. Each thrust filled that slippery vise, stretching, and making the thread hum with a sense of completion. When it was too much, when Claire couldn't hold back the waves of compelled ecstasy, she called out her hatred, cursing him to the pits of hell, between pleasured gasps and long moans. Shepherd just laughed and fucked her harder, pistoning his hips the way he'd learned his little Omega liked best.

With a wanton moan, she came, still calling out obscenities, full of coerced rapture until only his name was on her lips.

*"Shepherd..."*

The knot grew, his cock forced as deep as it could go the instant her muscles began clenching rhythmically to draw out his seed. Watching him grunt like a beast, Claire felt the thick spurted ropes of cream, lost in the rapture of her greedy pussy milking his cock until she was pooling with the stuff.

While the knot persisted, Shepherd looked into disoriented green eyes and demanded roughly, "Whose name did you call as you came?"

Claire could hardly breathe, was on the ebb of a powerful climax that shook her to her bones. She whispered, trying not to cry, "Yours."

"Because *I* am your Alpha." It was almost a roar. "You *want* to be fucked by me! Do you understand?"

Shaking her head, her lower lip quivering, Claire spoke the truth. "I don't understand."

Unfazed by the challenge, Shepherd coldly said, "Then allow me to show you again."

Once the knot subsided, he took her gently, coaxing and stroking, his thrusts slow and calculating. He played her body like a violin, drew out every possible sound a pleased female could make, gave her the type of orgasm that builds slow and burns long, watching her as a cat watches a mouse hole.

It continued for hours as he stripped away all her petty convictions until she was too exhausted to fight back, until her hands began to reach for him in a sex-induced daze, to stroke his back and trace the lines of his horrid tattoos. When his point had been thoroughly made, Shepherd held her against him and purred as he petted, rewarding the wayward Omega for coming to heel.

# 3

Shepherd could call it whatever he wanted—animal impulse, compulsion of biology, necessity of the bond—to Claire, it was still rape. She hated herself every time he coerced her to softly murmur his name in the dark, or reached out a hand to stroke the bulge of his muscle.

It was the same every day. He was almost constantly buried inside her womb. He took her when she woke, after she ate, roughly if she seemed irritable. And he always made her climax... simply to prove that he could. It left her boneless and complaisant, shut off the mind screaming at her to remember herself.

And the damn purr; Shepherd exercised it expertly when she paced in frustration or fussed.

Time became irrelevant. Claire was not even sure how long she had been underground, if it had been days or weeks. Anytime she wanted to know the hour she had to ask, and it eventually grew confusing. Night was day, day was night—everything was turned around.

Even the arrival of meals followed no set pattern, though she was never hungry for long. Shepherd was feeding her so much, in fact, it seemed sacrilegious when she could not always empty her plate. The man was fattening her up.

Random things arrived in the room for her use: products for her hair, a brush, clothing of a sort—all dresses worn only by the elite women housed at the warm levels nearest the top of the Dome—but no shoes or underwear. When Shepherd was gone, she slept. Almost the instant she woke, he returned. It was odd—like he knew—like he felt her cycles on his side of the thread. And always, before words were spoken, he took off his clothing, came to the bed, and lay with her.

Claire knew nothing about the man, but had memorized every inch of his body, the random placement of scars, the smoothness of his skin. And she knew how every inch of him tasted. None of the attention was out of affection—it was just part of the spell he would build. Though her tongue might lick his flesh, Claire never once returned any kiss he tried to press against her mouth.

That was one thing he couldn't take and couldn't force.

His expressions were another study, Shepherd conveying much with his steel eyes. Claire was learning to read his moods by their subtle shifts. When he arrived angry, eyes blazing and nostrils flared over something she had no knowledge of, he almost always mounted her from behind—hard and fast—roaring when he came. When he seemed his version of mellow, it was slow touches while he watched her face. What she saw then, the calculation, the intense concentration—it frightened her more. He was dissecting her piece by piece. A little pressure here, a little tug there... and poof, no more Claire.

Their schedules were markedly different. They never shared meals. In fact, she never saw him eat. The only thing he seemed keen to share with her was his bathing ritual, washing her being an act Shepherd enjoyed and took extensive care with. Once she was clean, he would rut immediately. Sometimes against the wall in the shower, as if he could not wait another second to put his scent back on his Omega.

It felt like her vocabulary had been reduced to only soft gasps or screams of, "*Shepherd...*" That was what he coaxed out. "*Shepherd...*" Another part of her died... "*Shepherd...*"

Lying spread on top of him, not knowing the hour or day of the week, Claire felt the anchor of his knot locked inside her and suddenly began to weep as if her heart was breaking.

With his hand stroking her hair, he hummed, half-asleep, "Why are you crying, little one?"

She was crying because he was killing her.

He hushed her and wiped the tears that continued to fall. "What would please you?"

"I want to go outside," she sobbed against his chest, so very tired of those four concrete walls. "I need to see the sky."

There was no answer for a moment, only the sound of his breathing. "Once you have become more settled in your new life, it may be allowed on occasion, but only under escort and only if you have a bellyful of my seed to scent you."

So she would be expected to mate with him just to leave the room. The exploitation was not missed. Her tears dried and her usual distracted dejection made the little string buzz out of tune. "I have done nothing wrong, and you have trapped me in prison."

Shepherd felt her resentment through the thinly formed cord, traced the line of her spine as he considered her opinion of *prison* and how it was far from the actual truth. His little Omega should be grateful. Life could be a whole lot worse for her. "It isn't safe for you outside this room."

Half aware of what she was saying, Claire lay lifeless and muttered, "Thólos is unsafe because you made it that way."

Silver eyes focused on the strands of midnight hair running through his fingers. "That is true."

With her cheek pressed to his heart, she said, "You're insane."

She felt a bit of a rumbling chuckle and just ignored him.

Shepherd palmed her rear. "You have not been this conversational in some time."

The knot was slowly beginning to loosen, his seed spilling out as the barrier receded. Feeling the gratuitous amount of fluid drip from her womb, she drummed her fingers on his barrel chest. "If I start talking, you throw me on the bed. What's the point?"

"I only quiet you when you fret."

"Like I said... crazy."

"Resisting is pointless," the male grunted, stroking her back to quietness when she seemed eager to wiggle away.

Resigned, Claire stilled and was rewarded with a purr, certain the man was trying to train her like some dog.

"You will find, in time, that the arrangement will naturally grow on you, little one." Shepherd spoke as if he knew, as if it were absolute. "Exercise patience."

Defiant, she growled against his naked chest, "My name is Claire."

He smacked her backside hard enough to sting.

Her head flew up, green eyes blazing. He chuckled, the sound masculine, and musical, and thoroughly entertained. She hated it.

"Don't spank me like a child!"

Silver eyes playful, he refuted, "If you act like one, I will answer accordingly."

"My name *is* Claire. Claire O'Donnell. And before you unleashed hell in Thólos, I was an artist. I had a life and friends... my own home... things you must imagine an Omega worked very hard to achieve in a world where we are prized for mates but lowest in the hierarchy. You took all that away, stripped every one of us of what we were, made the masses so feral that I had to go into hiding. You might have me trapped, but I will *always* be Claire."

Seemingly unconcerned with her rant, Shepherd cupped the curve of her hip. "What sort of art?"

Scowling, she answered bluntly, "Illustrations for children's books."

"Given your previous celibacy it seems a bit ironic, don't you think, Miss O'Donnell?"

"Why, because I didn't breed with the first Alpha who sniffed me? I wanted to find a good mate, and the men I've met tend to be…" her eyes held his as she spoke her feelings, "pretty terrible."

Shepherd's expression was not threatening, his silver eyes remained languid, but in a growl, he harshly explained, "You chose to enter the Citadel. You exposed yourself at great risk. You must have known you would never be allowed to return once I knew what you were."

"I was hoping a man known as *The Shepherd* would have honor," Claire grudgingly admitted.

Voice almost lazy, Shepherd replied, "And I did the honorable thing, did I not? I fought a mob and saved you from violent rape. I gave you a choice. You chose me and I claimed you. Since then, you have been protected and cared for while others suffer under the Dome."

"A choice?" She practically choked on the word. "You pair-bonded to me without even courting me first! There was no choice."

"You wish me to court you?" He seemed intrigued.

The brute totally missed the point, completely disregarding her accusation. Grinding her teeth in frustration, Claire buried her head against his chest and tried to pretend Shepherd was not there, that his cock was not growing flaccid inside her, and that the damned hum was not in her chest.

~

IT WAS THREE DAYS LATER, at least, she thought it was three days, when Claire woke up to find a large sketchpad, two brushes, and a set of watercolors resting innocently on the bedside table. The new things were like a magnet. She rolled out of bed and snatched them up greedily. Yesterday's dress was pulled over her head, and within minutes, she was on her belly, legs kicking behind her, the paints mixed, and the beginnings of a view coming alive on the paper.

She spent hours rendering her favorite flowers, the red poppies that bloomed in the Gallery Gardens, drenching them in sunshine under a blue, dome-free sky.

"Your talent is greater than I imagined."

Just about jumping out of her skin, Claire looked over her shoulder, pressed a hand to her heart, and shrieked, "How long have you been there?"

"Long enough," Shepherd answered, already crouched at her side.

Nervous, she scooped up her paints and brushes before the giant stepped on them or got in a mood and took them away. Everything was cleaned in the bathroom sink. When she was done, Shepherd sat on the bed, his elbows resting on his knees, the drying artwork leaning against the wall by the bedside table.

"What time is it?" Claire asked, closing the bathroom door behind her.

He was hunched over, staring at the painting, a strange look in his eye. "The sun is rising."

Edging nearer the display, she reached out a hand to center her work. When she glanced toward the resting behemoth, she found his eyes held a trace of amusement, as if he found her behavior endearing.

Claire took a step back.

"You were going to smile," he grunted, as if he expected her to do so on command.

Green eyes, almost the same shade as the stems of the poppies, turned back to the painting. She knew it made no difference whether she smiled or not. "If I smiled now, I wouldn't mean it."

"You do not like your gifts?"

Hands fisted in the stuff of her skirt, she nodded. "I like the paints. You know that."

Standing, Shepherd moved toward his desk. "Paint another one."

Claire didn't paint, that mood had passed.

Sitting like an overgrown hulk at the small desk, Shepherd accessed his COMscreen and ignored her. Claire began her ritual pacing, a caged animal denied the room to run. Darting a glance at the back of his hated head, she suspected his inattention was some ruse. That, at any moment, he would turn around and pull out his cock.

But the exclusion continued—as if he were trying to break her down, confuse her... doing it subtly until she just cracked.

Breathing irregularly, her fists clenched in her hair, pulling black locks, she repeated over and over inside her skull. *"I am Claire."*

"Come here." The order was issued in a moderate voice, Shepherd having not even turned his head in her direction.

The last time she ignored a summons, he'd fucked her three times in a row, even as she begged him to stop—left her spent and replete until she could do nothing but lie still and stare at the wall. Moving to stand at his side, her hair wild, Claire did as she was told.

A large hand enveloped the entirety of her hip, pulling her a few inches closer before the mountain turned. "Your brooding is making you upset."

Why was she being reprimanded for having feelings? Normal humans who were not psychopathic murderers had feelings. And normal people did not do well for weeks on end in the same fucking room with only a monster for company!

Working his massive thumb into the hollow below her hip bone, Shepherd took in her disturbed expression. "Sing something for me."

"Uhhh…" What? Sing? Claire did not want to mate, and that was the probable outcome if she refused. Scowling, she rubbed her lips together and tried to slow down her thoughts long enough to think of a song. Nothing came to mind. "What kind of song?"

"Something soothing."

He was trying to get her to self-soothe. Well, he could go fuck himself. After a minute or two of deliberation, with the same steady pressure of his thumb moving against her skin, Claire settled on a well-known ballad older than the time of the domes. It was sappy and portrayed romance in a totally untrue light, but she had always liked it.

Though now she knew better. There was no such thing as true love—of that Claire was certain—only indoctrination, chemicals, and bastards who kept you locked in rooms.

By the time she neared the end, her voice had grown desolate. The brooding had been replaced with despair. There was never going to be a hero. The growing cord of the bond made it clear that she would only ever have the large Alpha seated before her. A man whose face she hated with her whole heart.

"Kneel."

The pressure of Shepherd's hand gently suggested she follow the order on her own, or he would press her down. Degraded, she went to her knees and looked up into his silver eyes, her lower lip trembling, certain he would punish her for thinking such dark thoughts.

When all he did was take her head and put it in his lap, she breathed out in relief. He petted her as he worked, Claire silently crying onto the fabric at his thigh, confoundedly comforted as he played with her hair.

There was a knock at the door. Surprised, she moved to get up. With a hand on the back of her neck, Shepherd kept her as she was, barking for the caller to enter. She should have known... it was all just a show for when his Follower came to call.

Since estrous had ruined her, no one had been in the room, no one had seen what she had become. Peeking for just a second, she saw the same Beta from the first day. The men spoke in a coarse language that meant nothing to her, Claire's face pressed against Shepherd's thigh.

The meeting extended until her knees began to ache, that weight ruffling the hair at the back of her skull never giving an inch. Placing her hand at Shepherd's thigh, she scratched gently to get his attention, aware that if she pushed away, he would retaliate—especially as another male was watching.

"Shepherd," Claire whispered his name against his leg, intruding in the men's conversation.

It had worked. The hand on her skull stroked down and lifted her chin until their eyes met. "Yes, little one?"

He looked clinically focused, and she was unsure if interrupting had been such a good idea. "My knees—"

Shepherd simply pulled her up to his lap and began absently rubbing her kneecaps, continuing the conversation with his officer as if it were nothing. Her face flaming, Claire was unsure which was worse: kneeling at his feet like a dog, or being forced to sit on his lap like a child. If either man noticed her discomfort, it was not addressed.

The Omega looked to the Beta, measured his stiff posture and unsmiling face, noting how his attention never darted her way. He was much smaller than Shepherd, hardly taller than her, but seemed to have a whipcord quality to him that made Claire suspect he was very dangerous.

The meeting drew to a conclusion, and for a split-second, the man's vibrant baby-blues flicked toward her.

Shepherd growled so aggressively Claire jumped. The Follower bowed, a submissive stance, and left without another word.

Already pawing at her, turning her startled face toward his, Shepherd forced his Omega to meet flared iron eyes. She saw intense possession, the kind that made her stomach knot. Those hands, so large, began to rub, arranging her just as he wanted—stroking a breast, his scarring mark on her shoulder, circling her neck.

"Why were you looking at him?" It was spoken lowly, heavily laced with disapproval.

Claire answered, a line growing between her brows. "I have not seen anyone else in... I don't even know how long I have been locked in here."

"So you find it acceptable to openly stare at other males?"

Her scowl deepened, her voice confused. "Yes..."

Shepherd barked, his scarred lips snarling, "Your behavior is unacceptable. I gave you paints; you didn't thank me. I gave you comfort; you stared at the Beta."

Claire snapped. "I don't want fucking paints! I don't want to bow at your feet and be held like a pet on your lap. I want to go home! I want my life back!"

Angry, he shoved her off his thigh, letting her topple to the floor. Landing on her hip, she looked up, big eyes wide in her pale face. Everything in the cord between them was jostled badly... worse than her bones from the fall. The mountain was furious, slowly rising to his feet before her.

He looked about ready to crush her and she closed her eyes tight, anticipating the blow, welcoming an end to it all. There was silence, only the sound of her labored breath. Ten seconds passed and no move was made. When she finally cracked open an eye, Claire found she was alone. Shepherd had left her so soundlessly that not even the creaking door had dared whine.

Letting out a puff of air, she sagged back against the floor, her heart hammering away. It hit her then… there had been no slide of a metallic bolt shutting her in.

The door might be unlocked.

Panicked, totally shaken by the look of murder in her mate's eyes—*not mate,* she reminded herself—Shepherd's eyes. She stood and ran for the exit. Pulling the lever, it mercifully turned, and an empty hallway was right there before her.

Left or right? She didn't know the way, but she smelled Shepherd's scent clearly in one direction and bolted like a frightened rabbit down the opposite path. Before the city fell, she had run often around Thólos' many parks; not just for exercise, but to ensure she would be faster than any who might try to catch her. The weeks of lockup had done little to her speed. She ignored the painful thud of her bare feet against the floors. Tears were streaming down her cheeks, her breath ragged as she tried to keep inhalations to a runner's steady rhythm. Twisting and turning, she followed the sound of water. She found a ladder and flew up the rungs, oblivious to the sound of men's shouting voices, unaware of the dash of Followers trailing behind her. She flipped a hatch, eyes blinded by her first glimpse of bright sunlight in weeks, and scrambled out of the darkness.

She darted down a random causeway, winding in and out of alleys, climbing to higher terraces, her body steaming in the chilled lower region's weather. She came to a crossroads, heaved, and spat bile on the ground. Before her sat a broken bridge between two quarters, a massive, unscalable gap separating her from the nearest escape. The temptation to jump and end it all was so tempting. No more Thólos, no more Shepherd, no more falling into rapturous pieces when he fucked her, then hating herself afterwards.

But there were still the other Omegas... and she had let them down. They needed to know about the little blue pills, needed to know that Shepherd would not help them. It was that feeling alone that moved her feet again.

Claire ran for miles, ran in a crazy pattern that would make no sense to any who could smell her, ran until she vomited and fell in a pile against iron girders. Then she saw him, and he might have just been the most beautiful thing her eyes had ever beheld. A Beta, a stranger, was reaching down to help her... leading her sobbing body away from all the cold and pain.

He told her his name was Corday.

# 4

Claire woke on an unfamiliar couch with actual sun on her face. Head aching, she sat up and looked around. The Beta's one room accommodation was small, sparse like hers, with little more than necessities and only a single, wilted, air-scrubber plant.

Corday himself was standing in the kitchen, frying eggs from the smell of it.

"Do you like coffee, miss?"

God, she had not had access to coffee in months. Already salivating, she nodded, her green eyes so wide it made him chuckle. The young man walked over with a lopsided grin, handing her a plate and the steaming beverage. "Sorry, I don't have sugar or milk."

She couldn't care less. The mug went to her lips, Claire sipping with a contented sigh. "Thank you."

"Just eat up. When you're finished, you can shower and—not to make this awkward—but you might want to put on some of my dirty clothes to mask your scent."

After all the running, all the sweat, she reeked of Omega. His offer was extraordinarily kind, assuming he was not just cornering her like the last man had.

Reading the troubled look on the woman's face, Corday added, "I'm not going to hurt you."

Suspicious, she asked, "Why are you helping me?"

"I'm an Enforcer."

She shook her head. "All the Enforcers are dead. I saw the Inter-dome Broadcast, the security footage at the gates of Judicial Sector. Shepherd's contagion killed them."

There was little Dome-humans feared more than the disease that had reduced billions down to a few million in one generation. That had forced skirmishes for supplies. The Red Consumption had destroyed global culture and left life safe only under the careful management of the Domes. Knowing Thólossens had seen his brothers and sisters-in-arms die coughing up blood, knowing that a pile of unconsecrated corpses waited in a section under lockdown, knowing potential Judicial Sector survivors would have been burned alive once quarantine procedure began, drained his smile away. Corday grew sad, his face suddenly seeming so very young. "Not all of us, miss. Some were on patrol outside the Judicial Sector before quarantine lockdown."

Her lower lip started to tremble. "My name is Claire."

"Are you okay, Claire?" Corday asked carefully, looking at a woman who showed all the reactive signs of abuse.

God, it was so nice to hear someone say her name. Whispering, she shook her head, "I'm not okay."

Skirting the couch, he sat as far from the shaken woman as the sofa would allow. With his hands on his knees and brown eyes soft, he suggested, "Tell me what happened to you."

She knew that the second she said the name *Shepherd,* Corday would kick her ass out on the street. She hated to lie, but she needed a shower and warm clothing to survive in the Lower Reaches.

But maybe she didn't have to lie. Maybe all she needed to do was start at the beginning. "The chem pushers are selling counterfeit heat-suppressants. They look just like the little blue pills... but they are not heat-suppressants. They're fertility drugs. They cause us to go into estrous unexpectedly, where we are unprepared and exposed."

"And this happened to you?" Corday asked, gently urging her to continue.

Claire didn't say yes or no, she didn't have to. The huge tears dripping down her cheeks were answer enough.

Realizing she was close to falling to pieces, Corday nodded and promised, "I'll look into it. Now finish your lunch." His boyish grin returned, and he backed off to return to his stove, teasing, "I had to fight six Alpha females to get those eggs."

She forced a laugh at the joke, the coffee going back to her lips. But it was hard to enjoy. The unshakable paranoia that Shepherd would burst through the door at any moment made her stomach churn. Or worse yet, Corday could be lying, waiting for an Alpha he could sell her to.

With her mind running in circles, she watched the young man. There was no projection of attraction. He was not sexually aroused. He was just a guy cooking eggs in his kitchen. He seemed genuine and harmless... he even smelled acceptable. But no one in Thólos could be trusted, not after the breach had unleashed chaos and the citizens became like animals.

The invaders had just come from the ground like ants—spewing from the Undercroft, from sentences for crimes deemed inexcusable—all of it so precise that Thólos' government fell within hours. All of it easy because the population was terrified of the transmission which looped on Interdome Broadcast.

Everyone watched accelerated signs of Red Contagion, the symptoms of that great plague known even to the youngest, decimate the very men and women sworn to protect Thólos citizens.

Shepherd threatened to infect them all should any resist.

The city turned on each other. Once peaceful men and women dragged anyone they found questionable to the Citadel to be disposed of. And there she was, forcing cold eggs down her throat, terrified Corday would turn on her.

She didn't approach him to give back the plate, just set it at the edge of his counter before scampering toward the lavatory to bathe. Under unheated water, Claire scrubbed every bit of Shepherd off of her body, knowing Corday had smelled the Alpha scent she was saturated in... mortified the little string in her chest seemed to twang as if pulled taut by a demanding pair-bond.

She closed her eyes and could practically hear Shepherd raging, his angry breath coming in long roars. Then something far more disturbing ran under her skin. If she felt his fury, he felt her abject terror. Because of the tie, Shepherd was still with her, there even at that moment in the shower, sensing her though the link. Hyperventilating, Claire mentally repeated, *only instincts*, and forced her eyes open to prove that nothing but discolored tiles surrounded her.

Shepherd wasn't there. He wasn't watching her, ready to rip out her throat.

Turning off the spray, Claire dried with a towel saturated in another man's scent—a man who had not once tried to hurt her... at least not yet. From his laundry, she pulled out the most pungent pieces, dressing in a sweater he must have exercised in and a pair of sweatpants that, knowing guys, probably had not been washed in weeks.

Standing at the mirror, she found queer green eyes in the reflection and wished she understood why the face looking back at her was filled with regret. Disgusted with that woman, Claire spun around and returned to the living room. Corday was still standing in the kitchen, eating his own meal. He nodded, his mouth full.

"I have no way to barter or repay you for the clothes right now, but when I can, I will." Her voice sounded nothing like her, it was the voice of a stranger.

When Corday saw her move toward the door, he swallowed quickly and approached with caution. "Ma'am, you're in shock. I don't think it's a good idea for you to be wandering the Dome. What you need is to rest, get your bearings. You will be safe here, if you need a place to regroup."

Everything he said seemed so sensible, even the weight of his hand on her shoulder, steering her back to the couch. Mechanically, Claire lay down. He covered her with a blanket and sleep hit her hard, a corner of her mind still marveling at the feeling of sun on her face.

BAD DREAMS BEGAN that very first night. Claire was running through Thólos, through smoke and evil. The buildings she climbed were ruins, many burning. Everything was decimated, just like the photos of Pre-Reformation War cities on visual in the Archives. No matter which direction she turned, she could not escape the mob at her back. The jeering faces of raging Alphas, violent Betas... they wanted to rip her to pieces because everything was her fault. She had sent the monster into a rage. She was the reason Thólos would know even more suffering.

Hands began to grip her clothes but she pressed forward, lungs burning as she tried to find any path through the smoke. She took a wrong turn, found herself trapped atop a broken viaduct, hounded and petrified. But then he was there in the darkness, waiting for her. Standing like a mountain, Shepherd reached out, beckoning her to him with the flick of his fingers.

With the dogs at her back and the devil before her, she did not know where to turn. All she could do was jump to her death.

Claire woke screaming.

Corday rushed from his bed, clicking on a torch to offer something besides the enforced dark of Thólos curfew.

"It's okay. You're safe, Claire." His voice came out soothing.

She threw her arms around the stranger and held on for dear life. "He'll find me here," she whispered, trembling. "He's already looking."

"He won't find you here. Do you understand? It was just a bad dream. Whoever he was cannot force you anymore. You're free, you get to choose."

*I get to choose?*

The words resonated, and she began to calm. Leaning back, wiping the snot and tears from her face, Claire fought to pull it together.

Illuminated by the small light, Corday asked, "Would you like me to sit up with you?"

Shaking her head, she answered in an unsteady voice, "No... I feel better now. Thank you."

She was lying, of course.

There was no more sleep that night. She simply sat on the couch and started at shadows. It was only when the sun came up, when she could feel the light, that Claire found the courage to shut her eyes.

CORDAY LEFT a note on the coffee table notifying the sleeping girl that he'd gone to garner provisions. With so many dead, it did not take long to find forgotten shoes for feminine feet in a closet where neighbors dwelled no longer.

On the causeways, Shepherd's Followers marched, hyper-vigilant. Corday made sure to keep his head down, to bypass all screening. Several people were pulled aside at random. That was nothing new, but that day Shepherd's men seemed only to target women—pulling off scarves, exposing covered hair, sniffing them up close. A few Alpha females grew riled. As it continued, even Betas began to show their teeth.

Messing with women was a sure way to start another round of riots. The females alone, Alphas especially, would react instinctively. If their children were near, they might be even more aggressive. Then there were their mates. Alpha or Beta, no one liked to see their woman harassed.

The air was tense as he passed by mob after mob. Corday was eager to return to the skittish Omega with his freshly gathered supplies.

She was awake, her head turning toward the door the instant she heard his key in the lock. When it was only the Enforcer offering a calming smile, Claire let out a breath and shook her head, as if she felt her reaction had been foolish.

Showing his worn catch, Corday said, "I found some shoes that might fit you."

"Those aren't very pretty," she tried to banter, but her voice came out flat, and what should have been funny was unnerving. Claire tried again, forcing inflection and a smile. "Thank you."

"It's Thursday. The power will be on in this zone tonight." He locked the door and set the shoes on the floor near the woman. "Rather than just watching the paint peel, I have a collection of old films. If you like, we can watch one."

"Okay."

While Claire pulled the *new* shoes over borrowed, stinking socks, Corday took a seat at the far end of the couch, the pair of them like mismatched bookends. He lifted the remote. When the screen came to life, all that played was the Thólos Interdome Broadcast. Unfamiliar correspondents looped every five minutes, detailing which sectors would receive fresh rations the following day, locations of supply pick up points, faces of wanted *criminals.*

Claire heard nothing, the entirety of her attention was on the date stamped at the corner of the screen. "Five weeks..."

Corday didn't need to be a genius to grasp what the woman had muttered. Five weeks, that was how long she'd been trapped.

She was trying to hide her horror, so Corday inserted the stick that held his precious films and chose something lighthearted most people would recognize. It worked. Thirty minutes in and Claire's shoulders lost their rigidness.

"I used to watch this with my dad when I was a kid," she offered, glancing at him with a small, half-felt smirk. "He loved this movie."

Corday gave her a crooked grin. "Your dad sounds like he has excellent taste."

"He did," Claire agreed, her face less tragic. "He was a really funny guy. Sooo Alpha, though."

They both snickered, knowing exactly what that meant. Alpha parents were fanatical about their children. Over-involved, bragging constantly... generally an embarrassing pain in the ass.

"What about your mom?"

"An uptight Omega with no sense of humor... she left when I was twelve."

That was very unusual. Children typically made Omegas incredibly dedicated parents. Besides, the pair-bond would have compelled her to return to her Alpha. Corday wanted to ask, it was all over his face, so Claire just spit it out—it was old news, after all.

"She found a quiet place near the Gallery Gardens and took a bottle of pills—overdosed. She couldn't stand a life tied to someone she didn't like."

"I'm sorry."

Shaking her head, her dark hair swaying, Claire said, "Don't be. In the end, she got her choice. I respect that." Looking back to the screen, she asked, "What about you? What are your parents like?"

"Both Betas. Dad was sent to the Undercroft when I was a kid. He, uh, stole things. Mom raised me. She died the day Thólos was breached."

Green eyes looked back at the man on the couch, at the one who had been kind to her. The lines between his brows spoke of grief. "I'm sorry."

There seemed to be an understanding between them. "Me too."

Both looked back to the projection, laughing at all the right parts, neither one-hundred percent sure if the other was faking. When the credits rolled, Corday made them dinner, surprised to find the kitchen had been scrubbed clean in his absence. He watched the back of her head, saw her nervously play with her hair, and wondered how on earth the world had become what it was.

IF CLAIRE SAT on the floor *just right* and angled her head, there was a thin patch of sky the surrounding structures did not block. Direct, delicious sun warmed her skin, but something in all of it was hollow. Corday had not told her to leave, and she had to admit she was terrified of even stepping outside. It seemed so ironic that all she had wanted was to breathe fresh air, and now that she could... she could not. But she could look out that window, crouched down low so not a soul but the birds flying overhead could see her.

Eyes on the clouds, Claire felt her mind slowly grow quiet,

sighed deeply, and enjoyed the warm rumble of ambient noise. It took almost an hour before she was startled out of her daydream, to panic at a sound that shouldn't be there.

Shepherd's purr was all around her.

Certain that the behemoth was standing behind her, her head flew around, her eyes frantically searching the small studio apartment. No one was there.

But he *was*...

Claire knew—logically—she was alone, but she could practically smell him in the air. Heart racing, she pulled her knees under her chin and went back to her view, determined to control *her* mind. The harder she fought, the warmer the worm in her chest grew. Over and over, a soft little tug came to the thread. It was the strangest sensation, as if the beast was utterly calm now, calling to her almost gently.

Claire didn't trust it for a second.

Shepherd was an aggressive man—in conversation, in behavior, in bed. There was no 'gentle' unless it served him. And the kindness she'd received was always calculating. He had no feelings—or if he did, they were so twisted up in megalomania they didn't really count. Whatever he thought he might gain by trying to lure her with something as elusive as a soft invitation through the bond, she was not going to comply. Claire was going to keep that window and that little slice of sky, rejecting darkness and isolation.

A few hours later, she was back on the couch, reading a book she had pulled from Corday's small collection. It was the first time her eyes had met paper in ages. Underground, she had never once touched Shepherd's books—as if his forbidden texts might infect her with his warped view and evil.

It felt good to do something normal.

At dusk, Corday returned. They exchanged customary pleasantries, Claire waiting for him to show her the door. Once again, he seemed unconcerned that an interloper was sitting quietly in his apartment's only room. Corday attended to his own things, she went back to the book, and before she knew it, the lights were out and she was lying back on the couch, prepared to face a night awake in the terrifying dark.

Should she sleep, vivid dreams plagued and tormented—the same scene over and over. In every nightmare, Shepherd lurked in the dark, violent strangers' hands reaching to grasp and hurt her if she didn't run toward him, if she didn't climb higher up the wrecked tower.

The viaduct that could carry her to a better zone, the thing she had raced toward—it was always broken. There was no escape. To her left stood her great nightmare, to her right, blurred faces of the ones eager to watch her bleed. She could feel it in that towering damaged causeway; the icy air rushing up from the lower reaches, the sweat on her face from the run. Then there were the mercurial eyes. Steady eyes. Determined eyes.

From the shadows, Shepherd would reach out a hand to her, silent in the din of wrathful screams, and crook his fingers. To Claire's horror, each night her feet moved one step closer to the thing she feared most.

She would wake in a cold sweat, surging from the couch just to make sure Corday was there. Fortunately, the Beta slept like the dead, snoring just a little. It was a sound that brought her great comfort. Whispering so she would not wake him, she talked to herself, explaining her fear wasn't real. Dreams were nothing more than the influence of the pair bond.

She was free. She got to choose.

When the urge to vomit passed and the fevered trembling ended, Claire would lie back and try to think of nice things. Every night, as she stared at Corday's ceiling, the boy's snores eventually turned into the sound of far more masculine breaths the moment sleep came upon her again. The sensation of a warm hand stroking her hair to soothe her, her unconscious desire to hear only a moment of purrs... One small slip and the dream would invade again; a dozen times a night, a hundred? It felt like a never-ending loop.

The sun would rise and so would Claire, more tired than the day before. Corday noticed it too, she could tell by the way he darted subtle glances at her, how he skirted the walls and made sure not to get too close. Neither of them spoke of her degradation. After all, what was the point? It was not until the fifth day—when Corday told her that he would not be back until morning—that the Beta reached into his pocket and pulled out a circular, white pill.

"This will help you sleep, if you want it."

With a conciliatory smile, he left it on the counter and wished her a good day. Claire didn't touch it, found herself far too mesmerized by the round pharmaceutical and how much trouble they had turned out to be in her life. The temptation to drop it down the sink was as strong as the temptation to swallow it immediately.

All day that little pill stared at her. Her fingers curled at the edge of the counter, Claire crouched down to be at eye-level with the little white temptation. What if she took it and sleep did come? What if the dream came with it, and she could not wake up to save herself from taking those final steps towards a man the manipulative pair-bond was twisting into a savior? What if she took a whole bottle of pills?

In the end, when the dark came, she did not take the little white pill. She hid it instead. Lying in the darkness, buried under heaps of blankets, Claire closed her eyes and the same movie played on repeat in her mind. Silver eyes, an outreached hand, villains and smoke... only that night, each time she woke there was no snoring anchor in the corner of the room for her to pace her heartbeats to. Curled up and delirious from days without rest, she felt she was going mad, hearing things, confused. As the hours stretched by,

Claire realized with a creeping apprehension that it was Shepherd's raspy breath she kept imagining in the corner, not the Beta's snores, Shepherd's hand she almost believed was stroking her hair.

She felt in her bones that if she could only hear a few moments of that purr, untroubled sleep would come at last.

# 5

"Shepherd's genetic markers do not match any prisoner on record. I am telling you." Brigadier Dane was adamant. "He was not incarcerated in the Undercroft."

Corday had heard a thousand explanations. Not one of them was possible. Outside the Dome spread one hundred kilometers of frozen tundra in every direction, the location of Thólos chosen specifically so any potential diseased wanderers could never survive approach. Everything inside was self-sustaining, and only twice in his lifetime had shuttles been permitted to land. All on board had been female, citizens from other biospheres invited to Thólos Dome to keep the gene pool fresh.

Those who came never left, just as those who had left to serve the same duty on foreign soil would never return.

Scans for all new arrivals were vigorous. There was no way any unexpected life-form could have passed the gates. Even so, the last exchange had been nearly a decade ago.

Voicing his opinion to the few Enforcer stragglers gathered in secret, Corday disagreed. "The man is covered in Da'rin markings.

He was branded by the gangs in the Undercroft and labored down there long enough to organize outcasts into an army, to have constructed numerous tunnels that had gone unnoticed all throughout Thólos."

Brigadier Dane was not exactly a fan of Recruit Corday. Her patience with the young man was slender. "Then explain why he doesn't exist on record."

Corruption was a disease even the Dome could not filter out. Jaw rigid, Corday said, "Because someone threw him down there *off record*."

"If that was the case, others would have known. You can't just march down those tunnels dragging a man behind you. The security protocols alone would have been logged. If a soul had gone missing, people would have noticed. What you suggest would require a conspiracy of epic proportions."

There was one man in the room who had the power and the clearance to know. Several sets of eyes turned to Senator Kantor, all of them demanding he confirm that no such atrocity was possible.

The old man raised a hand to silence petty arguments. "I'd like to say it isn't possible, but I can't. Just as it should not have been possible for those trapped in the Undercroft to emerge, for our government to fall, or for our people to have gone mad. There is much about the insurgency we don't know. At this point, the identity of the Followers' fanatical leader is less important than discovering where he has stored the contagion."

Speaking because nothing made sense, Corday sighed. "Brigadier Dane's intel would explain Shepherd's attack on the Senate and why he's hung the corpses from the Citadel. It might be an act of revenge."

Brigadier Dane narrowed her eyes. "Or just the act of a psychopath..."

Twenty-seven bodies in various stages of decomposition

polluted the filtered air with stink. Men and women who had served the Dome, chosen by the people, swung in the updrafts.

Then there was the one name no one dared mention. Even after all those months, there was still a complete lack of information on missing Premier Callas—the unelected head of the Thólos government. All that was known was that the Premier's sector had been locked down in the first moments of the breach, a steel barricade cutting his residence off from the rest of the Dome. Shepherd's Followers ignored it, citizens no longer kept vigil there begging for sanctuary, it was just another shut gate with gods only knew what on the other side.

Brigadier Dane had more to say, the female looking to the last subordinate she expected would actually support her theory—to Corday, her expression distrustful. "But it doesn't explain how he came to be armed with the Red Consumption, or how the disease was smuggled into Thólos."

Grey hair shaggy without the clean trim he'd sported in office, Senator Kantor shook his head. It seemed hard for the old man to speak, to formulate exactly how he was to explain. "Before the doors were sealed, several strains of Red Consumption had been collected for study, the secret of its keeping only accessible to the highest tier of government. Thirty-four years ago, there was an accident in the lab which had been charged with creating a vaccine. The strain had aggressively mutated. A tech was infected. In a matter of minutes, the entire lab was locked under quarantine." Senator Kantor seemed utterly sad, as if reliving the memory of something truly unspeakable. "I watched the security feed. Incineration protocol failed. The souls locked behind the gates, they suffered... before they died."

Horror sat on the faces of those huddled in the dark, the group speechless.

Swallowing, trying to wrap his head around the fact that the very plague which had ripped apart humanity had been knowingly stored inside the Dome, Corday breathed, "And the mutated strain... how did it get out of the lab? How did it get into Shepherd's hands?"

Frowning, Senator Kantor replied, "I don't know. The lab is off the grid, sealed. Even I never knew where it was."

If one of the most powerful men in the Senate lacked that knowledge, and with the majority of his colleagues dead or missing, this new information left the ragged Enforcers with nothing but more questions that could not be answered.

Seeing so many struggling men and women consumed with even greater doubt left Senator Kantor squaring his shoulders and taking on the tone of an orator. "Friends, there is still much we do not know, and speculation without fact to support us will only breed argument. We go one step at a time, and trust the gods will lead us to salvation."

Face grim, shaken like the others, Corday offered a worthy, immediate goal the group might sink their teeth into. "I know where we can begin. I have learned that the chem pushers working the causeways are selling fake heat-suppressants. Omegas in hiding are going into estrous while unprepared and most likely exposed. They are being brutalized."

Senator Kantor frowned, seizing on to the offered duty. "Where did you hear of such things?"

Looking at the Alpha, Corday tried not to let his lingering disgust show in his expression. "A few days ago, I came across a very frightened Omega female, collapsed mid-deck."

Brigadier Dane eased a step closer, an intrigued arch in her brow. "What did she look like?"

Corday shrugged his shoulders. "What's that matter?"

"It matters," Senator Kantor explained in a level voice, pulling a leaflet from his pocket, "because there is a very large bounty out on this woman."

It was a flyer, similar to every other wanted sign littering the Dome. The young woman was smiling, her waving black hair tousled as if by an updraft, her green eyes sparkling, gentle and inviting. Claire O'Donnell looked lovely and vibrant... and though the version Corday had met was shattered and frightened, she was the Omega who was sleeping on his couch.

It all started making sense. The women were being harassed in the food lines because everyone was looking for *her*. And the bounty itself was a king's ransom. "What's she wanted for?"

Senator Kantor's lips went into a line and he shook his head. "I don't know, but she may have information valuable to our cause."

Corday could not take his eyes off the photo. He took a deep breath, let it out of his nose, and muttered, "Then you better come to my apartment." Glancing at the Senator, he added, "But you must understand, she is not going to be comfortable around an Alpha right now. And if you show her that leaflet, it might just send her over the edge."

Senator Kantor was already walking towards the exit. "The rest of you are dismissed. Corday, you will take me to her immediately."

It was almost dawn when she heard the key in the door. After a night of hellish sleep and total exhaustion, Claire was jumpy, bolting towards the wall when another man—an Alpha—came into the room behind Corday.

"Don't come near me!" she snarled, looking for anything she could use to strike him with. Settling on a lamp, she clutched it so hard it shook.

Senator Kantor and Corday waited by the door so Claire might feel a bit less cornered.

The older Alpha exercised the kindest voice, soft soothing eyes, and years of experience playing to a crowd. "Do you know who I am?"

With lips pressed in a line and eyes narrowed to slits, she nodded. "You're Senator Kantor." The man known as *Champion of the People*; beloved by many for his outreach to the proletariat, laboring for the greater good in the Lower Reaches.

"I am not here to hurt you." He cocked his head at the young Enforcer. "Corday says you need help. I'd like to see what I can do."

Her sweaty grip tightened on the lamp. "I don't want you coming any closer."

"I can stay over here." He smiled softly, even backing up a few steps to sit on a stool by the kitchen counter.

It seemed to appease the Omega, and she slowly lowered the makeshift weapon. From the dark smudges under her eyes, Corday could tell she had hardly slept, could smell the lingering tinge of fear in the air. There was a standoff, Claire silent as she watched the Alpha like a hawk. Senator Kantor waiting, letting her do what she felt she needed to.

When several minutes had passed and her chest stopped heaving, the old man began. "You were taking the counterfeit heat-suppressants and went into estrous in a place that was dangerous."

"Yes."

"What happened?"

Rubbing her lips together, she took a deep breath. "What matters... the only way you can help me is to find a way to protect the hidden Omegas. They are starving... they need food."

"I need to know what happened to you before I can figure out how to help you all."

Her back was pressed so sharply against the wall, Claire's shoulder blades dug into it. With an expression that grew positively wretched, she fought to say, "It was dangerous to take our share at the designated areas. More of us were getting picked off every day, and those of us who did get food... it was never enough to feed us all. So it was decided that I would go to the Citadel to ask in person for help.

"I was taking the pills, covered in clothing that had been on a rotting corpse to mask my scent. I climbed the steps and found him. He would not acknowledge me, so I waited." She drew a shaky breath and stopped.

Corday picked up for her, saying cautiously, "And you went into heat in the Citadel..."

Claire nodded.

The young man continued, "And someone took advantage."

She tried to explain, but she just could not get that name past her tongue. "There was a riot. He killed a lot of people and carried me off."

Both men noticed that she had not once said *Shepherd*—that she continued to refer to Shepherd as *him*. It was Senator Kantor who posed the question as delicately as he could. "And Shepherd was the one who took you?"

Claire began to cry, whimpering as she fell to pieces. "He refused to give us our share. Instead he demanded I tell him where the Omegas were so they could be taken and used by his men. He forced a pair-bond... kept me locked in his room for weeks." Her hand went to her chest, her fist knocking against it. "And I can still feel him, right here."

They were stunned, both slack-jawed.

A pair-bond... the man was searching for his mate.

Corday shook his head as if it were impossible. He could understand why a villain like Shepherd would rut her through a heat, but to actually pair-bond with a stranger seemed extreme. A bond was forever. There was no known way to break it without the death of one of the pair. And the aftermath was messy—oftentimes the living partner could never pair again. He'd taken Claire for life. No wonder she was so terrified. A man with the power to take over an entire colony, with devoted Followers at his back, was hunting her down and bonded to her.

She opened her eyes and forced herself to stop crying. "I have to tell the Omegas. I have to go to them."

All Corday could mumble was, "You can't go outside, Claire. This is Shepherd we are talking about. His influence under the Dome is almost absolute."

"I can't abandon them. I should have gone sooner, but I…" She didn't need to say she was afraid, that fact was obvious.

"You are a very brave woman." In a voice encouraging and strong, Senator Kantor spoke his piece. "What you tried to do for the others was incredibly courageous, but you cannot do it alone. Let us assist you. Together we'll find a way to help the Omegas."

"How?" Large green eyes went to the soft-spoken older man.

"For now, we'll get them food, proper pharmaceuticals... but there will need to be a long-term solution. How many are there?"

Shaking her head, she wiped her eyes. "There were around eighty-five the last time I saw them. But it's been over a month, it could be half that number... I have no idea."

"Where are they?" Senator Kantor asked.

Her face grew instantly hard and threatening. Claire straightened her spine and said nothing. She would speak to the Omegas first, they would decide before she revealed the location to anyone. Period.

The woman's challenging expression was not missed. Senator Kantor raised a hand and added, "I mean them no harm."

She growled, a bit of her old spirit coming through. "I don't trust *any Alpha*."

"I understand." And he did. It would be impossible to expect a woman who had been through what she had experienced to expose others to the same potential fate.

"Give me a few days to consider all options, to get some food together as well." Senator Kantor stood from his stool, Claire already lifting the lamp again in warning. The Senator nodded a goodbye, and left.

The day passed in silence between Corday and Claire, but that night, they watched another film together on opposite ends of the couch, a bowl of popcorn in the middle. Knowing her penchant for comedy, Corday had chosen his favorite, and it seemed to peel away the suspicious attitude that had made Claire restlessly pace all through the day.

When it was time for bed, she seemed settled and Corday went to sleep certain she was stronger than she had been before.

She was.

Once Claire heard his snores, she climbed silently from the couch, stole his coat, and left to find the Omegas. It was dark, the tower lights snuffed, Shepherd's manipulation of the power grid enforcing curfew. Memorizing where she was so she could find her way back to the rambling structure, Claire ran—from shadow to shadow—all the way to a squalid site caught between zones: a frost-covered scrapyard on the lowest level, where every breath came out like fog.

The forgotten dump had been filled, abandoned, and shut up before she'd been born. Nobody went there, and the government had never re-purposed the site. Like all things deemed unclean, and due to the fact it was in the frigid Lower Reaches, the area was generally avoided. It was perfect for the Omegas: shelter to sleep in, enough water in the air that it could be collected and drunk without having to draw water in the upper levels and carry it down. But it was an icebox. They had no power and no heat.

"It's Claire!" A shout went up once the black-haired girl made it through a crack in the wall, Claire staggering closer to the women crowded together for warmth.

Gulping for breath, she hung her head between her knees, trying to speak even though winded. "Blue pills, fake..."

Someone brought her water, a match was struck, and a precious candle lit. Huddled around the light was a sight that made Claire's heart ache. The Omegas were skeletal, and so many were looking at her with eyes totally devoid of hope. But with the light, expressions changed. Some bloomed at her arrival, others fell dark with suspicion. Worst of all was the flat out envy... and Claire understood the reason. Shepherd had been feeding her. She was healthy. She had been given food while they had had nothing.

It was Nona, one of the elders respected by the group, who spoke first. "Sweet goddess! Claire, I've been so worried."

Her green eyes looked upon the familiar heart-shaped face, half-hidden by lank salt and pepper hair. "How many are left?"

"Last head count was fifty-six."

Claire felt sick. Fifty-six... practically a third of the remaining Omegas had been picked off while she had been imprisoned by Shepherd. "I have so much to tell you." Her voice grew stronger. "If you have not already figured it out, the blue pills are not heat-suppressants... they are fertility drugs. I went into my cycle right in the middle of the damn Citadel."

Gasps of horror, too many staring with pity, shamed Claire.

"There's more. Shepherd will not help. He refuses to send rations and wanted me to disclose your location so that everyone could be taken, segregated from the population, and readied for his Followers."

"But isn't that what we want?" a redheaded woman by her side hissed.

Claire looked Lilian dead in the eye, saw the miserable state she'd been reduced to and said, "You would be imprisoned and offered to a stranger in estrous, bonded to a man of his choosing. He told me so himself."

"But would he feed us?"

"Is that what you want?" Her arched eyebrows went up. Claire wanted to rail, to berate the woman, but she did nothing more than shake her head and continue. "I have also met with Senator Kantor. He offers food. He wants to help us."

"How?" several voices asked in unison.

"He needs a few days to get a plan together. Once I find out what it is, I'll come back and tell you. Then we can all decide."

Nona put her hand on Claire's shoulder. "You are not going to stay? It's dangerous for you out there. Don't you know there is a huge bounty out on your head? Amelia saw the flyer two days ago."

Claire scowled, but the news was not exactly surprising.

Lilian poked the flesh of Claire's cheek. "You have grown fat. Shepherd's men were feeding you."

Brushing off the fingers, Claire barked, "I was trapped in a room for five weeks!"

"But they fed you!"

"Quiet, Lilian," Nona snapped at the instigator. "You're hungry, not stupid... you can tell from her altered scent that Claire has been pair-bonded. They would feed what they want to keep. Instead of remaining with her mate, she escaped and came here to help us all."

Claire was mortified.

Did she really smell different? When more eyes began to shine at her in the light of the candle and noses began to sniff, all she could do was try not to shrink back.

The question was tossed around. "Which one was it? Who claimed you?"

Answering quickly, Claire muttered, "It doesn't matter."

Lilian, her lips curled in a nasty sneer, laughed under her breath. Claire tried to remind herself that the redhead was starving to death, lived in a constant state of terror. Her feral behavior was understandable.

"I better go." Claire pulled Nona into a hug. "Expect me back in a few days."

It felt good to smell and hold someone so familiar, someone she knew cared about her. When the extended embrace came to an end, Claire left, climbing through the dark causeways of Thólos all the way up to Corday's apartment.

He'd never even known she'd been gone.

# 6

With his head ducked low between his shoulders, Corday walked across the shadowed causeway, the man ahead in the flapping coat eyeing him like fresh meat.

For two days he'd watched the chem pusher peddle to so many citizens it seemed staggering how freely the drug rings operated now that the Enforcers were off the radar. The thug made absolutely no secret of his unlawful business, almost taunting whoever might challenge his actions to dare speak it to his face.

Without greeting, Corday grunted, "I need your heat-suppressants, the little blue ones."

"Sure thing, man." It was obvious, apparent in the tone and cadence of the chem pusher's speech, that the dealer was an Outcast. By the dilation of his pupils, one who sampled his own wares. Sagging jowls bouncing, he pulled out a bottle. "Gonna cost ya. Going rate's a kilo of fresh produce and five rations of meat."

"That right?" Corday shook his head, trying to avoid noticing any family resemblance in a convict the same age his father would have been. "I have something far more valuable than food we're willing to trade… if you can manage twenty or thirty bottles."

Yellowed eyes narrowed. "Why do you need so many?"

Corday gave the man the most perverted of grins. "Let's just say, we like to keep our Omegas begging for it. If you supply, you can partake."

"A man after my own heart." Chipped, brown teeth on display, a knowing smile accompanied the pusher's question, "How many did you catch?"

Corday shrugged. "Enough to keep half the zone's dicks wet, so long as they're locked in estrous."

Scratching his chin, the chem pusher cleared a great deal of phlegm from his throat laughing. "Shepherd's Followers slaughter any man caught with an induced Omega. A wise businessman might look for more than just meds…"

Voice disinterested, Corday asked, "Such as?"

"What you really came here for. Partners. My gang ain't afraid of Shepherd or his Followers. We can supply you and keep business running smooth."

Hearing Shepherd's name thrown about casually, brought a sneer to Corday's face. "Fuck Shepherd."

"Sky-breather... without men like us at your back, Shepherd *will* fuck you."

Cracking his neck, Corday muttered, "He doesn't scare me."

Breath which stank of rotting things slid like grease up Corday's nose, the thug leaning nearer to taunt, "That's cause you ain't never seen him kill, or watched psychos bow to kiss his feet."

Meeting those yellowed eyes, Corday stepped far too close for comfort. "You must think us *sky-breathers* are pretty stupid. The racket ain't nothing new. But, unlike you, we weren't dumb enough to get caught and crammed in the Undercroft. I said fuck Shepherd, and I meant it."

The man flat-out guffawed. "You're one cocky little motherfucker. If your stock is any good, I'll get you what you need, kid. As much as you need. And you'll get us exactly what we want. That's how an alliance works. Or do they call it a trade agreement under the Dome?"

~

"THEY REALLY MUST THINK every last law-abiding Enforcer is gone," Brigadier Dane muttered under her breath.

The idiot on the causeways was either mentally challenged, or outright shameless of his crimes, acting as if consequence no longer existed. Not once had he suspected that Corday slipped a tracking device onto his person, not once had he even seemed wary. And even now that the creep was back in his cozy, dingy hole, she could hear the man laughing, the sounds of grunts, and hoarse, animalistic noises in the background.

It was hard to listen to. The Alpha female was fully aware of what was going on behind the concrete walls bad men thought would keep their flagrant secret safe.

What Corday had claimed to possess—Omegas kept like livestock—these men had in quantity. And they were being used even as the thug from the causeway plotted with his chums just how he planned to slice up the cocky kid who had such a mouth, laughing at how easy it would be to double-cross the boy, and how much they would rake in offering something other than used, slack pussy to the men lining up outside.

Corday's continuous issue with insubordination aside, for once the Beta Enforcer had done something right. The atrocities committed against those females had to be stopped. All the men inside had to be wiped from existence. And order—even if it was only a small step back to the way things were before—had to be enforced.

Things had gone to hell under the Dome, the beauty of a functional system going up in smoke at the first sign of real trouble. It shamed Dane to see her brethren so weak, to know that the precious survivors of wars and plagues could still be reduced to nothing but the animals humanity had become before the Domes. Thólos Dome had been the bastion of civility. The greatest Dome on all the continents. What had been accomplished under the glass—the flourishing culture, the beauty of life beyond mere survival—was now abandoned by Erasmus Dome, by Bernard Dome, even by the poorest Vegra Dome. One hint of plague and any chance of support from the outside vanished.

The issue had to be solved internally. Shepherd and his Followers had to be removed. The contagion had to be destroyed. And the infection—men like the thugs Dane twitched to kill—purged. An example made for others to follow.

A day or two of surveillance and her team would demolish the upstart syndicate. Brigadier Dane smirked at the thought of a much-needed victory, eager to see the look on the wretches' faces when she shoved something unwelcome inside them—something pointy—to see how they liked it.

CLAIRE WAS GAUNT, blinking rapidly as she kept as far from Senator Kantor as the small space would allow. With Corday gone, the Senator had remained to question her in his absence, so they might discuss options for the Omegas.

The options, it seemed, were limited. But anything was preferable to the other outcome. Namely slavery, rape, or murder.

But help came at a price.

Senator Kantor was wise enough to keep his distance, to speak gently to the shifty-eyed woman pacing madly back and forth. "You must tell me about Shepherd. What you might know could save us."

Just hearing that name sent her attention to all the corners, as if the Alpha could be conjured with only a word. Stopping her feet, Claire wrung her hands. "I keep telling you, I can't. I don't know anything."

"You can do this," Senator Kantor urged. "*Any* information you divulge will help us all."

"You don't understand." Impatiently pushing her hair behind her ear, she tried her best not to trip up the words. "He didn't *talk* to me..."

The look of pity in Kantor's expression first inspired her anger, then shame. After what had happened, that look was one she would receive until the day she died.

The Alpha coaxed out the subtleties of what he needed. "We can just talk about the man, your observations."

"Okay..."

Senator Kantor started off simply. "The Da'rin markings, do you know what they are?"

Quoting what she'd been taught in school, Claire said, "Outcast tattoos—markings to depict whatever crime a prisoner was incarcerated for."

Nodding, Senator Kantor offered further insight, "Yet most are earned in the Undercroft, given from one inmate to another—a testament prisoners coax into patterns under the skin."

"Coax?"

"They are not made from ink. Da'rin is a parasite."

Brows drawn tight, Claire asked, "You purposefully *infect* convicts?"

"The men in the Undercroft live without sun, are exposed to difficult conditions. We subject them to a beneficial symbiotic relationship so they might tolerate the environment they labor in. And, should they escape, they are unable to hide amongst the general population. Not only because they are branded—you see, sunlight makes the marks burn."

But Shepherd openly wore his arms and neck displayed wherever he went, his large flexing muscles detailed with black for all to see. "That doesn't make sense."

The old man sighed. "The patterns Shepherd chose hold great meaning amongst outcasts. It could help the resistance if we had a better understanding of the man... if you could describe the images we have not seen, we might build a profile, learn his secrets."

Of course she knew Shepherd's marks by heart, could almost feel the heat of them moving under her roving palms. Face red, Claire stammered, "The ones on his arms, the ones you've seen. What are they?"

"A tally of the men he's killed."

Her embarrassed blush drained away, leaving her ashen. There were so many symbols swirled over the Alpha's flesh, hundreds of filigreed marks, thousands, and they extended over his chest, his back, his thighs and buttocks... even his...

Her fear came back stronger than before, the link buzzing as if to question why she remained scared and alone when her protector longed to care for her.

Senator Kantor stepped closer to regain her attention. "Is there anything you've seen amongst the tallies you might consider noteworthy?"

Just looking at the man, tears running down her face, Claire drew a blank. "He's covered, everywhere. The patterns mean nothing to me, just edges and swirls." All those times she'd traced fingertips over them in the dark, she'd been unknowingly admiring the death of another of Shepherd's victims. "I didn't know..."

The door opened, Corday returning to find Claire incredibly disturbed, her head in her hands.

"Claire." The Beta rushed forward. When she didn't panic, he drew her down to sit before her unsteady legs gave out. "You're safe here, remember? You don't need to be scared."

Something about Corday being in the room unhinged her tongue, Claire blurting out pointless observations in her horror over the marks. "His Followers speak another language. I never knew what they said." With a tired laugh that was disturbing in the extreme, she listed the only thing that was absolutely correct. "He likes to read. He holds my hair as he does it, so if I move, he'll know. I have to be very still."

Corday whispered the question, "What happened if you moved?"

"The book became less interesting." Claire quieted and turned her head towards the Senator, defiance drying her tears. "I was kept locked in a room. I had no exposure to anyone but him. There were no windows, everything was grey. The man never even shared a meal with me. Now, I've answered your questions, you answer mine. Beyond supplying true heat-suppressants, what will you do for the Omegas?"

The Senator, in dire need of a shave, offered a smile. "Once the numbers are assessed, separate cells of two or three will be smuggled to safe houses that can be defended and monitored."

Claire's ears pricked up, something in Kantor's statement sounding awfully familiar. "Why not just send food to where they are now? There is no need to move the group or break apart women who rely on one another for support."

"We can discuss that option, though I believe it leaves you far more vulnerable than entrusting them to our protection."

When had the government ever protected Omegas? Her kind practically had no rights without a mate to speak for them. "You will do nothing until I talk to the Omegas. They must decide," she said.

"Claire," Senator Kantor pleaded, stepping closer to the female who clearly had lost her faith. "You need to trust us and stay here where you are sheltered. We can approach your Omegas."

"No." Her voice sounded less like a frightened child and more like an angry woman. "I appreciate everything you offer, but even Shepherd couldn't drag the location of our hiding place from me. This plan you propose is their decision, and I will speak to them first."

"You haven't slept in days, you hardly eat..." Corday grew stubborn, squeezing her clammy fingers. "Wandering around Thólos in this state will get you killed. If you have to go, then take me with you. A Beta will be less threatening, and there is safety in numbers."

Taking her fingers from his hand, she considered. Coming to a decision was easy. "We'll go tonight, just you and me."

Both men seemed appeased.

Sheepish, Claire asked a favor. "I'm going to need clothing that can mask my scent. Everything here I have already worn... I cannot smell like an Omega."

Nodding that he understood, Corday went to his dresser and pulled on a heavy sweater. "I'll go for a run. You can wear these when I return."

Lashes lowering, she whispered, "Thank you."

Senator Kantor left, Corday his companion.

Alone, she stood from the sofa to prepare.

She needed a cold shower, all that freezing water would help clear the cobwebs. Claire cranked up the tap, eager for a deluge. She sighed the instant pipes groaned and her sleep-deprived mind mistook the noise for something very different. The effect was immediate. Under the spray, eyes closed, where there should only have been cold water streaming over her flesh, the heat of large hands replaced it.

Roughened palms flowed over the line of her spine, soothed the dip in her lower back... the air full of appreciative grunts. Those same hands, callused and familiar, stroked her soft belly, stole upward to hold the weight of her breasts, thumbs circling pert nipples until they were so sensitive Claire whimpered. The thread pulsed in her chest, generous slick dripping down her legs once the growl sounded a third time.

All around her, low breaths echoed deep and hungry, the heat of his chest pressed to her back, the thickness of his cock grinding at the cleft in her buttocks.

Two fingers were pushed into her mouth.

His order at her ear to suck, and Claire's eyes rolled back in her skull.

Pressed to the tile, nipples chafed by grout, Claire's tongue hungrily twisted as it was told to. The head of his cock, searing hot, prodded insistent where she ached. His was not a slow entry. Shepherd speared her, his rhythm erratic, filling the small enclosure with Claire's muffled cries no matter how he finger fucked her mouth.

Forehead against the tile, hardly able to breath, Claire came with a shriek. Everything inside her clenched, slick ran like a river, and the hallucination ended.

Phantom hands were gone.

There was no Shepherd.

No growls.

No licentious grunts.

All there had ever been was the sound of the pipes and her inadequate fingers working her pussy.

Shaken, she looked down at her hand, horrified to see what she'd done. She was going crazy, every other thought running out of control. In a panic, she reached for the soap and began to scrub away the pheromone-laced slick before the whole apartment reeked of Omega arousal.

She was in the kitchen when Corday returned. Looking up from the simple pasta she'd prepared for dinner, Claire offered a smile. "Welcome back."

Good and sweaty, Corday's cockeyed smile was quickly hidden when he pulled the pungent sweater over his head. "Just let me grab a quick shower. We'll eat, then we'll go."

Nodding, smiling in gratitude for his effort, she announced, "Dinner will be ready when you're done."

Once Corday had disappeared behind the bathroom door, she retrieved the little white pill that had been hidden away days ago. Crushing it to a fine powder, she mixed the drug into his serving.

Claire knew no amount of soap could wash away the pheromones lingering in the bathroom. When he took longer than usual, red up to her ears, she tried to ignore Corday's muffled grunt, ashamed she'd put him in such a position.

Another stifled noise, an extended curse, and the sound of the water ended.

By the time Corday emerged, her embarrassment had faded back into familiar fatigue, and she offered the dish.

Between the run, jacking off in the shower, and the sleeping pill she'd hidden in his food, Corday was out cold in less than an hour. Claire dressed in the sweaty clothes he'd prepared for her, threw a blanket over the Beta who'd been so kind, and left to find her Omegas.

THE HARSHER CHILL of the Lower Reaches was underscored by light flurries dampening Claire's clothes. The distance was far, her pace dangerous for an exhausted woman about ready to drop.

It seemed they had been anticipating her, a small group of Omegas already at the cracked entrance, candle in hand. Doubled over once safely inside, Claire struggled to catch her breath, croaking, "Senator Kantor has a plan. He can provide food and real heat-suppressants."

"How?" It was Lilian, the redhead, who brought the candle closer.

"That is what we must discuss. He wishes to break us up into smaller cells, smuggle us to safe houses where armed Enforcers could stand guard. Or, should we demand it, they will bring rations here."

"The Enforcers are hunted down in the streets." Deriding, Lilian snorted, "They'll all be dead in less than a year. Who would bring the food then, Claire?"

Too tired to be patient, Claire stood up straight. "I'm only offering options. The group must decide for itself if they want instant slavery or difficult freedom."

It was then Claire realized no more Omegas had come to join them. Nona was nowhere to be seen. The only faces around that candle were Lilian and two very unfriendly looking women.

"We have already decided," Lilian snarled, swinging a rock in her fist.

The world spun, sharp pain erupting beside Claire's ear. Broken pavement and scattered refuse scraped her legs, her listless body pulled deeper into their shelter. Trying to focus past the ringing in her skull, her unsteady eyes searched for Nona in the crowd, only to find the older woman restrained, struggling to get free.

She called out to her, begged the Omegas not to give in to fear, and felt a hand fist her hair to wrench her away. Dragged to a storage cell, Claire was shoved inside, the sound of something heavy heaved to bar her only exit.

Disoriented, surrounded by the dark, her green eyes stared blankly at cracked walls.

They were grey.

Her broken laugh echoed back at her. Tasting blood in her mouth, she turned so the icy ground might cool the throbbing lump growing on her skull.

But there was no time to rest. She had to get up.

It took great effort to uncurl from a ball and crawl to the door. Standing hunched, Claire screamed out her story, told them not to lose themselves in desperation and panic, to think rationally and see that Shepherd would never pay a bounty, that the whole thing had been a trap just to snare her. To stop before they all made themselves slaves.

She could not budge the rubble blocking her in. She could not scream loud enough.

Claire only had so much voice, and as it left her, so did her ability to differentiate fantasy from reality.

As she slid down the wall, the dream began.

So much running, the wave of madness at her back, but Shepherd was there holding back the dark, his arm upraised. She ran straight for him, close enough to smell him before her feet skidded to a halt. There were screams, furious screams of the Omegas at her back. The wave of noise was getting closer. Terrified eyes went back to Shepherd, back to the man standing like a stone in the chaos as he crooked his finger.

She took another step.

The dream began again.

Light came on in her cell, the single dangling fixture above her flickering in its sorry state. The hum of the old bulb and the filament inside drew her to her scraped knees and then wobbling feet.

The mob. She could hear them, their shouts closing in. Any moment they would come for her. She would run, because she always ran. And she would find him, because he was always there, waiting.

Again and again.

Her head turned towards the door, where it seemed inevitable his large form would fill the portal, that she would see the same roughened armor, the same Da'rin markings crawling up his neck... those eyes.

The intensity with which Shepherd stared seemed unnatural.

Whatever he saw in her expression made the giant crouch down, as if to make himself seem smaller. The Alpha reached out a hand, slowly, so as not to frighten.

He'd never crouched in the dream before.

Claire closed her eyes, certain she had finally lost her mind, then that sound came... that long pined for purr, loud and confident, reassuring her that all was well.

"Come to me, little one." Even his rough voice seemed perfect, melodic as the words passed scarred lips. Coaxing, non-threatening, he added, "You will not be punished."

The thread was pulsating, whispering to her as it did, tempting her to step forward and take her Alpha's hand. That he was calling her. That he missed her.

Claire had no idea what made her say the words, but they came softly, like a confession. "You've been haunting my sleep. Every time I close my eyes, you're there."

"You've been in my dreams, as well." Shepherd crooned so deep she imagined she could feel the vibration change her on a cellular level. "You've been singing to me, little one."

Dazed, she pulled in a breath, smelling the scent that was supposed to be with her—the familiar musk of that Alpha. "What did I sing?"

A smile was in his eyes, the skin at the corners crinkling. His fingers flicked, beckoning her, and Claire found herself mesmerized by the movement. "Come."

In the distance, there were sounds, frightening things of the mob from her dreams. Soon she would have to run... or she could choose to end it.

It took three weak steps before she was standing directly before him. Looking at the male who, even crouched, was at her eye-level, Claire did not take his hand. Instead she sagged against him, demanding in an exhausted voice, "Purr."

He did, turning to study the disoriented woman resting her head on his shoulder, weighing the beauty of her extended groan broadcasting that there was nothing else in the world that had ever been so soothing as the noise rumbling from his chest.

Massive arms wrapped around her the instant she began slipping to the floor.

Shepherd stood.

Claire didn't see the blue-eyed soldier take up position as guard. She didn't know Shepherd took off his coat, or feel her body being stripped of clothing that reeked of another male.

She was laid in the heat of his coat, wrapped in the scent of the Alpha. Unfocused and uncaring, she felt his body settle between her thighs, Shepherd a furnace compared to the cold room.

"You are lost, little one. I will bring you home."

She mumbled a reply, her vague mind in agreement. Warm hands, callused and reassuring, ran down her stomach, spreading her legs wide. Before she could complain, the firm press of lips and the flicking dart of a tongue ran over the part of her no one had ever touched in such a way.

Shepherd tasted her, ensuring she'd remained untainted by another... purely his.

Finding her uncorrupted, the Alpha growled savagely. At the sound, her body bowed, her pussy responding with a stream of slick. Shepherd noisily sucked it all into his mouth, swallowing, lapping madly.

There was nothing gentle in the way he scoured her clean.

A choked cry and Claire's eyes flew open. All she could see in the haze was his face buried between her thighs, his eyes closed as if the feast were perfection. He sensed her attention, gun-metal gaze flashing. The lower part of his face hidden, Shepherd continued to devour her even as he growled, "You have been exceptionally disobedient. A difficult and defiant mate."

Panting, crying out when he flicked her clit, Claire argued with the apparition, "It's your own damn fault! You're a tyrant. You expect things I don't understand. I hardly know a thing about you. You don't listen... keep me locked underground. How would you like to live in prison?"

Shepherd chuckled evilly, gripped her hips to still her writhing, and gluttonously pulled her dripping cunt closer.

Fighting gasps and throaty moans, she accused, "All you ever do is fuck me!"

She felt his teeth skim her folds, his lips curling into a smile. Shepherd's answer was rich, licentious. "I *greatly* enjoy fucking you."

She wished he'd disappear and the dream could end, but not until she fought her broken voice to accuse, "You force me."

He rebutted, his teeth lightly biting the little nub his thumb exposed from its hood, causing her to twitch frantically so he might prove his point. "I always ensure you feel pleasure when we mate."

Breathing out an unhappy moan, she whined, "That is not true."

"I punished you once by rutting you without your gratification, and ascertained it was not the best way to discipline your bad behavior. I have not done it since." Once the words were finished, he attacked her with rapid flicks of his tongue, a pleased growl coming from his smiling lips when his little one began practically sobbing from the attention her trapped hips could not escape.

When Claire was right at the cusp of falling further into delirium, Shepherd licked a trail up her body, leaving her aching pussy neglected so he might pin her down. A nipple was captured, suckled almost too hard until the bud lengthened. Distantly, she heard the grate of a zipper and then sucked in the heady smell of potent Alpha musk once his member was exposed. The bulbous head butted against her, and ever so slowly he eased into a place that was fragile and tight from neglect.

With her distracted, Shepherd tried to take the one thing he had not been able to coax from her yet. He captured her parted, moaning lips to tempt out a kiss. It woke her from the spell, her black lashes flew open.

It was not a dream.

All she could see were the lust-filled silver eyes, challenging her to participate even as Shepherd dipped his tongue into her mouth. He invaded—so she might sample how perfect she tasted—and began to thrust.

She tried to take her mouth away. To prevent it, he cupped her cheek, running his lips over hers as much as he desired, knowing she recognized what he'd done, how he'd defied her last barrier, and fought for the kiss she continued to deny him.

The feel of his cock—it was all so intoxicating, consuming, and infinitely disturbing. Claire grew frenzied once he began pounding with vigor. Borderline violent, Shepherd fucked in earnest until she was writhing and crying out, needing release, needing sleep, needing him to give her all those things and more. Turning her head to the side, his palm braced her cheek so that his lips could suck a trail down the exposed side of her throat.

The feeling of his mouth, the rasp of warm tongue on cold flesh, and frustration blended with delusional ecstasy. The second her pussy clenched and her undoing began, he shoved in deep, his knot swelling huge, stretching her mercilessly. Claire's orgasm raged so hard it hurt, her pussy milking him desperately as Shepherd bared his teeth and bit down brutally atop the scar on her shoulder—the scar that made her his. A crunch sounded, teeth broke skin, and blood began to flow.

Claire's throat could only offer a silent scream, her agony ignored as he ferociously tightened his jaw. With her trapped by his massive knot, there was no escape, made worse when her pussy spasmed and blended pleasure into the pain with each spurt of hot come the Alpha dumped inside her.

The Omega was sobbing when it was finished, bleeding badly, and so overcome that she no longer knew where she was.

"Shhh," he whispered, licking at the running blood, hushing her gently while she wept. He gave her the purr she'd wanted, petting and stroking, his lips at her ear. "Now you may sleep, little one."

Everything had been too much. Too much fear, too much heartache, too much anger, too much desire. Overwhelmed, Claire closed her eyes and gave over to the thing her body needed most. Shepherd tucked her limp arms into the sleeves of his coat. Hitching her about his waist, his knot still joining them, he walked out the door, her naked body and their joining covered by the drape of worn leather.

Outside the waste facility, the Omegas were being herded onto transport prepared to take them to the Undercroft, a few snarling, others screaming, but the majority simply scarfing down supplement bars his Followers were passing out.

Claire missed it all in her dead slumber.

# 7

Claire felt no warm haze, no fulfilling sense of contentment upon waking. Instead, a deep-seated ache drew her brows tight, only growing worse when she shifted. Someone had run her over with a transport rig, wrung her out... left her wasted. Confused, her lashes parted, and Claire saw nothing but subterranean gloom and walls of concrete.

It was the smell that brought it all together, the nest of familiar, soft blankets rich with the scent of her mate.

*Not mate...* Claire had to remind herself. *Shepherd.*

She hated that his stink offered reassurance in her discomfort, that the thread was humming delightedly, telling her it was okay to feel weak so long as he was nearby to watch over her... that everything was back as it should be. The worm pulsed and grew warm in her chest. It was that manipulative pair-bond which had distorted her in the first place—Shepherd's influence, which had broken her apart day after day when she ignored her mate's call to return—that led to exhaustion and hallucinations. Now it was writhing in contentment, spinning a web of the seductive lie of shelter and safety.

It seemed stronger than before, that cord humming between them felt tighter in her chest. Was it because of his total victory over her? Or maybe because she had stumbled straight to him in her craving for sleep? Claire didn't know. All she knew was that her struggles, her denial and stubbornness, had been for nothing.

They were bound. Even in her hiding, he'd exercised control.

That grey-walled room was not shelter. It was her prison. Shepherd had her in his cage, she was back under his thumb... and she would probably never leave that room again.

Swallowing down distress, Claire recognized his great weight dipping the mattress at her side, her thigh flush to his back as if she'd pressed near while she slept. Shepherd was facing the wall, his elbows on his knees, staring forward, lost in thought.

Licking dry lips, Claire thought to scoot away, only to fall back to the pillows with a curse. The pain was great, shooting from her shoulder so sharply it was all she could do to breathe.

The broad expanse of bare muscled back rippled, Shepherd turning his head to look at the recaptured woman. His silver eyes were blank, the Alpha's air not one of impending punishment, nor was it one of offered comfort. He seemed static, yet those mercurial eyes were watching her as if she were troublesome and easy to crush.

Abashed by such an expression, Claire glanced away, her attention turning to the blood-soaked gauze at her shoulder. Unsure why she felt guilty under his appraisal, why she was tempted to apologize, she focused on the task of peeking under the bandage. What she found almost made her retch. The wound may have been cleaned and dressed at some point while she slept, but it was an oozing, sluggishly bleeding mess, swollen and bruised and utterly disgusting.

No wonder it hurt so badly. Shepherd had maimed her.

He reached out a hand, pulling back the gauze to see the bite mark for himself. He seemed pleased. "That will scar nicely."

It would scar horribly... twenty times worse than the last mark he'd made.

Unforgiving silver eyes bore down on the woman, watching as she pressed back the dressing and tried to calm her breath. "Perhaps now you will remember that you have a mate," he said.

Tired of intimidation and fear and silence, she forced her body to sit up. Ignoring the agony of an unresponsive arm, her green eyes flared, her small hand covering the dressing as if to shield it from him. Appalled, she growled, "*You will not be punished*? Then what is this? How would you like it if I tore a chunk out of you?"

Shepherd raised a brow and challenged, "I am your mate. You may mark me if you wish."

Something in his words caused a jolting craving to chomp so strong her lips peeled back from her teeth. With a snap of speed, Claire rolled out from under the blankets, her nails already digging little red moons into Shepherd's biceps as she scrambled to the position so she might sink in her teeth at the juncture of shoulder and neck.

Somewhere in the haze of action, she recognized the beast was holding still, that no great swiping arm had sent her flying in response to her aggression. Her instinctive reaction had been so very quick, so mindless, that she only caught herself a second before punching her mark into the proper patch of skin.

An unexpected wave of dizziness made her vision swim, overwhelming nausea snapping her out of madness.

After a shaky breath, reason returned.

Confused by how badly she still wished to bite, how everything inside her told her it was her right—that she *needed* it—Claire slumped, exhausted. Shepherd's hands were already on her waist, steadying her as she dropped her forehead to his shoulder.

Flesh to flesh, he smelled like he was hers, the thread gratified by his proximity.

Why did it have to feel so good when he pulled her closer, holding her so that she might find her strength?

After a minute, she clumsily unhooked her claws from his arm, back in control of her urges, stubborn and resolute to resist. But her head was still spinning when she glanced up. Liquid mercury watched as he always watched her, like a wolf licking his chops. She made a move to climb off his lap and return to the warmth of the bed, but his arms held her firm, settling her body where she straddled his thighs.

A finger traced down her spine, a reminder she was naked... a state he had seen her in so many times there was little shame in it.

"There are topics that must be discussed." It was said conversationally, but his expression was daring argument. "To begin, you will tell me where you have been for the last eight days."

Her voice seemed to catch, worn from screaming at her sister Omegas so this very scenario might be prevented. "I was offered shelter after I collapsed in the street, by a man who was kind to me, who listened, and who tried to help."

The heat of his massive palms kneaded deeply into her lower back, pressing her closer. "Who was this man?"

Claire shook her head, frowning and bracing herself to receive punishment for the words she was about to speak. "I won't let you kill him because he was noble."

There was the slightest of squints above a warning smirk. Shepherd's voice crooned, oddly complacent, and a total lie. "Perhaps I wish to reward the Beta whose stench saturated your clothing. After all, he tended to my runaway, foolish mate."

"No. You wish to know how to reach Senator Kantor so you

might string him up from the Citadel." Claire knew the Omegas he'd captured would spill every word she had told them in their fear. They might have lost themselves in despair and starvation, but Claire had been made stronger by being fed as Shepherd's pet, and she would not give the Alpha information to help hunt down anyone who might resist his occupation.

Threading large fingers into her hair, Shepherd began to comb out the tangles. "Do you know where he is?"

"I do not. He came to me. But even if I had learned his location, I would not tell you."

"Do you think that your loyalty to those men will save them?"

She straightened her spine and fought to keep sadness from weakening her voice. "They were the only ones who offered to actually help, who wanted nothing in return, respected me as a person—not an object... I will not say a word that might help you hurt them." After a sniff, she raised her chin, all defiance and haughty determination. "You may have the Omegas under your control, you may have me back in this room, but you will never claim my integrity or honor."

A finger traced the line of her jaw, his silver eyes almost soft as they searched her face. "You are still so defiant."

"I am still Claire."

Unexpectedly, the purr rumbled, soaking into her, soothing her rankled belligerence. When Shepherd spoke, it was indulgent. "You are... wayward and foolishly noble... I find it is not disappointing."

Why was he looking at her gently? Why was he saying nice things? Narrowing her eyes, suspicious even as the purr made it all better, Claire tensed.

Shepherd's thumb brushed her lips. "Did you miss me, little one?"

The dark fan of her lashes lowered, Claire was unwilling to answer. She had missed him. Missed his smell and the purr, missed the calm he cultivated with precision. But her desire for such things was only the result of the bond. She had not missed the constant feeling of being trapped—watching day by day as more pieces of herself were peeled away.

"Answer me, little one." He used that power he had, making the thread knock about in her chest.

Looking lost, her emerald eyes met his. "You have invaded my mind."

"And your body," he added, holding her a little firmer.

"And my body," Claire agreed, her expression brokenly resigned. "Is that what you want to hear?"

Pinching her chin so she could not look away, he warned, "You will not run again."

The pair-bond had grown so overwhelming that even if she did, there was no chance for true freedom. The dreams, the waking hallucinations, Shepherd would be with her no matter where she tried to hide. But knowing that and accepting it were not the same thing. Claire wanted freedom, she wanted to choose.

"Shepherd," she spoke his name, a thing that was rare unless in the throes of passion. "I needed to breathe fresh air. I needed to see the sky."

His purring ceased.

"The sky," Shepherd spat the word as if the idea were overrated. A deep breath rattled in his chest. "You think you know what prison is, little one. You do not. In prison, one is surrounded by the worst possible breed of men. If I wanted food or water, I had to kill for it. Shelter, supplies... everything was hard-earned. What you call rape is nothing compared to what the dregs indulge in. You live in safety and comfort. I tend to you and soothe—see to your needs." His voice grew utterly disgusted. "And still you pine for your sky."

Shepherd had never once shared personal opinion. Intrigued at the strangeness of such a statement, Claire's brows furrowed and she said, "I can't decipher which of your Da'rin markings explains what crime put you in the Undercroft."

Ignoring her hinted question, Shepherd smirked. "That term you use for it—the Undercroft—I find it amusing. A poetic word used to describe a place of darkness, filled with the pleas of thousands scraping at the doors to get out. And as for crimes... crime is irrelevant. I was never condemned to your Undercroft. I was born there."

Shepherd was a man who remorselessly created suffering—one who understood the dark workings of the human mind as if they were second nature—but such a monstrous history could not be true. Claire stared, looking for the flaw, for the lie.

Tight words betrayed his irritation. "You claimed to know nothing of me. Now I have spoken, and you are mute."

She inched her face a little closer, a line growing between her brows. "Females are not sentenced to the Undercroft. They labor on the farm levels, segregated from men until rehabilitated. What you claim cannot be true. Such an act is against our laws."

Shepherd laughed dryly. "Your laws? What do you know of the cage you live in and the false histories you've been trained to recite?"

Cheeks flaming from his mockery, Claire shrank back. "So in isolating me from the world, your goal is to make me deranged like you?"

The question seemed to momentarily confuse him. After a brief pause, he answered, "I want you to become amenable, to stop resisting, and to look objectively instead of with bruised emotions that will never serve you."

"And I am just supposed to forget what you've done?" Hurt sat in her eyes, Claire listing his sins. "You took me against my will, offered no help to my cause... only seized for your own. You have captured the Omegas and even now hold them captive so you might give them away to strangers. *You* see us as objects.

How can you not understand why I feel so resistant, why I am afraid?"

He purred, almost inaudibly, once she claimed to feel fear. So intent on her expression, so very concentrated in his regard, his hand cupped her cheek. Large thumb stroking soft skin, he explained, "Your own kind betrayed you. Do not waste your thoughts on those who are unworthy."

She could feel her eyes well, knew he would not let her look away, and forced herself to ask, "Were any of them hurt?"

"No wounds of consequence. Three will be hanged."

Horrified, Claire whispered, "For what reason?"

Shepherd hardened his expression, flexing the arm that chained her to his lap. "They attacked my mate and tried to sell you to me... thought to barter a life I already own to ensure their comfort. Do not imagine they had any regard for the others either. Those women had no intention of returning to share the spoils."

Claire clutched at the hand he held to her face, pleading. "Please don't kill them. Lilian and the others were starving, afraid, and desperate."

"So were you"—his narrowed eyes flared—"more afraid than they were. And you were, and are still, trying to be their champion."

Looking down, full of sadness, Claire muttered, "I am a piss-poor champion."

"You did fairly well considering the odds," he acknowledged quietly. "Your flaw was assuming there is good in Thólos, when there is not. That is why you lost."

"I know you're wrong. Some of those women are my friends. They *are* good people. Those who attacked me... I don't know them well, but I would rather show mercy than condemn desperate, starving women tempted by the lie of food you broadcasted on your leaflet."

"And that is why you are weak"—it seemed almost a compliment—"and why I am strong."

"You are stronger than me," Claire acknowledged, studying the Da'rin markings on Shepherd's shoulder, unsure how many dead were represented in that patch of skin. "You're faster, have power, but you lack something great. And you will never find it in the life you live."

"Do I?" It was as if he knew what she was going to say, found her opinion juvenile and cute. "Do you speak of love?"

She shook her head, black tangled hair waving around her shoulders. "Not love. Anyone can love."

"Then what, little sage?"

"Humanity... the source of joy. You may have had it once, but whatever life you've lived has eaten it away."

He hummed at her, unconcerned with her judgment. "I understand humanity at its basest level, and have far more experience in the world than you do, little one. The way the citizens are behaving—such as those women I am going to hang no matter how much you may beg or cry—proves the point that they were never good, even before starvation. Suffering merely draws out the true nature of each life festering under the Dome."

"The way you speak, you make it sound as if you believe you are offering enlightenment by knowingly crafting misery," Claire scoffed, shaking her head, surprised he had not just started fucking her to shut her mouth.

It was the same stormy fury that rolled through his eyes when her words displeased him. Claire was still afraid—afraid of the monster who could so easily crush her, afraid of the effects of the bond—but Shepherd seemed tranquil and almost willing to let her speak.

"The books you keep," she breathed softly, looking to the shelving across the room. "You have such a strange collection... a veritable training manual on how to be a dictator. But then there are soft things: poetry, writings by great spiritual leaders and virtuous human beings. Do you read them to try to seek what you are missing?"

He stated with pride, "I am *The Shepherd*. I lead the flock."

She whispered the words, mesmerized by the exchange, "Through terrorism?"

"Your naiveté is like that of a child. Under this Dome, injustice runs rampant. Thólos is a cesspool filled with corruption, greed, apathy, and vice—a breeding ground of lies. Weakness must be purged, deceptions exposed, and punishment suffered."

Her thickly lashed green eyes went wide. "This is some kind of trial?"

"You have grown wiser, Miss O'Donnell."

The fact he had used her surname was chilling. Her end of the thread began to hum out of tune, the connection to such a creature unwanted and abhorrent. "You don't want power at all... you want the city to wallow in what your breach has inspired. You want to watch us squirm."

A conceited smirk, an evil thing, distorted scarred lips. "Continue, little one."

Slight understanding of the man and his reasoning came together. "You think you are some kind of champion... like Premier Callas, or—"

Snapping in anger, Shepherd cut her off, "Your precious Premier is no more. I ripped him apart with my bare hands, and caution you against speaking his name in my presence."

To be Premier was to be the ultimate servant of Thólos: a hereditary position held by the family that had erected the Dome, and served until death. They were immaculate, lived wisely, and led by example. Yet Shepherd's hate was personal... unexplainable. Claire had to know. Heart racing, she tempted fate, and whispered, "Why?"

"Your Enforcers are dead, your Premier rots in pieces, and soon every Senator will swing outside the Citadel so that all Thólos might breathe the true stink of their corruption." Shepherd placed his lips to her neck and pulled in her scent, flexing his hips to press his growing erection between the soft legs wrapped around him. "So you see, there is no one to save you. You have only me."

At those words, panic surged, her mind racing past the point of dread. If Shepherd hadn't started purring at that very instant, she might have begun to scream.

Large hands went to his belt. He felt her tremble and resist as he withdrew his member, restraining his weakened mate on his lap easily. Feeling the feminine curves nurtured by the food he'd provided, he gave a hungry growl. The instant she was remotely wet enough, he lowered her down on his straining erection.

The pace was almost languid. Her head buried against his shoulder as he lifted and lowered her, Claire's panic broken apart by distracting debauchery.

There would be no escape, all her fighting had been for nothing—these things he whispered in her ear.

She would not show her face, or her silent tears—her only view the sight of his thick cock, shiny with slick, infiltrating her body, just as his taunts penetrated her mind.

Shepherd stroked a hand up to grip her neck, pulled her closer until her breasts were flush to his chest, the location of their bond in contact. He held her so wet, green eyes were compelled to meet his. "Kiss me."

Claire felt it begin all over again. "No."

It was his show. It was *always* his show. Her life was his, her body too. But her lips were her own.

Her defiance only excited Shepherd more. With a low, animal growl, what had been unhurried became an all-out carnal attack. He turned them about, bouncing her on the mattress to pound the scented, pretty hole that sheathed him so perfectly. She screamed, filled the air with sobbed moans of his name. Shepherd held her by the nape, felt the strength of her climax lock on to his cock as he swelled and secured her to him. And though his hips were trapped by the knot, it did not stop the pad of his thumb from grinding against Claire's swollen clit.

He was merciless, pushed her past pleasure and to a point of overburdened sensation.

She tried to writhe away from his finger, the friction too strong, but could do nothing, pinned as she was. Begging in breathless catches of sound, Claire panted, "Shepherd, please stop."

Watching her lips form the words, dissecting the tortured desire and uncontrolled pleasure, he rubbed even faster. Snarling like a beast, still painting her womb with spurts of cream, he demanded, "Who do you belong to?"

There were tears leaking from eyes squeezed shut as she jerked and twitched from his abuse of her clit and the cramping orgasm, prolonged too far. "Pleeease, please stop... I can't..."

"WHO DO YOU BELONG TO?"

She was going to die; it was too much, the sensation so great it was agony. Everything went white, as if the world was made of nothing but blinding, horrid light that stripped her bare. Back arching, she sucked in air, like the first gasping breath of a newborn, and felt another wave of devastating contractions in her core. With a face full of pained pleasure, Claire gasped, "I belong to you!"

"That's right, little one," came a voice as if leagues away. The pinch on her nerves abated and she sobbed when the over-strong, extended climax began to abate. More waves of hot semen burned her from the inside when Shepherd purred, "You belong only to me."

The punishment had been brutal, and it took him almost an hour to soothe her trembling muscles and ragged breath. Eyes shut tight, Claire burrowed into him, pressing hard, worried that should the contact vanish, she might cease to exist.

With a stroke down her hip and back up again, the monster explained in a low, soft rumble. "If I ever smell another man's scent saturating you again, I will hunt down the male and rip off his limbs while you watch... then I will fuck you in the pool of his blood."

Her fingers simply clawed where she clung, digging in deep. "When you speak that way, it frightens me."

Strangely, he hushed her as if comforting a child, gathering her tighter in his embrace.

# 8

He just couldn't believe it. Shaking his head, hurting for her, Corday fought boiling anger. Rumors had spread like wildfire, varying stories of how an enclave of Omegas had been rescued.

That was the term Dome Broadcast used to describe it. *Rescued.*

And Claire was gone. Deep in his gut, Corday felt responsible—that he should have known the Omega would do what she felt was best—and hated himself for not seeing the signs.

Waking up on that lumpy couch, a crick in his neck from the odd angle, he'd realized at once what she'd done. Leaping to his feet, cursing up a storm, Corday had run out the door.

There had been no need to search, his hours racing through the city wasted. Had he simply turned on his COMscreen, a distorted version of the story—including footage of emaciated women accepting food—would have played on repeat. There had been no shot of Claire, or even Shepherd for that matter. But a short Beta known to be Shepherd's second-in-command was featured, offering blankets to the Omegas and directing Followers to see them to safety.

A lie.

Corday didn't know how Shepherd had found them, but after seeing the flyer and the outrageous bounty, he suspected that one of Claire's friends had betrayed her.

The thought broke his heart.

The Enforcer knew Thólos, understood what she was up against. Innocent Claire was too idealistic, too sweet, and no matter how willful she was, still Omega. She saw the world through the eyes of a caretaker, a nurturer—not a warrior.

From the look of the icy grounds surrounding the capture, from the steam of starving women's exhaled breath, it was the freezing Lower Reaches that had sheltered Claire's group—a dangerous place where more than just the subzero weather could kill you.

Corday had made his way into the mist to see for himself, disguised as a looter to pick through the warren, blending in with the rest of the vultures already poaching the meager goods left behind.

Claire's smell lingered in the air, heady with anxiety, powerful from the sweat she must have worked up when she ran to her friends. Corday followed it, ignoring the deserted personal items scattered around the rooms, the garbage. The trail ended at a closet, where—once the door was pushed open—he found trapped air that reeked of sex. Shepherd had fucked her the moment he'd found her. That was clear not only from the smell, but the sight of the discarded sweater and pants Claire had been wearing. His clothes—the ones Corday had specially prepared for her earlier that day.

Crouching down, he lifted the fabric and brought it to his nose, pulling in a breath of the Omega, bowing his head, feeling like a failure.

It could not end this way.

He may have failed Claire, but her information about the pills had brought to light other Omegas in need, and the Enforcers—led by Brigadier Dane—were already preparing to strike. Corday would help them like he'd promised. After all, what was the point of resistance if one didn't actually fight back?

CORDAY HAD a difficult time finding respect for a woman like Brigadier Dane. Dane's arrogance and short-sighted need to constantly remind him about his father's crimes and subsequent incarceration had set them at odds from the first moment he'd met his commanding officer. But something had changed in Dane during the months since the city fell. It was clear that the Alpha female harbored the massive weight of survivor's guilt. Dane tried much harder, spoke much less, and seemed as grimly determined as Corday to right at least one wrong if she could.

The weather was nasty. Even at midday, it was almost dark, the swollen sky over-dome just as unwelcoming as the guards outside the chem pusher's den. When Corday arrived to join Dane's tactical assault, he could smell drugs cooking, the bitter, chemical tinge tainting the air. More so, he could hear the drugged, needy calls of the women, begging for release from wherever the saggy faced dealer had them locked away.

There were about twelve men on the premises. Half were armed with Enforcer-grade artillery they should not have had access to. Guns slung over their shoulders, faces devoid of emotion, the thugs were habituated to the vileness surrounding them. From Dane's intel, the Enforcers now knew which sleaze ran the show; an older, stocky Alpha named Otto. The Brigadier's orders were to keep him alive for questioning.

They needed to know who had supplied those men with those

guns. Were they affiliated with Shepherd's Followers? Were there other cartels with artillery that could be confiscated?

Customers were already shuffling in with offerings to trade, twitching with the need to knot a heated Omega. It seemed something as simple as a fresh piece of fruit or a bag of rice could get an Alpha or Beta laid. There were stockpiles of food, crates stacked in a guarded corner that could be put to better use once impounded.

Taking down these men might potentially fund the beginnings of a true rebellion.

Led by Brigadier Dane, with Corday at her back, the team of twelve armored Enforcers breached the concrete compound in tactical formation. All targets were eliminated without question, the infiltration choreographed to a precision even Shepherd would have admired.

While Dane took down the men bent over tables cooking drugs, Corday's team turned a corner and passed into the back of the building. Nearing where the Omegas were corralled, the Enforcers, like all humans, found themselves susceptible to the lust-inducing pheromones mixed with the stink of human filth. The animal inside Corday sniffed, instantaneously enticed, while the human who controlled such urges found all he saw repulsive. The view was sickening. Six women were chained to the wall, collars around their necks like dogs. Two were so emaciated from the continuous estrous, Corday was not sure how they were still breathing.

Each captive was equidistant—just a bit too far from the others to touch. A few were still being rutted by Alphas; oblivious to the soldiers bearing down upon them. There was no mercy with the city a war zone. A single shot to the head and the offenders died, too caught up in the knot to disengage. In the end, only three of the savages—including the necessary Otto—had been taken alive and bound in the middle of the room. The Enforcers began unchaining

Omegas, preparing to move them as soon as possible before one of the officers instinctively fell into a rut from the pheromones.

There were things Corday had seen in his short years as an Enforcer, crimes so vulgar he just could not believe anyone was capable of committing them. It turned out that the horrors in that Omega kennel were only the beginning. Behind a chained meat locker lay the spent bodies of numerous skeletal creatures. The emaciated corpses of eleven murdered Omegas, bruised, beaten, gazing out of lifeless eyes at the nothing they had become were haphazardly piled up, frozen from the cold that kept them from rotting.

Brigadier Dane stared, the Alpha female slack-jawed, seeing one little girl who looked so much like her missing sister, it took her a moment to register the shouting of her men. Tearing her eyes away, she rushed toward the outcry. One of the Omegas, a female freshly caught and still free of the drug's full effect, held a shard of glass that dripped with blood. Naked, she stood over Otto and his thugs, sawing through the bound gangster's neck until her hand bled.

She'd killed their source of information.

Corday was talking to the Omega in hushed tones, trying to soothe her, to get her to drop the glass, but nothing seemed to get through her zombie-like expression. "Shh-shh, it's all right, put down the glass. We're Enforcers, and we're going to get you someplace safe, ma'am."

Looking to the youth holding out his hands as if to placate her, her broken voice managed, "They killed my Doug, my baby."

"Please, put down the glass."

Glazed eyes rolled back to the dead men who had chained her up, who had taken her life. There was not even a moment of hesitation. She jammed the bloody weapon so deep into her throat, the gush of blood was immediate.

Corday rushed forward, putting his hands to her neck.

Brigadier Dane knew there was no way to save the female from the gaping slash she'd sliced into her own throat, no matter how hard the frantic Beta tried. But there had been ways to save all the females piled up in that meat locker—had the Enforcers taken notice, had they acted months ago. Instead, they had been too busy mustering, plotting, and doing nothing.

In the hearts of all who watched, all feelings of victory faded, dripped away as that Omega's blood stained the floor. Dane crouched down and closed the dead Omega's eyes as she spoke their prayer.

When the incantation to the Mother Goddess of Omegas was complete, Dane's voice hardened. Orders were barked. The tower of food was disassembled and loaded onto transport. The heat-addled Omegas were carted away.

The bodies had to be left behind. There was nothing that could be done for the dead.

All the drugs were dumped, spilling together, filling the air with noxious fumes—the perfect recipe for the absolution of fire. Corday struck the flame, destroying the counterfeit heat-suppressants, the methamphetamines... the evidence of atrocities and the Enforcers' part in purifying it. But the shell of the building still stood.

Thólos was fireproof.

TIRED, Claire stretched her legs out from under warm blankets and pressed her feet to the ground. She felt… off, saturated with the lethargy that comes before illness, and was grateful Shepherd was not in the room to paw at her as he always did when she woke. He had punished her for her resistance, had frightened, then placated, back to his old tricks of trying to warp her mind.

Sitting on the edge of the bed, she rubbed the sleep from her eyes and frowned at the ache in her shoulder. In the room, everything was where it had been the last time she had been locked inside. Except her painting of poppies. It was skewed, the paper less crisp, as if having been handled repeatedly. Denying her impulse to center it, Claire studied the flowers, certain Shepherd had done the same in her absence.

Considering the great rage which had blared from his side of the link at the onset of her escape, there was no sign of such wrath about the cell. No furniture was broken. Her meager things were exactly where she had left them, almost as if she had never been gone. Even the bed sheets were the same; stale, unchanged in her absence.

Moving at a snail's pace towards the bathroom, Claire peeled off the gauze on her shoulder and stood under warm water. It was hard to move her arm without pain, shampoo stung her wound, and she found herself gritting her teeth at the discomfort it caused her simply to become clean.

As if he had known she would want to bathe upon waking, there was a sterile gauze pad and tape waiting on the counter. Wanting to cover the ugly mark so her churning stomach would stop threatening to spill each time she looked at it, Claire dressed the bite. While pressing down the tape, mindful of the bruising, her eyes caught something that shouldn't be. The small bin they used for their laundry displayed one of her dresses peeking out near the top. Considering she had been gone for eight days, it struck her as strange. Pulling it out, her brows shot up. The fabric smelled of her, but it reeked of Shepherd's semen... as if he had been sniffing it as he masturbated before coming on her clothes.

The idea brought an unwelcome twinge between her legs, and Claire unthinkingly dug deeper, only to find almost every item of her clothing had been treated the same way. Why would he do that

—or, more importantly, why did it smell so good? Realizing she still had the first dress pressed to her nose, a wave of embarrassment made her cheeks burn. Claire quickly stuffed the offensive laundry back down.

Cool water was splashed on her face and the fever seemed to pass.

There was something about the act he'd committed. In all her days of freedom, she had fought not to think of Shepherd, not to question how their separation might have affected him. Claire had not allowed herself to wonder if he had suffered as she had. Her denial of his call, her denial of the bond, it had twisted her. What had it done to him? Had he worried she might have been hurt? Even the bounty had stipulated she must be brought in undamaged to claim the reward. The man had placed a great deal of confidence in the greed of others... and it looked like his assessment had been correct.

Claire left the bathroom, left her flushed reflection, and began to pace.

Absently, she looked about and found her earlier assessment was incorrect. The room was just not right. It began with the bedding, it was unsatisfactory. It had to be replaced. She stripped it off, feeling slightly better when fresh linen was laid out. Her painting had to be moved, to be centered. A headache began to pound, the lump on her skull throbbing. She began to pace some more. One moment she was hot, the next cold. Yet no matter if she sweated or shivered, she was thoroughly uncomfortable.

Worry for the Omegas agitated the forefront of her thoughts. Shepherd had assured her no one had been wounded. But what of Lilian? What of her cohorts? Had he murdered them? Was he stringing them up that very second?

Claire's stomach rolled, and for a moment she felt truly ill. The feeling passed, swamping her with dread and leaving her empty.

This was it. Green eyes appraised drab, grey walls, sweeping the room. This was her life—a life tethered to a man obsessed with keeping her hidden away; who was going to hang three women because they had tried to collect the bounty he'd offered. A possessive monster who wielded evil as a tool… a fiend who would say terrifying things and then cuddle her back to a sense of false comfort.

Shepherd was admittedly evil. They were incompatible—in needs, in ideals—in the very makeup of their souls. And they were pair-bonded. Forever.

Before she might cry, Claire tried to lose herself in cleaning the room, slowed by her arm and distracted by her worry. No matter how she scrubbed, nothing seemed clean enough. But the worm was pulsing, indulging in her crazy behavior, whispering to her of how perfect this was, of the beauty of that grey-walled room, of the prowess of her mate and how clever he was in retrieving her.

By the time Shepherd arrived, Claire was resigned, sitting at the table with her head on her arms. Her mate had a tray for her, and looked over the room with approval upon finding that his female had occupied her time practically. They did not speak. Claire simply sat up, pushing her hair behind her ear, and frowned at the food.

It was a beautifully arranged chicken breast, drenched in a savory sauce thick with mushrooms and garlic. Exactly the kind of cuisine Claire loved, but something about the smell was off. It had been difficult to eat during those last few days of freedom, a side effect of fighting the bond, and she felt uncomfortable even as she reached for her fork. The man was purring, he smelled of rich Alpha, all things that should have brought her comfort, all things her body and mind had demanded when she'd been in hiding. Even so, she could hardly force half of the dish down.

It should have been good. She should have been hungry.

Feeling unwell, Claire pushed the food away and felt she might vomit. He stood beside her, reached down to pick up the customary vitamin she tended to forget, and waited for her to take it. Eager to just get it over with, she tossed it into her mouth and gulped the water. When it was done, when the pill had squirmed down her throat, she began to gag.

A warm hand came to the back of her neck and pushed her head between her knees, the purr increasing in volume and strength. The wave of nausea passed, but left her in a cold sweat. It had to be the stress, or maybe she'd picked up a bug. All Claire knew was that there was no fucking way she was swallowing another thing.

"I must check your claiming mark for signs of infection." It was not a suggestion, it was a command, and she knew it.

"Can you just give me a minute?" Claire grumbled, doubled over and not at all eager to straighten.

"I will retrieve what is required. It will take several minutes, which you may use to collect yourself."

The weight of his hand left her neck and Claire watched his boots disappear. Sucking in slow, cooling breaths, she managed to uncurl and wiped the sweat off her face with her forearm. By the time he returned, she'd lolled back in the chair, staring at the familiar concrete ceiling, still feeling like shit.

The beast approached. "Sit up straight."

A new tray was set down, filled with various medical instruments and two prefilled syringes. Eyeballing the strange assortment, Claire tensed when Shepherd slid the strap of her dress down. The gauze was pulled carefully away. Swabs soaked in hydrogen peroxide ran cool over hot skin, making the angry bite fizz. She looked away, unsure if she was going to puke. Everything he was doing seemed to be as concise as possible, to minimize discomfort, the hulk bending down and handling her gently.

She sat still through all the poking and prodding, extremely unhappy with the event, and just about ready to lose her cool and hide in the bathroom. Ointment was smeared over the mess, fresh gauze taped down, and then he stuck a digital thermometer in her ear and nodded at the result.

When those large hands went to grab one of the syringes, Claire stiffened and asked quickly, "What are those?"

"This is an antibiotic." Shepherd held her arm as if she might yank it away and injected her quickly. Claire watched the needle leave her skin, a tiny bead of blood welling. When he came at her with the second one, his grip tightened and he stabbed it much harder into the meaty part of her bicep. While she gave an irritated ouch, he pushed in the plunger and said frankly, "And this is a much purer form of the fertility drug you had in your pockets when you came to the courts."

"*What*?"

Claire was already shoving at him, beating at his arm with her fist to get him the hell off. The Alpha just ignored each blow and pressed a sterile cotton ball to the injection site, rubbing until her arm ached.

"YOU FUCKING BASTARD! HOW DARE YOU!"

Seemingly mellow, he explained, "That was your second dose. The first injection was administered upon your arrival twenty-four hours ago. That is why you feel ill."

The stomach acid, the cold sweat, the fever... it was exactly how she'd felt waiting in the courts, magnified by ten. Only this time, she was not terrified. Instead, she was about ready to kill him. While she screamed every obscenity she knew until red in the face, Shepherd simply held her arm and continued to knead the injected drugs into her muscle.

She was not due for another estrous for at least three months, five if she was lucky, and this jackass was forcing one on her.

"Why would you do this?" she spat at him. "*Why*?"

Without remorse, he explained, "Your body was too weak

during your last heat to accept fertilization. You are stronger now. The chance of successful impregnation is much more likely."

"So you pump me full of drugs to breed me like a horse? Do you have any idea how fucked up that is? I have been pair-bonded to you for less than two months. This is insane! *And I would have cycled naturally in the spring*!"

Shepherd spoke, completely unconcerned by her outburst, "Time is a factor, and as an Omega, motherhood will only bring you joy."

Claire was about to start tearing out her hair. "Shepherd, get the fuck out of this room! Take your poison and short-sighted assumptions about Omegas and LEAVE!"

When she saw laughter between his lashes, she lashed out and slapped him as hard as she could. All her violence accomplished was her stinging palm, Claire squeezing her fingers into a fist to cradle the offended digits to her chest. He seemed calm, as if completely expecting her tantrum, and stood through it as she railed and tried to get up from the chair.

When she was a disheveled mess, hair wild and eyes threatening murder, she felt another wave of horrible feverishness, worse than before, and growled like a beast. "I hate you!"

"You are hormonal."

Of course she was hormonal, he'd been pumping her full of hormones!

It came out from between tightly clenched teeth. "You are a pig... a bad mate."

"I guarantee that you will like me much better in a matter of hours," he cooed evilly, the backs of his fingers reaching out to stroke her cheek.

Claire jerked away and burst into tears. She didn't know if this was some sort of fucked up punishment or just another part of her life he had in his control. All she knew was that everything about what he'd done was not okay.

When he tried to pet her hair, she slapped his hand away and shrieked, "*Don't touch me*!"

She bent over, hid her face in her skirt, and sobbed. Shepherd stood by through the good ten minutes it took before her wailing distorted into gasping hiccups.

"If you will stop this crying, I will take you outside and show you your sky," he offered, his jeering replaced with subtle enticement.

She stayed bent, her face hidden, and slapped at the air in his direction. "Go to hell."

The thread, the little link between them, had been so happy, so full and warm, only an hour before, but now the thread was only pain, like a razor blade in her chest. She hoped to god it hurt him as much as it was hurting her, that the damn greasy cord was a two-way sense of torture. But then she remembered that he was only a psychopath with no heart, incapable of human emotion... that he was torturing Thólos on purpose.

Thinking about her mother, Claire understood everything that must have been going through that woman's head all those years... eating away at her until she just couldn't take it anymore. Her father may have been a decent man, but even Claire could see that her mother had not wanted him... that she'd longed for the female Alpha next door that she could never have. How freeing her suicide must have been. Control of her destiny, of the one thing the pair-bond wielding Alpha could not decide for her. The idea was growing increasingly appealing.

"I do not approve of the direction of your thoughts," Shepherd growled, low and threatening.

Claire ignored him.

Large hands circled her arms and pulled her up to stand.

Refusing to look at him, she sniffed and turned her head, staring pathetically at the far wall.

"We will go outside. You will see your sky and you will feel better." It was a command. "This emotional response from the medication will pass."

It was like he had no idea how people worked.

All the signs of a steadily encroaching heat cycle were there: trembling shivers, cold sweat, her digestive tract shutting down. All the cleaning, the need for the room to be ready... Shepherd was right. In a few hours she would be begging him to fuck her.

Covering her mouth, another wave of nausea came.

He let her go, watching as she ran to the bathroom to vomit. Between her stomach vacating retches, she distantly recognized that he was holding back her hair, that his hand was stroking her back. Everything she had eaten was expelled until nothing but bile came up. She felt so utterly sick and so completely debased, sitting there on her knees with the very cause of her torment the facsimile of comfort.

"Why are you doing this?" she breathed, even as he wiped a cool towel over her face.

"I desire offspring. A legacy."

"You're sick." Rational thought was returning and Claire struggled to crawl out of the cradle of his lap so she might reach the sink and rinse out her mouth. "Even you must see that this is no place for a child."

He spoke with assurance, watching her brush her teeth and looming far closer than was comfortable. "Pregnancy will calm you into the rightful state of mind. There is no need for you to be upset, little one. I will provide you both with safety and comfort."

Spitting, she snarled, "Safety? You just poisoned me. Comfort? I live in a concrete box!"

His deeply warning silver eyes narrowed, Shepherd was clearly losing patience. "It was necessary, and it will only be beneficial to you if, in your coming estrous cycle, you should conceive."

"Do not make it sound as if your actions benefit me. I would be completely at your mercy. Pregnancy would make me actually *need* you!"

"You are already completely at my mercy. No more sulking." He took her by the scruff of the neck, the purr he'd incessantly offered never wavering as walked her back into the bedroom. "We will walk now."

Claire was not stupid. "Don't pretend this is an act of kindness. You want me to leave the room so others can come in and prepare it."

"You are very clever, little one. A good trait for the mother of my progeny."

"And you are very evil," she answered back, eyeing the mountain before her with abject loathing.

Shepherd seemed to grow, to spread out into the dim darkness of her prison. "I can be. But I am also a man, and I expect a child from the one I chose as mate. It is unfortunate the timeline does not please you, but it is what I wish." A large palm was extended for her to take, not exactly an act of politeness, and not exactly a threat. "Now come. I will escort you outside."

Claire had no coat and no shoes, so Shepherd wrapped her in a blanket, wiped her face and smoothed her hair, purring loudly to keep her from snarling. There was absolutely no one in the halls he led her through, as if he had prepared and ordered off any men who might have encountered the Omega who belonged to him. Walking the labyrinth, Claire memorized every turn, each little landmark, building a map in her head, ready to bolt at the first opportunity. Through it all, Shepherd maintained an unrelenting clamp on her hand. She wasn't going anywhere.

Their silent journey ended at the lower terrace, near the base of the Citadel—a disappointing segment which offered little in terms of the view beyond the fog-coated Lower Reaches. The blue-eyed Beta was there, armed and staring straight ahead, but no one else.

Feet freezing against the ground, a stiff wind pressed the fabric of the blanket against her legs, all discomfort was ignored by the unhappy Omega. Though it was dark, there was an expanse of sky far above, surrounded by towers reaching up to brush the top of the Dome.

If she squinted, she might make out the stars.

Claire ached, her heart a deep-seated, rotting piece of meat encased in ribs damaged by the worming thread. Absently, she began to rub at the spot, staring through tears, sick, and nearing hopelessness.

Shepherd stood behind her, flush to offer body heat, toying with her hair as it blew in the gusts. Every part of her longed to shove him away, to pull her hair from his fingers, but she knew that screaming at him in a rage in the room was the extent of the disobedience Shepherd would allow. Challenging him in front of a male, his subordinate Follower, would not end well for her. He had so much more to threaten her with now that chemically induced estrous approached. If she pushed him hard enough, he might go so far as to let his men mount her, and she was terrified at the thought of being shared like a whore.

A torment was coming. She was young, fertile, and Shepherd's scent advertised virile male. They were extremely biologically compatible. He would create life within her. As if it were already an actuality, Claire looked down to her flat belly and pressed her hand to where, in less than a week, a baby would be growing.

His nose was at the back of her skull, Shepherd breathing deeply. "You are feeling better."

"Does it matter how I feel?" she asked, low enough that her words were kept between them.

Tugging gently on her hair exactly the way he knew would calm her best, he answered, "It matters."

"I will never forgive you for this."

The man purred louder, his arm slipping about her middle like an anchor.

Turning around, eyes level with his chest, Claire put her hand on the relative part of his body where her own worming thread was hooked. Lifting wet, spiky lashes to look into expressionless silver eyes, she openly wept. "This is where you are tied to me, where the bond is threaded. Perhaps you are incapable of feeling what you've done, but I do know this: pair-bonded Alphas are supposed to care for their Omegas. But you do not... so why pair-bond to me? If all you wanted was a child, you could have injected me with your drugs and seeded me just the same. Why make me carry the burden of an unfulfilling bond? Why ruin me so I might never be happy?"

He did not look away, but she got the feeling he was trying to look through her. After the space of three breaths, Shepherd spoke. "You are young and believe that you understand the world from your short-sighted, idealistic perspective. You think you know much more than you do," he explained as if he were some great eloquent teacher, the music of his voice unaffected by the wind. "Sometimes, it is as unsophisticated as a man simply wanting to because he could, saw a chance, and took it."

The giant was talking in circles, giving her nothing at all. Claire took her hand from the place where she hoped he might feel something—some hint of regret, something for her beyond the idea of a possession. "I will fight estrous."

"You will try." A finger hooked her chin and brought her attention higher. He was serious, his expression conveying his point. "But I am your mate, and I will see you through this heat. I will tend you and give you pleasure, and when it is finished, you will give me what I desire."

"If I fail to conceive, will you drug me again?"

Tucking back a strand of her hair, he nodded and softly answered, "Yes."

Locked in that silver gaze, Claire muttered, lost and shaken, "My feet are cold."

"I am aware, but I want you to experience your sky for as long as you can." He rubbed her back as if to warm her and continued almost gently, "We both know you cannot be trusted, little one. Therefore, you will not be seeing it again for quite some time."

A large warm thumb was already there to wipe away the angry tears he knew would fall at his verdict.

CORDAY PRESSED his back to the wall behind him and tried to ignore the chemically induced begging of the women locked in the room at his back. Only six Beta Enforcers had been allowed to remain on scene at the safe house, rotating who had to enter the room to force-feed the Omegas heat-suppressants every four hours. They did what they could to block out the pheromones, wore masks drenched in pungent oil, moved as quickly as possible. Even so, it set the Betas into the rut and each man had been tested. Two had been dragged outside to breathe clean air when whoever was watching through the pane of glass saw the change come over their comrade.

It was not intentional, and not one of the women had been touched. The compulsion was simply an act of nature they prepared for with checks and balances. The Enforcers tending to the Omegas worked as a team for that very reason. But even with their careful nursing, one of the females—a body that was little more than skin and bones—had already died from lack of nutrition and unseen internal injuries.

No one knew what her name was when they buried her in an

overgrown terrace lawn, as deep as they could dig before hitting structure. Her story was unknown, another Jane Doe left to rot by Shepherd's occupation. The Omega had dark hair like Claire, a similar small frame. As the dirt had been laid over her, Corday felt sick, had almost cried, and went back inside before it was done, unable to look any longer.

Twelve hours had passed since the Omegas' first dose. Through the small window, Corday could see the sky had grown dark and braced himself. He would be next to enter the room reeking of chemically exaggerated estrous.

An alarm beeped, and the Enforcer who would watch over him as he shoved medicine into the women's mouths said, "It's time, man."

Nodding, Corday stood, took the offered mask they'd drenched in stink, then grabbed the pills and water. The door was opened and he moved forward, unconsciously holding his breath to start from left to right.

Their jaws opened willingly to suck his fingers. It was getting them to swallow that was almost impossible. He had to purr brokenly, which forced him to breathe, and practically drown them until they managed to swallow the pill. He made it through all five, felt the fever, and backed away even as his cock began to throb so hard it hurt. Once outside the room, he practically ran outdoors, his mind full of Claire and the moment of weakness he'd had at the apartment when the bathroom had smelled so damn good and had made him so fucking hard.

The fact that, even at that moment, he wanted to reach into his slacks and jack off, filled him with self-loathing. Corday fought it, stood in the cold for over an hour... just as all the other Enforcers who had been in the room had. Eventually, he found himself, grew flaccid, and went back inside to continue his watch. He prayed to the god of the Betas that he would not have to go back into that room.

The prayer, like all his others, was not answered.

It took almost three full days for the Omegas to come out of estrous, and five more trips into the pheromone-laced hell for Corday. As the females came to their senses, they were confused and scared... most having been so high they hardly remembered what had happened to them. The ones who did remember were inconsolable or blank—like dolls with nothing inside. The Enforcers gave them food, each man assigned shifts for suicide watch.

Another Omega died by morning, the most vacant one... cause unknown. It was Brigadier Dane who sighed and said it seemed like the girl had just decided to stop breathing.

Corday buried her, knowing at least that her name was Kim Pham, right next to Jane Doe. That time, he cried like a baby.

# 9

As they stood on the terrace, Claire suffered the first stirrings, the first warning sign it was time to fight estrous. A wave of warmth banished the cold, the blanket around her became uncomfortably hot, itchy... she tried to hide it. Her attempt to feign normalcy made no difference. Shepherd sensed the change at once. Without a word, she was lifted and swiftly carried back to her cage. Once the door was locked, she scampered off, forcing space between them, where she began pacing back and forth. Her march continued for hours, her stomach sour, her mood foul. The male seemed content to let her wring her hands and pace to and fro, noting she refused to even glance in the direction of the provided nesting materials, or at the table full of food prepared to see him through what might be a lengthy seclusion.

The knots in her gut twinged and soon she was breathing hard, pressing her hand to her belly, worried what his drugs were doing to a body nowhere near ready to ovulate.

A calming, muted voice came from the corner. "The discomfort will pass. There will be no long-term damage."

Claire threw the unwelcome presence a long, vicious growl, hating how he spoke as if he could read her mind. He ignored her disrespect, merely sitting like a gargoyle too big for his chair.

It was infuriating.

She wanted him to leave the room, unaccustomed to being near a male in those uncomfortable moments of pre-estrous. Forcing herself to ignore the intruder, Claire employed a catalog of tricks she'd learned over the years, small distractions that might ease the madness. Feverish, she found her hands in her hair. She braided her locks, paced, unbraided, breathed—over and over. The delicious smell in the air—the scent of a far too near Alpha—she pretended was something else: orange blossoms from the orchards her dad loved to visit. Every summer of her childhood, he'd purchased family admission to the highest level of the Gallery Tower so she could play in the dirt as little girls had once played before humanity retreated under glass for survival.

Each precious weekend had cost her father a month's wages.

Needing to crack her neck, her bones growing looser, Claire absently rolled her damaged shoulder. Instant pain stopped all movement. She'd forgotten. Looking down at the bandage, she trilled her fingers over the gauze. It hurt much less. Muted pain receptors signaled that full estrous was almost at hand.

Fear sharpened a clouding mind. Claire forced more thoughts of orange blossoms, ignored the need to pop joints, and tugged at her hair.

But time marched just as she did. Movements that had begun in a brooding, stiff cadence grew into something languid. Frustration spiked, diminished, leveled. And no matter how hard she tried to concentrate, her thoughts grew muddled.

At the sound of a purr, Claire began absently humming. Something soft came under her touch. Bedding, all fluffy, all new, lay in her arms. Once she realized she had mindlessly begun organizing the nest, she dropped it all, scattering the temptation, and stumbled back as if burned.

Shepherd chuckled. "You are doing fairly well, little one, but you will not last much longer."

Her head turned slowly toward the unwanted presence. Finding Shepherd naked, Claire's thought process slammed to a stop, her attention drawn to the bulging grandeur of his stiff cock.

Green eyes began to dilate.

The Omega had endured remarkably. She had denied and ignored him with a will deserving admiration. But there would be no more time wasted. Based on her behavior, Claire's reaction to the injection was stronger than predicted, her temper and outright aggression almost cute as she fell further in. Shepherd had found himself watching, hypnotized, as she sang under her breath and muttered about fields of orange trees.

"Come to me," he beckoned gently. "Let's end the charade. Allow your mate to tend to you."

She spat, measuring him as if she were the greater dynamic, "What, so I can kneel at your feet, Alpha? *No*!"

When the beast began to stand, to look at her as one looks at prey, the angry Omega stood her ground, showing teeth.

As he approached, she held her breath, determined to make a point that she could resist his scent and presence. Claire could prevail.

Shepherd went to his knees, purring beautifully and stroking her hips. His nose found the apex of her thighs, the heat of his breath hypnotic. "Is this what you wish, for me to kneel to you?"

His nearness exacerbated the internal chemical issue she had been fighting so well. Watching him, knowing he had approached, had knelt, to further his agenda, Claire whimpered. Standing rigid and uncomfortable, she fought the urge to touch him so hard, her muscles shook.

"Your eyes look very beautiful this way, little one," Shepherd crooned, mesmerized by the green irises slowly conquered by the encroaching black of her pupils.

He was not holding her. She could just walk away. One step, then another—it would be simple. Instead she grimaced, feeling that first sharp cramp of estrous slick. He smelled it at once and silver eyes flared. Rising with a flowing grace, Shepherd rubbed against her, pulling her dress in a swish of fabric over her head.

From the Alpha's chest came a demanding growl, the male relishing the way his mate's body doubled over at his call. For hours he had controlled his need to posture and pace so that she could have her short-lived victory. He had tested himself instead of descending into the rut and forcing her along. Now slick openly dripped down her legs. Now every fiber of his being needed to fuck her.

Shepherd wrapped a hand around the scruff of Claire's neck and pressed her lower. Fisting his cock, he rubbed the head of his manhood against her lips, spreading the heady fluid created to entice her into the frenzy. She stiffened, panted, the tip of her tongue flicking out against her will.

Swallowing, she keened.

"Is it not better when you don't fight what you are?" he asked, smoothing her black hair to expose hollowed cheeks to his view, hungry to watch her suck at his cock.

For a moment Claire remembered herself. On her knees, debased before him, Shepherd's cock slipped out of her lips and she looked as if she might weep. "What you have done is wrong."

The pads of his fingers burrowed against her scalp. "I am giving you life."

Unable to stop running her nose over the heat of his groin, she panted, "I already had a life. You destroyed it."

Feeling the fury, lust, and vehemence blend with wretched need,

Claire clawed her way up his body. Dilated eyes wide and burning, she growled at the male. The noise had hardly left her throat before Shepherd spun her about and pressed her back into the mattress.

Arched, struggling to sheath the mountain cramming his throbbing cock into the pussy that wept for him, Claire entered full estrous. The cord was plucked to harmony, her insides eager for that first true sip of what her pair-bonded mate promised to give. Shepherd hooked her legs over his arms, allowed her to scratch and cling as he attacked, ramming fast and deep, staring into blown pupils while his little one howled.

He had enjoyed her during the Omega's first heat, but something was far more fulfilling in this second estrous cycle. Shepherd was as high on her pheromones as she was on his, knotting her with shouted roars each time her pussy clamped down and wrung his cock for fluids. Words were spoken they could hardly remember, shrieks of ecstasy and feral violence. Claire was so much stronger than before—nothing compared to him, of course, but she had no reservations about attacking if he did not please her. And Shepherd loved it, loved how he had to pin her down, secure viciousness, and overtake his prey.

Claire slept in spurts, always lying on top of him, no matter how he tried to tuck her against his side. When she woke the first time, she looked down at the mess of blankets and just knew they were all wrong. Shoving at the warm mass in her way, she snarled until it shifted, yanking soft materials out from under the Alpha.

As she designed the nest, the heat of a nearby body lingered at her side. Shepherd sniffed her often, running his fingers through the dripping fluids that ran sluggishly down her thighs, stopping only to hand the Omega pillows or whatever she demanded next. When it was done, Claire pushed him back into what she had built and took what she wanted—a thing she had never done before. Riding his cock at her pace, watching him and relishing the way he eased that horrible internal itch, she came powerfully, loving the look in his eyes when she grinned.

The Omega prowled over him, her black eyes utterly absorbed in his body. It kept him hard for days. When she grew tamer, as the overblown reaction to forced estrous lessened, she would stay still long enough for him to scent her, for his big hands to rub the puddle of come that had leaked out of her womb all over her skin, to feed it to her as he purred and gave affection.

When her high was near its end, Shepherd moved in her gently, his silver eyes watching every tick, seeing that she smiled softly and gasped in pleasure with each thrust. He put his lips on hers.

Even caught in estrous, she repeatedly refused his kiss.

Shepherd found it very displeasing.

With her small, conquered, exhausted, and distracted in orgasm, it would be so simple to take... but he needed her to come so he might knot her. He needed her to cry out—because once she did, once he had her fully trapped where she could not resist, he was going to force what was his due.

Eager for his due reward, his hips snapped, he clutched her too tight. Mouth at her ear, Shepherd howled, "COME NOW!"

Something in his tone, the absolute command, and Claire spasmed. Eyes rolling back in her head, her climax crashed too soon and too hard. Shepherd's knot swelled huge behind her pelvic bone, the beast groaning loudly with each gush. With her mouth open in a silent scream, he took advantage. Shackling hands held her in place, as if the female would panic. His rough lips crashed down.

She tried to turn her head, body twisting. No matter how he teased her tongue, how he sucked her lips, Claire would not engage.

Issuing another stream of semen into his Omega, Shepherd lifted his head and found her eyes hooded, distant. Growling, frustrated, he demanded, "Kiss me, little one."

Full lips came again to hers. When Claire locked her teeth, he grabbed her jaw and brought her face back to his. "Look at me."

It was the rough-hewn voice that broke through the haze of orgasm, Shepherd desperate and almost human. She glanced at the source, confused. A ragged scar ran diagonally across what was still a beautiful mouth. She found a strong jaw. She looked at him as if for the first time, studied the Alpha who had taken her, who had drugged her to force a child into her womb—the one whose purrs almost brought her as much peace as the sky.

"Look at the man you claim to hate," snarled words were distorted by gnashing teeth, "and kiss me, little one."

Claire continue to stare, reaching up to touch, to trace the lines of her mate's face—the stubble on his jaw, his fine nose, and the aggressive lips with their arresting scar. She whispered to him. The great beast began to tremble, eyes clouding with what almost looked like physical pain.

She did not offer her lips, but she pulled his head to her breast and offered a tingling nipple instead. He sucked greedily.

TUCKED AGAINST HIM, his Omega slept far more deeply than she had after he'd broken her previous heat cycle. Carefully running his fingers through the dark mass of her hair, Shepherd purred, just as possessive as he had been from the first. Obsessive thoughts circled in his head, centered on the female in his care, on how to keep her, on how to continue. She was his. He was never going to share her. She'd stay in this room and he would pet and purr as much as was needed while the child he'd planted grew.

What was a sky compared to that? Nothing. The sky was nothing.

His little one stirred, and dark lashes fluttered open. Seeing his face, smelling the familiarity of his breath, Claire hummed sadly and put a hand to her belly. "I am pregnant."

"You are, little one. Your scent is already altering." He disregarded the look in her eyes when it was not exactly one of joy, and stroked her cheek. "You will provide me with a fine child."

Something about the way he spoke made her incredibly uneasy. The haze of lust was gone. The moments of tender words and untrustworthy proclamations passed. Automatically, the purr increased and the tugs on her hair resumed. Watching him with distrust, Claire filtered through the memory of the last few days, aware he had been patient with her initial refusal and outright drug-induced aggression. Shepherd could have debased her, but for hours he'd simply watched—until she began to drip, until the rut became unavoidable. Not that it absolved him of what he'd done, the manipulative bastard. She almost wished he would have just outright raped her.

He'd got what he wanted without her consent or approval, and been rewarded with a very willing bedmate in estrous.

"Are you going to keep our child locked in this room, too?" she asked, nervous that no matter what his answer was, it would not be good enough.

"No." The purr came full force.

Claire reached for his hand, holding his eyes as she pulled the roughened palm down her sticky body where it might rest over the life planted within her. It was almost impossible to bring herself to whisper, "Will you separate me from..."

The hand on her abdomen tightened over a womb cradling rapidly dividing cells, owning their combined genetics. "You do not need to worry over such things."

"That is not an answer." She rose to an elbow, growing indignant. "I was not ready for a child—certainly not with a man I hardly know—but you have done this, and I would know what you are going to do to us."

"Already the protective Omega mother. I find that pleases me." There was a strange glow in his eyes, as if the bastard was grinning, though his scarred lips remained neutral. Pressing her down into their nest, he purred, "I will not part you from our child."

But would somebody else? The man had ways of spouting half-truths. "Shepherd." The name was spoken like a threat.

There was a smile in his voice, a hint of something dark, as well. "Yes, little one?"

"Do not give me cause to hate you more."

He was charmed by the warning, and began to twist his fingers in a long strand of midnight hair. "No more talk of hatred. You are my mate, bound, and you will devote yourself to me."

Dark brows shot up and her jaw dropped. "You cannot force that."

The pad of his thumb traced her lips. "I can."

As if in agreement with the man, the thread began to bang loudly in her chest. There was to be no more talk, she was too tired to argue. The familiar weight of his hand moved from her belly to between her legs. Ignoring how Claire turned her head away, he began to stroke the little bundle of nerves, flicking it to entice it to swell.

Shepherd growled and purred as he played with her pussy. "Submit. I will be gentle and you will enjoy it. Once you are calm, you will sleep more."

THE ROOM WAS COLDER than the cell Nona had been locked in for the past six days. A guard, a brutish man four times her size, gestured to the empty chair across from a Beta she had seen on the premises. That Beta had led the men who'd dragged Lilian and her friends away days ago.

"My name is Jules. Take the seat, Nona French."

He had an unplaceable inflection and the startling blue eyes of a bully. She knew his type. Nona pulled out the chair.

"Your registration states you are a Beta, and according to your clearly fraudulent record, you have never been pair-bonded or conceived children," the man began, looking up from the file before him to meet the older woman's eyes. "Are you the one who taught Miss O'Donnell to live as a Beta?"

The woman had her own questions and was disinterested in the Follower's bullshit. "Where is Claire?"

The smallest of smirks came to the Beta's face. Placing his hands on the table, he took his time organizing his body into a position of subtle intimidation. "She is where she belongs. With her mate."

"The Alpha, Shepherd?" It was asked like a question, but they both knew it was a statement of disgust. She'd seen the brute carry her off, Nona spraining her wrist trying to fight free so she might save her. Her wrinkled lips turned down at the corner, and the old woman's hands mirrored his—a strangely antagonistic stance for an Omega. "He locked her in a room for five weeks. That is no proper mate."

Hard, unblinking eyes held hers. Jules clarified, "Seclusion is customary behavior when adjusting one's Omega into their new life."

She laughed right in his face. "I should not be surprised at your lack of civility, given what you are. No wonder she was too ashamed to admit who had claimed her. Does he beat her, too?"

"When you saw her, did she look beaten?" The man leered, leaning forward.

Nona answered calmly. "She looked terrified and unwell."

"How long have you known Miss O'Donnell?"

The severe-faced woman said nothing.

Jules was through playing games. "It is in your best interest to answer my questions, Ms. French."

"Or what? You'll lock me in jail so that I can be given away at my next estrous?"

"At your age, estrous would be unlikely. I would simply have you killed."

Tapping her fingers on the table, Nona smiled. "I'm old. And I lived on my terms. The threat of death does not overly concern me."

"What about torture?"

"Only one way to find out."

Jules smiled and leaned back in his chair. "I didn't say your torture. There are two Omegas in our custody too young to serve a purpose. It is them I will torture if you do not tell me what I want to know."

Nona's anxiety spiked. Lips pressed in a line, she nodded.

Looking back at the file, Jules began again. "How long have you known Miss O'Donnell?"

Her answer was vague. "We were introduced two years before her mother died."

"And you have been a surrogate parent?"

"I have been a friend," Nona grunted. "Claire is independent and did not need to be coddled."

Jules looked to her again. "So she is not aware that, when her father died, you funded the endowment that allowed her to pursue art over menial labor?"

"She is not," Nona answered, her lips tight. "As far as I knew, only the bank had access to such information."

Suddenly the tenor of the conversation altered. The air grew thick and Jules spoke with no smile or intonation. "It seems you have a strong personal attachment to the girl, which makes me wonder why you allowed her to enter the Citadel."

A deep furrow grew between Nona's brows. "We both volunteered, but I was supposed to be the one to go to the Citadel."

"Explain."

"She stole the prepared clothing while I was bathing. By the time I was aware of what had happened, she was gone. Claire is very protective of the ones she loves."

"Did no one try to stop her?"

"The group agreed with her reasoning." The woman looked away, her disappointment obvious. "And many simply thought she would be more appealing as our representative. It was a very close vote."

"Is that not ironic?" Bored, the man looked her dead in the eye. "Who was her contact to Senator Kantor?"

"Since you have already questioned the women who met with her that evening, I am certain you are aware that it was never mentioned in the brief conversation we shared." Leaning on her elbows, the older woman demanded, "I want to see Claire."

"No," the Beta answered flatly.

The interrogation continued, a list of assorted questions about Claire's history, her quirks—some so precise, such as her favorite fruit, that even Nona did not know the answer. The exchange was strange, and she wondered why Shepherd did not ask Claire these questions himself.

THERE HAD BEEN only exhaustion in Claire's short-lived freedom, and Shepherd had allowed her no rest upon her return. Between the eight days of insomnia and the chemical alertness of estrous, Claire was drained in a way she had never known. There was never enough sleep. Her former restlessness was replaced with haunting lethargy and an unwillingness to move from the nest. When she woke, she would be burrowed, completely covered. Once or twice, she snarled at the male reaching in to pluck her out from under all the covers so she might eat or he might dress her wound.

All she wanted was the dark and to be left alone. But Shepherd would appear no matter how much she hated the sight of him, the man dragging her to stiffly lie atop him. Too tired to complain, she lay limp, knowing he would cover them both and reproduce her burrow. Once total darkness returned, she would pretend the bastard was not there... or she would try. Shepherd would only let her rest for a short time before his seeking hands more than petted the lingering soreness from her body, fondling increasingly tender breasts and playing between her legs.

Claire did not want the attention, hated that his smell did things to her, that she craved it so badly she had a need to burrow into his side of the bed when he was gone. As if he knew what kept her constantly sniffing him, yesterday's shirts began to appear in their nest. Upon waking, finding them pressed to her nose, Claire would toss them out and curse him to hell.

Shepherd would put them back when he returned.

It was almost a game. That morning, Shepherd raised the stakes. Claire threw one out and woke to find two in its place. When she realized what he'd done, she giggled, a sound that made the secret observer in the corner perk his ears, never having heard her sound for joy. Unaware she had an audience, she threw his things on the floor and burrowed deeper, still laughing.

There was a swat on her rump, and she shrieked in surprise. Twisting, shoving the blankets off her head, Claire sat up, hair a mess, and found him standing over the bed, demonstrably dropping the clothing in her lap.

At the blush on her cheeks, Shepherd was the one chuckling,

prowling over her to sniff at the bedraggled woman. "You think your rejection of your mate's scent in this nest is funny?"

She had not spoken to him—even to ask the hour—in days. Too tired, too confused, still angry, she frowned, unsure of his tone or intention.

"Is your protest a silent way to communicate your preference for the real thing?"

It seemed almost as if he was flirting. Claire cocked a brow, croaking, "No."

Shepherd fisted the blankets and drew them over their heads, pulling her against him as he rebuilt her burrow. Settling back, hating that he was not taking the proper position, and instead looming over her, Claire felt his hand move between them. His fist was pumping, and it took her a minute to realize that he was stroking his cock. A few small grunts, a warning growl when she tried to move away, and his hand moved faster until he groaned low and long. Splashes bathed her naked belly and breasts, fluid pooling until it dripped into the nest and scented the confined space far more strongly than any used shirt.

As if she was in estrous, he rubbed it into her skin, pressed it between her resistant lips, and made sure his seed got everywhere. Something about the act, that he'd done it for his own pleasure and none of hers, left her feeling neglected. He left her as soon as his scenting was done, Claire frowning at his back. Peeking out from her burrow, it took mere minutes before she was tempted to exchange the darkness of her blankets for the subterranean dimness of her cage.

Her bare feet padded silently to the dresser, green eyes sneaking a glance at the Alpha working at his COMscreen. Dressing, oblivious she lacked an urge to wash his semen away, Claire began to do what she usually did in her waking hours underground; she paced.

Her joints were stiff from so much sleeping, and the walking did little to ease her black mood.

Shepherd seemed content to ignore her. She was trying to ignore him, but as the hour progressed, she began unconsciously edging a little bit nearer.

Staring, Claire found his COMscreen bizarre and unreadable. Sighing, bored, she popped her lips and yipped when a great arm swooped out and snatched her out of the blue. Once she was tucked across his lap, Shepherd went right back to whatever he had been doing, trapping her in a cage of overly muscled limbs.

She had been so quiet and he had seemed so focused. It had not been her intention to invite interaction. She squirmed against his chest. "I'm hungry."

An answer came. "No you're not. You're restless and desire attention."

What she was, was irritated. "Why aren't you purring?" The jerk could at least do that. For fuck's sake, it was the only thing he was good for.

Claire could not prove it, but she was fairly certain he was laughing at her, despite his silence. "If I purred, you would not have been coaxed nearer."

Rubbing at the soreness in her shoulder, she narrowed her eyes.

Smirking, he went on, "Your mood swings are mildly amusing, little one."

"What is this?" She gestured toward the screen, unwilling to be baited, and far more willing to be aggravating.

His attention went back to his work. "If you were meant to read it, it would be in your language."

Claire simply rolled her eyes. Lesson learned. She would pointedly keep her distance to avoid this situation in the future.

"No, you won't."

When he responded to private thoughts that were none of his business, she snapped, "Stop doing that!"

Ignoring her, Shepherd's finger went to the screen and tapped until something new flashed, bright and pretty. Leaning forward, she eagerly reached out to take hold without thinking. He began to purr and she to smile as she looked at an image of her family.

"Your father was an Alpha." It was clear that that was who had all her attention in the photograph, that it was his face her finger ghosted over. "Your mother was an Omega."

*Obviously...*

Claire was trying to ignore the distracting man, to focus on something worthy, seeing the patch of blue sky in the background, as they all stood together in the orange grove.

"My mother didn't like my father," she taunted, pointing out the parallel to their situation.

Shepherd mocked her right back. "And to avoid her fate, you sequestered yourself away, became something unnatural."

Her dark head swung around to face the man who could not possibly understand. "There is nothing wrong with celibacy and self-control! You might think I am beneath you, but your short-sighted view of Omegas is pathetic and limiting. It shows very much what kind of mind stands behind the charisma and insane agenda. I made it *years*! Years, Shepherd. And you ruined everything."

Seeing the building fire in his eyes, Claire realize what she'd done. She grew nervous he would react to her outburst, and instinctively covered her belly to protect what was hidden inside.

His tone hissed a forced sort of neutral. "And what was this great plan you saw for yourself? How were you to find a mate when you lived in seclusion and behaved like a Beta?"

Defensive, she grumbled, "I was courted... on occasion."

Shepherd's tense physical response was clearly displeased. "Betas?"

"Betas respect my boundaries. Alphas are dangerous and take without asking."

"And you lied to them about your dynamic."

Scowling, Claire clarified, "I just didn't say anything about it. Being an Omega should not be what defines me, any more than the color of my skin or the level in which I was reared."

"Your mother's suicide had a strong impact on your thinking."

Claire shook her head and gave a cynical sigh, not at all surprised he had researched her history. "I find it funny how often in my life Alphas have tried to equate my subversive behavior with my mother's death. I am not the only Omega to feel this way—many of us do. And if you Alphas had a lick of sense, you would take time to talk to us instead of just spreading our legs for your own amusement."

"Was your father unkind to your mother?"

Claire looked back to the screen. "He doted on her, but it didn't matter. She was in love with someone else."

That stopped him at once. He began to gather her hair in his fist, pulling her head back to force her attention. "You will love no one but me."

Every feeling inside made her long to spit out the truth, to scream that she did not love him at all. But she could smell the aggression, the dominance and anger, and knew speaking was dangerous. Their conversation was at an end, the point driven home a moment later when his hand slipped under her skirt and the growl was made.

# 10

Corday's assumption was accurate. Betrayal by those closest to Claire had allowed Shepherd to abduct his friend. Standing with the masses gathered before the Citadel, he watched three emaciated women being shoved forward to be gawked at and heckled by the crowd. The Omegas had been charged with theft and battery, Shepherd himself shouting their sentence as the terrified females were dragged, then propped up so each might have a noose fitted around her scrawny neck.

Tens of thousands had come to watch the sentencing, Dome Broadcasts having announced the upcoming executions for days.

Thólos Dome had once been the pinnacle of evolved human culture, maintained and exalted no matter the ruins left far behind and far away—the greatest of the Domes. Capital punishment had not existed before the breach. The worst male offenders were sent to the Undercroft, the females to the farming levels to labor. And now the city was enamored with such morbid pageantry, cheering for their conqueror, and hungry for blood.

It was an extravaganza, a visual warning to remind the population who was in charge. It was a sham.

Shepherd postulated, eloquent and captivating, listing the three Omegas' sins, calling them cowards and aggressors—rattling off a record of crimes so ridiculous Corday found the crowd's gasps preposterous. How could they not see what this was? Could they not grasp that those skeletal women were terrified and pleading... that they had been gagged so their shrieks would be nothing but noise?

Shepherd approached the Citadel's archway—turned into a macabre scaffold—large and terrible, the Da'rin markings on his arms flaunted as if the pain they caused him were nothing. The convicted Omegas sobbed pathetically, their eyes darting over the crowd in search of deliverance, mercy... anything.

"Lilian Hale, Xochitl Ramos, Barb Guppy, you have been found guilty and are sentenced to death by hanging."

Shepherd himself, the monster who had Claire in his possession, kicked each support from under the terrified females' feet. They fell —a short drop, their toes kicking a few inches from the ground. Through it all, Shepherd watched them jerk and thrash, fixated. Fifteen agonizing minutes passed before the last of the women stopped twitching.

The rabid crowd lost its edge when the women's uncovered faces turned grotesque shades of purple, the corpses' eyes bulging. Two of them had wet themselves and, in the end, it appeared as if Thólos recognized and began to suffer the fear Shepherd had intended to inspire. The three bodies were left there to swing in the breeze, exposed to the birds when Shepherd turned his back and walked away. The mob began to disperse.

With hands deep in his pockets, Corday moved on. Some part of him had hoped Shepherd would have Claire at his side, that he would flaunt her, though deep down such an idea was ridiculous.

But Corday needed to see her, to know she was okay. For her to see him, so she might know he was fighting for her.

There were so many unanswered questions, so much that weighed on his shoulders, and when he closed his eyes each night, it was her in that grave he saw being covered in dirt—Claire's green eyes, staring dead and unblinking at the sky, which haunted him.

Shepherd was a psychopath. It had been two weeks and Corday was not sure if his friend was even still alive. The temptation to approach, to ease just close enough to see whether he carried her scent, took Corday's feet up the steps and into the Citadel.

It was madness, he knew that. He had totally lost his mind. But with the crush, with the fanfare and the rowdy froth of the crowd, he was unseen and unnoticed. The stink of the room was intrinsically gross. With unwashed males and a few of the more nasty Alpha females, the air was laced with an aggressive musk that mingled into a pungent stench that would warn off the vulnerable and timid. Corday could imagine Claire walking into such a place, could see her being swallowed up.

She had claimed a riot broke out at the start of her heat, that Shepherd had killed a lot of people to claim her. If it was in the midst of this group, she was lucky they had not started ripping off her limbs.

But Shepherd had fought the mob for her...

That was the one part Corday still could not wrap his mind around. Shepherd was a killer, the type to enjoy the bloodbath. He'd just murdered three women. So why fight for Claire, why pair-bond?

Edging through the crowd, mimicking the savage behavior of those shouting for more, Corday went unnoticed. He only needed to get within fifteen feet before he smelled the scent Shepherd wore with pride. Claire's slick—Shepherd's trophy—was fresh, as if he'd only just had her before executing the Omegas Corday's gut told him were responsible for turning her over to the brute.

It was all too surreal, too double-edged. But Claire was alive. In that, Corday found reassurance. So he must remain strong for her—for all the oppressed—and he, like the other Enforcers, would find a way to end this madness.

Gritting his teeth, he left the Citadel.

SHEPHERD FOUND her under her burrow again, fast asleep in a circle of his scented garments. His Omega was almost always sleeping, a side-effect of the early stages of pregnancy. Turning her into the curve of his body, he saw her grimace, draw in his scent, then come awake startled.

Pensive, she began to sniff at him, scowling deeper each time she did. It was impossible to miss her displeasure at whatever she found. Stranger still, she made no secret of her appraisal, climbing over him until her nose was breathing in the air exhaled from his mouth.

Revulsion sat thick in her eyes.

Shepherd let her climb out of bed to approach the bathroom, where he could hear her turn on the shower. Her new ploy, the extensive cold-shouldered silence, continued. Claire was not going to speak to him. She simply marched back in the room with her hand over her nose, her silent way of telling the Alpha to wash off the smell.

"Explain your issue," Shepherd growled, watching her grimace deepen.

Her tongue was sharp when she lowered her hand. "You stink of many hostile Alphas... you contaminated my nest."

He rose from the bed, narrowing his eyes at the disgust on her face. "Your tone is undesirable."

Claire wiped her face clean of her unfriendly expression, needing him to wash, refusing to give him a reason to fuck her while he smelled of the very squalid men who'd almost raped her in the Citadel.

Her heart picked up pace. An off note vibrated out of tune from her end of the thread. "Please don't touch me while you smell like… them."

The way she whispered the entreaty, the odd fear in her eyes, made him frown and skirt away from where she stood, pleading. Shepherd moved into the bathroom.

She stripped the bed in a flurry, bunching up all the offensive sheets to dump by the door. New, unsatisfactorily scentless bedding was put on at once.

Claire was already burrowed when he came back, smelling only of soap and Shepherd. His hand ran over her cloth-covered body. "Come out of there."

She twisted and sat up, finding the monolith naked at the side of the bed.

Piercing silver eyes dissected her trepidation. It was worded as a question and a lure. "Do you still find me offensive?"

In many ways, yes. "No."

He cocked a brow, challenging, "Are you certain? I do not wish to contaminate *our* nest."

Unwilling to invite negative attention, she moved to her knees to nose his stomach, hoping the action would satisfy him enough that he might leave her in peace. "You smell as you should."

It was another one of those new games of his, Shepherd's crafty ways of drawing her out, the manipulation to earn attention outside of her persistent anger. Climbing over her, arranging her body so their skins were flush, he reached for the covers and pulled them over their heads, recreating the soft, dark burrow she liked best.

Feeling her nose at his neck, hearing her absently sniff, it was clear his Omega was appeased—even humming her strange music, contented when his fingers started to manipulate the muscles along her spine. Soon enough, Claire was utterly tranquil, her soft breaths revealing slumber was a heartbeat away.

A rasping breath preceded, "What have you done in my absence?"

Half-asleep, she grumbled, "The same thing I am trying to do right now."

"I have other plans for you."

He felt her body tense, the Omega expecting to be manhandled. A catch of breath hitched before a tone devoid of emotion seemed to strangle her words. "I'm tired."

Correcting her, Shepherd flexed the arm strewn across her lower back and answered with his own low reassurance, "It is natural at this stage that your body feels lethargic while it adapts to its new task. This malaise will pass."

It seemed like such a predictable explanation for her reluctance.

Claire put her chin to his chest and glanced towards the man burrowed in her nest. He ran his palm up her body until it rested flush against her cheek. Watching her reaction, knowing she thought darkness concealed her, he found her expression was not grimaced in the miserable distrust he'd stomached since her return. Instead, it was softly rendered into a state of the resigned acquiescence she refused to show where she thought he might see it.

Taking time to trace her lips, to watch her close her eyes and find a moment's peace under his touch, Shepherd wondered aloud, "You are still angry with me for inducing estrous, even though you were well-cared for during and since."

Claire stiffened, her face forming back into a reflection of sadness. "I suspect you desire a specific answer. I am too drained to figure out what it is."

There had been little conversation between them in their short acquaintance. Most dialogue usually ended the instant Shepherd no longer found her replies acceptable. The frustration of fighting to be heard had passed into disillusioned acceptance. As things were, Claire possessed little interest in anything but sleep.

In that dark little tent of blankets, she looked towards the sound of his breath, chewing her lower lip and wishing that moments like these, the times he would seem gentle, were her reality, that the dark nameless warmth and male body was someone else.

Speaking through the purr he projected gently into her smaller body, he asked, "Beyond leaving the safety of this space, what would lessen this *discontent*?"

"A window."

Burrowing the pads of his fingers against her scalp, rubbing just enough so she'd close those unhappy eyes, all seemed so much better when his mate almost leaned into his hand. "There are several shelves of *windows* waiting across the room, which you have pointedly ignored."

"I don't need to learn how to be a dictator. I don't want to be anything like you."

Shepherd smiled. "I agree. You would make a terrible Follower and would require constant punishment for insubordination."

A palm cupped her face and brought it fractionally higher. His voice in the dark breathed, "You are smiling."

Was she? No, she could not have been. "And how do you punish your Followers?"

The pad of his thumb traced over her forced pout, Shepherd teasing, "Would you prefer corporal punishment over being physically attuned to your proper course?"

There was a stifled coughing noise, and Claire moved out of his palm and pressed her face to his chest. A shudder wracked her body, Shepherd feeling her lips curve against his skin. And then it escaped —a second burst of strangled laughter.

The purr returned in full force. "And now you are laughing..."

"Of course not." She cleared her throat, trying her damnedest to keep her lips from twitching.

The pads of his fingers skimmed her ribs. Claire flinched, stiffened, and then bit her lip to stop her forced, laughing shrieks. "Shepherd!"

"Yes?" He trilled his fingers over her flank as she shied and tried to slip away, only to be caught in all her blankets.

They twisted as he mercilessly tickled. All the while, Shepherd noting each slip, each little quake of a giggle to escape. He seemed alive, full of a new, unusual energy as his ribs expanded and contracted above her in rapid, excited breaths. "Little one, you are alight again."

Automatically sucking her lower lip in her mouth, Claire grunted, "You're smashing your baby."

His weight shifted, and thin branching crow's feet developed outside his eyes as Shepherd observed the female trapped beneath him.

Scarred lips pressed to her neck, the behemoth sucked in a deep, rasping breath. "I favor you this way, little one."

His body flexed against her, and suddenly the massive killer was playful, setting his hip between hers. Immediately unsettled, Claire realized she had behaved badly in her fatigue. She had invited attention, she had engaged... and he seemed very happy about it. Taking her hand, he put her palm on his chest and drew it down the length of his torso, arching into the compelled touch like a spoiled cat.

Claire watched her fingers on their course, wondering idly if he even registered, or cared, that it was only his force on her wrist which continued the caress. She wondered if the thread spoke to him as it did to her. What manipulations was it working in his mind?

The ripple of knotted muscles over Shepherd's ribs, the hard line of his belly, so much mass and heat. Her eyes traveled up to find him watching her clinically, gauging her expression. The moment became far more confusing, as did the light furrow of his brow and the almost intrigued expression surrounding his liquid mercury eyes.

His body shifted, Shepherd drawing Claire's palm higher until it rested against the swirl of tattoos on his thick neck—the forefront of his Da'rin markings. He sniffed and growled low, releasing the pressure of his hand on hers. "I am sore here."

The beast stilled and waited, covering but not crushing her, his complaisance urging her only to stroke him. It seemed a reasonable thing, but she hesitated. Touching him in coitus while her mind was on another plane was one thing. Giving him relief simply because he wanted her to... she was resistant to offer it.

When his hand moved to her breast and began to knead the mound of flesh, Claire stiffened, bracing as she understood his point. His erection had been growing between their bodies and was already pulsing and ready. She could rub him, or he could fuck her.

He was giving her a choice.

Her small hand reached for the covers, to recreate the wrecked burrow, then her hand went back to the thickly muscled nape of his neck.

The beast released her breast, growling low and long at the feel of her hand kneading his spine.

The sensation of touching him seemed so very bizarre. Thinking of it as a chore, considering the act clinically, Claire let her hand recognize where there was tension in the musculature, where she could feel scars. The more she dug in, the deeper his purr became. It seemed the behemoth was nearing sleep, his weight settling a bit more atop her, but that was not what distracted Claire's attention. It was the still hard meat of his cock, and how it would jerk, as if Shepherd were flexing a muscle every so often, butting against her sex. Secondly, her breast, the one he'd caressed in the unspoken offer, was sensitive, and the nipple distended to the point where it ached. Claire had to take great care, as she rubbed Shepherd's neck, to ensure the mound of flesh did not come into contact with him, that the inappropriate thrill when the peaked nipple scraped heat was ignored.

It was maddening.

Even in the early stages of pregnancy, her body reacted to his nearness far more strongly than it had before. Where there had been disgust, Claire began to feel stirrings. It was only a physical reaction, but it felt like a betrayal of her very self when revulsion disappeared and her mind tried to shut off the torrent of endless internal reproofs.

That was why he'd done it, she was certain. Pregnancy made her crave the nearness of the father, almost inspired the interest Shepherd seemed to demand. A long worried breath passed her lips. The giant shifted just a little. As if some threshold had been crossed, some test finished, he seamlessly began to ease the head of his cock into her supine body. Claire pretended it was unwelcome even as she continued to stroke his neck.

She moaned.

Her expression hinted that she found his callused fingers distasteful, but the flush on her cheeks gave her away when slowly he returned his large hand to her swollen breast.

There was something under the surface of the act she could not put her finger on, something in the way the pad of his thumb circled her flesh, his cock still slowly pushing inside her, as if testing the waters. It was too much, as if he was waiting for some revelation, some great moment, and like a bucket of cold water Claire realized what had happened.

Shepherd had never made the growl.

There was no derision, no mocking of her confusion and instant panic, only the satin movement of his hips thrusting forth until her slick passage was filled to the brim. They shared breath. Shepherd rolled his hips, watching her eyes in the dark as Claire came to terms with what had led her to tremble. Her body had broadcast the scent of slick, and he had acted instantly to fulfill something her mind would have never allowed.

She had wanted him.

His warm fingertips left her breast to trace her lips, the line of her jaw, Shepherd watching her hooded green eyes close completely.

The seduction seemed organic—missing the measured calculation he usually employed—but Claire's mind was in turmoil, and she had to do something. It was like a flash of inspiration, the only way she could fight back, because his new dominance over her body had to stop somewhere. He might be drawing soft gasps and murmurs from her lips, but she had the power to think of another. At first it was almost easy, her little mental defiance. She thought of the one person she knew Shepherd hated, his unknown nemesis—she thought of Corday.

Like the flow of a river, Shepherd turned them both until her burrow fell away and he was holding her above him. There was no dark shelter where her face and feelings could hide, he had exposed her... but so long as her eyes remained closed, she could maintain defiance and pretend.

He rolled his hips even as he commanded her, "Little one, you will look at me when I fuck you."

The weight of his gaze drew her attention, and automatically the fan of her lashes lifted. Claire looked through passion drugged eyes.

Green found shining silver. All thought disappeared, the image she'd tried to maintain vanished as if it had never existed. There was only Shepherd.

"Good girl."

Large hands lifted and lowered her hips, the pace still slow, Claire braced on his massive chest to do as she was compelled. Leaning into his touch, caught up, she sucked his fingers. Shepherd angled to hit the place she presented, drawing out her gasps until she began to keen softly. Being pleasured by the Alpha had always been a sensation of mind-bending carnality, but at that moment, all she could register was shining silver and soft touches. In combination with a long hum, her pussy twitched and clasped Shepherd's cock like a fist, drawing the Alpha deeper, enticing him to spill. He did, groaning as he yanked her writhing hips flush against his so he might knot deep in her core.

With the splash of heat in her belly, she was humming, contented. Shepherd pulled her closer, chest to chest, groaning long and loudly as another wave of come shot from his cock just as her pussy clenched for more.

They were locked together, and would be so for some time by the feel of it. With her cheek to the damp skin of his chest, Claire listened to his heart. At moments like that, the thread no longer seemed greasy. It seemed clean, and even when she pretended it was not there, it hummed, singing to her.

Painful self-loathing returned.

There was no comforting purr when her mind grew anxious, no pets to soothe her tension. Shepherd wanted her to recognize the quality of their exchange. Shifting as if to put distance between them, Claire felt the huge bulbous anchor hooked behind her pelvic bone reminding her resistance was pointless. Trapped, she tried to be still, to allow the waves of castigation to burn each and every vein.

In a voice almost laced with compassion, the male offered, "Your reaction was not unnatural."

It began to feel as if the whole thing had been planned, down to the very breath she drew to speak. "And your neck," she began in a voice full of self-hate, "does it still hurt?"

"Your touch eased the pain." Feeling her bury her face against him as if ashamed, he ceased the lesson and offered a purr, allowing his arms to come around her, to cradle her as she needed but could not ask for.

IT WAS NOT MUCH LONGER, perhaps only a handful of days, before Claire began to sleep less and to grow anxious when left alone. She no longer found joy in her hours of seclusion as she had before he'd infected her with poison. Instead, isolation left her edgy. When Shepherd was not present, time dragged by. She found herself longing for his return no matter how much she denied it and hid in her burrow, praying for sleep to eat up the hours as it had before.

Ashamed of herself, she tried to hide her relief when Shepherd came through the door, did her best not to look at him too long. It didn't make any difference. He knew that very first time, and it showed in the intensity of his curious expression when he smelled the air in her direction. He responded to it with a smile that crinkled the skin at the corners of his eyes, and by immediately taking her body with a practiced, calculating sensuality, watching her obsessively with those all-seeing eyes. It was as if he knew what was warring inside her, knew that she was losing—grasped that Claire found it harder to hate him, and struggled even to hate herself.

When she fell to pieces and the shame knifed into her, she began to cry as if lost. Shepherd played his hand, behaving seemingly patient, and continued the manipulative assault on her convictions by comforting her with deep purrs even as he mounted her, fucking the Omega until she forgot she had been upset in the first place.

The culmination of her ruin was the perpetual attack that persisted even in her sleep. Claire's dreams were filled with soft things, warmth, and the scent of her mate... his voice, the feel of his roughened hands slipping over her skin. The dream grew stronger nightly, and to her horror, she awoke half aware and throbbing for him to fill her. She instinctively reached for him the third or fourth time she'd awoken in that state, trailing her hand down his muscular body, pressing closer in her dazed need while she hummed in the dark. Shepherd responded with absolute enthusiasm, rolling his silken weight on top of her and groaning long and deep to find her already dripping wet. In that dreamlike mating, Claire could not get enough of his skin, cried out for him when his cock replaced where his fingers had been exploring, and held him as if he were hers, as if he were precious. When a corner of her mind rebelled, she shut it off, unwilling in that moment to recognize her failing, needing the fantasy just once where she was happy. And just like that, she lost another part of herself to a monster.

As he moved inside her, the thread resonating in joy, she realized how easy it could be—how dreamlike, how intoxicating—if she would only forget and submit. When she urged him to go faster, to give her more than slow, soothing thrusts, she came apart underneath him as he pounded away, the bond throbbing as powerfully as her pussy when she burst apart. Shepherd knotted deep, the sounds he created, the transcendent quality of his iron eyes, making it clear it was the most fulfilling orgasm he'd ever known.

He praised her for hours afterward, stroking and purring, and she wished he would not speak. Claire did not want to hear how well she had pleased him or how beautiful he found her. It was making her remember that she was Claire and he was Shepherd, and all the things he had done, and all the ways she had failed in so short a time.

When she woke again, he was working at his desk, breathing in and out in a rhythmic purr that seemed so commonplace she hardly noticed it anymore. With him shirtless, Claire could see every line of his muscles, the dips and curves of a man built to break things. All that strength covered in a testament of murder...

Pulling a dress over her head, she sat at the edge of the bed and watched him.

Shepherd turned and looked at her, approval obvious between his lashes.

How far she'd fallen. Mortification made breath difficult. "How are the Omegas?"

The change in her captor was immediate. All trace of amusement vanished, and in its place was the hardness and dominance he exercised expertly. "They are exactly as they should be."

"Subjugated and imprisoned?" Claire challenged, standing up to force herself to pace. She should have been pacing for days... why had she stopped pacing? Why had she not asked sooner? What the fuck was wrong with her?

"Come here."

Her barked answer was immediate. "No."

She needed to go back to the status quo, to remembering to hate the father of her baby, not to admire his body... never to allow pleasant feelings for him. She should be wishing him dead, not prizing his attention. Wringing her hands, she marched, pointedly ignoring the giant rising from his chair to subdue her.

A meaty hand locked on her shoulder atop the claiming marks Shepherd had inflicted and tended each day. The discomfort of compressing tender flesh made Claire wince. She pressed her lips into a line and refused to look. Heat rose from his body, seeped into hers, and the smell—the necessary scent—forced her to close her eyes and focus to maintain defiance against a man who was her foe, not her lover.

"You will cease this at once." His voice was not hard.

"I will not."

His tone dropped considerably, it *promised* things. "Little one..."

Trying to shrug out of his grasp only enticed Shepherd's anger.

That was good, wasn't it? He had been too gentle, pretending he was not a beast who imprisoned and poisoned her. She needed to see the dragon, to hear the angry growls, to feel the thread buzz badly out of tune.

The fan of black lashes lifted, she looked him dead in the eye. "I will not stop."

"Your fear of change and this acting out is beneath you."

Frustrated, Claire clenched her fists. She wheezed.

A voice dripping reason came from lips that had tasted every inch of her skin. "If you wish to mate, you do not need to pick a fight to justify your desire to yourself. That is what you are doing, little one, expecting that my reaction will be to respond by mounting you—because you do not want to acknowledge that you are already wet and ready."

That was not what she was doing! Was it? A look of horror came to her face when she realized that she did smell of slick, that she was incredibly aroused... but she was also angry. She put her head in her hands, to hide her face, wishing she could just explode. "You do not understand me at all!"

"Then tell me what the point of this tantrum is?" he challenged in a mellow voice, still refusing to show the anger she wanted so badly to foster. "There will be no change to the Omega situation. You know that. I know that. Conversation on the topic is pointless and basely inflammatory... you desire my reaction, and we both know what you want me to do."

Claire started yanking on her hair.

Shepherd spoke again, "If you do not ask in this instance, then I will not give you what you want."

A sly smile, a nasty hateful grin, came to Claire's lips. She lowered her hands and looked into the unaffected silver. "I can tell you what I want! I want the Omegas to be treated as humans, not livestock. I want them to have the choice in whom they mate—to be safe and fed, and not treated like sex toys for your disgusting Followers!"

He still sounded so calm, but the embers were igniting. "I caution you to carefully consider your next words."

Her eyes fell to the expanse of his chest, staring hard where the thread was attached. She thought of the needle he'd jammed into her. She thought of his promise on the roof. "I am starting to remember myself. I will find a way to be free."

In one quick yank, he shook her roughly. "*You will never leave this room*!"

The customary discord was back, a shrill piercing pluck at the cord. Claire breathed in relief to feel it as Shepherd yanked her towards the bed. She was thrown down, the giant looming tall over her. But he did not touch her, only glared, his chest heaving, as if he wished to rip off her head. Then he turned and left, locking the door loudly to make his point.

Her victory was short-lived when uncomfortable loneliness set in. He did not return to her. At length, the blue-eyed Beta brought her next meal and Claire understood she had been upgraded to solitary confinement.

She was pregnant, her scent no longer enticing to his men. Shepherd could avoid her as much as he wished and have his peons bring her food... and she would simply have to endure it.

As she ate a dinner of lamb and roasted potatoes, she began to cry, missing Shepherd's presence and hating herself for it.

# 11

It took a bit of creative thinking to learn the location of Claire's domicile before the occupation. All network systems in the Dome had been terminated, even COM towers were destroyed to ensure the population had little means to communicate or muster outside of face-to-face contact. All that was left was emergency hardware.

Shepherd's manipulation of the information and communication networks was practically complete, but not total.

There were still databases, servers filled with the information of the residents on each level—that was what Corday needed to access. Most of the Enforcer offices were currently occupied by Shepherd's Followers. Corday had scouted dozens. The few locations he'd found abandoned were in very hostile regions, the sectors' inner workings picked clean or totally demolished. But after two weeks of dangerous reconnaissance, he got lucky.

In the burned-out husk of a small, mid-level Enforcer station, Corday discovered one minuscule directory office untouched by the riots. The COMscreen functioned and, by some fucking miracle, booted when plugged into a battery.

Working quickly before anyone passing might notice his presence, Corday collected the former address of one Claire O'Donnell. Wasting no time, he shut off the valuable resource, tore out the memory cube, and climbed down seven levels to brave the cold neighborhood Claire had called her own.

The Omega had lived too near the slums for her home to ever have been considered safe. Everything was poorly maintained, sandwiched tightly, and painted in a faded wash of color. Her apartment had been ransacked, of course. Windows were shattered, knickknacks destroyed and anything of value gone. What remained was shoddy furniture and walls of expensive paper books.

In all the *things* taken, few books had been stolen.

The novels she adored had spines distorted by frequent use. Smirking, Corday found her favorites almost cliché, his lip twitching when a dog-eared copy of a pre-Dome romance was in a position of prominence. With careful fingers, he pulled it out and looked at the worn cover.

It was creased, it smelled like soapy vanilla. Returning it, Corday moved into the small space's only bedroom.

Everything was in the shade of robin's egg blue, styled in the simplistic, comfortable atmosphere Omegas required. The bedding still smelled of her, though it looked as if one of the rioters had rolled about in the linen. Taking a seat on the narrow mattress, Corday picked up the family photograph from her bedside table—her parents and Claire when she was just a girl. An Alpha father's hands rested on his little girl's shoulders. Beside them was a woman with a tight smile, a forced expression that tried to convey joy below surrendered eyes.

Claire was the image of her father, the same distinctive looks, the same black hair, but she had her mother's small frame and swanlike quality. She appeared fragile, but Corday knew she was stronger than she seemed.

Setting the photograph back, Corday began to poke through her collection of worthless jewelry even the looters had passed up. Under the lining of the small velvet box, he felt the outline of a ring and pulled back the fabric to find a worn gold band.

It was a wedding band. The same one worn by her mother in the photograph.

Without thought, Corday took it so he might return it to Claire. Because he *was going to see her again.* His Omega friend was sneaky and smart. She would find her way. Claire would not end up like the glassy-eyed Omegas the Enforcers had set free, the ones begging for some Alpha to claim them and give them a sense of purpose and relief. No... Claire was different.

She had to be.

CLAIRE WAS unsure how many days had passed, what the hour was, how long she'd slept, or why she was always exhausted when she woke. Shepherd had not returned once since their fight.

There was no one to talk to, no soothing scent. There was nothing to do but obsess about the room and try not to think about how very lonely she was.

She cleaned every surface, going so far as to pull everything out of the dresser and refold each item with sharp corners. Even forcing distraction, more than once, she unwittingly allowed her thoughts to circle on the Alpha, tempting her to recall his more pleasing points.

The root of the issue was palpable. Claire wanted him back—his soothing purr, the heat of his body in her nest. Life was muddled by enforced seclusion, off-putting and confusing.

After shutting the last drawer, ready to move on to the bookshelf

—what Shepherd had called her *window*—Claire turned and squeaked. A woman was standing behind her, so close they could have been touching.

Green eyes wide at seeing a stranger, Claire stammered, "Hel-lo," wondering for a moment if she had lost her mind and begun hallucinating.

A smile, the lovely, polished, practiced grin of nobility, spread across pink lips. "Hello, pretty."

Claire could smell that the female was not what she seemed. The exotic beauty was an Alpha, but so delicate that the brunette could almost pass for Omega. Backing away, Claire found blue eyes tracking her movement and a small, amused smirk on those lips. "Who are you?"

The coolness of the woman's fingers made Claire instantly pull her head back. It did not stop the smirking woman from tracing her nail over the delicate skin under Claire's jaw. "I am Shepherd's beloved."

That string in her chest, the chain, writhed at those words. Pressing a hand defensively over her belly, Claire choked out, "I am Claire."

"Claire," a wealthy, accented voice drew out the pronunciation of the name.

A glint was in those oval eyes, something unwelcome and treacherous. The Alpha was dangerous, looking at her like a piece of meat, countering each step Claire took backwards until the Omega found herself trapped against the bed.

The intruder purred, "Be still, Omega."

Claire's voice dropped, her shoulders grew stiffer, and she said it again, "My name is Claire."

Pain burst across Claire's face. Pressing her hand to her bleeding lip, she stared in shock at the stranger who'd struck her.

"You're drenched in him." The Alpha female sniffed. "Lie on the bed and spread your legs so I may see."

"I don't know who the fuck you are, but back off!"

There was a tutting sound in the air. "You can obey, or I will have Shepherd force you."

"Then get him to force me... I don't spread just because an Alpha bitch commands it."

Before she might escape, an unyielding hand circled Claire's throat. She was forced back until her knees bent and the Omega's back hit the mattress. Clawing at the grip crushing her windpipe, Claire stared up into the unblinking blue eyes of a killer—what she saw there inspired more fear than she'd ever known.

The woman's hand stroked under Claire's skirt, fingers jamming inside her to swirl painfully around her dry womb. The brunette drew them out and tasted. "You are pregnant. How interesting."

A second hand came to grip Claire's neck. A tighter squeeze and her world began to go dark.

"Svana." It was one word, spoken in a very dangerous tone.

The brunette cocked her head at the man standing in the door.

"My love." Svana smiled. "Your plaything's eyes are the wrong color. My eyes are blue."

"Release the Omega's throat."

With a playful smirk and a quick flourish of her fingers, Svana let Claire go. Coughing, sucking in air, Claire scrambled back, wide eyes looking at Shepherd, looking at the man who, though bonded to her, stood by and did nothing. Everything was wrong, the cord was jangled, and with horror, Claire witnessed total love in the expression Shepherd offered the Alpha female approaching him.

The exotic beauty petted her mate's chest. Svana purred, "I have missed you. Get rid of your toy. I only have a few hours before I must return."

Cupping the woman's face, Shepherd explained, "The Omega is not permitted to leave this room."

Svana shrugged her shoulders. "Then she can join in or watch. What a pity I missed her last cycle. We have not shared a heated Omega in some time."

Shallow pants, that was all Claire could manage as she pressed herself against the wall and realized how truly depraved the man who had hooked an anchor into her chest really was. Now she understood. No chemicals from pregnancy, no pair-bond could change it. She was nothing to Shepherd. She had been manipulated to care for a monster who loved another—to be what the female had insisted: his plaything.

"Claire, you will go into the bathroom and remain until I come for you."

He had spoken her name. Dumbstruck, Claire stared at the two of them, stared as Shepherd—as her mate—touched another female affectionately.

When she made no movement to follow the command, a furious head snapped up and his silver eyes narrowed menacingly. "Go."

She obeyed. Each step felt like walking on glass, but the pain was a blessing, a gift from the goddess of the Omegas. Claire's mind began to clear, the influence of the cord began to weaken, and she began to feel *nothing at all*.

She closed the door behind her and sat alone. Staring the future dead in the face, she knew just what hell looked like.

The sound of the two Alphas fucking was nothing. Breathing was nothing. Where she had been slowly settling into life in that little grey room, she was now free of such petty things as further existence. A great crack ran through her chest, a fissure that bled vile, noxious gas into the air while Claire sat there in the dark, the music of evil coming through the door. There was nothing left for the greasy thread to hold onto. There was nothing left inside her... but she was still horribly Claire.

Later, Shepherd woke her where she slept against the wall. He pulled her up and sat her on the lid of the toilet so he could press a wet towel to her split lip. She looked him dead in the eye, a fierce, penetrating, nightmare of a gaze. When he said nothing, she began to laugh at him, loudly, the noise saturated in judgment.

He was pathetic... disgusting. And he was dead to her.

The expression that came was one of confusion—the look a small boy cornered by bullies wears. It was perfect.

A hard voice growled, "Svana is dangerous."

Claire only laughed harder, the hoarse sound ruined by the damage to her throat. She laughed until her face was red, until her insides hurt. She laughed until she had to push past Shepherd and puke in the sink. Standing straight, she wiped her stinging mouth with the back of her hand and, still snickering, walked out of the bathroom and into a room that, if she had any reason to breathe, would have smelled utterly tainted.

It was just four grey walls, every crack known to her—a box with nothing in it.

Her nest was a wreck, so Claire lay down in the middle of the floor and closed her eyes. It almost felt like she was merging with the earth, becoming one with the endless, lifeless room.

It was beautiful.

When she woke, it was bright outside, Claire felt it in her bones. She stared at the ceiling imagining the way sunlight must glint off the Dome. She was alone again. Food was on the table waiting for her. Standing, she took the plate, carried it to the bathroom, and flushed everything down the toilet. Dropping the vitamin, her lips sounded out the word, "plop," as it fell into the swishing water. The empty plate was returned to the tray and she went right back to her warm outline on the floor. A whole day passed.

The door opened. Her listless eyes found the blue-eyed Beta had come with another tray. The Follower moved past her as if she did not exist.

Devoid of feeling, Claire croaked, "I don't know your name."

Deadpan, he answered, "I'm Jules. Shepherd desires that you do not forget the vitamin."

The empty tray was taken. He walked by without even looking at her.

The door was locked and Claire made sure she followed Shepherd's mandate. She flushed all the food, and unquestionably, did not forget the vitamin. After all, now that she was hollow inside, it was nice to have the grey room to herself. She showered, changed her clothing, brushed her hair... all the things living people were supposed to do. Then she went right back to that spot on the floor to rot.

Inevitably, enough time passed. The sound of combat boots thudded against the ground and the devil was crouching over her. A purr sounded and Claire opened her eyes, entirely unimpressed.

She felt nothing.

Shepherd picked her up, her body hanging limp, and took off the fresh dress, putting her in the bed. The sheets must have been changed. Either that or she had lost the pattern of Shepherd's scent. Everything just smelled flat. The man slid in beside her, naked, and eased up close. As he did everything he wanted, taking what she never offered, he pressed his chest to hers and growled.

Nothing.

He spread her legs, growled again, and let his fingers dance between her thighs. Whatever he was doing, Claire only stared at the ceiling, seeing instead the overcast night sky. She did not make a noise when a foreign presence pushed uncomfortably into her unprepared body. She just lay there through all of it, unsure how long he tried, how hard he worked... because she didn't care. An odd stretch let her know that the sweating, grunting thing had knotted.

Still nothing.

While their bodies were locked, she heard the distant sound of a low, raspy voice and ignored it. There were tugs at her hair, the smooth strokes of hands. Claire yawned. Sleep was immediate.

WALKING through the Undercroft where her kind had been locked away, Nona maintained her ramrod spine despite the two large Followers yanking her about. She had not been troubled or questioned for weeks, and wondered what asinine things they would waste her time with now. When the door opened and she was pressed into the room, even she could not hide the quirk in her brow or the sudden feeling of dread when she found it was not the Beta, Jules, who sat at the table.

Even seated, the Alpha was massive.

"She seems to think standing as you do serves a purpose as well. But you are still Omega and you know that resistance to one such as I is pointless," Shepherd explained, his voice conversational, though the nature of his expression was anything but pleasant.

Nona took a seat without being asked, old enough to know better than to engage male taunts.

The man began. "You are the de facto leader of this Omega pack—"

Nona interjected, "I am not. We function as a democracy."

"How have you found the provided accommodations?"

"Prison-like," Nona answered, watching him just as callously as he watched her.

Shepherd was not impressed with her bravado. "I have supplied you with clean water, wholesome food, warm blankets, shelter..."

"Your rationalization is faulty." Nona tapped the desk. "All those comforts are only to prepare the Omegas for slavery to a stranger."

"You are the one who corrupted her into thinking the way she does."

Now that was interesting. Cocking her head, Nona asked, "Excuse me?"

"Of the eight Omegas pair-bonded since arrival into my keeping, all have accepted their place—behaving as they should."

It was foolish to smile, one good swing and he could rip her head off her shoulders, but Nona allowed the expression. There was a catch to his statement, an underlying irritation that exposed his own less than perfect relationship. "There is nothing I can tell you that would make Claire be what she is not. I have droned on for hours about the foods I know she likes, her hobbies... all questions you could have asked her yourself."

"Your only use to me, old woman, is information that will help settle my mate." Contemplating how easily he could crush the old woman's throat, Shepherd warned, "Do not think to posture or advise."

"Then get to the point."

The slight flaring of his silver eyes, the sudden stink of hostility—he was far less steady in his aloofness than he pretended. "I am beginning to suspect you have outlived your usefulness. There is room for your body to swing next to the other Omegas."

"If there is something wrong with Claire, I would do anything to help her," Nona argued, more than happy to honestly express her anger. "Whatever insight you seek, just ask."

"My mate has grown withdrawn."

Scowling, Nona wondered how the hell he could possibly be surprised. With her lips in a line, she waited for the man to continue.

Shepherd leaned nearer, barking, "Are you going to say nothing?"

"I am unsure what you expect me to say," Nona maintained. "That is not a word I have ever heard used to describe Claire. She is usually quite vocal. Whatever she is now, you have created in your treatment of her."

"At the separate deaths of her parents, what drew her out of her melancholy?"

"Time, and the support of people she loved."

It was clear the answer was unacceptable, that the giant had reached the end of his patience.

The man made her sick and the sentiment was obvious in Nona's accusation. "Do you behave this way with her, as well? She won't respond to it."

"I am very careful with Claire."

Something in his words made her feel he was lying, or that he was careful in the way one holds a newborn kitten—an unnatural way to behave with a mate. Sniffing the air, leaning forward to make her appraisal obvious, Nona found very little of Claire's scent on the man. "And you have studied her like a specimen, with information gathered from outside sources. Why? To manipulate the situation to your liking?"

"Of course."

"Apparently your strategy has failed." That was it. "There is nothing I can say to help you, Alpha."

Shepherd's glare threatened torment. "There will be no food for any Omega over the next three days. All will be notified that you were the cause of starvation."

~

How funny the world was. Everything was in reverse. Claire sat in a chair, her head resting atop her palm, while Shepherd was the one pacing. Back and forth, back and forth. He was like an agitated dinosaur.

Claire made a noise.

The great hulk stopped and looked at her. He spoke.

She heard nothing.

Her thin fingers began to drum against the table. And again the beast prowled. Eventually, he tugged her up, as he had done with every visit, and he took her dress. It was the same: the mattress at her back, his useless growl, and then whatever tricks he had thought up to seduce her body. Shepherd thought to be clever, smoothing a great portion of lubricant on his jutting cock before he began the rut. He thrust this way and that way, just like his disturbed pacing. He tried everything to get a response, even trying to coax a kiss from her slack lips, to whisper in her ear, to caress and stare into eyes that were far away.

"Little one, come back."

She would never come back. Not to him. Not to the beast who had made her want him once and betrayed her so thoroughly.

Claire fell asleep while Shepherd was still moving inside her.

Eventually, the Alpha figured out what she was doing with the meals delivered while he was away. Not that it was hard to discover when she did not even look at the food he brought her. His mate was growing wan, dark circles under her eyes, and no matter what he pushed between her lips, she would not swallow. She would only stare with those dead eyes, stare straight at him, daring him to try and make her eat.

As he slammed his hand on the table, the metal groaned. Claire stared right back, and lazily spat out everything in her mouth, letting it fall into her lap. There was a roar, the entirety of her tray thrown across the room to slam against the wall. A paw wrenched her from the chair, a blanket wrapped too tight around her. Shepherd had her in his arms. The metal was thrown back, her concrete walls disappeared. They passed a fire extinguisher she had seen before, a blue door, a room full of COMmonitors, only that time there were men in the room, men in the halls—Followers saluting the giant who ignored them as he stormed past.

The sound of boots on concrete stairs, grunted orders Claire ignored, and a door opened to blasting cold. Atmosphere, fresh air... she'd seen such things lying on the floor staring through the ceiling. It was nothing special. Claire closed her eyes.

Shepherd was having none of it. Great arms shook her, jarring her body until her eyes opened. He set her down on her feet and backed away so that she had to stand on her own. Claire did, knowing something that no other man on that terrace knew. A mind could learn entirely new things almost instantly when it was utterly devoid, eyes saw minutiae that thinking minds missed. She stood on her own two feet and looked up at the snowing sky... feeling the large white flakes melt on her cheeks.

Snow that thick was a sign the Dome had been damaged, the arctic creeping in. The engineers responsible for colonial safety had failed.

Hadn't they all failed?

Seeing her stand, the beast drew a relieved breath behind her.

No one could have known what she was going to do. Not one of them could have suspected it. Under the pretense of a yawn, Claire cracked her neck, and rolled her shoulders in a way that loosened the blanket. Then, in a burst of speed, she darted like a hare and bounded over the edge of the Citadel terrace to fall into darkness before any could reach her.

The inertia of limp bodies absorbed force far differently than stiff flailing ones. Claire knew that. What she didn't know was that even high fluffy piles of snow really, really hurt when you jumped off a building to land in one.

There was a general outcry above her, but the fresh powder sucked her in, hiding her long enough to slip down an icy corridor only someone as small as an Omega could fit through. Then she did what she did best. Claire ran.

From above, it looked as if she had simply vanished. Since she was already dead inside, she may as well have.

# BORN TO BE BROKEN

---

ALPHA'S CLAIM, BOOK TWO

**ADDISON CAIN**

# 1

By the time she'd found his home, Claire could little more than crawl. Scratching at the portal, fingers numb, she slumped to the floor. When the door cracked and squinting eyes showed in the dark, had she the capacity, Claire would have laughed. Never had a man looked more shocked.

She was filthy; stringy hair wet from snow and sweat, limbs badly scraped from her fall. About her throat, a bruise tellingly shaped in a handprint circled like a sad necklace. That was nothing compared to the state of her feet when he tried to help her stand. Torn and bleeding, more skin had been worn away than was sound. Corday hoisted her from the ground, her freezing body flush to his, and locked the door.

"Claire!" He vigorously rubbed his hands up and down the trembling woman's back. "I have you."

It's a good thing he did; once the door locked her eyes rolled back in her skull, Claire unconscious. Corday rushed her to his shower, cranked on the heat, and stood with her under the spray. Her lips were blue, and no wonder considering that temperatures on this level of the Dome had grown near freezing. The Beta stripped off her ruined dress and washed every rivulet of blood from his friend, finding more bruises, more wounds, more reasons to hate Shepherd.

The gauze at her shoulder he'd left for last, grateful at least something had been tended to. But as it grew saturated, he grew worried by what was hinted at under the bandage. Peeling it back, Corday cursed to see what the beast had done to her. Shepherd's claiming marks, the tissue red and distorted—even after what looked like weeks of healing, her shoulder was a fucking mess.

The monster had mutilated her.

The water turned as cold as Corday's blood. He pulled her out, dried her the best he could, and tucked Claire into the warmth of his bed. There she lay, naked and badly damaged, a little color coming back to her hollowed cheeks. One at a time, he uncovered limbs, tending scraps, bandaging wounds, doing his best to preserve her modesty. That didn't mean he didn't see them, the telling bruises mottling her inner thighs.

She looked almost as bad as the Omegas the resistance had rescued…

It frightened him. Not one of those women was thriving. Even safe, they deteriorated—hardly spoke, hardly ate. More of them had died, and though the Enforcers could not pinpoint the cause, Brigadier Dane was certain with all that they'd suffered—the children and mates that had been taken from them—they had simply lost the will to live.

Claire had to be different.

Left arm, right arm, both elbows sluggishly bled. Salve and bandages were the best Corday could offer. But there was nothing he could do for her throat; the mottled yellow-brown bruises were not fresh. The Omega's injuries grew far more complicated with her legs—both kneecaps were grotesque; one gash deep enough to require stitches. He did his best with butterfly sutures, closing the gap of torn flesh, lining up the skin so that it might stand a chance of mending. Her joints would swell—that was unavoidable—and he hesitated to ice them as she was already shivering and still cold to the touch.

"You're gonna be okay, Claire," he promised. "You're safe with me."

Claire opened bloodshot eyes; she looked at the Beta whose face she could read like a book. He was scared for her. "It doesn't hurt."

"Shhh." He leaned down, smiling to see her awake. Stroking the wet, tangled hair from her face, he said, "Rest your throat."

She complied, and Corday worked quickly to finish, disinfecting every abrasion on her outer thighs, knees, and shins. Her feet were a different matter. There was little he could do, and she would hardly be able to walk in the days to come. He picked out the detritus, noting how she didn't move or twitch even when a fresh wave of blood followed a large chunk of glass once it was pulled free. He wrapped her feet tight, and said a prayer to all three Gods that the open wounds would not fester.

Once it looked like she was asleep, he rose.

Claire's hand shot out, her bruised fingers clawing into his sleeve. "Don't go!"

"You need medicine," Corday soothed, weaving his fingers with hers.

Claire held tighter, disjointed and afraid. "Don't leave me alone."

Brushing a pile of bandage wrappers to the floor, Corday did as she wished. He slipped under the covers beside her, offering body heat and a safe place to rest. Claire let him hold her, laying her head on his shoulder, still.

Ashamed to ask, beyond pathetic, she whispered, "Will you purr for me?"

Such a thing was an act of intimacy between lovers and family, but there was no hesitation in the Beta. Corday pulled in a deep breath and started the rumbling vibration at once. The sound was a little off—the act being something he was unaccustomed to—and though it lacked the richness of an Alpha purr, it was infinitely comforting in that moment.

"That's nice." Exhausted, Claire sighed. "Please don't stop."

Corday thumbed a spilling tear from her cheek. "I won't, Claire."

In the voice of a broken thing, Claire began to feel more than endless choking malaise; she felt disgust… for herself. "I hate that name."

HUDDLED CLOSE TO HER FRIEND, like children whispering secrets, Claire woke. Though her body ached, she was warm, surrounded in a scent of safety, and grateful for the boyish smile Corday offered once she'd pried her sticky lashes apart.

Cautious and gentle, he smoothed her tangled hair. "You look much better."

They were so close she could see the night's stubble on his cheek, smell his breath.

He seemed so real.

Sucking her split lower lip into her mouth, Claire felt the sting. Tasting the scab left when that woman, Svana, had struck her for refusing to spread, made the nightmare real again. It was as if Svana were in the room with her, as if the Alpha's hands remained wrapped around her throat.

Claire struggled to breathe.

Corday broke through her growing terror. "You're okay, Claire. I'll keep you safe."

It wasn't a dream, it was real. Claire grew to understand that the more Corday spoke, the more he touched her, the more she felt the sun on her face.

How had she even come to be there?

She *was* separated from Shepherd, in a great deal of physical discomfort, naked, and Corday had taken her in, despite the fact that she had drugged him—lied to him.

She had to remind herself out loud; she had to make herself remember. "I jumped off the back terrace of the Citadel… crashed into snow."

"And you ran here," Corday finished for her.

She had, before air had even returned to her lungs she'd scampered up and fled. "I ran as fast as I could… right to your door." Voice breaking, trembling something fierce, Claire sobbed, "I'm sorry, Corday."

Seeing her panic, he tried to calm her. "There is nothing to be sorry for."

"I drugged you," she whispered. "I lied. And now he'll find you. He'll hurt you."

"He won't." Corday grew earnest and severe. "You can trust me. There is no need for you to lie to me again. I can't help you if you lie."

"If I had taken you to the Omegas, he would have killed you, just as he killed Lilian and the others." Claire looked to the pillowcase lightly crusted with her blood. "He punished me… I'm pregnant."

Corday already knew. He'd smelled it almost the instant Claire had been in his arms. There was only one way such a thing could have come to pass. Shepherd had forced another heat cycle.

There was very little he could say, little he could do, but one thing Corday could offer her. He looked her dead in the eye and asked, "Do you want to remain that way?"

What a question… Claire had to think, recognized she had been clinging to the Beta to the point where it must have made his shoulder ache. Easing her hold, she measured the little bit of human that she still was, and knew she had not wanted a baby yet. More so, she had foolishly allowed herself to develop an attachment to the monster who had filled her womb, a monster who was using her like a broodmare—a beast whose lover had tried to kill her.

Claire pressed her hand to the tiny life growing inside her. She could rid herself of the issue; abortion was a common practice, probably accessible even now. She could have Shepherd carved out of her.

After a shuddering breath she admitted her horrific truth, "I don't feel anything, you know. Inside… I feel nothing at all."

He gave her space, offering a lopsided smile. "I know it might seem like the world has ended for you, Claire, but you are free now. You're a survivor."

She could not help but sadly smile at a man who would never understand. "Survivor? What kind of future do you see for me? I was pair-bonded to a monster to be his toy, drugged into an unnatural heat cycle, impregnated against my will so I would grow devoted, and then forced to listen to the Alpha who was supposed to be my mate fuck his lover—a very scary Alpha female who wrapped her hands around my throat, who shoved her fingers inside me right in front of him."

He couldn't stop a grimace. "Shhh. This can be made right."

"It's okay for us both to admit there isn't going to be a happy ending for me." Claire sat up, holding the sheet to her chest, empty. "I have no future, but I can still fight for them."

Brushing back her hair, wanting to pull her nearer, Corday restrained the desire to embrace the sad-eyed woman. "If you step outside that door and try to take on Shepherd, you won't win."

"I won't win… but I *am* going to act out." A goal, something to cling to, hardened her voice. Claire sneered. "I'm going to do everything I can to make noise. And if they catch me, I'll make sure they kill me."

"Please listen to me," Corday grew urgent, afraid to scare her off should he say the wrong thing. "Let's talk this through. The best thing you can do right now is grow stronger. "

"I intend to." She nodded, knowing he misunderstood. "Shepherd once told me there is no good in the people of Thólos. He was wrong. This occupation has stripped away our pretenses; it has made us naked to our nature. Don't you see? Integrity, kindness—it exists here…" Claire closed her eyes, nestled nearer once again. "You, Corday, are a good man."

He didn't hesitate to pull her flush. "And you're a good woman."

Resting her cheek on his shoulder, she sighed. She might have been a *good woman* once, but the truth was, she was not a person anymore. She was a shadow.

"I want you to know that while you were gone, we uncovered the distributors of the counterfeit heat-suppressants. Omegas were rescued. They are recovering and protected. The drugs were destroyed; every last man paid for his crimes."

There was a flutter in Claire's chest, a moment of feeling she tore to pieces before it might infect her. "Thank you, Corday."

"You are a part of that, you know?" Boyish eagerness, a desire to see Claire pleased, infected his grin. "Your determination—you fought for them. They have you to thank for their freedom."

"I didn't do anything but get raped and cry about it."

"You're wrong." Corday took her cheek, made her meet his eye. "You stood up to the biggest monster of them all. You have escaped him twice now. *You* are strong, Claire."

But she wasn't. "No… you don't understand. The pair-bond, the pregnancy… I started to care for him, to need him." Saying it out loud made her mouth taste of vomit. "I was weak."

Corday knew none of that was her fault. "Given the circumstances, what happened was only natural."

"I don't know what it was… but *it* was. I stopped seeing a monster and wanted the attention of the man. And once he'd persuaded my affection, he made it the world's sickest joke. I should be grateful, I guess. Listening to him with her… it ripped the pair-bond out. He can't control me now."

The total lack of emotion in Claire's voice disturbed Corday. Whatever Shepherd had done had damaged the Omega, and a part of him wondered if every expression she was making was only because she was supposed to remember things like breathing and blinking.

Oblivious to the apprehension in her friend, Claire continued. "I get it now. This breach was not about gaining power. We're his puppets, falling rabid at the snap of his fingers. We dance on his stage. Shepherd, his Followers, they're punishing us all for…" she scoffed under her breath, "for blind ignorance. For allowing what was done to them."

"You are free of him, of his lies, and his evil, Claire. Remember that."

"The Dome is cracked. It's snowing outside. Not frost, *real snow*. We are not free of him, not when we let that happen. We let this all happen."

"We can take back Thólos."

Claire's breath hitched. "Not so long as he is alive."

"Your Omega escaped through a broken drainage gate. Blood on the scene shows the direction in which she fled and that her bearing was not affected by broken legs. The trail was lost when she slid below mid-level and moved out over accumulating sludge."

"How much blood?" Shepherd demanded, skimming the report in his hand for anything relevant.

"Considering the distance she fell, minimal. Internal bleeding may be an issue."

His unforgiving gunmetal glare caught the light. Impatient, Shepherd growled, "She has not eaten in almost a week. She will not have been able to manage a great distance malnourished, shoeless, and bleeding."

"Was she suffering from morning sickness?"

Shepherd turned toward his desk, his attention going back to the report. "Hunger strike."

Jules, unsurprised by such a statement, remained blank. "When she is returned, what are your expectations of Miss O'Donnell?"

Exceedingly irate, Shepherd hissed, "For her to resume her duty as my mate."

Only psychological damage would lead a pregnant, pair-bonded Omega to hunger strike and jump off a building in madness. Jules grew blunt. "And if that's not possible? Whom do you intend to serve as surrogate Alpha to see to her until she delivers your heir?"

Muscles straining, Shepherd warned, "You presume much, Jules. She will be returned and her behavior corrected."

Jules was second-in-command for a good reason—he was shrewd and willing to act. Employing candor, he stated, "Without physical contact the Omega will willingly accept, she may miscarry."

Shepherd was not to be gainsaid by man or woman. His final order was issued. "You are dismissed."

Grasping that the situation was beyond his original assessment, Jules saluted and removed himself from the room.

Shepherd took to his desk, alone. Memorizing the reports

flashing on his COMscreen, every so often he habitually glanced behind him, expecting to see Claire pacing. But she was not there. She was gone… He knew in his bones that his mate had sought out the *noble* man who had offered help. The Beta would take her in, tend her, comfort her, touch her. The very idea another might hold her… act as a surrogate… infuriated him.

Gnashing his teeth, Shepherd swore. The Beta would die screaming.

Had Shepherd not purred, growled, stroked, followed every instinct to rouse her back from her stupor? He'd even tried to explain. *Him*! The Alpha, the strongest who was never questioned, had tried to reason with an Omega. But she had not even blinked.

She'd slipped so far out of his grasp.

It was her vocation to stay, to be devoted, to love him, to obey. Had he not seen to her needs? Had he not given her nice dresses and the best food? Had he not spent hours simply petting the girl until she was completely content? What was one unpleasant situation compared to that?

*Had he not saved her life in more ways than one?*

Impregnating her ensured her survival, justified her maintenance to his followers. No one could question the safekeeping of his baby. More importantly, it gave her purpose and distraction. Shepherd could not tell her in so many words—she was not one of them, remained far too determined in her ideal of *goodness* to comprehend the greatness of his calling. Furthermore, the reasoning behind his actions was unnecessary for her to know. Shepherd knew if Claire realized the true nature of what was coming, she would only fret more. She would cry for her pathetic citizens instead of giving all her attention to him. Direct treachery was best: it kept him in control of her fate. But she was willful, so damn obstinate with her foolish romantic notions.

Shepherd's fist crashed against the table. He roared, upended the entire thing until papers flew and his COMscreen cracked against the cold floor.

Svana's unexpected arrival had been infuriatingly problematic. Not only was she displeased by what she had found, Svana would have ripped Claire's beautiful eyes out had Shepherd not pacified his beloved once she'd seen what he'd kept hidden away. You don't reason with provoked Alphas, you show action. Had he not fucked her loudly, broadcasting his favor to ensure the territorial female did not view the Omega as a threat, Claire would have been murdered the first moment he left her alone. He had done what was necessary, for both of the women.

It was the price to keep Claire.

Yet he had lost her anyway, even before she had run. Watching her mentally slip away, his rush of anger, his outright fury… it was the same rage that had burned him when he rose from the Undercroft to murder Premier Callas… only to find the leader of Thólos—the man who'd sentenced his mother to the Undercroft—was richly laced with the scent of Svana's sex.

Shepherd had drawn a deep breath, momentarily stunned as he processed what could not be—until he understood what Svana had done.

The speech he'd prepared for his greatest enemy, the one perfected night after night caged underground, was forgotten. What should have been a quick death, the body to be displayed, ended in blood dripping from the ceiling, Premier Callas' entrails flung all over the floor.

And then came pain far more horrific than any agony his Da'rin markings might produce. His beloved had defiled herself, purposefully tainted her body by mating with the enemy.

Shepherd had confronted Svana, the woman he had loved from the first moment they'd met in the dark, the ethereal creature who was his whole life, who held his soul in her beautiful hands. The woman who had set him free, empowered him to gain control of the Undercroft—the very woman he'd killed for, suffered for, ached for.

Since their first sexual experience, Shepherd had only ever lain with the occasional estrous high Omega his beloved had procured for them—so they could fulfil the animal urge to rut together as they were meant to. For lesser beings, Alpha/Alpha pairings were difficult, as there was no pair-bond, and it was in their natures to challenge for dominance. But the two of them were beyond such sordid behavior. Or so he'd thought. He had never wavered… not once.

She had.

She had fucked the Premier, thrown what they had aside for some distorted ploy, as the final undiscussed crux in her plan. As Shepherd heard her speak on the matter, as she convincingly painted a grand scenario, he could not bring himself to question what she'd *never mentioned.* Svana had planned her seduction all along. Though she held Shepherd and spoke of her love, he was attuned to her; he could smell what was wrong in her scent. What had been done was even worse than he'd originally believed; Svana had chemically forced an unlikely ovulation. She wanted to bear the child of her enemy… to have a traitor's lineage continue the line—a man who wasn't infected with Da'rin, who was born with superior bloodlines—a man who might even be the carrier of the *alleged* antibody to the Red Consumption in his veins.

Not like Shepherd, who didn't know which of the countless prisoners who'd raped his mother had fathered him. His blood had not been fostered through generations with access to secret science and inoculations against disease. Instead, he was disfigured by Da'rin that burned in the sun and would always mark him as a castoff.

She had not voiced it, but Shepherd interpreted the truth. Svana found him wanting in the most primal of ways.

All those years, Shepherd's fidelity had been one sided. Svana did not hesitate to admit she'd taken other lovers. Hadn't he? After all, were they not Alphas? Was it not their right? She had stroked his chest and smiled so perfectly, reminding him that what they shared was beyond the physical. They shared a great destiny, an eternal spiritual bond of love.

Gutted, Shepherd had fulfilled his duty to his loyal Followers, to the dead mother he hardly remembered. Thólos fell, everyone playing their part to perfection; yet he was less for it. The world had shifted, he had achieved greatness, but what was he left with? Nothing. A big black hole where the light had gone out. He was incomplete.

But then he smelled something untainted hiding under the poignant stink of decay. Like a gift from the Gods, Claire was delivered; unlikely virtue born out of the filth of Thólos. A lotus. Claire, with her convictions and her timid bravery, walked up to a man like him—stubbornly waited for hours, a lamb amongst the wolves—to beg for help from the very villain inflicting suffering on the friends she would save.

One breath of her and he would have taken her, heat or no. The Gods had simplified his spiritual culmination by delivering her in estrous.

As he'd rutted the willful, strange thing, Shepherd found she wriggled so wonderfully, felt so perfectly snug encasing his cock, that he had to ensure she could never leave. As Svana had claimed their *devotion* was beyond the physical, their love divine, Shepherd felt perfectly justified in taking Claire, in creating a corporeal mate—an attachment that would only benefit the unruly Omega. He bonded to keep Claire for himself, his reward for service to the greater good of mankind reborn. The green-eyed little one's purity was now his own, her nearness succor. In Claire, Shepherd had regained that missing piece, the covetous need to possess something innocent, achieved.

Yet, now his bonded mate was gone with his child in her belly, wandering a city that was destined for plague.

The Omega would never come back to him willingly, not while the pair-bond was so damaged. Shepherd would have to return Claire by force.

He could almost hear the echo of her words in the air: *do not give me cause to hate you more.*

What had gone through the mind of the Omega he'd found unconscious on the bathroom floor? He'd anticipated anger, but found something impaired far beyond his reasoning. His coupling with Svana had left Claire unresponsive and empty—left the cord so fractured, all Shepherd could feel from her was an echo of desolation.

It was not a sensation he enjoyed.

No amount of attention or space had made a difference. Glassy eyes looked at him with judgment and hatred no matter how he tended her, touched her, or purred. All her favorite foods had been prepared, new dresses put in her drawer… she had not even noticed.

Claire O'Donnell belonged to him. Shepherd would find her, drag her back… and force feed her if he fucking had to. He would make her adore him like she was supposed to. Because she was his, only his, and he did not share his things. Ever.

He had even prevented the sharing of her body with his beloved. Was that not something?

Corday had rushed to carry out his mission for the resistance, eager to return to Claire. It wasn't because he didn't trust her to stay put, it was because he didn't trust her at all. The look in her eyes when Senator Kantor had arrived to guard her had been nothing but calculating. There was none of her former fear or skittishness, her reaction numbed as she sized up the Alpha.

The Senator could see the change in her as well, Kantor reacting with cautious courtesy. They exchanged pleasantries, Corday made them coffee, and then he left to meet Brigadier Dane. Corday's duties kept him out past dark, and the Enforcer was utterly unprepared for the sight that met his eyes when he returned home.

Claire was asleep, curled up on the couch next to Senator Kantor, who was boldly purring in the dark.

A stab of something unwelcome drew Corday to frown. "Did she ask you to do that?"

"No. I knew what would lull her to sleep," Senator Kantor answered in a hushed tone. "Rebecca struggled to fall asleep too. I learned a lot tending my wife in the years the Gods blessed me with my Omega."

It was taboo to speak of deceased mates. Corday was surprised to hear the Alpha mention Rebecca—especially considering the sad circumstances of her long ago murder by Kantor's political adversary. It had been a sensation and had led to Senator Bergie, several of his staff, and even Bergie's son being incarcerated in the Undercroft.

Unsure what to say in response, Corday lit a few candles, and dragged a seat over from the kitchen, his face grim as he looked at the sleeping girl. "How was she today?"

"Better once she ate—less catatonic, more cognizant." Senator Kantor studied the wasted thing. "Miss O'Donnell's physical reaction after having parted from the father will be complicated. The pair-bond and the pregnancy will make her ill."

Corday had faith things might turn out better. "She told me the pair-bond was broken. As for the pregnancy, I will take care of her."

Senator Kantor shook his head "It doesn't work that way, son."

Shooting a look at the Alpha, Corday ground his teeth. "We'll see."

"Now that you are back, the three of us need to have a discussion." Senator Kantor sat straighter, smoothing his sleeve. "Get dinner in her first; afterward the two of us will explain."

It was unsettling to be ordered around in his own home, but Corday nodded and went to the kitchen. Simple fare was prepared. There was some fresh fruit for Claire, an apple he'd bartered for a handful of batteries.

When all was ready, Corday carefully took Claire's limp hand, stroking her fingers until her bleary green eyes popped open. It was obvious she was confused. For just a moment she jerked from his nearness, ready to run. Then it began. The rich rumble of an Alpha purr took Claire from startled to angry.

The glare she gave Senator Kantor would have been funny had her scent not turned so rancid with fear. "You can stop now."

The old man conceded.

Over dinner, the men chose silence. Claire did not. "Is there another bounty?"

Corday was not going to lie to her. "Yes."

She forced down another salty bite. "And?"

"When we observed the Citadel, there was a line of citizens dragging in women of your description."

Claire cringed. "That's disgusting…"

"From what I could see, the Followers were letting them go, but citizens are starving." This was Corday's chance to explain why Senator Kantor was really there. "The bounty on your head could keep a family fed for a year. We have to keep you hidden."

The old Alpha broached the greater issue. "And not just from Thólos."

Claire cocked her head. "What do you mean?"

"I need you to understand that what is said cannot leave this room."

He'd insulted her. "I never told Shepherd a thing. Never," she said.

"Dissention could be our greater enemy." Ruffling his grey hair, elbows on his knees, Kantor sighed. "Many of our people believe that unification under the Follower's governance would satisfy Shepherd. The fact is, these citizens are numerous and growing more loyal to the dictator's regime than we could have imagined. Our own ranks, even some of our brothers and sisters in arms, have been tempted to the other side. Once ensconced, they cannot be reasoned with. Your appearance within the resistance might offer too great a temptation for any straddling the line. Corday and I both believe they will vie to give you back."

"We would never let that happen, Claire," Corday interjected, desperate to explain once he saw the look on her face. "Ever. Do you understand?"

Senator Kantor dared to squeeze her hand. "We need our troops focused. We must find the contagion. To do that, you must stay hidden. No one can know you're here."

Claire sat silent, processing such information. When she finally spoke, her words were not gentle. "You seem to be a wise man, Senator Kantor, but can't you see that time and further suffering will corrode those loyal to you no matter what? My pregnancy is the key to your success. So long as I am running wild in Thólos with his baby as my hostage, he won't infect the population—not at the risk of infecting me. Now is your chance to strike. Use me and rebel immediately."

"I disagree… Shepherd's treatment of you has been appalling, negligent in the gravest of ways." Solemn, Senator Kantor denied her. "If we move prematurely, he might release the contagion. I cannot risk millions of lives, your life, on a maybe. I'm sorry,

Claire. Until the Red Consumption's location is uncovered, the resistance will make no move."

The line of Claire's mouth grew sharp. Sitting taller, she looked at both of them as if they were simpletons. "It's not the contagion that keeps us in his power. It's our own cowardice. Every day our people do nothing, the bastard is proving his view of our behavior is correct. The Dome is cracked. Don't you see the weather will kill us long before any virus might? *We* have to take back our city, or we die trying."

Senator Kantor put a hand on the Omega's shoulder. "Thólos' citizens are not soldiers. They're scared and have no comprehension of combat. You must understand; many are watching their families suffer, their children are dying."

Claire shook her head, swallowed her outburst. "No one in this city is a civilian anymore, there is no neutral. Either you are with Shepherd, or you are against him."

"It isn't that simple, Claire."

She looked to Senator Kantor, lost. "Isn't it?"

A deep sigh preceded Senator Kantor's explanation. "You are still young and will learn in time that things are not always as they seem."

Claire cocked her head, her previously glowing image of so highly regarded a Senator distorted by the sad impotence of such a man. "Shepherd once told me the same thing… You just echoed the words of a madman."

Senator Kantor offered a conciliatory smile, his look of pity disarming. "I'm asking you to trust me."

Corday understood what riled her; bone deep, he felt the same away. "We make progress every day, Claire. I swear it to you."

Claire looked to her friend and could see he had faith in the Alpha charged to lead the rebellion.

"I understand." And she did. She understood that the longer they waited, the more people would die—that the world was a nightmare where the men and women who'd once sworn to uphold the law might hand her back to a despot for food that would only last so long.

She understood perfectly.

She hurt; everyone hurt. And it had to end.

Once Senator Kantor had left, Corday took her hand, and led her back to the couch to rest. When he had her to himself, Corday smiled and pulled a gift out of his pocket.

"I have something to cheer you up." The Enforcer, his face dimpled, held up what was pinched between his fingers. "A few weeks ago I went to your residence. Everything was pretty smashed up, but I found this hidden under the lining of your jewelry box."

He slid a band of gold on her finger.

The gold was warm, but Claire's reaction to it utterly cold. "This was my mother's wedding ring."

As a child she'd hated the sight of it, still angry her mother had abandoned her, too young to accept what had happened. Claire had forgotten she'd even had it tucked away. Now it fit, just like her mother's disappointment in life fit. Holding up her hand to view the grim thing, she saw the correlation to her mother's impetus—a pretty, sparkling reminder that one could always choose.

"Thank you, Corday."

He took her hand again, stroked her fingers, and promised, "I want you to know that I understand the way you feel, but he's right. If the Senator's life was not gravely threatened, I don't know if I would trust even him with you."

Claire wasn't sure what to say. "Why haven't either of you asked me about Shepherd?"

Corday started to purr, scooting closer to put an arm around her shoulder. "Considering that you escaped once, anything he'd allowed you to hear may have been planted to mislead the resistance should you get free again. I hate to say it, but every move that monster makes is… brilliant. There is nothing you can give us."

No one was on her side, and though she tried to hide her look of hurt, it didn't matter. Corday saw.

She chose to tell him things anyway; she needed him to hear her. "He was born in the Undercroft, his mother incarcerated by Premier Callas. His lover's name is Svana."

The Beta listened, Claire's words confirming what Brigadier Dane had conjectured. It would explain how Shepherd had been incarcerated off record, but the thought of a woman being thrown into that hell… that his own government had done such a thing, just could not be. Could it?

Claire continued, eyes far away as she blathered on. "Svana has an accent I've never heard before—like she's not from here."

"There are a thousand kilometers of snow in every direction outside this Dome, Claire. Outsiders cannot wander in."

"Just like women cannot be thrown in the Undercroft and entire cities cannot fall overnight?" To Claire it seemed there had to be more… dark truths about themselves that had to be recognized. Meeting her friend's eyes, she confessed, "I don't think Premier Callas was a good man. I'm afraid Shepherd's harsh opinion of us might not be wrong."

Corday's arm tightened around her. "Are you saying you agree with him?"

"No," she answered quickly. "No. Evil cannot change evil. Maybe his underlying motivation was once principled. I know he thinks it is, but it's not."

"That's right, Claire," Corday reaffirmed, worried to see her so lost. "Shepherd and his army are delusional."

Cheek to his shoulder, she agreed, "Aren't we all a little these days…"

# 2

Claire was not a violent woman. She did not know how to fight. She was not physically strong.

But she wasn't defenseless. Claire was fast and clever. She just needed to find a way to use those traits to further her agenda. Deceiving Corday *again* did not sit well with her, but his loyalty, his intentions, were tied up in Senator Kantor's leadership.

Maybe the Senator's plan would work… perhaps rebels could uncover the location of the contagion. Then what? Rally the people over a series of hard years while the Dome continued to crack and more snow fell? Claire was not going to wait to find out.

Feigning complacency, smiling when she was supposed to, Claire acted the part of a submissive Omega and fervently agreed when Corday asked for her promise to stay inside. Admitting she was terrified of being given back, that she trusted him to protect her, it only took two days of good behavior before he finally left to attend his duties.

Despite the pain each step cost, once alone, she began to pace and plot.

The monster himself had told her she'd failed because she believed in goodness in a city where there was none. He was wrong. Claire knew that she had failed because she hadn't tried hard enough, thought big enough because, in the end, she'd expected someone else to save her.

How very Omega.

How fucking ironic that the champion the women had chosen had been Shepherd! Laughing under her breath, sickened, Claire gripped her skull.

Nona, the other Omegas—not once had Corday mentioned them. It was the other Omegas, the one's he'd freed that slipped into conversation here and there. He was trying to shore her up, show that there was hope, but he never mentioned her friends.

Claire knew why. Corday was afraid the temptation to go to them would undermine her promise to stay put. He was right.

Just as he'd threatened, Shepherd had stashed those women in the one place no outsider could get to—the Undercroft. Claire was certain down to her bones.

Getting in would not be easy. Once inside, her quest would grow impossible unless… Claire could encourage the Omegas to stand as a pack and fight.

No one was going to save them—they would have to save themselves. All Claire could do was give them their chance.

In a way, Shepherd may have even done Claire a favor. He'd have seen to the Omega's basic needs, wanting them healthy enough for his men. After so many weeks with food, the women would be stronger, and Claire had a feeling that with starvation no longer clouding their judgment, they would also be very angry.

Anger was the only sentiment Claire seemed to understand most days. Anger was a great motivator.

Turning to pace in the other direction, her elbow winged Corday's bookcase, knocking a mess to the floor.

Bending over to clean up, Claire froze.

An Enforcer data cube…

Information on Shepherd might be there. Maybe even Svana's name was tucked into inside an Enforcer file.

Claire plugged it into Corday's COMscreen and typed out the name 'Shepherd.'

Nothing.

'Svana.'

Nothing.

This resource was too valuable to ignore. There had to be something on there she could use. Claire just needed to think. She needed to slow her mental chatter, to breathe. A cold sweat came as her finger tapped the screen, spelling the name of the only criminal Claire knew. The COM flashed, beautiful chocolate eyes staring back at her.

Claire knew the contemptuously smirking face on that woman's credentials, every angle of it. Even though it had been years, Claire still knew how she smelled, what her laugh sounded like. Leaning nearer the screen, the Omega almost smiled.

The next hour was spent absorbing every single detail the data cube contained on one repeat felon. Maryanne Cauley had amassed quite a record: assault, larceny, burglary, arson… her file was massive. From the looks of it, the stunning lawbreaker had gone from cocky repeat escapee of farm labor to… nothing. Her file just stopped—no record of further incarceration, no address, no date of death. She had just disappeared.

If Claire had not known what had been done with Shepherd's mother, it would not have felt like a very… *disturbing coincidence*.

She did not know what made her do it, but her fingers typed out one final name: 'Claire O'Donnell.'

It only took a moment to see the flaw on her citizenship registration. If Maryanne Cauley still lived, Claire knew where she'd gone to ground.

CORDAY HAD COME BACK to find his apartment cold and empty, lifeless where there should have been a small Omega resting on the couch. Corday had hated leaving her, but she had sworn so faithfully, admitting that she could hardly walk on her feet, that he had believed her.

Claire had fooled him. Claire didn't trust him. Claire had left him… again.

There was a note:

*Dear Corday,*

*I can't live a lie and stay hidden. Not the way things are now. I want you to know that no matter what happens, I chose – fully aware of the consequences.*

*Love,*

*Claire*

She had signed 'love' but there was no apology. He knew where he stood and the position was painful and deeply upsetting. Knowing her obsession with the Omega situation, Corday folded up the letter and shoved it in his pocket. Zipping up his jacket, he went right out onto the causeways and fought through the snow to where Brigadier Dane secretly sheltered the leader of the resistance.

Banging on the door, Corday refused to let up until the woman answered.

Dane glared. "You shouldn't be here."

Corday did not wait for an invitation, pushing his superior officer aside as he growled, "Like hell I shouldn't."

"Have you lost your mind?" The door was swiftly locked, the

invading cold air shut out. "Showing up here in broad daylight endangers us all."

Looking back at the soldier, Corday deepened his scowl. "It's dumping snow outside, no one's on the street and my tracks are already being covered. Where is Senator Kantor?"

"I'm here," a voice sounded from the dwelling's back room.

Ignoring the snarling Brigadier Dane, Corday pulled the note out of his pocket and stomped over. "She left."

Senator Kantor set down his COMscreen and took the note. One brief read over and the old Alpha shook his head. "I'm sorry, Corday. It's not like we could have locked her up."

"Claire is going to do something crazy!" Practically tearing out his hair, Corday snarled, "We've gotta stop her."

Senator Kantor shook his head, his tired eyes bloodshot and sad. "We cannot risk exposing ourselves on a manhunt. We both know she recognized we couldn't help her. Do you understand that, kid?"

"She's going to get herself killed!"

Speaking in a low voice, the Alpha tried to convey sense and a much needed measure of calm. "The Omega is pregnant, she's pair-bonded and mentally detached. She doesn't have much time left, and she knows it."

Rubbing his forehead as if he could wipe away his frustration, Corday demanded, "What are you saying?"

"I am saying that Claire is fighting what must be a nightmare inside her. Her timeline is short and she is making her choice."

"I told you. The pair-bond was damaged."

Senator Kantor dropped the fatherly tone in place for one far more authoritative. "*She's* damaged. Her determination is the only thing keeping her together. You try to cage her, or stop her, she'll fall apart. And that would only open her up to his influence again. It might be best to let her do what she needs to do while she can still do it."

"We both know she's going to try to get those Omegas out of the Undercroft," Corday hissed. "It would take an army and she's just one girl."

Senator Kantor fully understood what was at stake. "She has an advantage, a hostage, and you don't know where she is. Nothing can be done. Believe it or not, my bet's on her."

"He'll KILL her."

"Read the letter again." Senator Kantor handed the crumpled page back. "No one can comprehend the consequences like she can. She's a grown woman who's made her choice, just like we ask our brothers and sisters in arms to make every day."

"This is fucking insanity!" Corday stormed out of the room, the note crushed in his grip. "I'm going to find her. I'm going to bring her home."

Brushing past a frowning Brigadier Dane, Corday found himself caught.

His arm in her grip, Dane's face was red and her hiss nasty. "You will do no such thing. Return to your home. Cool off before you jeopardize the entire resistance with your impulsive stupidity. Think, for once. Whatever this Claire has planned, distracting her or getting yourself killed won't help anyone."

Corday was strongly tempted to violence. "You don't know Claire."

"I don't, but I know you. And I know when you're wrong."

THE WEATHER WAS ABSOLUTE SHIT. A blessing and a curse, as it seemed Thólos was hiding from the unfamiliar storm. No soul walked the streets to pester her, and though falling snow made the path difficult, the trek left her soaked to the bone and shivering violently.

In all the years since Claire had last walked the midlevel promenade, she'd forgotten much. The tight dwellings were still celery green, but it took her some time to remember which window had once housed a flower box full of red poppies.

There were no splashes of color now… no flowers. Soon even the withering trees would be nothing but sticks. All there was, was that too cheerful green peeking out from clinging frost, broken windows, and refuse.

Three flights up, third domicile on the right.

Standing face to face with a once familiar door, Claire jiggled the handle and found it locked. Running her fingernail around the frame, she felt a bump in the crack—a spare key hidden just as it had been when she was a girl.

The inside was dark. No one was home.

In place of the woman she sought lay junk: wires, filters, air scrubbers, pipes, and whirring machines piled all over the room. The selfish magpie had stolen them right out of the Dome's infrastructure, and by doing so had weakened everyone else.

It was unspeakable, infuriating and, worst of all, after reading her file, Claire was not remotely surprised.

Mouth sour, Claire stripped off her wet clothes, hung them to drip in the galley kitchen, and helped herself to something dry. It was night before she finally heard the scratch of a key in the lock.

A tall beauty slipped into the chilly room, rubbing her mittened hands together. It only took the woman a second to spot Claire lounging on her couch. "You should not be here."

"You always were such a cunt. You know that, right?" Claire snarled back.

"That is a big word coming from you, little girl." Cocking her head to the side, blonde hair moving like a waterfall behind her, the Alpha changed her snarl to a provocative purr. "Do you have any idea how much you're worth?"

"Don't get too excited. He won't pay you… Shepherd hanged the last batch who brought me in, Maryanne." Claire looked at what had once been the smartest girl she knew and saw a stranger. "Fact is, he takes offense that anyone would expect payment for returning what's his."

Shoulders tight, Maryanne eased closer, eyeballing every corner of the room. "Did anyone see you come in?"

"No."

"That means at least three people did."

Claire let out a breath. "My face was covered and I'm sure you can smell for yourself that I am nothing special right now."

Full lips smirking, Maryanne lifted a handful of Claire's hair for a sniff. "True…"

Claire took Maryanne's hand, the hand of who had been her closest childhood friend, and held it. Large eyes pleading, she whispered, "I need your help."

"No."

"Why?"

Maryanne pulled her fingers free and sauntered off. "You have no idea what these guys can do to you, Claire. Whatever you did, just find a place to hide and wait it out… but don't drag me into it."

"Actually, I do know what they're capable of," Claire spat at Maryanne's back. "I'm pregnant with Shepherd's child."

"Fuck me!" Maryanne spun in horror, staring down at the diminutive Omega's belly.

"I wouldn't, remember," Claire teased, trying to mimic the mischief of their youths. "You were all over me during school. That's why we aren't friends anymore."

"Shut up, bitch." Maryanne laughed, unable to suppress a wolfish grin, "You wish. It was Patrick Keck whom I wanted to fuck… and I did. Often."

"Then you disappeared. You were my best friend and you never even said goodbye." And that had hurt a great deal. More so because Claire knew Maryanne had been capable of so much more than the mayhem she'd accomplished. "I read your file. Is it true you broke into the Archives?"

"Several times… only got caught once. Shoveling pig shit for a year was worth it. You have no idea how much some folks will pay for something as mundane as forbidden, tattered books."

"How did you get in?"

Maryanne licked her teeth and motioned to herself in a sweeping gesture. "This girl's got skills."

Claire grew serious. "And I need them."

The woman edged closer, trailing her fingers down Claire's tangled black hair, cooing, "You can't afford me, sweet pea."

"I know. Which is why I hate to do this." Claire looked for a moment like she might lose her nerve, but she drew a deep breath and began. "The Omegas are locked in the Undercroft. I need to set them free, and you're going to help me, or I am going to tell Shepherd you laid a hand on me. He will rip you to pieces, because I'm not only carrying his child… we're pair-bonded."

Maryanne turned full Alpha. "I WON'T FUCKING DO IT!"

"You will."

The blonde paced towards the window, checking for the twentieth time for a sign of trouble. "Goddamn you, Claire. Goddamn you and your pointless humanitarian bullshit. You always were a goody two-shoes when we were kids. It was disgusting then, and it's even more pathetic now."

"But I was never a pushover." Claire took Maryanne's arm, her expression one of desperation. "I am sorry, but I need you. I need the *skills* you have that I lack. If you do this for me, I will never bother you again."

A deadly look came with the question. "Why not just ask your mate?"

"He's the one who locked them up." Claire pushed her hair behind her ear and stood her ground. "Like you, he's blind to what is right and wrong."

Maryanne cursed. She raged for hours, trying to talk Claire out of such madness, but the outcome was inevitable. Maryanne Cauley had no choice, and she knew it.

They fought over the plan vehemently. There was no time for reconnaissance, the pair blind to what may or may not be waiting. Diversion was one thing, but what Claire intended was insanity. But it could be done, Claire knew it in her bones. She could make it work. She had to, because if she did not give her all, risk everything, then nothing would change.

In the end, it was a shot in the dark at best… suicide at worst. But Claire, it seemed, had come to the right woman.

Maryanne Cauley knew the Undercroft—she knew entrances, she knew secrets—and though she refused to speak of why, it was obvious that once upon a time, Maryanne Cauley had been disposed of down in that dark place.

Shepherd's mother was not the only woman thrown into hell.

At dawn, Claire was exhausted but determined. Maryanne swore up and down and yanked Claire to bed when the Omega would not stop yawning. Once under the covers, it was so simple to fall into old patterns, Maryanne braiding Claire's hair just like she had when they were little.

Hoping the answer would not be as disappointing as she anticipated, Claire sighed, "The way you talk about the Undercroft, the look in your eye every time I say the name Shepherd… You know him."

"Everyone knows him."

No, it was much deeper than that. Claire rolled over to look her friend in the eye. "Don't lie to me, Maryanne. He scares you. He scares you because you *know him*. Somehow you were once involved with that monster. Are you still?"

Maryanne tried to be flippant. "Involved? I should be asking you that same question. After all, your romance is probably going to get me killed."

"I am not mated to Shepherd by choice." Claire would not let herself blink or stutter. "I went into estrous unexpectedly in front of him. He forced the pair-bond."

Maryanne had the decency to look stricken. "Don't take this the wrong way, Claire, but this is Shepherd. He's a powerful man. It seems a little strange that he would bond to a woman he didn't know… I mean, he's a warlord. People probably give him Omegas for Christmas."

Svana's words echoed in Claire's head. '*We have not shared a heated Omega in some time.*'

"They do… I don't know why he bonded to me, and the one time I asked, he gave only pointless, empty words." Her green eyes grew harder, as did Claire's demand for answers. "My question, Maryanne. How do you know him?"

Pursing her lips, Maryanne confessed, "I, um, needed friends once."

"I was your friend. I would have been, had you not run off… and"—Claire sighed, knowing Maryanne well enough to see she was not exactly an innocent—"done the things you did until you got thrown into the Undercroft."

Maryanne snorted. "Before I found a way out."

"From Shepherd."

"My services in exchange for my life." The girl who had never felt guilty about a single trespass she had committed in her life looked at her old friend with uncustomary regret. "I was the one who recovered the access codes to the Judicial Sector and the Citadel."

Brows drawn tight, Claire hissed, "How could you?"

"I didn't know their plans for Thólos. I swear."

Claire didn't want to hear it. "What did you think he would do once freed?"

"He was already free…" Maryanne whispered. "How do you think I got out?"

Claire's brows shot up. "What?"

Maryanne snorted at the small woman's naiveté. "Sorry, bitch, but we've been screwed for a long time."

"Do you know where he keeps the virus?"

Smirking, Maryanne shared a hard truth. "If I did, do you really think I'd be here, stockpiling and preparing for the end of the world? Listen to me, Claire, they don't know about this place. I wiped it from the records almost a decade before I was tossed downstairs. I have enough food, enough air scrubbers to get through almost a year. You don't need to follow through with your crap plan. You can stay here with me. Should the worst happen, all we'd have to do is wait until the virus did its work."

Claire shook her head. "The Dome is cracked, Maryanne. You'd freeze to death as the ecosystem fails. It's like he planned for people like you. We're all going to die. We're all going to die if nothing is done."

THEY WERE BOTH ANXIOUS, tired… just like everyone else in Thólos. There was no point in further argument. Instead both Claire and Maryanne fell into hurried preparations. Things needed to be built for Claire's scheme, and technology learned. Maryanne's explanations, the way she could make something dangerous from nothing, reminded Claire just how out of her element she was.

Rudimentary bombs, how to override basic access panels—

Maryanne was teaching her instead of just making them herself, wordlessly reminding Claire that their association would soon end and that the fumbling Omega would be on her own.

When all the tools were ready, Claire showered, scrubbing off any lingering trace of Corday's scent. Maryanne was in that bathroom applying lipstick as if they were planning an outing, not an attack against the tyrants holding the city. Blinking at the mirror, Maryanne froze, jaw agape at the sight of the Omega's naked body.

The Alpha touched without asking. "What is all of this?"

Claire didn't need to look down to know what Maryanne found so disturbing. "The price of my freedom."

Careful fingers traced the yellowing handprint over Claire's throat. "And your neck?"

An incoherent noise, a mockery of speech got stuck in Claire's mouth. "It's nothing."

Maryanne took her chin and turned Claire's face to meet her own big brown eyes. She smiled, teasing. "Your feet are disgusting. You're bleeding all over my floor."

And the pain was a blessing, the perfect distraction. "Shepherd didn't allow me access to shoes. I had to run in the streets barefoot."

"Does it hurt?"

"Yes. But it doesn't bother me and it won't slow me down."

Maryanne crouched to see why fresh blood was running down her old friend's shin. "Your knee needs stitches."

"Nothing I can do about that right now."

"Sit down, I'll do it."

It was so backwards to have Maryanne Cauley be the one to tend to her; as kids it was always the other way around. Watching the fully grown woman pull a needle and some metallic thread through her skin, feeling the pinch and burn, the world seemed so very strange. "Whatever happened to your mom?" Claire asked.

"Who fucking knows," Maryanne muttered as she made another tight stitch. "Probably OD'd years ago."

Claire just hummed, distracted. "My dad died four years back. Roadway accident."

"Your pop was always pretty cool."

Claire had to agree. "Yeah… I'm glad he's not here to see this."

Maryanne rubbed her lips together as if she wanted to say something but thought better of it. Instead, she stood and gathered clothing appropriate for the mission and shoved the horrid black garb of Shepherd's Followers towards Claire.

The Omega didn't balk, just dressed silently while Maryanne squeezed her limber body into a matching uniform.

"You know, Claire," Maryanne was dead serious, knotting her hair to tuck under a cap. "Underground there's a whole 'nother world. Those who follow Shepherd are beyond dangerous."

"Whatever they are doesn't matter."

Maryanne's voice fell flat. "What I am trying to tell you is, pair-bond or no, they have an agenda. Shepherd might just kill you."

Claire had no illusions on that score. "I'm counting on it."

"I could save us all this trouble and kill you right now," the Alpha offered.

"That's awfully sweet of you," Claire teased, standing on tiptoe to press a peck to her friend's ruby lips. "But I will already be dead to you after tonight. Give me what I need and you have my word."

Maryanne tucked a loaded gun into Claire's pocket. "Promises, promises…"

"And, Maryanne," Claire added, forcing a playful smile. "You look like a slut in that outfit."

# 3

"This is the entrance to Purgatory." Maryanne pointed to the map alight on the screen between them. Tracing the snaking tunnels that lay right below the concrete footpaths of the Lower Reaches, she said, "This floor is for administration and separated from the true Undercroft. If your Omegas are being kept in this shithole, Shepherd would not stash them any lower than here. Not if he wanted to keep them alive."

Claire stared down at the COMscreen. Seeing her people locked away like livestock brought a wave of unbearable sadness. The Omegas slept ten to a cell, segregated by age, and there were less than the fifty-six that had been taken. Three Shepherd had hanged, the remainder Claire assumed had either died or been pair-bonded and dragged away. There were hardly even forty, and one was in estrous, isolated and being rutted by a stranger… the girl only sixteen.

In her heart, Claire had been terrified Shepherd may have allowed his men to inject the Omegas with the same drugs he'd used on her… to set up a brothel of mindless estrous sex for the taking, and she had to admit she was marginally relieved to find he had yet to stoop so low.

"Looking at them like that isn't going to change anything, sugar pie," Maryanne cooed, crouched at her side.

"Even you must see how sick this is." Frowning, Claire looked away from the COMscreen so her friend might meet her eye. "Don't let me down."

"I'll get you in. Then I'm gone."

Claire nodded. "For your own sake, I suggest you run fast."

As per their agreement, Maryanne tapped into the system and hacked the prison's upper level controls. Handing over the technology, she gave Claire patchy dominion of Purgatory's security systems.

"You need to know, small fry, not every castoff was released when Shepherd staged his coup. There are paths in there you don't want to stumble down. If you get lost… you let Shepherd find you." With those final, frightening words, Maryanne gave Claire a quick kiss and disappeared.

Claire had to make the next move alone. Holding a device constructed from duct tape and a few stolen circuits, praying to her Goddess that their plan worked, she flipped the switch.

Scattered explosions went off, all four of the handcrafted bombs Maryanne had distributed functioning flawlessly. Right on cue, Claire began phase two. As her friend had promised, the Followers on screen rushed towards the disturbance with alarming precision. When the soldiers were separated and in halls or elevators, she trapped the men with updated overrides to the systems they would have to countermand at each terminal.

Lips a hair's breadth from the screen, Claire took control of the prison's internal communications system. "Omegas, the doors to your cells are unlocked. Anyone who would prefer freedom to Shepherd's slavery, claim it. The guards are scattered, trapped, but I can't hold them for long. Band together, I'll lead you out. Do not forget your sister being held in the room at the end of the corridor." Venom dripped from Claire's voice. "I don't imagine Shanice dreamed her first heat would be spent mounted by a soldier three times her age."

On her small monitor, seven women, Nona included, stood and rushed out of their cells. More stood to watch, afraid but rallying. Over lingering seconds, the numbers began to grow, women throwing back the bars and racing out to join their sisters. But Claire's attention was elsewhere; a band of Followers had already overridden control and broken free.

Lacking the skill to manipulate the system with the same finesse as Maryanne, Claire cried, "Four Followers have made it through. You have to stand up for yourselves! If you want out, you must fight back!"

At first sight of the unwelcome Alphas, the Omegas fell upon them like locusts. More Followers tried to grab at the women, only to discover supposedly weak Omegas attacked in packs. Even the strongest male could not stand against forty enraged females. Gunshots were fired, two of Claire's sisters fell—but all four of Shepherd's soldiers were destroyed as the group forced their way forward. By the time they descended on the room where the estrous high Omega was being rutted, the pack had fallen into a frenzy.

The rutting male was ripped away, torn apart by teeth and claws.

They scooped up their sister, and followed every last direction Claire shouted over the speakers. In less than five minutes, women began to flood the very passages the Castoffs had employed the day they broke free.

Once they had pushed past the final doors, Claire stepped out of the darkness and called out to them. Nona reached her first. Over the sound of shouting, Claire yelled hurried instructions into the woman's ear. One nod of understanding, and Nona took Claire's COMscreen.

Claire pushed her crude trigger's final button.

Blinding flashes preceded cloying green-grey smoke—it filled the prison's access road to the point where Claire could no longer see Nona, she could not smell her, and she would not have the chance to wave goodbye.

The screech of tires and trucks packed with Shepherd's Followers skid to a halt outside the causeway. In moments, armed soldiers had created a perimeter; the only plausible exit blocked.

There was no turning back. This was the end.

Claire recognized the blue-eyed Beta leading the men, watched him squinting when the billowing smoke parted just enough to show who'd dared strike a blow at Thólos' new regime. With a gun held to her temple, Claire walked forward until she was exposed to Shepherd's men.

Eyes sharp, Jules commanded, "Put the gun down, Miss O'Donnell."

Seeing them so close, so organized, the Followers were exactly as Maryanne described—killers, remorseless, walking nightmares—and she was just one woman standing up against far more powerful men.

Raising her chin, defiant, Claire shouted over the fray, "Every Omega here gets to walk away, or I pull the trigger and kill Shepherd's child."

Ignoring the accumulating smoke, Jules marched to the edge of the barricade. "And how far do you think they will they get?"

The Beta was expecting an answer; Claire did not give one. All she did was stare right back into those unsettling baby-blues.

When long minutes of silence continued, when no further move was made by the female, Jules finally seemed to understand.

Claire smiled.

"Now that I think about it," the gun still pointed at her skull, Claire took a deep breath. "Putting the women in the Undercroft was actually an excellent idea. I think we'll stay… without the debauched visitors and scheduled rape, of course."

"Do you really think a handful of women will be able to hold the prison from us?"

"Yes."

A strange look passed through the man's eyes. He looked about to speak but was silenced by the sound of heavy footfalls approaching from the shadows.

The nightmare was coming.

She felt him before she saw him. Her eyes never left Jules, but it took every ounce of Claire's self-control not to step back into the blanket of smoke and ruin her plan when Shepherd emerged in her periphery.

"Little one," Shepherd's voice was soft and enticing, flowing just like the vapor at her back. "Point the gun at me."

He was so very big. Even with a good fifteen paces between them, Claire had the impression that all he needed to do was reach out to drag her back to hell.

Though she was afraid to look his way, though she kept her attention anchored in the vibrant blue of Jules' stare, Claire's words were for Shepherd. "If I thought I possessed the skill to aim and be certain a bullet blew right through your skull, I would not hesitate to shoot you. But I've told you before, I'm not stupid. Pointed where it is, I don't have to worry about missing."

Shepherd took a step closer; Claire stiffened.

Showing her teeth, she forced herself to look at him. "Your approach is making it very tempting to pull the trigger. If I die, your child dies with me. Stop. Moving."

With her attention on him, Shepherd paused, guiding the conversation as if they were having an afternoon chat. "It is good to see that you are mostly uninjured from the fall, and that you have been eating."

"I didn't fall, I jumped." Claire lifted her chin higher, exposing the bruises blotched across her pale throat for every last Follower to see.

Only with some great effort was Shepherd able to speak levelly. "You have made your point. I will even admit I am impressed with your little coup. But it's over now."

"I don't give a fuck what you think!"

A stifled bark came from the Alpha, his mouth curved into a snarl. "I know you are angry—"

Her voice dropped low, coarse as she hissed through clenched teeth, "Angry does not even begin to describe what I am. I have been defiled, manipulated, betrayed, and broken. *I am way past angry.*"

"Everything that was done was necessary," Shepherd countered, taking another intimidating step closer.

"You may have had me for a moment there, but your woman opened my eyes to what you really are." Fierce, Claire's lip curled in threat. "I should be thanking you, Shepherd. Your horrible lesson of insurrection was an inspiration. You taught me that even the weakest can rise up against tyranny with the right encouragement. Well, I'm rising up against you and the perversion of your ideals."

She had stood there long enough.

Trembling so hard she was certain every last man there could see her fear, ready to do what she did best, Claire took a backwards step into the smoke.

Shepherd countered, struggling to rein in his rage. "Do not make me come and collect you, little one. You may get injured, and I would prefer that not be the case."

"What are a few broken bones and a potential gunshot or two?"

She pressed her free hand to her heart, Claire's face the image of anguish. "They wouldn't matter. I feel nothing. Nothing at all."

Even Shepherd could not deny the echoing truth in the fractured bond; it was like she wasn't even there—the greater fragment of her spirit simply gone. But she was more at that moment than she had been when her every hour was spent in a stupor underground.

She would recover.

Looking deep into such pain-filled eyes, Shepherd spoke in a voice of certainty, of authority. "Your place is with me. You will return to your mate."

"You are no mate to me." Claire spat on the ground between them. "I will stand with my people on my terms! If Thólos is to suffer, your child and I will suffer with it."

Shepherd was going to reach for her, she knew it. Claire spun, black hair flaring as she darted into the smoke. Shepherd was so very fast for a man of his size, and Claire could feel him and his Followers bearing down on her. But out of the dark, thin arms reached for her.

The embrace of an old friend was followed by a sudden loss of gravity.

Maryanne Cauley had come back, a cable propelling them high above the Lower Reaches before the raging giant or his men had even seen where Claire had gone.

The amount of security protocols that had been overwritten during the Omegas' escape was extraordinary. All the surveillance footage had been wiped, many of the mechanized doors manipulated to trap his soldiers still malfunctioning. Purgatory's grounds had been turned into a maze that took Shepherd's most skilled Followers over an hour to penetrate, only to find there was not even one Omega inside.

The females had vanished as if teleported by the smoke.

Seven Followers dead, twenty-four trapped, and one man barely breathing. Claire's plan had been either extremely well-coordinated, or she was gifted with sheer dumb luck.

Deceitfully complacent, Shepherd turned to his second-in-command. "Explain to me, Jules, how an Omega female who paints pictures for children's stories accomplished this feat with only four days to plan?"

"I can't. Not yet, sir." The Beta stood at attention, unsmiling and severe. "We tracked the Omegas to the sewer access and know they went north, but the scent…"

"Was lost in the waste they rubbed all over themselves," Shepherd finished, knowing exactly what they would do. His lip curled. "And they are armed with weapons taken off our fallen men."

"Weapons they do not know how to use," Jules offered.

"Those women went on a rampage and killed five Alphas with their bare hands. I am fairly certain they will learn how to fire assault rifles in no time." A strange feeling came to the pit of Shepherd's gut, the sensation quickly ignored in favor of the satisfaction of clenching his fists until joints popped.

"We have profiles and photographs of all known surviving Omegas. The odds that one will be seen are exponentially higher with so many. They will be found."

"The situation with Claire takes precedence over retrieving the Omegas. Her escape route was divergent. She must be moving through Thólos as we speak. Assign our best trackers, and when she is found, no one approaches but me."

Jules knew the female had been serious about ending her life; it had been the only reason he'd not disarmed the quaking woman at first glance. "Cornering her would not end well. Her mental state is unbalanced. Miss O'Donnell is a danger to herself until her desperation recedes."

Shepherd cut a dangerous glare at his lieutenant. "What is your point?"

Intense blue eyes sat static in a face devoid of emotion. "Your appearance turned her fear to rage; her finger tightened on the trigger. I had a measure of rapport with her; you did not."

The slight flare of Shepherd's nostrils, the intake of breath, was nothing compared to the growl that stained his reply. "Her entire plan hinged on distracting us with the ploy. She did not pull the trigger, she ran."

Jules did not baulk. "Her success will give her confidence, and may lead her to expose herself to needless danger in order to fulfill her agenda. Shall I create a situation she'd want to resolve? We could draw her out on our terms. Miss O'Donnell could potentially be captured before any more trauma accumulated."

Shepherd momentarily considered the suggestion before he shook his head in the negative. "She is too clever for that."

"Where do you think she'll strike next?"

"I do not think she will strike at all. Not one of her bombs killed a Follower. She could have executed all our comrades trapped inside. Casualties were kept to a minimum. As far as we know, she never fired the pistol or pointed it at anyone but herself. No matter the show she put on, Claire O'Donnell is a pacifist. Her ideal would be to inspire, just like she threatened."

"If she exposes herself to the public, they will bring her in," the Beta assured.

"Her faith in the scum of this city is far more dangerous to her than any gun. If they knew of our bond, the people of Thólos would not deliver her home. They would rip her to shreds."

Curled together like kittens in Maryanne's bed, Claire slept with one hand over her belly and a troubled frown on her brow. Maryanne watched her fitful sleep, certain again that she'd lost her mind for going back to drag the obstinate fool away.

After witnessing the showdown with Shepherd, watching as the hulking killer spoke as softly as he could even though he was clearly furious, Maryanne couldn't wrap her head around it. When she'd been forced to work for him, she had seen him at his most ferocious, and it was nothing compared to the cautious demeanor he displayed to his mate.

The man was fucking terrifying. But just for a moment there, Maryanne had seen it. He'd been desperate.

Pair-bonds were strange things, a condition Maryanne had purposely chosen to avoid until the day she died. Who would want to give up their freedom and be tied to another person forever? The very idea was repulsive. Sex was sex—and Maryanne loved sex—but the urge to forge a tie, to bind oneself… no thank you!

As an Alpha female, options of whom you could fuck ranged far and wide, and fear of getting knocked up was basically non-existent. The only way to ovulate required the use of hormone injections or a male Omega in heat to inspire such an event. Maryanne didn't have a thing for scrawny guys, which was good, since the likelihood of finding a male Omega was pretty dismal. It was Beta boys she preferred, though a girl now and then had been fun, too.

Being born an Alpha had been a boon. She was stronger, aggressive, quick, and able to move through society in a position people like Claire coveted. The small thing in her arms had always resented her dynamic, even when they were little. Maryanne couldn't blame her. Once Claire's scent began to fill the room with sweetness instead of just little kid stink, the world started treating her like she was made out of glass. That was half the reason Maryanne had dragged her into more… interesting pursuits.

Childhood shenanigans had been good for Claire.

Or were, until Claire began to hide what she was under the practiced mask of a Beta—the pills, special soap. It was sad to see someone try so hard to be something else.

Considering the alternative of being bonded in a heated stupor with no real protection if the Alpha went against the Omega's wishes, it was understandable.

After all, look what had happened to Claire's mom—the paragon of the downside. It was no surprise Claire had never embraced her true nature. Looking at her now, Maryanne wondered if the dark-haired woman even knew the absolute finality of her bond with Shepherd, and the lengths to which he would go to recapture his mate.

Or he would just kill her… he probably would kill her after tonight, at least.

Grinning stupidly, Maryanne thought back on Claire's taunts and the burning vehemence practically rising like flames from the giant. Maryanne would have paid good money to watch that show. If she wasn't so anxious that Shepherd was going to rip the wall off the side of her den and come to fetch back his very unbalanced mate, she would have probably laughed at how perfectly Claire had owned him. She'd got her prisoners out, she'd stood alone against the Followers, she'd even threatened to kill herself and probably would have… simply to give the Omegas more time to follow through with the second half of the plan.

But Claire had always been a stubborn, sentimental fool.

A little fool who was clinging to her in sleep with a face so full of misery, Maryanne almost didn't recognize her. Claire was ten kinds of messed up. It was more than the scrapes and bruises, or the gross state of her feet; it was something in her makeup. The Omega female stood like a marionette missing a few strings—not at all the spirited girl she had been when they were kids. A small part of

Maryanne wanted to ask what had happened. The larger, more reasonable part, was determined to wash her hands of this trouble as soon as possible. Whatever was going on between Claire and Shepherd, whatever had caused Claire to provoke a man of his size and deadliness, Maryanne did not want to get dragged into it.

*Defiled, manipulated, betrayed, and broken...*

Well, that happened to everyone. Apparently it was just Claire's turn. Threading her fingers into the tousled, sooty hair, Maryanne began to comb out the knots.

Claire pressed nearer, a whimper catching in her throat. "*Shepherd...*"

And that was the final reason Maryanne would not be able to keep her. Everything went back to that pair-bond. Claire might be fighting it, might be fueled by rage and pain, but eventually she would waver and crack. It was inevitable, a tie of souls or some such nonsense. So long as she was running wild, Shepherd would hunt her, be fixated on a rampage, and Maryanne was not going to get trampled when nothing would change the outcome. She didn't owe Claire a damn thing; in fact, the way it looked now, *Claire owed her*.

Maryanne closed her eyes and cursed Shepherd to hell.

When she woke, there was no need to make a complicated decision regarding her lodger; Claire had made it for her. The little black-haired Omega was gone.

It was strange to walk through Thólos.

Claire may as well have been walking through the apocalypse. Everything she saw was far worse than the nightmare where the rabid pack was chasing her through the streets. Nothing seemed alive. No stores were open, no restaurants offered food. Buildings stood in shambles, broken glass and debris scattered about. Even bodies were left in the streets to freeze.

As her stroll continued, the warmth of Maryanne's bed leached away as if Claire had never known the comfort. She wandered, confused… wishing she could unsee all of it. In less than a year, the city had become a wasteland, another world that poisoned all it touched with frost, ice, and loss.

Shepherd's plan had been a success. Thólos was destroying itself, and all the man had to do was sit back and watch.

A whoosh of breath left her lungs and Claire stopped walking. Hunched against the wall was a dead child—blue, frozen—a little boy no older than nine.

Kneeling over the stiff corpse, Claire reached out and brushed back his matted hair, wondering how Shepherd could think this child's death would satisfy his plan. What great lesson would society learn by a lost life no soul would remember?

Slumping to the kid's side, mimicking the body's posture, Claire tried to find a reason for any of it. Tragedy in Thólos was nothing new. Since the occupation, orphan children died all the time.

More children were orphaned every day.

This was the new norm.

And who took them in? Where were they to go?

The people failed. Claire was not even sure if she could justify it anymore, not after seeing this. Leaning her head to the side she rested her cheek on the dead boy's hair and stared forward. There was no pleasure in her freedom or her view of the sky… there had not even been a sense of victory at her success freeing the Omegas.

Even in Maryanne's company she had only played the part, falsified emotion on instinct.

Closing her eyes, she let out a breath, ruffling the stiff brown hair under her lips. There was no point in being Claire anymore.

Instead, she would be nothing, as hollow as Thólos had allowed itself to become.

It was the sound of a sob that woke her, and for a moment she thought it was from the boy she slept against. Waking abruptly, her bleary eyes darted around and found nothing—just the same empty alley and the same piles of icy garbage. The only difference from before was the darkness, a thing her eyes adjusted to quickly after so long underground.

Oblivious to the freezing cold, Claire stood, ignoring the crack of stiff knees. Her pillow, the forgotten corpse, sat as rigid as before, the child staring forward into the same future as hers… into nothing.

Claire claimed him, and with more strength than she felt, she hoisted the boy up on her back, the corpse's limbs not easy to manage.

Not a soul disturbed her as she walked with her macabre prize through the streets of hell.

# 4

Corday looked over the newly freed Omegas, silently observing as they assembled a living space from piles of garbage. The mid-level Incineration Plant no longer created compost for the farm levels—not since citizens had taken to dumping their garbage in the streets. Now rotting mounds of muck protected an enclave of frightened women. Every breath stank of putrid food, mold, and things better left undescribed.

One thing it did not smell like was the young Omega still writhing through estrous, the girl moaning and begging for relief.

Corday was admittedly not an expert on Omega heat cycles, but whatever had been done to her, her sobbing response could not have been normal.

He kept his distance. The other Omegas also gave her a respectful berth, the group huddled together for warmth, gnawing on the rations he had provided.

An old woman, Nona, had come knocking on his door. It was Claire, she said, who'd directed her to find him. It was Claire who'd promised the resistance would feed and supply the freed Omegas.

It was the name Claire that made him come running.

He'd taken supplies without the permission of his commander. Brigadier Dane was going to kill him, and he was going to tell her straight to her face to go fuck herself. He was not going to let Claire down.

When he'd arrived the previous night, the Omegas had been… hostile. They were filthy, reeking just as badly as the garbage heap they'd chosen to shelter in.

Nona had warned him the women were dangerous, that they were armed and might shoot any male on sight. She had even warned him not to follow her back once she'd procured supplies.

Corday was having none of it. He needed to see Claire.

But Claire was not there. Even hours after the women had settled in, their liberator failed to show her face. The night dragged on, morning came, afternoon, Corday stiff from leaning against a slimy wall.

Had Claire been captured? Had the tyrant killed her?

Nona gently told him that Claire's plan required her to arrive from a different path; that the woman most likely was waiting for dark before she moved; that she had always been overly cautious when away from the safety of the group.

Corday scoffed. The Claire he knew was reckless. She was also badly hurt.

Over and over, Nona reminded him that if Claire had been taken, Shepherd's men would have already come for them.

Claire O'Donnell was out there.

And so he waited past the point of exhaustion, exasperation, and flat out fear. Evening fell. At first Corday thought his eyes were playing tricks on him. A two-headed hunchbacked beast staggered down the plant's dark garbage chute. Milky eyes stared right through him; they never blinked—just as the mouth beneath those dead eyes gaped in a fixed expression of hopelessness.

It was the face of a corpse.

Hidden beneath it sat a much dearer countenance, the struggling woman's eyes half-covered by a curtain of black tangles.

"Claire!"

Corday rushed towards the Omega and her burden, unraveling the frozen limbs of a cadaver unwilling to release its host.

Claire did not seem happy to see him. In fact, she didn't seem herself at all. "I found that boy alone in an alley, Corday… forgotten."

Once the dead child lay safely upon the ground, Corday pulled her against his chest. Warmth of his cheek against hers, stubble scratching, he breathed, "Nona came for me. I know what you did."

After the atrocities Claire had seen in the city, the attack on the Undercroft… facing Shepherd, seemed to have happened in another life. "The city's become a horrible place. I saw things… What's happening to us?"

Existential talk on the human condition could happen later. Tugging her towards the Omegas' fire, Corday urged, "You're freezing, Claire. Sit."

Nona ran over at first sight of her friend, the older woman throwing herself around her. "Your mother would be proud. You know that, my girl?"

Claire didn't want accolades, she just wanted to collapse.

There was no shyness. Corday ignored the watching women and tugged Claire down to rest between his thighs. Arms and legs wrapped around the girl's shivering frame, he put his chest to her back and purred.

The Omegas were openly confused by the state of their hero. Where was the confident deliverer who'd faced down an army? Why was she letting a Beta male hold her in an intimate embrace?

Why wasn't she speaking?

Nona smoothed the hair off Claire's forehead, watched her

young friend close her eyes, and waited until Claire's breath became steady in sleep. Only then did she sniff.

Cautious not to wake her friend, Nona mouthed the words, "She smells pregnant."

Corday nodded and whispered, "She is."

It should not have been possible—not when Claire's last cycle had come the day she'd entered the Citadel.

Pressing her thin-lipped mouth in a frown, Nona's heart broke. "Shepherd has done this to Claire. This is…."

Corday cut her off. "I know," he tightened his hold, "but she won't be alone."

Nona's severity lessened, she even smiled at the boy. "You care for her."

Corday did. "Swear to me you won't let her leave when I'm gone. Swear you will keep her safe."

The inevitable was unstoppable. "She is pregnant and pair-bonded, Corday. Even if you tend her constantly, she won't be able to stay for long."

Looking Nona dead in the eye, Corday chewed out each word. "Shepherd damaged the pair-bond. It has no bearing now."

Older and wiser, Nona spoke as gently as she could. "That is not possible… what he damaged was Claire."

"So you'll just let her wander back to Shepherd?" Corday would be damned first.

"You are not an Omega. You can't possibly understand the finality of a pair-bond." Nona began to smooth Claire's hair, looking at her friend with pity. "The only way for Claire to be free, is with Shepherd's death or hers. I guarantee she knows that, no matter what she may say."

"But…" Corday chose denial. "Claire told me…"

Her friend had always had misplaced altruism. "She would want you to have faith." In a hushed voice, Nona confessed, "I know better than to give you false hope. But know this, so long as she is pregnant, she is precious to Shepherd. That makes her safe."

Corday pulled down the scarf around Claire's neck. Nasty bruises sat on display. "Would you call this something treated as precious?"

Nona took in the marks, tears gathering in her eyes. Words were difficult. "It's more than just the pair-bond. Everyone here knows she is mated to Shepherd. They will not trust her. They will drive her off."

Corday glared at the collection of women stealing glances in their direction. "Claire saved their lives."

"Listen to me, boy," Nona urged, fervently whispering. "That does not mean every Omega in this room deserved it. It would only take one to bring us all down again."

Had the Omegas not learned? "The women who turned her in last time were hanged by Shepherd. I watched their executions myself."

"You and I both know that fear makes people do very stupid things."

"Then she comes home with me."

Nona, her face full of compassion, agreed, "That might be best."

Looking down at the sleeping woman in his arms, Corday felt shaken… because he knew what was wrong with his scheme. "But she won't stay unless I lock her in."

Nona nodded. "I think you're beginning to understand. Keep purring. It will calm you both."

PUZZLE PIECES WERE HIS SPECIALTY. Jules understood the finite operation that motivated people, he was second only to Shepherd in that particular skill. He was also the only other person who'd had any access to Claire over the last few months. He knew what she smelled like, even pregnant. He knew her voice and had pegged her at once for a brooder.

She was almost sweet in her misguided agenda, and Jules grasped exactly what had drawn Shepherd so strongly. Claire was an enigma, all wrapped up in a little moral bow.

Claire was everything Shepherd falsely believed Svana to be.

His commander had never *lived* amongst Dome civilization, not like Jules had before he'd been imprisoned. Shepherd's rearing underground—surviving the extreme of Undercroft society—had wired the man to thrive in acute circumstances. No matter how preternaturally brilliant Shepherd was, his lack of empathy in dealing with conventional people was obvious. Yet he was an amazing leader, drew men to his standard, could see the world in a way others could not.

He'd freed the outcasts… even before the breach.

*One man* had driven back the nightmare underground. Shepherd had organized a feral population, given slaves purpose, hope. Yet, like all prisoners, if Shepherd wanted something, he took it, and God help you if you disappointed him.

Shepherd remained incapable of understanding Claire's *hesitations.*

Even for all the Alpha's aggression, there was no one in the world Jules admired more. His respect even withstood the flaw in his superior—Shepherd's universe began and ended with Svana.

The fact the two Alphas were lovers was no secret. Even Jules had witnessed Svana's enthusiasm for Shepherd for years. He knew the story of how she had drawn him underground, approached Shepherd as if she were an angel with her passcodes and rare food. At the time they'd both been young. Perhaps they had seduced one another—two miscreant wild things enslaved by the system. But where Shepherd had been born in hell, Svana had come from heaven.

He practically worshiped at her feet. He had made himself the mission for her, built her an army.

She claimed to be special, chosen…

Worst of all, it was true. All of it.

She owned something no amount of money could buy: a valuable bloodline.

Svana was the key to freedom, to a new world, to a land where no one would look down on them for Da'rin—where no one would hiss the word 'outcast.' With her help, all of them would be heroes, redeemers, saviors.

They would all be reborn.

Svana had not been born in Thólos Dome. Instead, she'd been *gifted* to the people of Thólos…

None of this was public knowledge, of course. Very few knew Svana had arrived on a transport two decades ago as part of an Interdome trade of viable females. Even less knew who that child in rags really was. Her adopted parents didn't know, and from Jules' investigation, even Premier Callas was not privy to such information. The secret belonged to Shepherd and to the chosen Followers of the man sworn to lead them to freedom.

Svana was cunning on her own; she used her position to develop access to everything… secrets, money, favors—even lovesick teenaged Shepherd.

It was a fancy she'd grown out of. Shepherd, on the other hand, had been entirely unaware of the fact that his beloved had moved on. She knew what she was doing, feeding his regard for her, nurturing his devotion. It seemed pathetic, had you not seen what the two of them could accomplish together.

That Jules hated. She was necessary for the plan. Shepherd, all the Followers, *needed* her.

But she also needed them. Without Shepherd's army, there was no way the woman could reclaim her birthright. Svana was the only surviving offspring of Greth Dome's ruling family; a monarchy that had been deposed and disposed of. Insurgents had killed her parents, and had foolishly thought to extend mercy to a little girl considered too young to remember.

Svana may have been small when her life under Thólos began, but she had been coached to corrupt from birth. But, just like her parents, she believed herself beyond reproach.

The affair with Premier Callas… Whether the Alpha admitted it or not, Shepherd had been forced to face a glimpse of what she truly was.

In response, Shepherd had acted against his beloved; he took an Omega mate. A fact Jules had known Svana would not be pleased about once discovered. Was this not the very reason Shepherd had kept the Omega obsessively hidden? Not a soul was allowed near her, and even Jules had been cast out for only looking once… until recently.

The Beta did not know what had spurred Shepherd to take quarters away from his room for days; he didn't ask. He had instead been stuck dealing with an irate ruler who possessed far less patience, and a pregnant Omega who looked heartbroken each time he brought her another of the blasted trays.

For reasons unknown, Shepherd had reduced Claire to a position of breeder, not mate. Jules accepted it and did his duty. It was less than a week before the lieutenant opened the door to find Miss O'Donnell on the floor, altered, and trapped in a room with an odor Jules had smelled in his leader's quarters before—the spiced scent of Svana's Alpha slick. The Omega who should have been nesting was as far away from the bed as she could get, so still she seemed corpse-like. It was the only reason he'd spoken when she asked his name.

On closer inspection, it had been impossible for Jules to miss the split lip and the discoloration on Miss O'Donnell's neck. Even more, he had recognized the look in her eye when Shepherd approached outside Undercroft; every nuance of her expression Jules had read with precision. The Omega was devastated—not just afraid—emotionally crippled, and clearly suicidal no matter Shepherd's denial on the subject.

And that was where the issue lingered. Jules presumed the obvious assumption was correct. Shepherd had mated with his long time consort… and he was aware of their habit of sharing heated Omegas.

Claire had reacted badly to whatever the Alpha female's visit had inspired.

The situation was irreparable in the allotted time. Shepherd's denial and Svana's vindictive nature had done the damage. If what Jules suspected was true, Miss O'Donnell now had good reason to hate the man beyond just the initial fear of her situation and misunderstanding of his true agenda. Even more, Shepherd's current demands that Miss O'Donnell be returned to resume her position as his mate made the situation far more complicated.

It would almost be more convenient if the little Omega just died, the entire situation being nothing but troublesome. But she was carrying what would be Shepherd's heir.

Claire was important now.

THE GROUND WAS hard beneath her, the unyielding floor setting her hip to aching. But there was the smell of safety… a well-known Beta. They were wrapped together, covered in his coat like an overripe bug cocoon.

She cracked open an eye, finding Corday already watching her, his expression too controlled to read.

Claire admitted guilt. "I knew you'd help Nona if she used my name."

Corday put his lips to her forehead; he held her tighter. "She told me what you did. You held a gun to your head, Claire."

She had done that… and she had been very scared. "I did."

He could play the belligerent game just as well as she could. Still holding her, he moved his face until their noses were touching. "Claire, please."

Claire glanced to the side and absently worried her lip. "I'm not sorry for setting these women free."

"I don't want you to be!" Urgent, Corday whispered so the spying women might not hear. "What I want is for you to trust me. You don't need to fight alone."

But she did… both Corday and Senator Kantor had explained their position. "I am not going to attack Shepherd or his pig army. The Omegas are free, it's done."

"I don't believe you."

Still bone tired, Claire sighed. "I give you my word that I will not attack Shepherd. Such a thing would be pointless."

"Look at me," Corday urged, face grim and determined. "Swear it."

She held his gaze. "I swear I will not attack them."

The Beta seemed satisfied. "How long has it been since you've eaten?"

"I ate at your house."

Frustrated, he squeezed her. "That was three days ago, and you threw up afterwards."

"I had more important things to worry about than food."

"Claire, you are not superhuman."

No. She did not even feel regular human. She felt quasi-formed and misshapen. “I will eat.”

A twitch curled Corday’s lips. “Good.” He sat her up, rubbing at her neck when her bones cracked. “And while you are eating, I am going to ask you what other crazy schemes you have planned. You don’t need to keep secrets from me, Claire. Let me help you.”

They had an audience, several sets of eyes watching their low, murmured exchange. Corday went to pillage through the crates he’d brought. A piece of fresh fruit and a packet of protein rich supplement in hand, he returned to her.

Others approached Claire.

A few even sniffed the black-haired Omega, backing away quickly as if she might taint them once the rumor had been confirmed.

If Claire noticed, she did not react.

Corday could see that Nona was right. No matter what she had done for them, Claire would not be tolerated by the pack for long. “Come home with me, Claire.”

Claire looked to the man offering her an apple as if he’d gone mad. “I can’t put you in that position. No.”

“Then I’ll come here every day until you change your mind.” The Beta took her cold fingers and urged, “I want to take care of you. When you come to your senses, I will take you home.”

Claire mumbled, looking to the fire, “Should the time come, I look forward to going home.”

It was Nona who’d sat quietly through the exchange, who’d touched Claire’s arm in understanding.

It was time for Corday to go. Claire stood, pulled him into a hug, dismissing the man as she teased, “Next time you visit, bring decent coffee.”

He chuckled.

Suddenly serious, she gripped the fabric of his coat. “And if you are foolish enough to get caught, I will charge the Citadel to get you out."

Corday's laughter faded. "That's not funny."

"I wasn't joking."

Frustrated, running a hand through his hair, Corday argued, "You set the Omegas free. You moved mountains. It's time for you to rest."

Claire agreed. "Nona would not allow anything else. Now, get out of here, Beta. No boys allowed."

Corday did not want to go, but he gave her space, swearing he would return.

With the Beta gone, Nona placed an arm around her young friend, the old woman muttering, "He doesn't understand."

The broken Omega whispered, "He doesn't need to know."

THERE WERE ONLY four in the room: Corday, Brigadier Dane, Senator Kantor, and a stranger.

"There is a new member come to join the resistance." The typical exhaustion that had aged Senator Kantor since the Dome's fall, lifted. The pleased Alpha gestured to the beautiful woman at his side. "We made contact with my niece… This is Leslie Kantor."

Smiling softly at her uncle's heartfelt relief, the brunette Alpha female reached out her hand in formal introduction. "It is a pleasure to meet you, Corday."

There was a glint in the older man's eyes, a long lost spark returning when Corday grinned and took her hand. "It's rare we get good news. Welcome."

Dwarfed in her layers, bundled up warm, Leslie offered, "And I hope I have more to buoy you. Before Shepherd's invasion, Premier Callas had been my betrothed. Our circumstances had yet to be announced." She waved a flippant hand. "These things have to go through the proper channels, be approved by the Senate, and so on. In the interim, Callas arranged for me to have deputy access to everything. As it was done in secret, Shepherd's men are unaware that I can infiltrate their communications network."

Corday's mouth gaped. "Holy fuck…"

"Yeah, son." Senator Kantor chuckled. "Holy fuck."

This changed everything, gave the resistance an actual chance. "Do you know where he's hidden the contagion?"

Leslie shook her head. "No. The language they communicate in, it's difficult to understand. But that does not mean we can't crack it. I just need time."

But this was still great progress. The secrecy of the meeting began to make sense, no one could know Leslie Kantor's secret. She would have to be hidden, the information restricted. Corday said as much. "No one can know about her. If Shepherd got wind, it would be an easy thing to revoke her access."

"Agreed." Senator Kantor had Corday's next orders. "If we kept her here, too many people would see her. We can't have questions raised. I'm entrusting my niece to you, Corday."

The honor bestowed on the low ranked Enforcer came at a very bad time; however, there was no way to refuse such an important mission. Claire needed him, but the entire population needed the intel Leslie might uncover. Corday shared his news. "You should know sir, the Omegas were freed. Today we've struck two victories against Shepherd."

The Senator genuinely smiled. "I told you my bet was on Claire."

"You did."

And that was it.

~

JULES FROWNED, a rare thing, and listened to the audio surveillance of Thólos' pathetic resistance headquarters. The hunt for Claire had been waylaid when report arrived that a certain Alpha female had presented herself on the resistance's doorstep.

Svana—Leslie Kantor—had a different part to play in the fall of Thólos. She had a specific mission that had nothing to do with playing rebel. And if she'd known where they were all along, why not pass that information to Shepherd.

Jules knew exactly what the bitch was up to.

Svana was hunting Claire. Of course she'd know the Omega had escaped. It was the reason he'd had the Alpha female followed since Shepherd's mate had gone missing.

And now she'd lead them right to the resistance.

The woman was truly foolish to think this act would go unnoticed. Shepherd might have lauded his beloved, but Jules did not find her cunning clever. Oh, she was useful and she was powerful, and for that reason alone, Jules had not engineered an accident for her years ago.

But she was trouble.

No matter the plan or the promises, the female was self-serving.

Jules didn't trust her, and was eager to prove that she needed to be curbed. It was the reason he chose to follow them, to make a preemptive visit to the listed domicile of one Enforcer Corday.

It wasn't difficult to breach the building. All it took was the acquisition of one terrified rebel and a few minutes of torture to learn the location of Enforcer Corday's home, and a few well-placed distractions for the dubious couple working their way across the city. While the Enforcer and Svana were still meandering through the dangerous city streets, Jules opened the door to the sad little apartment.

That first breath of air… and the Beta froze. The room was saturated in Miss O'Donnell's scent—the couch, the bed, he even found her bloody dress tucked in the bathroom hamper.

Svana could not have intended it, but she had delivered Jules right to the Beta who'd taken in Shepherd's mate.

Even if the Omega was not in the domicile, Enforcer Corday had access to her. Miss O'Donnell's retrieval was imminent.

Bugs were placed, the surveillance team handpicked by Shepherd's second-in-command, situated nearby. The job was done quickly. All that remained was to report personally to Shepherd and explain the *complicated* situation.

# 5

Entering Shepherd's den, Jules could scent his commander's extreme agitation. "I have picked up the trail of your mate."

Shepherd's demand for an answer was immediate. "Where?"

The Beta detailed his report, handing Shepherd a dossier on a young male. "Since Miss O'Donnell's disappearance, as a precaution, I have had Svana shadowed. Today, *Leslie Kantor* chose to contact the resistance—inadvertently she led us right to their doorstep. While she was there, a Beta by the name of Enforcer Samuel Corday was charged with her protection. I personally went to the Beta's residence to bug the location before he could return with Svana as his ward.

"Miss O'Donnell was not on the premises. Her scent, however, permeates the dwelling. I also found the shredded dress she was wearing when she leapt off the roof. Enforcer Corday is the Beta with whom she found refuge before her assault on Undercroft. I believe he knows where she is. By tracking him through the grid, he will lead us straight to your Omega."

Looking up from the photograph of the handsome male, Shepherd let the weight of his glare run over his second-in-command. "You can confirm that Svana approached rebel leaders of her own accord?"

"Yes." And that was the greater issue, in Jules' opinion. "The niece of Senator Kantor has offered her passcodes to help the resistance."

The stiff set of Shepherd's shoulders, the pulse of danger in the air, warned him the Alpha was not pleased with the news. "Did she?"

"Svana is acting autonomously for purposes of her own." Jules, his chin held high, ignored his leader's silent dismissal of Svana's unsubstantiated misdeeds and outlined the remainder of the report. "She will have recognized Claire's scent the moment she entered Enforcer Corday's domicile."

"That will not matter. Claire will be recovered immediately." Shepherd could always tell when Jules had something more he wanted to say, it was in the shiftiness of his hardened glare, and the uncomfortable lines around his mouth. Standing, his huge arms crossed over his chest, Shepherd's own posture made it clear his subordinate had better get to the point. "Speak."

Jules explained in the same steady monotone that displayed acute sincerity. "Aside from the threat of Svana, Claire O'Donnell is willing to kill herself, brother. By starvation… a bullet to the head… she will find a way if she wants to."

The single step closer put Shepherd within the distance to behead Jules with little more than a flick of the wrist. Eyes flared, Shepherd threatened, "You presume to tell me what she will and will not do? You presume much lately. I am quite certain I made myself clear before."

The Beta was loyal; it was his duty to speak. "You are responsible for Claire O'Donnell's current state. Your open infidelity has altered what you created when you chose to pair-bond. That kind of hatred will not disappear simply because you drag her back."

The beast emerged. An arm bulging with muscle struck, slamming the smaller man against the wall. Dangling Jules by a grip on his throat, Shepherd roared, "You do not know of what you speak!"

Gasping, his boots high above the floor, Jules grunted despite the grip of the giant, "You allowed Svana to manipulate you into dishonoring your pregnant mate. You are responsible for what broke her, and must recognize the consequences of what you sanctioned. I cannot return her as she was."

Jules was thrown clear across the room. Before he might break the man's bones, the bellowing giant's fists attacked the wall instead. Huge chunks of concrete broke off, his knuckles tore, and blood flowed, but Shepherd's outburst did not exorcise such rage.

When the provoked, panting monster spun to face the Beta, eyes full of murder, he found Jules standing, loyal and unmoving as always. Shepherd poked Jules roughly in the chest. "I should kill you."

Before answering, Jules wiped a trickle of blood from his mouth. "For speaking the truth, brother?"

Shepherd rolled his shoulders, snarling a defense, "I did what had to be done and sent my mate from the room so she would not have to watch as I pacified Svana."

The Beta outlined the facts. "In choosing to *pacify* your former lover, you destroyed any potential for Miss O'Donnell to be your mate the way you seem to wish her to be."

"And you think given the fact that you once had an Omega wife, your opinion has value?" Shepherd's face was red, his pulse thundering at the bulge of his neck.

Jules offered an alternative. "The only way you will gain influence over the Omega is to give her what she wants."

A minute passed, a minute where Shepherd had to fight every

instinct that told him to crush the Beta for questioning him. "Explain."

"Her profile is one of a martyr. If you offer to leave the Omegas and her *allies* in peace, you have a bargaining chip—influence over Miss O'Donnell you can wield to gain compliance and the behavior you prefer. If approached correctly, I expect that she will agree to return of her own free will in exchange for the lives of the others. Suicide will no longer be an issue, giving you time to progress the pregnancy that may soften her hatred towards you."

Shepherd detested what he was hearing, but there was wisdom in his second's words. "Is there more?"

For once, intonation, bitterness, inflected Jules speech. "I didn't only have a wife. I also had two sons."

There was a hint of remorse in Shepherd's retreat. Ignoring his bleeding knuckles, the Alpha pulled on his coat and left the room. "I shall lead the surveillance of the Beta personally."

Jules radioed an underling to clean up the mess and repair the wall, as usual, three steps ahead.

As ordered, Corday had escorted Leslie Kantor to his apartment. The journey had not been simple. In fact, it seemed that every causeway they'd tried to walk contained some obstruction or Follower presence that required the pair to choose another path.

It took hours of doubling back just to make it a few steps forward. It didn't help that Leslie Kantor did not have a clue how to fend for herself. The female, though charming, had no business on the streets.

Corday could hardly believe she'd survived as long as she had.

He did not voice his opinion, but she could sense it. When they were finally sequestered and safe in his apartment, she admitted, "I have been sheltered since the city fell. My family's housing holds a secret panic room that was stocked with enough food and water that I had little need to leave."

If only everyone had owned such a luxury. Sizing up the woman, Corday asked, "You were alone in your bunker?"

Eyes downcast, Leslie nodded.

"That must have been hard."

"I didn't know my father had been hanged outside the Citadel. I didn't know my mother had been strung up beside him." Tears fell free down her high cheeks. "I'll never forgive myself for not trying to find them… I should have sought my uncle sooner."

Leading her to his worn sofa so the weeping woman might collect herself, Corday said, "Your parents would have wanted you to stay safe."

Rubbing her eyes, Leslie sighed. "I will do anything I can to help the resistance. Shepherd must be stopped."

A smile was offered in agreement. "And we will stop him, but we cannot make a move until we uncover the location of the contagion. That must be your priority."

"I'll do my best."

"We can start tonight."

"Of course. Just let me clean up first." Leslie glanced down at the fine coat that had grown grimy with their crossing, at the scarf, the mittens, and began to strip the layers away. "The scent of your mate leads me to believe you'll have some fresh clothes I can borrow."

Corday stood and moved to the kitchenette. "I don't have a mate."

Leslie smirked, coquettish and feminine. "I just assumed… Omega scent is on your coat… and in this room. But I can see it's a sore topic. Forget I said anything."

"No, it's okay." Gathering food so they might eat and get straight to work, Corday said, "Claire just sleeps here sometimes."

Leslie bit her lip, eyes sparkling. "And she sleeps in your coat?"

The charm worked, Corday was amused. "And sometimes in my coat, yes."

"I pegged you as a cuddler." Leslie stretched her arm across the back of the couch, looking over her shoulder and bantering as if they were friends. "She's a lucky female to have the attention of a man who fights for what he loves."

With a half-hearted smirk, Corday shook his head. "It's not like that. She couldn't even if she wanted to… or even if I wanted to. My friend was pair-bonded to a stranger, someone who mistreated her. Any kind of physical relationship is off the table for now."

"Pair-bonded?" The woman went deadpan, cold calculation slipping into her expression. "That is unthinkable."

Corday gave a sorry shrug. "So you see; it's not what you imagine."

Leslie shook her head, contemplating something monumental. "It cannot be the case that this *stranger* pair-bonded to her."

Corday brought over their rations, plopping down beside his guest. "I wish it wasn't. She's a wonderful girl whom I like very much… even though she's as infuriating as she is sweet."

Leslie's smile returned, her bearing once again playful. "What is she like, your Omega?"

Corday gave a small, caustic laugh. "Stubborn. Determined to be a one woman resistance."

Patting his thigh, Leslie warned, "One woman can't stand alone against Shepherd's power."

"I hate to admit it, but she's done pretty well so far. She's accomplished more than we have."

Leslie inched closer, fascinated. "How did she stand up to Shepherd?"

There was little Corday could say. “By simply being Claire.”

The beauty at his side was unsatisfied. “Be cautious of her, Corday. Don’t allow yourself to foster feelings. If she is pair-bonded, as you say, then she could never commit to you.”

“Yeah, well… she ain’t exactly committed to her mate, either. He made that easy enough by allowing some psycho female to unhinge the pair-bond.” Corday scoffed at the irony. “Well, now it seems he woke the beast. The Alpha monster and his lover unleashed a storm.”

Leslie’s voice grew lower. “What are you talking about?”

“Claire broke Shepherd’s Omega prisoners out of Undercroft two nights ago.” Corday grinned, proud to the bone. “I’m starting to think the bastard doesn’t stand a chance.”

“What of the woman? Shepherd’s lover?”

Corday cut a glance at his guest, frowning deeply. “I didn’t say it was Shepherd.”

Leslie blinked, the picture of naiveté. “Not in so many words…”

“All I know is that the woman behaved like your run-of-the-mill sex offender.” Reaching for his COMscreen, Corday grit his teeth and growled. “Sounds to me like Shepherd and the Alpha bitch are a match made in heaven—or maybe hell is more appropriate.”

EVEN WITH THE popped collar of the leather jacket Claire had stolen from Maryanne, it felt as if the cold constantly cut right through her.

Cold was the only thing she could feel.

The Omegas were beginning to stir, the shuffling sound of movements soothing. Claire was glad to observe the group adjusting to freedom, even if it was in a reeking dump, even if she was not a welcome part of it. The women had maintained a respectful verbal distance, had asked very few questions, and had been as comforting as they were able.

That did not stop the troubled glances, though. To them, she was contaminated.

They could not have been more correct.

It was unsurprising that wariness should come from the knowledge that she had been claimed by the biggest monster of them all.

There was only one there who kept to Claire's side.

"Did they discover who you really are, Nona?"

The old woman wrinkled her brow. "I don't think so. Even if they did, they had little interest in me. Interrogations were only about you."

"That seems rather pointless." From the sound of it, Followers had compiled a file packed with random inaccurate information. Most of these women hardly knew her, and would have probably said anything they thought Shepherd wanted to hear. Staring dull-eyed at the fire, Claire murmured, "You need to make sure Corday doesn't find out."

"It's not exactly like he can put me in prison, dearest," the woman whispered, pulling Claire to rest her head in her lap.

"But when the city is free…"

"We have other things to worry about now."

Claire sighed. "I wonder what happened to the others, the Omegas who were bonded?" Were they locked underground as she had been? Were they frightened? "I never saw anyone else. I don't know where they are. I can't help them."

"Shepherd told me that all had settled into their new place. You were the only one having difficulties." It was a subject that disturbed Nona as much as it troubled Claire. "Did you know he came to speak with me a little over a week ago? Your mate claimed you were withdrawn and demanded I tell him how to end your depression."

Hearing such a thing, Claire turned green, doubling over to vomit. That was the end of any mention of Shepherd.

Nona was a modicum of comfort, but Claire felt adrift—isolated even in the companionship of her kind. It led her to stand, to wipe her mouth, and to leave the Omegas' sanctuary without another word.

Though it was obvious she wanted to, the old woman did nothing to stop her.

Just like the last two days, from dawn to dusk Claire wandered Thólos like a wraith.

Her absences were hardly commented upon, but Nona was always there with a portion of rations she pressed Claire to eat. Once she had her dark-haired friend warming by the fire, she would talk nonsense; she would make Claire communicate, until the exhausted Omega forgot to keep answering.

For two nights straight, Corday failed to return.

If Claire noticed, if she was relieved or saddened, she said nothing.

Nona was not even sure her friend had any concept of time passing.

Claire was too beyond herself, too detached. But when she walked, the city seemed to open up to her—every path leading to some new awful landscape. The buildings were hollow because the dead were piled in the street. Marks of violence were everywhere, roving bands of looters still pillaging as if there were treasure to be found in the decay.

That was reality—exposed reality.

Half cognizant, Claire almost found her wandering had taken her right to the Citadel.

The black specks of Followers in the distance startled her out of her stupor. She drew back with such speed, she slipped on an unseen patch of ice. Heart in her throat, Claire fell into the gutter, scampering blindly until she zigzagged through the first open door in her path.

It took almost an hour to snap out of her panic, to look around at the wreck of a stranger's home and recognize why every frigid draught filled the room with whispers.

It was paper bowing in the wind. Overturned shelves, fallen books scattered over the floor.

Under her hand lay the words:

*He who does not know the evils of war cannot appreciate its benefits.*

Disgusted, Claire snapped the worn book closed to find Sun Tzu's *The Art of War*.

She wanted to throw it, to rip every last page from the spine, but instead found her eyes drawn back to the dog-eared pages. Sprawled on a pile of some dead soul's ransacked things, she read until it was too dark to continue. Then she slept, passing another night free of Shepherd, utterly lost, and broken inside.

When morning came and she woke stiff, Claire rose from her makeshift burrow and walked out the door as if she'd never been there. It was not until she was back at the Omegas' haven that she realized her bloodless fingers were still gripping Sun Tzu's masterpiece to the point they'd gone white.

She was staring at it like it owed her an explanation for being there.

Nona crept nearer to see. "What is that?"

Eyes on the book, the green-eyed waif muttered, "Sun Tzu said to appear weak when you are strong, and strong when you are weak." Claire began stripping off her clothes. "Go get the COMscreen. I need you to make me look strong."

In a building opposite the generic apartment Enforcer Corday dwelled in sat a seething Alpha—one on the verge of snapping. Shepherd prided himself on his steadiness, his focus and dedication to purpose, but at that moment, after bombardment, accusations and indignity, he was not at his best. Where the pair-bond connected, Shepherd felt some strange pulse. The force that burned and stole his focus condemned his rage. The sensation had denounced his actions often over the past months, brought with it severe discomfort. It was discomfort he bore, knowing that the final result made what were sometimes reprehensible deeds necessary for his mate.

He could tolerate the pain of the bond just as he tolerated the pain of such extensive Da'rin infection. Tolerating being challenged by a subordinate, even if it was a man he respected, was not quite so easy.

No one questioned him. He ruled the Undercroft, had toppled the Dome's disgusting government, and controlled an entire puppet population. His Followers recognized and bowed to such greatness, and no puny Beta had the right to dictate what was best… as if to share wisdom… as if to say that what he demanded was impossible!

Jules' insinuations looped on repeat in Shepherd's thoughts, the Alpha dissecting each word, finding the flaws in the other man's argument… determined to prove he was right and Jules was mistaken.

Shepherd would have his Claire on his terms. Everything would be as nature intended, Jules' idea of *consequences* be damned.

But there was a deeper message between the words, a sly list of allegations Jules would have to be corrected for.

'*Infidelity...*'

'You allowed Svana to *manipulate* you into *dishonoring* your pregnant mate…'

All this implied a breach in code: castigation. Jules had inferred

Shepherd was corruptible and that Svana pulled his strings. His second-in-command's gall was unspeakable.

Even aware of his simmering wrath, the blue-eyed Beta stood vigilant at his side.

Stuffing down bitter rage, unwilling to be seen as less than perfectly calm, Shepherd continued his surveillance and kept his growling to a minimum. Jules would be dealt with for his failure once Claire was returned. As Alpha—the creator of the bond—Shepherd would prove to the lesser Beta that his Omega would come to heel without pointless negotiation or bribery. That was the natural order of things.

Claire would be found, and she would submit. In time, she would love him.

But the bond whispered that she wanted to die, that she would find a way soon. And that possibility was the tiny mustard seed of doubt cracking his obstinacy.

In hindsight, Shepherd recognized that he should have coddled her after Claire's tantrum all those weeks ago. But he wanted his mate to see why she'd suffered the meltdown. She had to admit she desired him, responded to his presence, that things had improved. Shepherd had given her the space to consider such weighty insight—left her to feel the loss of the mate she needed—so that she would know without question what her true, natural feelings were.

So she would behave and adore him.

Even Shepherd had to admit that his attempt to condition, his rejection of her presence, must have made his mating with Svana seem deliberate—another punishment.

The feelings inside Claire once it began, the degradation, it could not have been worse.

Improvement did not come with time. Her terrible desolation had not abated with freedom or success; Shepherd could feel it flowing from her like an endless bubbling poison. Claire was past the point of despair. It was a thing he had witnessed countless times in the Undercroft—a cessation of spirit. But the Omega had spoken; her eyes had been full of fire when she faced him on the streets, a marked improvement from the vacant figure who had subsisted on air in his den.

And it was the Beta smiling at Svana that had roused her. Corday was the one Claire had run to, his food she'd accepted. He was the man Claire preferred to him.

Shepherd deliberated on such an outrage, frustrated further to see Svana playing the fine lady—touching Corday, wooing him gently, all the while digging less than subtly for information.

What game was Svana playing?

Svana had a great many strengths, but the Alpha female had a tendency to miss the minutiae. It was for that reason Shepherd was sure she had no idea he was watching, that the Enforcer's apartment had already been bugged… that Followers were listening to their would-be queen.

As the conversation between Corday and Svana continued, the stiffness of his second-in-command was impossible to miss. Jules found the whole thing distasteful.

Svana had no cause to get involved, to distract. Her only duty was to keep the contagion hidden and unleash it once their exodus began. If she were to be captured or killed in this ploy, the finale of their great insurrection, of their great revenge, would fail.

Worse, every minute Corday was stuck tending *Leslie Kantor*, he was not giving them the location of Claire.

Her interference was a disappointment.

Svana's initial displeasure with his keeping of a mate had been addressed, handled, and resolved. Shepherd had paid the price for Claire—a far steeper price than he had expected—ruining the Omega's growing affection. He had even fucked Svana in the same bed he shared with Claire, watching the Alpha female grow excited by the scent of his mate, a thing Shepherd hated allowing.

Breathless, Svana had claimed their mating to be the most glorious yet, satisfied when Shepherd's orgasm was finally achieved. As always, he'd ensured his knot remained on the outside of her cunt; Svana unwilling to let them be linked in a position that left either vulnerable—a long standing sexual rule between them.

Grunting as he gushed, he had offered the answer the female sought, *"Glorious indeed, beloved."*

Shepherd pulled out, lay at her side while she petted his broad chest. In a silken voice, Svana had purred out her absolution, *"I forgive you."*

The words had seemed unfair. Had Svana not herself fornicated and tried to lure her Alpha body into highly unlikely pregnancy with their enemy? Were not her very words the idealization that their love was beyond the flesh… a thing of spirit and destiny?

Shepherd had fucked her twice more, once almost immediately, simply to keep Svana from speaking on the subject, and again to ensure he'd exhausted her. There had been no more pillow talk. In the end, there had been no demands about Claire at all. As if the hiding Omega was of no consequence, Svana had simply dressed and left. All that was left behind was Alpha female scent saturating the air of his den, blending oddly with the sweeter smell of Omega.

No, that was not all that was left. The Omega who had only a few days prior begun to respond, who for once had been eager at last to be near him, had lain crumpled on the bathroom floor—everything between them left in wreckage—all his effort dismantled and ruined.

He had not seen Svana since, and now he was forced to listen to her subtle manipulations as she sat beside the hated Beta.

*"I just assumed... Omega scent is on your coat."*

Shepherd growled so violently at the presumption that Jules ordered the other Followers from the room.

*"It's not like that. She couldn't even if she wanted to... or even if I wanted to."*

Shepherd gripped the table, the wood beginning to buckle.

Did Claire want to have sexual congress with that male?

*"My friend was pair-bonded to a stranger, someone who mistreated her. Any kind of physical relationship is off the table for now."*

And if it couldn't get worse, like magic, it did. Svana's reaction to Corday's words was authentic. Shepherd saw her face through the feed, the beauty of her exotic bone structure lost the mask of Leslie Kantor. Svana showed herself. *"Pair-bonded? That is unthinkable."*

That disgust was genuine.

Outraged, Shepherd was forced to conclude Svana had believed he'd kept a female under lock and key in his quarters that was not his rightful possession. Rape was beneath him, as Svana well knew considering his mother's sad history, and Shepherd did not break his code, ever!

Vibrating with utter indignation, Shepherd felt energy build up, crest, years of anger threatening to seep out as a low endless howl of rage. Only one thing stopped the outburst, one phrase that carried him beyond explosion and straight into stagnant shock.

*"The little I know is that the woman behaved like your run-of-the-mill sex offender."*

Blood throbbed in his skull. Was that Claire's interpretation of Svana? Of him? She had called him a rapist once, and he had taken her when she was reluctant… but she was his bonded mate. Claire grew willing once she learned he took the time to pleasure her; the Omega relished their mating once she let herself enjoy it. Even the first time, he had not touched her without her consent. The one time he'd punished her physically, he had not hurt her. When she'd cried so pathetically afterward, he could not bring himself to do it again, even though it was his right as Alpha to correct her bad behavior and establish dominance. Never had it been rape. Her hesitation was due only to misunderstanding her position as an Omega, and her fear of her unfamiliar Alpha. After their time together, she had been coming around… he had painstakingly melted that ice.

He would not dishonor Claire, nor would Svana. His beloved had never touched Claire, he'd ensured it himself!

But he'd found Svana choking the life out of his mate… the Omega pushed back on the bed, her lip split and bleeding.

A new feeling, a sort of churning sickness stole his breath. Perspective shifted. Svana *had* come into his room and attacked a pregnant Omega clearly under his protection… but she would not have sexually assaulted her. It was against everything they stood for.

*But Claire had been very frightened; it's what drew you from the Citadel to rush to your mate.*

No! Such a thing was impossible. His beloved would never degrade herself in such a way. Perhaps this was based off Svana's suggestion that Claire join them in intimacy—the very statement which had sharply commenced the decay of the bond. Shepherd had not missed a nuance of Claire's reaction to those words, had felt her repugnance, her disgust pulse through their link.

She'd looked on him like he was a monster.

Consumed with separating the opposing factors, far too determined to maintain the status quo, Shepherd had not regarded the exchange's baser intent. How had he not seen? Svana had preyed upon the Omega so flawlessly… spoken every word to shame and debase. Thinking of it now, Svana's verbiage seemed so very beneath her, so calculatingly terrible.

The more Shepherd considered, the more he hated: hated Jules for daring to do less than he was ordered. He hated the handsome Enforcer Corday who had the audacity to feel fondly for his Omega—a man who spoke as if he knew Claire intimately. Corday couldn't *know* her. A base Beta could never have the bond that exposed Claire's very soul and perfection to her Alpha mate.

Shepherd *knew* her. Every breath she took, the music of her hum, her purity, her light. That was his alone.

The hate expanded, and even for the briefest of seconds, he hated Svana for effectively taking Claire away. The fleeting feeling of something other than reverence for his beloved confused him. Mechanically, Shepherd looked to the only other person in the room, as if the man might have the answer.

All was written in the smaller man's flat expression. Not one word spoken had surprised Jules.

Placid despite the tempest inside, Shepherd rose. "Once the Enforcer is asleep, pull Svana. I desire a private meeting."

"Yes, sir."

Shepherd's eyes narrowed. "What? No unwarranted opinions?"

There was no hesitation or fear of imminent recourse. Jules spoke openly. "I only stated facts. I have not shared with you my opinion."

"By all means, Jules, SPEAK!"

The sharp edge of the man's dead stare displayed more than enough. "Choose an Alpha surrogate for Miss O'Donnell."

Rising from the chair, all the waves of provocation, the violence Shepherd had been restraining, flowed out in the simple phrase. "I would kill anyone who dared to touch her."

Jules rebutted, unflinching, "Not anyone."

# 6

The other Omegas probably thought she was insane, and maybe she was. At this point it didn't matter anymore. Claire knew her time was almost up, that the group was starting to chafe at her presence, that her behavior was a threat to them.

Claire understood exactly what was happening; that was the very reason why it was so important she hurry.

With the city's shops stripped clean of *valuables*, it wasn't hard to find the 'nonessentials' useful for her ploy. With Shepherd in power, COMscreens and networks were beyond Claire's reach but, like the book in her back pocket, paper had power.

A printed leaflet embossed with her image stared up at her; reproduced over and over again until no more paper could be found.

Nona had been brave enough to join her. To find the machines and make the copies… Through the madness, the old woman had not left her side, not once. Her friend had even helped as Claire created what would ruin her in the eyes of the world.

Senator Kantor had warned Claire of the consequences should

anyone learn who she was to Shepherd—of the potential outcome should the resistance get their hands on her. The conversation had been burned into her memory, had carried her away again and again over the silent hours she walked the city.

There was no great hero to stand for what had once been Claire O'Donnell; even her own people found her useful only as a commodity.

So be it. If that was what she was to be, she would make them all eat it. She would sell herself, choose how to manipulate the product, before she was out of steam.

Claire was not a leader of men or a great orator. She was an Omega who enjoyed painting pictures for children, who once believed she had a future full of promise. Now she knew there would never be a loving mate or smiling children. Distorted and ruined, she was just a faceless statistic in a city full of nightmares and indifference. Well, not anymore. She had nothing left and nothing to hide. So Claire created the voice she'd lost, the last piece of resistance she could manage—something horrific from her weakness that could give others strength.

Nona had captured the brutality of the image perfectly.

Though the flyer was black and white, something about those large, enthralling eyes pierced brilliantly as the girl on the flyer stared forward. It was the profound expression of pain, the tracks of tears, the defiance, all balanced with the set of her mouth and the obvious cut in her lower lip. Claire stared out at the viewer over her shoulder, displaying the violence of her scabbed claiming mark—the grotesque thing still bruised like a rotting flower. Her chin was cocked high, her black hair pulled back so the damage to her throat was exposed. She was absolutely naked, the fullness of one breast round above thin ribs, the nipple just covered by the arm clasping her hair. The world would see her as she was: captivating and beautifully tragic.

It was her handwriting, the feminine script her final statement to Thólos:

*I am Claire O'Donnell.*

*I am your mother, I am your sister, I am your daughter.*

*Look at me.*

*I am what you have done to yourselves.*

*I was pair-bonded to Shepherd against my will. I carry his child.*

*I fought back.*

*I fought back for you.*

*Each Thólosen who does nothing stands with evil. There are no excuses. Confront the abuse perpetrated on the streets, stand up to rape and violence.*

*Do not turn a blind eye again.*

*Do not make me stand alone.*

Claire fled the warehouse as soon as the dark gave her cover, racing her own shadow like a wild thing. For a body that was strangely listless, she flew through the streets, sheaves of paper clasped to her breast.

It took all the dark hours of the night, multiple trips back and forth to gather more stacks of paper Nona handed off to her. The flyers were placed on the tops of buildings to blow in the icy wind like garbage through the streets, to continuously rain down on common areas where in only a few hours citizens would congregate.

Her portrait was like a virus, almost unnoticeable as it infected Shepherd's system, her image blowing about like leaves.

When her body gave out and her vision began to blur, Claire dropped the last armful of flyers from the highest causeway she could reach. Once it was done, she crawled like a wounded animal into the nearest building. In a dark corner she collapsed, oblivious of where she was, and uncaring.

It was simple enough for a man of Jules' skill to enter the apartment of the sleeping Enforcer. Svana was collected, and from the monitor in Shepherd's hand, it was clear that Jules' appearance had been somewhat surprising to her. When he crooked his finger, she swept from the room with her customary air of superiority, head held high like the royalty she was.

Shepherd kept her waiting, entering Corday's domicile, finding it typical, small, and full of the trappings of city life. The Beta was asleep on his bed, snoring just loud enough to make the continued assurance of his slumber simple, the Enforcer completely unaware that the very terror of Thólos slipped through the darkness like a demon to stand over him.

Claire's scent was rich in the room. Even, to Shepherd's extreme antagonism, rising from the bedsheets. Watching the handsome Beta, his lips parted in sleep, the predator awakened. The beast licked his chops, ready to tear out the throat of his prey. But the giant needed the naïve young Enforcer alive long enough that the fool might lead him to Claire. Once that mission was accomplished, he would personally tear Corday limb from limb, relishing each scream. Staring down at the Beta, Shepherd could already imagine the tactile pleasure… feel the warmth of blood running through his fingers.

Moving away before he could give in to the temptation to carry out such a punishment before its due time, Shepherd forced himself to ignore the other traces of Claire lingering on the bed: the long dark hairs on the pillow and smears of her blood on the sheets.

In the bathroom, Shepherd found the dress she'd worn when Claire refused to eat, ripped and ruined, stained from wounds accumulated from a highly dangerous fall—a fall that could have easily killed her.

Shepherd did not know how long he stood in that dark cluttered space clutching that dress, wanting to rip at the fabric just as badly as he wanted to take it with him. But no sign of his visit could be left behind. Stuffing it back into the laundry container, he noticed the waste basket brimming with wrappings and white paper of used bandages, blood soaked cotton balls, all the signs that the Beta had tended her wounds.

It made him want to squeeze the man's neck until he felt his vertebrae pop apart.

The very air in the apartment was offensive.

Corday's smell had scented his female once before. It was clearly his sweaty clothing she had been wearing when the Omegas had turned her in. Worse was the odor of Svana's musk, picking apart Claire's sweetness in a gross reminder of what had been created in his den when all his weeks of dedicated exertion to draw out his Omega were spoiled by an action as rudimentary as sex.

Through his inspection, his ire only grew, and Shepherd knew he had to leave before the stink of his outrage escaped his carefully buttoned coat and high collar. Vanishing like a phantom, he moved at last to confront his beloved, finding her unaware of his entrance into the dark apartment chosen for their private meeting.

Closing the door to face down the subject of his anger, Shepherd addressed her with a blank expression. "Greetings, Svana."

Svana purred over her shoulder, her voice full of the richness of their shared history. "Must I remind you, Shepherd, that you do not summon me and leave me waiting."

Ignoring the lack of subtlety in the reprimand, Shepherd stepped closer. "How very beautiful you are this evening."

She smiled, her lips curving up like a cat lapping milk. "Am I not beautiful every evening?"

The warmth of his hand came to her shoulder. "Enforcer Corday is a fortunate acquisition. Exactly when did you infiltrate the resistance?"

"My love?" Svana's hands were already slipping up to cup his neck, to press to the small amount of warm exposed flesh so that nothing might be between them. "Are you not pleased at how easily they trust me? I can control them… mislead them."

The feel of her body under Shepherd's palms was familiar. "Nothing but ourselves could stand in the way of our success."

At once the soft, luring quality of Svana's blue eyes went sharp and narrow. "It is unlike you to make such a reference, especially towards myself."

Shepherd hissed. "Your undiscussed appearance amidst the resistance was unsanctioned."

At once, Svana moved out of the comfort of his touch. "I am not a child to be corrected, Shepherd. Remember to whom you are speaking."

Watching Svana in the dark, the shine of moonlight over the perfection of her face, did not bring him peace. Instead he found himself growing aggravated that there had still been no outright mention of Claire. Did she think he didn't know? That she would keep knowledge from him, purposefully, again… that she would presume not to admit her doings… it did not sit well in his gut. "Equivocation does not suit you. Let us speak plainly on the subject and be done with it."

The way she stood, with the city backlighting her silhouette, the silken tone of her voice, all of it was to allure. "Can it be that you are displeased with me?"

His large hands came to the lapels of his heavy coat, gripping tightly as he spoke. "The Followers overheard every word of your conversation with Corday, and nothing relevant towards our mission was even pursued. What is it you seek to accomplish in this game?

You risk exposing your identity and purpose to chase the scent of my mate."

"Mate," she spat the word, revolted. "When I had originally heard of your toy, I figured it was some passing fancy to fill the hours you could not spend with me. Finding her pregnant was staggering enough, but I can hardly believe what that fool downstairs described. You *pair-bonded* with something so beneath you!"

"You have had many lovers to satisfy your body. I chose to have only one. I could not rightfully keep Claire without bonding. Accepting her as my mate keeps her in my power and in line with the Gods' plan." Sucking in an angry breath, Shepherd took a step nearer. "Furthermore, you should take care where you would point that finger. *You* attempted to produce an heir with Premier Callas!"

It was a rare thing for Svana to display surprise, but it crept into the corners of her expression.

Shepherd did not wait for her to speak. "Did you really believe I was unaware of your attempted conception? I smelled the effect of the drugs on your body. It did not go unnoticed by my Followers, either."

"It was necessary, Shepherd," she argued at once, fisting her hands in his shirt. "His genes house a treasure that cannot be lost—immunities, resistance to disease. Why should it have been wasted? What better revenge than to have Premier Callas' child one day leading our people?"

Shepherd reached out to run his fingers through Svana's hair, watching the brown slip right through his touch. "You would have preferred to carry the offspring of the man responsible for the corruption of Thólos. He threw my mother into the Undercroft. I would never raise a child of that monster as my own. What crawled out of you would never rule."

Svana's expression twisted into one of disgust. "So you seeded a weakling out of spite? I feel both honored and disappointed that you would act out so from petty jealousy, my love."

His own great anger fell back behind an alarmingly placid expression. "Was it not your explanation that our love transcended the physical? My desire for a corporeal mate should mean nothing to you."

The woman circled Shepherd in the dark, calculating her next move. Something seemed to register and Svana's eyes grew warmly seductive; she licked her lower lip. "It is not too late should you wish to breed me. Think of the greatness of our combined power. The necessary drugs could be found and we could begin at once."

"Even as glorious as you are, the chances of an Alpha female conceiving with Alpha male sperm are very slim—carrying to term even more so." Placing his great hands on her shoulders, Shepherd outlined what was unchangeable. "Claire will bear my offspring and serve as my mate, and you will rule at my side once Thólos is in ruins and my army has delivered Greth Dome from those who usurped your family's claim to the throne."

"The Omega is unsuitable. A foul creature of this city is unworthy of such an honor!"

Shepherd hissed, agitated that she would further question him on the matter. "Claire was untouched, her body pure and receptive. I was her first. That is only one example of how Thólos has not tainted her."

Svana laughed, scoffing. "An Omega of her age… No, dearest, such a thing is not possible. You have been fooled."

"Through the bond she can hide nothing from me." Where the flawless cadence of the words came from, he did not know. Nor did he miss the tiny shift in Svana's expression when he said, "I have absolute faith in Claire's former celibacy and her current fidelity."

"*Fidelity*. I see… you question my behavior." Svana understood his deeper meaning. Composing her face into an expression of pain she asked, "Are you trying to hurt me?"

"No, beloved." Shepherd bowed his forehead to hers, working to calm the torrent of anger before it swept him away.

Her body softened against his, conformed to his strength, seeking to mollify. "If you wish to keep a pet then I expect that you will share her with me."

The concept turned his stomach, felt incredibly wrong. "I am certain, given your introduction, that she would be unwilling to mate with you if asked. It is impossible."

Svana's derisive snort preceded, "It would not take long for the Omega to learn her place… one which is below me. She may have fought my initial touch, but you are her Alpha; her opinion matters little. She is nothing but a physical vessel for your needs."

"Initial touch?" It was like the spark of a forest fire, Corday's accusation, *sex offender*, wrecking Shepherd's last vestige of calm. It cost him a part of his soul to accuse, "You tried to touch her sexually and she resisted. That is why you struck her…"

Svana seemed unperturbed, shrugging. "She refused to spread so that I could taste… I merely wanted to confirm the scent of her pregnancy—which I did."

A surge of violence almost overwhelmed his control. He shook, felt the dagger of the link twist hideously in his chest. The female Alpha had dared to touch his mate inappropriately! Svana had hurt Claire simply for being defensive and sexually obedient to only him. Shepherd blinked, fighting not to reach out and break bone. "That is unacceptable, Svana! Beyond your needless attack of a weak and pregnant woman, such behavior is so very against your nature that I question if you have lost yourself. How would you even consider what you have done as appropriate?"

Her eyes narrowed; she showed her teeth. "You keep her to fuck her. What is yours has always been mine."

"I claimed her as a mate!" It was almost a roar but so soft it seemed strange that the windows shook with unseen force.

"And then unquestioningly fucked me right in front of her, proving she is nothing but a sorry replacement. Because I am the one you adore. The scrawny Omega is only a diversion you believe to be more important than she is because you foolishly pair-bonded in a moment of weakness." A purr came from Svana's chest. "I understand now that I have neglected you. The situation will be rectified, and from now on I will see to your physical needs. There need be no animosity between us."

Shepherd blinked, jaw clenched as he looked down. His beloved had reached out to lower his zipper, her elegant fingers pulling out the flaccid length of Shepherd's cock. Svana began to stroke. It was the anger that sent his blood pumping and made him stiffen in her grasp, the fury that pulled forth the low animal growl as he latched onto sensation to escape the unbearable realization of what his beloved had done.

Rubbing her thumb in smooth circles over the tip of his cock, she cooed and leveled him with a hungry stare. Caught up in the grip, in the way Svana knew exactly how to earn a response, Shepherd tore at the fastenings of her pants, already rutting her hand in desperation to redirect so much wrongness into something right.

The apartment they were in was in shambles, the stained mattress he pressed her to as disgusting as the rotting chain in his chest. Gripping his staff in his fist, he met her eyes, lined up with the opening slit of Alpha pussy, and shoved in remorselessly hard.

The immediate sense of victory he saw in her shining eyes was appalling. Gripping her legs and turning his attention to look out the dark window over the city he'd conquered, he rammed hard and fast, just as he'd done on Claire's nest to save the Omega's life.

Just as before, Shepherd found less satisfaction in rutting a female who did not possess the smaller frame and the tighter cunt that would milk him when she came, that would draw out his essence until every last drop had been savored. There was no musical voice sighing his name as if it were the most beautiful sound in the world. Alpha females did not respond that way; they were built to mate with Omegas, to be dominant… they hardly even self-lubricated.

Shepherd felt no humming connection, no mental depth, just aggressive, angry sex… and it was eating at him. Svana was performing well, making her calls and trills, spreading wide to show the beauty of her body. It was not enough. His abject fury did not abate, it only distorted, it left him in ruins, and Shepherd began to feel the unsettling wrongness grow with every thrust.

He did the unthinkable and flipped Svana over, to mount his beloved from behind so he would no longer have to look at her. She gasped, tilted her hips at his strength, and seemed to relish the rough handling. To keep her head forward, Shepherd fisted her hair, immediately noticing the tactile wrongness of it. It was not silky black, but a coarser brown, and his growl led to no surge of wetness that bathed his cock and beautifully scented the air.

The woman he rode was not his mate.

Even with his eyes closed, even thinking of another, all he could see was Svana… altered, seemingly tainted by what she had done, by what he knew and could not forget. Once she came, tugging at her clitoris in little flicks of her fingers, Shepherd could not continue for another moment. Pulling out, he tucked away his already softening dick.

Spinning about, she gaped at him. "Dearest… everything will be as it was. Come, let me soothe you. I know what you need."

Already she was reaching for his zipper again, leaning forward from the bed to take him into her mouth.

Brushing her hand aside, he continued to right his clothing. "No, Svana." Shepherd felt an impure film on his skin, everywhere

Svana's hands had crept over him unclean. "It was wrong for me to take you now. Your assessment was correct, we have surpassed physicality, and I will not defile our bodies by attempting to mate with you again. Things have changed, we must both accept that."

Her voice cracked. "You cannot possibly prefer another to *me*." Svana stood before him, demanding he see reason. "Especially a woman who defies you, who prefers the pretty Beta downstairs."

Shepherd lowered his chin to his chest, the deep furrow between his brows sinister. "Claire is unenlightened and misunderstands my purpose. The very fact that she abhors what I've done to her people demonstrates her worth."

"I am the one who loves you," the beauty pleaded. "Do you not see that she *hates* you? Has run from you… The Omega could *never* love a marked man from the Undercroft. You disgust her."

The sharp sting of Shepherd's tattered bond concurred. "But she is still mine, carries my heir, and is under my protection." He grew, cracking bones as he postured. "You will not touch her again, Svana. Do you understand me?"

"You will come crying to me when everything you imprudently created falls apart." Svana nodded, staring forward as if she could see into the future. "And I love you so greatly that I will give you the comfort you do not deserve."

Shepherd could not tolerate another moment of such spite. After what he had heard earlier, the lie spilling from her lips, it was painfully obvious Svana had never intended to let him keep his due. She'd expected that he would cast off the Omega. Nothing he had done had satisfied her—and like the monster Claire believed him to be, he'd stood by and let Svana debase his mate… even willingly participated.

Squeezing his eyes shut, he heard Jules' words echo for what felt like the hundredth time: *You allowed Svana to manipulate you into dishonoring your pregnant mate.*

Shepherd had accepted his beloved's liaisons, even though the revelation had dumbfounded him. He had even adored Svana despite her foulness with Premier Callas. The same respect was not wielded in his direction, her expectations contradictory, immature.

Every word Svana had spoken when they'd faced off over Premier Callas had been carefully chosen to extradite herself of blame, to justify her own actions. Now he understood—she'd never expected him to seek sexual fulfillment with another.

His beloved had taken him for granted, made his devotion common.

There was something so very cutting in the revelation. After all, her actions had led to his response… his needs apparently considered less important than hers.

Svana had never truly been concerned about Shepherd's feelings on the matter, and now she stood before him and openly lied.

Faith shaken, Shepherd nodded sadly. What had once been the adolescent who'd climbed atop him at her first urge and mated, swearing to be his forever, was not the woman he found he could not look at.

Shepherd left in disgusted silence.

Back in his room, he showered in water so hot his skin burned, found the discomfort cleansing, but still felt the taint of what he'd done—found the recoil of the bond, the violent sting, a welcome penitence for mating in a way that degraded them all. No stranger to suffering, he relished it as his due, just as he had each time he had purposefully harmed Claire for her own good.

A knock came to the door. One of his lieutenants entered to hand him something far more disturbing than anything else he had faced in the last grueling twenty-four hours.

Shepherd held a wretched piece of paper in his hand, unable to look away.

Even with the consuming sadness of Claire's expression, even with the arrogant tilt of her chin and judgment in her eyes, she was beautiful. But it was the marks on her neck, the split lip… wounds created when Svana had forced Claire to spread, that held Shepherd's attention.

*Look at me. I am what you have done to yourselves.*

"Sir," the Follower began, "these are blowing all over Thólos. Reports say they were discovered scattered at six locations so far. They have already been seen by the citizens lining up for rations."

Shepherd's unresolved anger, the long hours of poisonous rage, vanished at the realization of what her actions could mean. His silver eyes darted all over the page, absorbed every curve of a body that was only for his eyes… read her words… and could not look away from the complicated pain.

He wanted nothing more in the world than to hold her, to touch that naked skin, to do anything necessary to remove that expression from her face.

*I was pair-bonded to Shepherd against my will. I carry his child.*

Her message to the world, the exposed expression of her spirit—it was the final rebellion. Death was coming for her, and she was going to feed herself to the city in an attempt to show them all the truth of what they had become. The foolish, brave little Omega.

*Do not make me stand alone.*

There would be no sanctuary for Claire after this. She would not live long enough to know the pain of Red Consumption. Thólos would slaughter her, rip her apart like dogs fighting over a bone if he did not get to her first.

Knowing the Beta Corday had been with Svana and under surveillance all evening meant the man could not have known the Omega had done this. If the Enforcer did care for her, even a little, he too would know exactly what that flyer meant. Banking that once Corday saw the image he would impulsively run straight to Claire, Shepherd grabbed his coat and organized a team to make sure the Beta stumbled on that very flyer the second he stepped out his door.

The hulk addressed his soldiers, resolute and indomitable, with a mind as still as a frozen river. "A team must keep visual contact on Svana. Should she attempt to interfere or leave the Enforcer's domicile, I authorize interception and detainment."

"Yes, sir."

Not one man questioned him.

How could one female cause such havoc? Corday was furious, looking down with a scowl at the suggestive image. At first he saw only rubbish on the ground; most of it wet from the sludge, and then he saw familiar eyes.

Naked, she looked out at him from the page, marred and damaged, but so fucking proud. Then there was her message… her goddamn message! What the hell was she thinking?

As he made his way to her, Corday passed people on the street who had their own copy, whispering the name 'Claire' amongst themselves.

Corday moved as cautiously as he could through the city until the mid-level byways spread out before him. The flyer crushed in his hand, past pissed off, he found the Processing Plant shut up, desolate and lifeless, just as the Omegas intended it to look. But a careful eye could see the sentry with one of the Omegas' acquired automatic rifles guarding from the chute hatch. The way was opened for him and he went inside, barreling through the space to find Claire and shake some sense into her.

*"Corday has made contact with the Omegas. No visual on O'Donnell."*

Shepherd and a team of twenty had already surrounded the

clever home Claire had found for her pack. There was little view within. Even so, from Shepherd's invisible perch on the building opposite, he and Jules could see the females mulling about in the dim space… but just like the Beta Enforcer scanning the room, they saw no sign of Claire's raven hair amongst the herd.

# 7

Nona had been expecting the young Enforcer, and walked forward to greet him. "When you did not return, I was worried you'd been killed. Claire assured me you were not—said she could feel you still lived."

There had been no chance to sneak off with Leslie demanding so much of his time. Three days he'd worked on translating the Followers' written language. Every hour they learned more, but at the cost of time he needed to be with Claire. Had he been here, he could have stopped Claire's lunacy. "Do you know what she did?"

Nodding, Nona gave a tired smile. "I do."

Corday held up the crumpled flyer. "How could you allow it, Nona?"

"There is no stopping that girl now." Nona gripped his arm, trying to get the boy to see what was right before him. "There is no stopping what's coming."

Corday cocked his head and had to agree. "You're right. Claire unleashed a storm of trouble with this shit."

"Corday—"

He didn't want to argue with an old woman. Corday wanted to argue with Claire. "At least tell me she is here."

"She is with the boy."

Corday narrowed his eyes, teeth clenched. "What boy?"

"Her dead boy."

"Oh…"

"She buried him in the compost pile out back." When Corday shifted away, Nona gripped his arm again, stopping the Beta so she might speak her piece. "Claire only just returned. She is tired, don't expect much."

Not interested in wasting more time, Corday held his tongue, marching right through Omegas who were less than happy he'd called again. A reinforced door swung in, sunlight invaded, and there she was, head bowed over a freshly turned pile of dirt.

THE ANGLE of the building hid her from view, forcing Shepherd to shift from his perch and move like a shadow over the roof. And then there she was, still as a statue, less than thirty feet away, staring down at a small mound of snow-dusted earth. Captivated, Shepherd let out a breath, watching the Beta approach her.

It was as if she didn't register Corday—not until the Enforcer shoved the flyer under her nose. "What is this?"

The Omega brushed the hair off her face, rubbing her skull as if it ached. "A picture of me naked."

"Do you think this is funny?" Corday snapped, working hard to keep from raising his voice. "Do you realize what you've done, Claire? Everyone will know. There will be no safety in anonymity, EVER!"

She would not need anonymity, but she did need Corday to move. "You are standing on my boy."

After a quick exhale, Corday stepped off the mound, pulling her to him. He hugged too hard, his voice breaking. "Your message… it is going to cost you any type of life. You will be hounded until the day you die."

The Omega pushed away, sniffed, and wiped her tears with the heel of her hand. "I know what I did. I know you cannot understand, that our agendas don't line up, but I cannot wait for the resistance to stop dragging its feet. There is no hero, Corday. There is no savior. Thólos has become hell, and I cannot even heap the blame for it at Shepherd's feet. What has happened here, we did to ourselves. Either the citizens see what complacency in the face of evil has cost them, or they are all going to die."

Corday pressed his hands to his face to keep his frustration in check. "Are you trying to inspire a revolution? You promised me you would not attack Shepherd's men."

Claire took his hands, pulling them down so he could look at her. She looked like death, exhausted, dark marks under her eyes. "It is not an attack on Shepherd. It's an attack on conscience. It's an attack on the people of Thólos."

Why couldn't she understand? "They will hate you…"

"I don't care." Claire took a step back, her temper flaring. "I told you there was nothing left for me. Don't you get it yet? This is all I can give, so let me give it and stop being so goddamn selfish!"

He tucked a stray piece of hair behind her ear, saying, "Survival is not selfish. Citizens who hate the bastard will simply kill you for sport. This was suicide."

Claire's voice was flat, steady as she affirmed the obvious. "I know."

"Have you lost your mind?"

She licked her chapped lips. "Look at me, Corday. I'm running out of steam, I throw up everything I eat; sleep gives me no peace… I am already dying."

"You are not dying, you are killing yourself!" the Beta shouted, clutching her shoulders as if he might shake sense into her "If you would just rest… If you would come home with me, I could take care of you."

"No."

"Aside from Nona, the Omegas hardly tolerate your presence here. It's only a matter of time before you're cast out." Why wouldn't she see that he could cherish her? "Why won't you listen to reason?"

"I CHOOSE HOW TO SPEND MY LIFE! NOT YOU, NOT SHEPHERD, NOT SENATOR KANTOR, NOT THE FUCKING PEOPLE OF THÓLOS. DO YOU HEAR ME, BETA?"

He had never once seen her with such fire in her eyes. "You're upset."

Throwing her hands up in the air, Claire agreed, "Of course I'm fucking upset! All I want to do is scream. Knowing that all I can offer Thólos is a naked picture on a flyer makes me loathe myself. How DARE YOU reprimand the fact that at least I am trying to do something while I still can? Your precious resistance does nothing!"

"Claire." He reached out to hold her, soothing what made her tremble and cry. "Please…"

"I can't be what you want me to be," she sobbed against his chest. "I can hardly be myself anymore."

"I am sorry," Corday whispered, his heart breaking to see her so sad. "Don't cry. I will purr for you, and you can rest. Okay? I should not have shouted."

His offered low vibration began, Claire weeping like a child in his arms. Her arms went around him, her broken apologies lost in the wretchedness.

Muttering nonsense, Corday stroked her hair. "We'll go inside, we'll eat and you won't get sick… I will stay so that you can sleep."

He had to carry her and she let him, clinging to his neck as if he would disappear otherwise.

From a distance, Shepherd fought every instinct that told him to rush in and take her from the man comforting what was his. He hardly registered Jules' hand gripping his forearm, the silent reminder to be still and measure the consequences. Because it was clear now his second-in-command was correct. Even if he dragged her back, she would not survive in this state.

Claire had lost the will to live.

THROUGHOUT THE DAY, Shepherd observed her actions inside the reeking plant. Corday was correct in his assessment. The Omegas avoided her and Claire seemed utterly unconcerned as she kept to her corner, purposefully distancing herself. All but the old woman had turned on the very catalyst of their freedom.

Envisioning a long row of women swinging, their hanged corpses on display to any who would deny his mate, Shepherd measured each wary look they turned towards Claire, even hating the women who gently ignored the suffering, dark-haired girl.

They were all unworthy of her, every single one, just like this city of lies and evil.

The Beta did tend to her, made her eat and held back her hair twenty minutes later when it all came up. He fed her again, pressured the small thing to drink water, all the while holding her in his lap, chest to chest, her legs wrapped around his torso, as if she were a child or his lover. The second serving seemed to stay down and in minutes Claire was dead to the world, snoring on his shoulder.

It was impossible to hear the exchange between Nona French and the Enforcer, especially with the man's lips pressed against

Claire's hair. Eventually the Beta lay down, and the old woman pulled the man's long coat over the pair.

The dark arrived, Claire cried out in her sleep. When Corday's horrified eyes looked up to find Nona's sympathetic expression, Shepherd focused on the movement of the Enforcer's mouth and watched his lips form the words.

*"She just called for Shepherd."*

The absolutely crestfallen expression on the hated Enforcer's face brought a curl to Shepherd's own lips. The Beta might be the one holding her, but even damaged as the bond was, his Omega's mind was full of thoughts of her rightful mate. A sign from the Gods, a reminder to them all, that Claire was his.

CLAIRE WOKE LESS HAGGARD. "I am feeling better. Thank you."

In a voice so low that no member of the spying Followers could hear, Corday pressed his lips to her ear and whispered, "Claire, it's going to be over soon, we have access to their communications now. So hold on. Hold on until I can kill him. I swear to you I will."

Doing her best to pretend she wasn't ill, Claire nodded and kissed his cheek. "I have a great deal of faith in you, Corday. You are a wonder."

"And you will be free."

"I will," she acknowledged, eyes soft.

Slender fingers carefully pulled off her mother's wedding band. Under their makeshift blanket, she took Corday's hand and slipped the band on his pinky.

"What are you doing?"

"I want you to keep this for me." Claire smiled as she gave her token. "A reminder, so that you don't forget I'm rooting for you."

She was making him uneasy. "I can't keep this."

"I am only lending it," she corrected, squeezing his hand. "You are to give it back to me when Thólos is free."

He hugged her, felt his heart soar. "Claire. I have faith in you, too."

"You are my hero, you know."

Corday wanted to kiss her, was so very tempted to thread his fingers in her hair and pull her lips to his. But that was not what they were; that was not what she could be…

At least not yet.

"Now," Claire broke the moment, shy. "You need to get out of here before the sun comes up. If I don't feel you're safe, I'll worry."

Already untangling herself, she eased out of his embrace. Corday was not allowed to linger, Claire urging him to leave before light might make his journey dangerous. It was obvious he did not want to go, but she seemed so much better, her eyes more alive and a smile on her lips when she spoke.

The Beta retreated. The second he was gone far enough down the causeway not to hear her, Claire doubled over, and quietly lost her stomach all over the frost by the chute.

Corday did not hear her vomiting, nor did he see even a hint of the Followers that had surrounded him so flawlessly when he stepped out of her sight. He popped his collar to warm his neck, and shuffled off with his hands buried deep in his pockets—smiling.

Shepherd left Corday in the hands of Jules' team, his attention on his ill Omega and the change that came over Claire the instant the boy was gone. The false smile fell, and she moved far from the group and their fires to sit in solitude, as if invisibly drawn nearer to the place where Shepherd hid in the dark.

He could almost reach out and touch her.

Once comfortable, the female pulled a worn book out of her pocket and lay back to read. Shepherd cocked a brow. His little mate was reading a book he knew by heart, *The Art of War*. It was oddly endearing, the man imagining future conversations about the text.

What was her favorite passage?

Claire read while most of the women still slept; she read the same book she had read every day since she had found it, and let her eyes linger on memorized quotes. Sometimes she fancied that it was like reading a segment of Shepherd's soul. She could see his mentality in the book, his tactics, and sought vainly to understand—fixated to the point where she did not notice that Nona stirred.

The old woman prepared instant coffee, readying a serving for Claire.

"What wisdom do you have for me today?" Nona asked, pressing a steaming cup of swill into the young woman's hands.

Claire tossed the book on the ground as she always did when done with it, treating it badly. "According to Sun Tzu, great results can be achieved with small forces… But I choose to interpret that as: pissing off a bunch of women is a really bad idea."

The old Omega chuckled softly, eyes dancing as she watched Claire sip the coffee and grimace.

Nona stroked back Claire's dark hair and teased, "You always did love your cappuccinos, but I'm afraid that's the best I can do."

Looking down at the shitty watered down beverage, Claire tried to banter. "I have many reasons to hate Shepherd, but reason number one is that I have not had a decent cup of joe since I was run out of my home… the jerk."

Her friend offered a soft chuckle.

Claire took another sip of the steaming brown water. With Nona at her side, she sat in miserable stillness, her bloodshot eyes growing resolute. She did not know what was causing it, but her ennui was beginning to fade. What was replacing it was acutely painful.

She had altered… crushing indifference warring with an unbearable sense of loss.

She should have felt victorious—she didn't. She should have felt pride; she'd forgotten even knowing such a sensation.

Nona was speaking some nonsense about the coming sunrise, Claire robotically drinking the tasteless beverage. When the brew was finished, the cup was set aside.

It was time.

Claire stood up and just walked away, leaving her friend without a goodbye.

She would see the sky for herself, observe the sunrise alone. But it would not move her. The sky had lost its magic.

The old woman watched her go, watched as dark hair disappeared… and knew Claire had made her choice.

Outside it was cold, colder every day. Claire wrapped her arms around her body and stumbled away from the Omega's haven. There had been no direction in her death march, but somehow she found herself standing at the edge of the Thólos water reserve. The top had crusted with ice, covered in white as blank and colorless as she had become inside. But if she squinted, she could see through it to a world of water, where everything was washed clean.

Tucking a loose piece of hair behind her ear, she shivered and waited for the cloud heavy sky outside the Dome to glow. Just as it turned an off-shade of pink, Claire felt that if she allowed any pleasure from such a moment, pain would seep through instead. The only way to continue was to feel nothing forever. So she took a step forward, then another one, and alone out in the earliest gloomy light of the morning, Claire walked the ice.

There was no question of hesitation; her work was done. She had completed her mission, given everything she could. She had earned her release from prison. Air crisp on her face, the unmistakable smell of cold, it began to soothe where salty tears burned her cheeks.

Those first steps and the ice already began to whisper complaint. The next ten paces were met with misleading silence. Claire chose to fill the quiet with the customary Omega prayer whispered into the wind:

"Beloved Goddess of Omegas, great Mother who nurtures and protects, I thank you for the life you granted me."

It was not until she was standing near the center of the reservoir before the sound she anticipated arrived—the crushing threat of cracks and imminent death.

"I am your image. I am your delight. For you hold me in your care. Watch over the world—"

"*Do not move, little one*."

The first thought at hearing the sound of that commanding voice was that she should have known he would be there. The devil would have to witness her final moments. There could have been no other way.

Her focus left the horizon and moved down towards her feet, to the fractured pattern that bloomed under her stolen boots. Claire sucked in a slow breath, felt it stretch her chest, and glanced over her shoulder. "The city is a horror show and I don't have anything left. You win, Shepherd."

"You willfully misunderstand." The urgent coarseness of his voice was insistent… nervous. "Svana would have killed you had I not—"

Claire felt her mouth form a small smile at the man behind her. "At least I know what made you the way you are. It wasn't only your life in the Undercroft. It was her."

Shepherd held out his hand, his eyes wide and unblinking. "It was the only way I could appease her and keep you."

A look of pity—and it was pity she felt—saddened Claire's face.

"You tell that lie almost as if you actually believe it. The choice you made was not the only way; it was the way *you* chose. You chose to do that horrible thing… to do many horrible things… for her."

Shepherd's lips wavered, he looked confused. When he spoke next, it seemed as if the words were foreign to him, "If I was to offer an apology, would it make any difference?"

"No."

"Then I will offer this instead." He stretched his hand out farther. "If you return to me, I will give you what you want. I will leave the Omegas in peace and see that they are left alone. You have my word."

Claire hummed, her attention returning to the cracking ice under her feet.

He tried again, determined. "Svana will not be allowed near you; nor will I ever touch her in that manner again."

Claire ignored him.

Exasperated, he gritted out, "I will even allow you to see your sky."

She mouthed the words, spoke them as if the very idea meant nothing anymore, "My sky…"

"I will care for you."

Water fell from her eyes, ran down her cheeks. Her voice was so sad. "It almost sounds like you mean it… how funny."

It took a great deal of effort for Shepherd to manage the last inducement. "I will spare the Beta, Enforcer Corday, whose death will otherwise be very slow and painful."

That was the tipping point. The hazy quality of her green eyes sharpened and her soft lips pressed into a firm line. She listened closely.

"I am offering you the lives of forty-two people, little one." Shepherd employed a voice of reason, his purr rumbling to show sincerity.

Claire looked at his upturned palm, at the largeness of it, the lines and the calluses. She thought of Corday, of his vow to free the city… of everything that had been whispered between them in the dark. She thought of the child she felt utter indifference for, and put a hand to her stomach.

"That is right, little one, think of our baby."

She would never allow Shepherd's evil or that horrible woman to have the child, but she could buy Corday time. If he failed, she would kill herself and the life growing inside her before it might be born; she could do that, and she would. The smooth turn of her step, the little movement necessary to face the giant made the ice crack further, yet still she stood above what should have been her watery grave.

Shepherd knew she would say yes, that she would subject herself to him to save every life he'd mentioned. Claire could already feel it through a link that should not have been there; a burning barb knocking about where her lungs fought to expand. Her breath hitched painfully, and she fisted the leather of her jacket over her heart. "There is one more life I want."

"Who?"

Despite the invasion of the clawing worm, Claire sneered at the Alpha. "I will only tell you if you give me your unequivocal word that this person will *never* come to harm."

"And if I do this, you will return to me and live fully as my mate?" It was what he wanted, she could see it, feel her just a little bit more through the link, and he did not stop the malicious greedy evil that fostered his grin.

She felt his pleasure, glanced into rapacious eyes, and saw every ounce of his desperate elation. "Yes."

Shepherd nodded and crooked his fingers. "You have my word."

"Maryanne Cauley."

There was a flash of insight, a minute narrowing of the eyes.

The Alpha nodded in understanding—the slippery traitor… Maryanne Cauley, a prisoner who'd once sworn her allegiance to him in exchange for safe haven in the Undercroft, was the one who had helped Claire free her Omegas.

Claire took a step towards total abasement, cursing the Gods when the march to Shepherd did not shatter the ice and suck her down. The weight of her cold fingers she set in his, not returning the smile when the devil's hand engulfed hers. Shepherd touched her face, and she instinctively jerked away when the heat of his palm cupped her cheek.

His large thumb brushed away the line of tears. He knew she was in pain by the burden of the intensifying bond clawing its way past her resistance.

Intense, overexcited, he reached for her, unwilling to wait another moment to cart her home. Claire continued to fight the claim, clutching at her heart, battling to maintain the sense of endless nothing that had carried her to the ice. She did not want to be Claire anymore, oblivion had become her armor. If there was no Claire, there was no pain. Nothingness was her pride… then she remembered she had no pride. She had lost it all the day she started to care for the man cradling her in his arms.

As if he knew her thoughts, he gripped her a bit tighter to his chest and gloated. "Forty-three lives, Claire."

Her eyes screwed shut at his use of her name, the unwelcome anguish at the memory of the only other time he had spoken it ruining her. She lost the war—Claire felt something: the hurt and grief she had been unable to feel that day, and everything shattered.

~

HER PICK-UP HAD BEEN ORGANIZED with military precision. Shepherd held his reclaimed prize, purring loudly in arrogant triumph as he carried her through the subterranean halls towards his den.

It seemed a waste of noise. The purr was not soothing Claire. She was past comfort as the worm inside her swelled, each breath hurt, corrupted and hated.

The sound of the deadbolt, the finality of the moment, all this went past her as she fought so very hard not to show what she was feeling—not to give him the pleasure of acknowledging he had the power to hurt her again. But he wouldn't stop touching. He even pried her fingers from where she clutched at her chest so he might rub the heat of his palm where she was so very clearly pained.

Shepherd encouraged the meltdown because he knew what was tearing at her insides. "We will start afresh," he crooned, his huge hands pulling at the layers she was dressed in, stripping her clothing just as he stripped away her freedom. "My little mate."

Green eyes flew open, full of outrage, full of all the seething vehemence she should have screamed at him two weeks prior. "Mate? MATE? You are less than nothing to me! A deceiving monster I abhor. You are depraved; you disgust me! What you did was unforgivable. I HATE YOU!"

Even as she screamed, even as she beat against him, he stroked, he hushed.

Claire ranted, the stream of vileness bouncing off grey walls, until screams turned to great soul-wrenching sobs. She cried so very hard she could hardly draw breath. She begged him to kill her, cursed him to hell for tempting her from the ice, and only found the softness of the mattress under her back his answer to her pleas. Those great hands were everywhere, tracing the scrapes, the stitches in her knee, exploring every bruise, until Shepherd commenced his inspection with a long possessive stroke of his fingertips along the outline of his still healing claiming marks.

There seemed to be no end to the agony of the cancerous tether inside her. It twisted like an outraged alligator, tearing out her organs. She had her eyes shut tight, trying to will it all away, until naked lips came to her chest, to the very spot that had been so corrupted. Claire began to fight back, shrieking like a banshee. There was no stopping his penetration, or the throaty groan that escaped him at feeling her tight heat gripping his cock. Shepherd suckled her breasts, ran his teeth lightly over her neck, tried to kiss her mouth between licking away the tears and restraining her flailing.

The sounds from the beast, the soft noise that issued forth over the rending of her brokenhearted wails were those of a thirsty man who had finally been given water. Every stroke of her tight velvet channel as he thrust his cock lifted him closer to that unattainable heaven: to freedom. She was his again, trapped and tied, and he would take her any way he could—even if she hated him, even if she was only a slave to the bond. Because he needed her.

He growled so low and deep it made her flutter and ooze, made her shriek in horrified hatred, and he moaned into her mouth at the slick and scent. Taking what he needed, he rode her gently, spread her legs wide to see the thickness jutting from his groin enter her over and over. Rolling his hips and toying with her nub, he stole what he demanded and the wave blasted through her resistance until Claire reached a shattering, uncomfortable climax that made her arch and choke.

He drove her back powerfully against the bed, knotted as deep as he could, and shared her completion, filling her with heat, with his very essence, breathing hard at her ear as he groaned the words, "I love you, little one."

It did not lessen her pain. It only cut her deeper.

Claire keened as Shepherd held her through it all, still gushing, still knotted, swearing he would never let her go.

# 8

Shepherd had hurt her in his fervor, in his need to see her mated while the bond reformed… to ensure that she could not escape it. There was a little blood between her legs, as she had been dry and aggressively resistant when he first thrust. Even her mouth was swollen from his unwelcome kisses. New bruises were forming around her wrists and between her thighs.

Shepherd relished each one of the stinging scratches marring his own flesh, his reminder that she was his again—each wound a trophy, and testament to what was between them.

His little one had put up a good fight, but Claire had quieted over the hours, though not calmed completely. The thread in her chest was frazzled. It pained her, so Shepherd held her tight and kept the heat of his palm where her nails tried to scratch through her skin. The tears had ended and instead, she was in a trance, fighting sleep, yet clearly exhausted.

The purr never ceased, and though she gave him her back, Shepherd stroked and soothed, allowing her little defiance. She needed nutrition and hydration, yet he withheld his immense dissatisfaction at the state of her body to allow her some respite after her struggle —to let her think she might rest on her terms for a moment.

Unwilling to leave her, he sent out an order for medical supplies, and covered Claire from sight. Holding her in a grip of iron, he allowed Jules to set what was required on the small table beside the bed. When the door was locked, he found her still refusing to look at him. It didn't matter.

Shepherd had seen her reaction to food, was certain that she would hold nothing down as upset as she was, and took her arm. When the needle pierced a vein, she remained unresisting. Intravenous fluids were administered. While the IV emptied, he bathed her with soft towels, each wound treated and bandaged, the stitches grunted at, and her feet, a thing that made the beast openly angry, were wrapped in soft strips of cloth.

When the process was finished he gathered her again in his arms.

"I will build you a new world, little one—a kingdom worthy of you and our son." He whispered his distorted ideals, raking his fingers through her tangles. On and on Shepherd elocuted, articulating all he would accomplish, how he would be a legend, how he would do this for her.

In Claire's hazy understanding, Shepherd had never spoken so much and said so little.

On her belly, with her back to him, she found herself listening to the pipedreams of a madman until she could not stand it another instant. Rolling over, interrupting his game with her hair, she argued with that same passionate defiance, that same misplaced goodness that had yet to vanish no matter what had happened to the rest of her. "Do not use me as an excuse for the horrible things you do. I will have no part of it!"

He grinned, smiling darkly at her hoarse complaints. Hand molded to the shape of her belly, Shepherd patted where their child grew. “The very fact that I have you back proves the Gods side with me.”

Claire had cried herself dry, her chest was rotten mush. “You have me because I would rather save the lives of forty-three people than kill myself.”

“Shhh.” His hush was brushed over her chest. He kissed where their bond thrived. “Everything is mending and your sadness will fade in time.”

It was not mending, it was scarring.

There was a gleam in his eyes, confidence. “We *will* begin again.”

Lip curling, Claire laid out his sins. “You forced a pair-bond, drugged and impregnated me, fucked your crazy Alpha *beloved* in my nest…” She did not finish. Instead her pain surged again and Claire found her eyes could indeed leak more tears. “I recognize, Shepherd, that I am only here to be your toy. I’m a slave, a kept thing. I sold myself for them.”

It was predictable, the storm of fury in his eyes. What was surprising was the small dash of regret. Where he had been rubbing her chest, his hand moved to a breast and began to roll and pinch the nipple until the soft pink darkened and the bud elongated under his fingers.

Of course he would fuck her again no matter how unappealing Claire found the idea. That was always his recourse for her mouth. That was his answer every time she was resistant or unhappy.

Lying still, too tired after hours of struggling to put up a fuss, she remained limp… ready to get it over with.

The other nipple received the same treatment; all the while Shepherd watched her with that calculating gaze. A thumb traced over her lips and dipped just a bit between them to play against the flat of her tongue. The growl was made, the aroma of her slick scented the air, and his free hand began to play with her pussy.

Shepherd pressed his chest to hers, growled low and deep once more, watching so very carefully.

She closed her eyes and chose to ignore him.

With his fingers coated in her slippery fluid, he began to speak. "In the Undercroft, I had my mother for so short a time, I hardly can remember her face. She died from the harsh use of many men." A slippery finger slid to her puckered anus and Claire started. Shepherd slowly added pressure against her rectum, her breath catching at the uncomfortable cramp of that place being stretched. Wide eyes showed her distress. Claire reached down to grip the wrist of the offending limb, her complaint lost around the thumb still teasing her tongue.

When she had stilled, realizing he was not moving, not penetrating further, Claire watched him with absolute attention.

"As women never lasted long, prisoners took their pleasure from men in this way." The probing finger slipped past Claire's clenched ring. "Or by using the mouth of another. The beasts in that hole would howl in the dark as they gratified their bodies on the small and weak. The sounds of screams, of tortured begging—even the moans of those who took pleasure in such things—that's the lullaby that lulled me to sleep every single night."

The sensation he was creating was unpleasant, the tip of his finger wriggling. Claire tried to squirm but his weight was on her, and Shepherd growled again until more slick dripped down to coat what penetrated her rectum.

She whimpered.

"I was smaller than you are now the first time I was cornered. My back was to the wall, a man with sores on his face pulled out his member and reached for my throat. What he didn't know, what nobody knew, was that my mother had whored herself for a knife. I shanked my attacker. During the struggle, I earned the scar across my lips that you in your estrous called beautiful."

Had she?

There was a purr, a short offer of soothing as he pressed his digit further up her ass, knowing the stretch was unwelcome, but using it to make sure she listened to every damn word he said.

"I left his corpse strung outside my cell, his cock hanging from his mouth as warning to others. He was only the first, and I was surrounded by dark-hearted monsters. As I grew bigger, grew stronger, the small and feeble would come to me, offering their mouths or their bodies for protection from those same men who hounded them. I found them repugnant, weak, and beneath me. I killed several just to make my feelings on the topic clear."

The thumb in Claire's mouth stroked her tongue in little circles as he spoke. "One day, something from the light found me in the dark, a young woman with a knife of her own. It was already bloody."

Svana.

"She'd heard of me, had crawled into hell to seek me out. She gave me the means to rule and asked for nothing. Her visits were often, her affection splendid. Like me, her mother had been killed before her. Like me, her future had been stripped away.

"Her mind, the things she knew, were beyond anything I had been taught. She offered to share such wisdom, brought me books, found worth in the monster whom inmates feared. The angel even brought me the file with my mother's name on top." Shepherd nuzzled her cheek. "In that missing person's dossier was a photograph. My Beta mother, before the Undercroft rotted her teeth, had been very beautiful, like you. I hated hearing her screams."

Claire put her hand to his flank, she felt his pain break against her.

The Alpha continued. "I could not save her, and to this day could not tell you which one of the demons underground was my father."

Claire did not want to let his history touch her, but it was so pathetic she could not help but feel pity.

"I was not the only man trapped in that dark by corruption above. Like my mother, more than half of the men forced below were innocent enough, but inconvenient to the powers that be. I learned secrets from them, things you cannot imagine… if you only knew the infection creeping through the hearts of this city, little one, if you could read the stories scraped into the rocks below us."

Why was he telling her this? She began to struggle, and flinched when his finger inside her surged deeper, stretching her until she stilled.

"Open your eyes, little one." The growl was menacing, guttural. "You will look at me when I say this."

She did not want to look at him, felt invaded by that single, oversized finger, and the way he still teased at her tongue with his thumb. Jerking from the penetration, she met his gaze.

"These men, this rotten society—in your goodness, you fail to see the flaws. I could tell you things that would keep you awake at night. Everyone, man and woman, hanged outside the Citadel participated in, or knowingly ignored, atrocities. Like the imprisonment of my mother.

"And yes, years ago Svana became my lover, and I thought she was also, equivalently, my mate. I learned I was wrong. She is a driven woman, powerful, but you are the mate the Gods designed for me. Had you been dropped into the Undercroft, had I smelled you once, I would have killed every man who tried to touch you. I would have claimed you and dragged you to my cell, bent you over my cot, and fucked you where every convict might see through the bars… so that they all knew you belonged *to me*. Do you understand?"

There was no answer for such a barbaric statement.

Shepherd sniffed her, growled. With his finger still submerged in her ass, he worked his cock deep inside where she was wet and ready. She gave a little scream, muffled by his thumb as he began to rut. There was nothing tender, it was pure aggression, but it satisfied in a strange way. The overfull feeling, the way he left no place untouched as that uninvited digit squirmed around. She climaxed so quickly it was startling, felt his knot press against her quivering passage as he removed his finger from her rectum.

Claire screamed when her orgasm twisted into a tuneless vibration that wracked her bones.

When he shot his load against her womb, each spurt was matched with a roar. Head buried at her shoulder, lips at her neck, Shepherd pressed his chest to hers, to the place where they were tied. The cord sang, burned, ached, pleased, and consumed.

His thumb left her mouth, Shepherd pleased when he ground his knot inside her and his little one came again.

Crushed under him, his Omega moaned, lowered her lashes, and found sleep in the clinging arms of what may, had circumstances been different, been a good man.

"WHAT DO you mean she's not here?" Corday demanded.

"I mean, Enforcer Corday"—Nona offered a tired sigh—"that she isn't here. Claire slipped away days ago and has not returned."

Behind narrowed eyes, Corday's mind raced a mile a minute. The worry was making his stomach churn, and by the look in Nona's eyes, it was clear she was just as upset, only concealing it better.

As if trying to offer the young man an explanation, Nona said, "I think she simply decided to go home."

"To Shepherd?" he snapped, anger written all over his face. "Claire would never do that."

"She had been low on spirits, Enforcer. What I am trying to tell you is that she most likely went *home*."

"You are wrong," Corday spat the words. He had spoken to Claire only three days prior. The Omega had given him her ring… she'd made a vow. "Did those women run her off?"

"No, but they would have in a matter of days. She knew that."

The agitated Beta looked at the old woman as if she was stupid. "So she went somewhere else for shelter."

"Perhaps," Nona admitted, debating if it would be best for the young man to have something to hold on to.

"When did she leave, precisely?"

"The morning of your last visit."

Corday threw up his hands, growling at the ceiling. "Goddamn it, Claire!"

Nona took his shoulder again, squeezed his coat, and pulled him away from the gathering Omega crowd. "Sit!" The Beta male obeyed out of decorum, Nona glaring. "Claire did not want me to tell you who I really am. But I am going to anyway, because you are a Beta and I know you care for her, but you do not understand."

Nona made him be still, composing herself beside him. "When I was sixteen, I was abducted from my home, kept under lock and key for days until I was sold like cattle—bought by a man named David Aller, and forced into a pair-bond at my next estrous by a stranger twice my age.

"Once bonded, he revealed me to the public again, and my family accepted what could not be changed, even though I begged them to help me. I had no advocate; I was just a bonded Omega with no rights. When I ran the first time, I made it less than two weeks before I began to lose touch with reality. I was found wandering, confused, through the streets. The Enforcer that picked me up took me back to David as if I were a stray pet.

He beat me, a common practice for correcting renegade

Omegas. The beatings grew worse, and I ran again a few months later. It was always the same, that unwavering pair-bond to a man I hated persisted and controlled me. I tried everything, every hinted course, but it was the same nightmare. It was ten years before I poisoned him and acquired a new identity. I still dream of him, sometimes I think I hear him… and David has been dead almost forty years."

Jaw loose, Corday looked at the gentle, old woman and knew she spoke the truth.

"There is no way out of a pair-bond, no recourse for Claire. One of them has to die for her to be even marginally free. Killing Shepherd might have saved her, but her time was running out and she knew it. She just did not want to worry you… because she knew you had affection for her."

"Claire is stronger than you."

Nona agreed. "That is absolutely true."

"She told me herself that the bond was damaged. Why do none of you listen when she speaks? Why do you all assume?"

"Corday." Nona took the boy's hand and spun the ring on his finger. "Claire is gone. She gave you her ring so you would not forget her, because she had affection for you, too."

The man argued vehemently. "She swore to me that she would survive. I choose to believe she had a plan. We have all seen just what she is capable of. I have faith in Claire."

"I love Claire as if she were my daughter. I knew what she was suffering, what she had sacrificed for us, and I hope you are right. But if you are, the only way that would have happened is if she purposefully went back to Shepherd."

Gritting his teeth and glaring at her, Corday growled, "She would not have gone back to Shepherd."

"I agree."

Beyond frustration, Corday turned and left, furious with the old woman.

THE WARMTH of a large hand softly stroked back loose hair from her face, waking Claire from a dead sleep. The purr was light, enticing her to stir, and from the way the mattress dipped, she could tell Shepherd was sitting on the edge of the bed.

It was the smell that made her comply, the aroma of roasted coffee beans and something sweet. Blinking salt crusted lashes, she looked straight at the bedside table. Sitting in a white cup atop a saucer was a steaming cappuccino made by someone who possessed the skill to create the little pictures in the foam.

It did not take a genius to figure out he had been watching her in the processing plant. Shepherd had heard her conversation with Nona, and he had done this in response.

"Please don't tell me you kidnapped a barista," Claire groaned, sleepy, stretching forward to sniff.

"The chef I kidnapped months ago to prepare your meals needed company."

Claire could not tell if Shepherd was trying to make a joke. Scowling, she glanced up at the man still petting her elongated back and pursed her lips. From the look in his eyes it was clear the brute was absolutely serious.

He picked up the saucer to hand to her, using his other hand to lift and turn her to sit back against the pillows. Situated with the drink in her hand, she sipped and sighed, unsurprised when Shepherd moved the curtain of her hair over her shoulder to reveal her breasts for his gaze.

"Are you enjoying your coffee?"

Shepherd had never woken her unless it was for sex, and certainly not with coffee in bed. Claire did not trust him for a moment. "I am not going to thank you." But she did take another sip and melted… hating to admit that the drink was really fucking good.

Though his expression did not change, Claire was certain he was satisfied with her reaction to his offering.

Elbow on his knee, Shepherd watched her savor her drink. "Maryanne Cauley is in the Citadel as we speak."

Cup rattled against saucer, and the moment of coffee-induced comfort was gone. "You promised me you would not hurt her."

"And I have not." Shepherd's eyebrow arched. "But I will if she is here in some attempt to steal you from me."

"Considering how you collected me, I doubt anyone even knows I am here." Claire turned belligerent. "I came with you willingly to respect my end of the bargain, and I will not attempt to leave so long as you respect yours."

The purr came and so did a pet down her hair. "That is all I wanted to hear."

Claire looked to one side, debating. "Could I speak with her?"

Of course Shepherd was going to deny the request, he knew she knew that. With a deep sigh he took her empty cup and saucer away. "I do not wish to argue with you."

"Then you may as well go back to torturing Thólos, and I will sit here like a good captive and stare at the walls."

He shifted, leaned closer while Claire pressed herself further into the pillows. His lips brushed hers as he asked, "What is your connection to Miss Cauley?"

So close, Claire felt… torn. "Maryanne was my best friend when we were children."

He stroked her arm as if rewarding good behavior. "I find that difficult to believe. The woman is a thief and a prostitute."

"Like you," Claire said, frowning, "she too was once innocent…

Though, unlike you, I think she is trying to be good now. She is just not very confident in the pursuit."

"You are the one to hold all the goodness, and I will hold all the power," Shepherd purred, leaving a lingering, and ignored, kiss on her slack lips.

"As you say," Claire responded, her voice flat once he disengaged.

"Are you sore"—his fingers dipped under the covers to brush over her mound—"here?"

Any second he would make the growl and she would be spread under his rutting body. "Does it matter?"

The hand left her. Shepherd brushed the pout on her lips. "You will rest today. Food will be sent. If I find out you have not eaten, one of your forty-three will pay for it."

"You do not need to threaten them." Claire did not want to play such games. "I gave you my word."

"That pleases me, little one." Shepherd was so damn confident as he shifted from the bed.

He gave her a long look while she slipped back under the covers for more rest, then left silently, turning off the light.

The next time she woke, food was waiting on the table. She showered and dressed in one of the feminine dresses Shepherd seemed to think she should wear, and looked at eggs benedict. He had a chef somewhere in the compound just to make her food. She wanted to roll her eyes at the strangeness of the long ignored gesture, but had noticed it almost from the start. Canned veggies and mass-produced meat products had transformed into satisfying cuisine only a week or so after she had first arrived. The confirmation should not have mattered, but it bothered her that he had mentioned it, and now it had to be addressed.

What bothered her more was that the chef was probably safer down there than above ground. Claire even suspected he or she had been taken from the Premier's mansion. Shepherd was a thorough man. He would only take someone renowned… a celebrity. And he had done it to please her.

Claire ate every bite of that food, though it was too rich and her stomach was bound to rebel. The vitamin followed, and all the milk was drunk. Of course she threw it all up about thirty minutes later, but that could not be helped.

Customary pacing came next, her only form of exercise. Matters needed to be sorted now that her thinking had grown sharper. Shepherd knew of the Omegas, of Corday, and of Maryanne—the Alpha female having been the only one on her list that he was not previously aware of. The real question was how had Shepherd found her, which part of the branch had been first observed? Considering when he had come, it seemed that the answer was Corday. Which meant Shepherd would undermine every move of the resistance.

*The supreme art of war is to subdue the enemy without fighting. - Sun Tzu*

Shepherd had infiltrated the Enforcers… but it would have had to have been very recently. Otherwise she would have been collected that very first night.

Claire's bare feet stopped their limping shuffle, and she stood there, worrying her lip. The grate of the deadbolt drew her attention. The door swung in and Jules, bearing a tray, entered.

The blue-eyed Beta did not seem interested in acknowledging her presence, so she spoke instead. "Hello, Jules."

The trays were swapped and he grunted, "You did well outside the Undercroft."

Surprised he was engaging, even if he was not looking at her, she grumbled, "Not well enough if I'm back here."

The male did not respond, simply walked towards the door.

From her lips came a name synonymous with Satan in her mind. "Svana. That woman will ruin you all… You know that."

The man halted and turned his head enough so that she might see his profile. “It would be wise for you to choose your topics of conversation with greater restraint.”

Claire scoffed and looked at the suddenly still Beta. “You follow a madwoman.”

“I follow Shepherd.”

Claire actually smiled, a little wicked, and laughed at the man. “And he loves her. Your point is invalid.”

“The future is what matters, and your ignorant opinion matters little.”

“A fact of which I am well aware.”

At the door, he spoke over his shoulder. “Do not measure your worth by one minor success, Miss O’Donnell.”

“I agree. I measure it by my countless failures instead.”

“You fight for what you believe in, yet when you grew fragile, your answer was to seek out a meaningless death. Mine is to spend what years I have left working for a greater purpose. I will see the world altered, improved. You and I are not that different. I simply chose to be stronger and was willing to pay the price to enact change.”

She had no idea where the words were coming from or why they seemed so important. “Your logic is corrupted. I chose to die before I became like you. That makes me stronger than you are.”

The man faced her one last time, those striking eyes unsettling. “It does not make you stronger. It makes you a coward.”

Claire felt as if he had struck her, the storm in her words unleashing nothing more than a pointless whispering breeze… because there was an undeniable fragment of truth in his words.

There was nothing else to be said between them, the man dismissing her as if she were nothing. The door closed with a thud. She must have stood there for ages, staring at the metal, half numb. Eventually, she moved towards the food, chewed and swallowed with no idea of what she ate, nor did she notice that she did not get sick.

Thinking of that stupid book, *The Art of War*, of Sun Tzu and all he seemed to have accomplished, Claire remembered: *Thus the expert in battle moves the enemy, and is not moved by him.*

Jules had just done that to her.

So, how does one move a mountain? Her words were nothing to Shepherd, arguments ended in sex, but her actions had affected him more than once. On occasion she must have caused distraction in his pursuit. The monster even said he loved her, in his own twisted fashion. That gave her influence of a sort, now she just needed to learn how to wield it.

Her green eyes went to the watercolor of poppies still resting against the wall—a mindless project that had once made her cell a little more bearable. The unwelcome cord in her chest pulsed. She needed a reaction, something small, a place to begin.

Absently, she prepared her paints, her mind full of one image, one hard truth. There was no need for much color, the world was nothing but shades of grey under a bruised sky.

# 9

While still deep in her work, the door's hinges whined. Claire ignored the giant's entrance and approach, even his large hand once it rested on the table alongside her painting.

The beast leaned down with a low, displeased growl. "Throw it away."

Claire was focused on finishing the last details, the little flicks of her brush exaggerating the cracks in the Dome. "Why would I throw it away?"

She had painted her final morning of freedom; the moment denied her out on the ice.

It was stark and horrific in its implication.

His lips were at her ear, his breath fluttering her hair. "Have you done this to upset me, little one?"

The brush tip was dipped again until drenched in black paint. "No."

She felt his hand gather up her hair so he might pull her head back from where it hung over her project. Shepherd was not hurting her, or yanking, he simply unfolded the Omega, forcing her to meet his narrowed gaze.

He was stern as he searched her expression. "You will paint something else."

Claire set the brush on the table and furrowed her brow. "I like this one."

"*I* dislike what it suggests." He released her hair to take the offensive piece of paper, staring with rancor where Claire had painted her last moments of freedom… only to have changed the story to show the ice cracked open in a gaping hole—alluding that she had fallen through to her death.

"Fine," Claire challenged him, "I'll paint you instead."

Crushing the wet paper in his hands, Shepherd snorted. Once the painting had been thoroughly balled up and ruined, he threw it in the bin, found she still was willingly meeting his gaze, and slowly took the seat across from his mate.

He'd yet to strip off his coat or armor, looking just as he'd looked when Claire had first seen him in the Citadel—namely, intimidating and angry.

The hazy dreamlike high of estrous had made her find him attractive. Seeing Shepherd now, seeing him through her anger, disgust, and the effect of their re-established bond… it was different on every level. Already reaching for a fresh piece of paper, looking objectively at the subject of her nightmares, Claire's eyes darted over the Da'rin marks creeping up his neck and a lifetime of collected scars.

The silver of his eyes never wavered as he watched her take him in, though they grew a little hard when she squinted and leaned closer. Then her attention went to the paper and, like magic, the lines of his face began to appear.

Every few seconds, inquisitive eyes would glance back at the motionless Alpha, run over whatever part of the outline she needed to adjust, and then go back to the paper. Quickly, the line of his jaw, his closely shorn hair, were captured in shades of black. Concentrating on her work, Claire began to create his mouth, with the scar she had once called beautiful slashed across it. Had they not been marred, Claire would even admit Shepherd's lips would have been considered handsome—their fullness almost pretty. His nose, now that she looked far more closely, was not straight; there were places, small deviations, where it had been broken and reset more than once.

Tiny scars were in his stubble, all over his hairline and forehead.

Picture nearing completion, only one key feature neglected, Claire took a deep breath and made herself look into Shepherd's eyes. The silver was so familiar to her, she could have painted them a thousand times without looking, but every study would have been eyes focused on intimidation, on drawing out fear. At that moment his eyes were almost complacent, the animal aggression, the focus of a predator, contained.

As he was, it seemed to take ages to translate such an expression onto the paper. She tried, but her interpretation was never quite right.

How could anyone capture eyes like that?

"You are growing agitated," Shepherd commented, displeased when she began to glare down at the painting.

Again she tried to capture his expression. "I can't get the eyes right."

Slowly, his hand reached out and took the paintbrush from her stained fingers. The portrait was turned, Shepherd asking, "Is this how you see me?"

It seemed a strange question. Of course that was how she saw him, that was why she'd painted him that way. "I am better at painting landscapes."

His voice was odd. "You made me different."

"The eyes are wrong." Gathering up her supplies, she stood and rounded the table so she might clean her brushes. A large hand stopped her progress, pulling her closer. The paints were taken and set back on the table, his arm snaking around her middle.

Shepherd just looked up at her, regarded the dark-haired woman who'd painted him.

Holding her messy hands away so as not to smear his coat, she stood awkwardly, unsure why he was looking at her with such an expression. She had done nothing to soften him in the picture; every mar, every scar, every part of him was on that paper.

Shepherd pulled her to his lap.

Watching him as one watches a snake, Claire sat stiffly. He began to touch her face, to thread his fingers in her hair, and then those lips, the full lips she had translated perfectly, came to hers.

He was insistent even in a languorous slow kiss, even when she complained against his mouth, "I'm going to get paint on you."

Smiling into his answer, brushing his lips over hers he whispered, "Then get paint on me."

A warm tongue slipped in her mouth, Shepherd held her tightly… but she did not kiss him back.

His lips traced her jaw, tasted her neck, nibbled at her ear while her eyes were on the portrait on the table.

"Kiss me, little one," he murmured against her skin, smirking as he purred.

"No."

The monster softly laughed and retook her mouth with passion, bowing her body until the table met her back. The paints were under her, their color seeping into her dress. Shepherd didn't care; all he wanted was his mouth on her body.

Fabric tore under his hands, her dress split down the middle.

"The paints," Claire gasped, worried they were being ruined, trying to wriggle off her things.

"Are nothing compared to this." The man fumbled with his zipper, groaning as he nosed her breast.

Lips were at her nipple, his tongue flicking the bud before he moved lower and pressed his mouth to her mound. He attacked her there, tasting a place he had not enjoyed since he'd collected her from the Omegas. Claire tried to push him off, squealed as her legs kicked, but Shepherd held firm.

Leaning up on her elbows, Claire's jaw dropped, her hips jerking to escape something so intimate. He watched her every expression, all the while thrashing his tongue in her pussy and releasing his cock from his pants.

When her legs began to twitch, her breaths nothing but stifled gasps of air, he drank her up, seeming to know just where to move that tongue until Claire's face grew pained and she began to come. A shriek, short and stuttering, passed her lips as the tight winding coil the man had fostered snapped apart. In answer, Shepherd grunted into her, wove his tongue deep, stroking himself madly under the table.

Her groans grew rabid, his fist tightly gripping his burgeoning knot until seed splattered the floor. Air ripe with the smell of semen, he rode the high, tenderly kissing Claire's inner thighs and mumbling that she tasted delicious.

Falling back against the table, Claire stared blankly at the memorized grey ceiling, trying to ignore that her thighs were on his shoulders, that he was licking her clean, and that he had, once again, expertly commanded her body's response… as Svana had claimed the two of them had done to other Omegas.

That thought brought blistering heat to her chest, the painful knowledge inspiring instant anguish.

"What is wrong, little one?" Shepherd pulled his tongue from her slit. "I did not mount you. That should not have caused you pain."

Claire answered robotically. “It didn’t hurt.”

More soft kisses to her inner thigh and a strong purr preceded the promise, “I will replace your paints. You need not feel distressed.”

To win the war, she would have to wage a battle. Closing her eyes tight, she told herself that she could do this. “It’s not the paints. I was thinking of the Omegas.”

“They are safe, as per our agreement. My men watch over them from a distance.” Again he tasted her center, enjoying how she bowed from even a simple kiss over her pert nub.

Gasping, Claire answered, “Not those Omegas. The ones you shared with Svana.”

The man froze, hesitating before he spoke. “Why would you think of them?”

Claire forced her eyes open, lifted her head, and found Shepherd watching her very carefully. “I wonder if they were frightened or ashamed.”

Each word was growled. “They were all willing.”

“Somehow I think you misunderstand the meaning of that word. Estrous bends the mind.” She knew that better than anyone. “Did you speak to them before or after?”

“No.”

Then they were probably dead. “That makes me sad.”

Large hands accompanied an almost unsteady purr, Shepherd stroking her from her knee to hip. “Do not be sad, little one.”

Claire lay back, eyes once again on the ceiling. “I do not remember how to be happy.”

Leslie was on his couch, working on a COMscreen when Corday returned.

Her mouth was set and she was clearly displeased. "Another rendezvous with your Claire?"

"No." Corday stripped his coat, his back to the Alpha female.

"Yet you smell of her." Leslie scooted a little closer, her tone instantly light. "How is the Omega faring?"

Tired eyes, his face lined in disappointment, Corday could not muster any enthusiasm for Leslie. "Claire has—"

A knock sounded at the door, not Claire's timid scratches but an arrogant bang. Gun already in hand, Corday motioned for Leslie to move out of sight.

"I hear you breathing on the other side of that thing, Enforcer." The tiny view through the peephole showed an unwelcome woman. "Open up or I will simply turn the knob of the door I've already unlocked." Maryanne smirked. "I am trying to be civil."

Corday turned the knob, finding it was indeed unlocked, and opened the door far enough to point his gun at Maryanne's face.

Maryanne sniffed and waved her hand at his petty threat. "I saw you skulking around the Omega's trash heap. Low and behold, it *was* Enforcer stink she was wearing when she came to me. Now that I smell her on you, I see that I was right, as usual. Let me in, I want to talk to Claire."

Teeth clenched, Corday hissed, "She isn't here."

"Bullshit," the woman spat, looking over Corday's shoulder to peer into the apartment.

"You have three seconds to tell me who you are before I shoot you."

"Oh, shut up." The blonde pushed past him. "I'm here to see my friend."

"Claire O'Donnell is not your friend." But he felt a spark of hope that maybe they were… because he could smell traces of the Omega on the strange woman's clothing.

He closed the door and watched the woman look around, frowning when she saw no sign of Claire.

Maryanne dumped the bundle in her hands on the floor. "She left these clothes at my place. Feel free to thank me for returning your crap to you." Moving deeper into the apartment, her chocolate brown eyes looked straight at the pretty Alpha standing in the corner watching her like a hawk. "And what do we have here?"

Running a hand through his hair, Corday said, "That's my girlfriend, Monica."

"Nice try, Enforcer." Maryanne rolled her eyes. "But anyone paying attention knows Leslie Kantor's heart is pining for Premier Callas." Smirking meanly, the blonde looked at the woman and teased, "I slept with him twice to get out of jail time. He was awful… You dodged a bullet when he shot down your marriage proposal."

Leslie's expression grew dark. "Who are you?"

Turning her attention back to Corday and ignoring the spoiled niece of Senator Kantor, Maryanne growled, "I smelled you in her apartment, I smelled you on her clothes, this room is saturated in her, but she is not here or with her pack… so where is Claire?"

Corday showed his teeth. "What do you know of the Omegas?"

"Who do you think chose the location of their cozy new home? Claire?" Maryanne rolled her eyes when the man glowered. "Goddess save us, you really did think she broke them out all by herself…"

Aggressive Alpha females and dominant Beta males did not mix well, leaving the air full of tension and mistrust.

Maryanne had not come all that way to be disappointed. "I want to talk to her crazy ass. One last time, *Enforcer Corday*—that's right, I know who you are—where is Claire?"

Lip curled, shoulders tense, Corday hissed, "Claire is missing, okay? I don't know where she is!"

For a moment Maryanne looked worried, studied him as if there was more to the man's outburst. "I don't think you are lying." That left the most likely outcome. "Then she is probably dead… or Shepherd has her again."

And that was exactly why Corday felt such desolation. "I don't think Shepherd has her." If Shepherd had her, then the tyrant would know of his own location, the Omegas would be gone, and Leslie's access to their communications would have been terminated.

"You make a good point"—Maryanne covered her doubt with a cocky smirk—"because if he did, you and I would both be strung up from the Citadel… Unless, of course, we and her little pack of Omegas were offered in trade for compliant behavior. The little twit is stupid enough to fall for that, you know."

"She wouldn't go back to him." There was no way. Every feeling inside Corday knew better. He'd seen what the monster had done to her… what she had been forced to live through. Touching where her ring circled his pinky he walked back to the door, opening it so his *guest* might take a hint.

Before she left, Maryanne faced Corday one last time. "I know her better than anyone else in the world. I also know she wanted to kill herself… That's why I am going to pray that she did instead of considering the horrible alternative. Thank you for *nothing*, Enforcer Corday."

He slammed the door.

Corday turned towards Leslie, found the outspoken woman awfully quiet.

The strange woman's warning scratched at his composure. "If Claire is in Shepherd's possession, if she struck some reckless exchange for our lives, then he knows about you. If all this is true, then every piece of information you've uncovered is compromised… useless."

Leslie looked about ready to break something.

# 10

Claire was still sleeping, restless under the covers on the bed beside him. It had taken a great deal of effort to get her comfortable after Shepherd had found her holed up in the bathroom vomiting upon his return. Hours of soft touches, bland broth, and her agitated growls eventually turned to snores. Once Claire had finally lost consciousness the thread seemed to harmonize, leaving Shepherd able to work as he lay at her side.

Reports on Enforcer Corday's movements were less than pleasing. Svana was still holed up in his apartment, and irksome Maryanne Cauley had come calling, looking for Claire.

Neither woman's agenda was clear. Svana was toying with the resistance, for what purpose Shepherd was uncertain, but she was up to something.

In the years of their relationship, there had been no secrets, no dividing line between them. Ordering Jules to continue with her constant surveillance had been… difficult. Studying her motives as he'd studied the Senators, their families, their work, for years, troubled Shepherd greatly.

This woman was not that same revolutionary he'd loved with every last fiber of his being. Worse, not knowing where she'd stashed the contagion, having had all the usual places searched, made him uneasy.

She wanted to remind Shepherd that she had the power. Knowing he was watching her flit around the Beta's apartment was her less than subtle way of reminding him she was in control.

She played her games with the resistance. Leslie Kantor wanted them to find her valuable, even passing fragmented information that could potentially undermine Shepherd's control.

Svana was taunting him.

Why?

There was more to this than her anger over Claire.

So far just Maryanne Cauley had thrown the only wrench into her plans.

*...when he shot down your marriage proposal.*

How did a woman like Maryanne possess information even Shepherd had never heard whispers of? Why did Svana just about reach out and break the blonde's neck?

Most importantly, why hadn't Svana noticed the immediate look of suspicion the Beta Enforcer had shot her way once those words were out in the open?

Challenging was not the right word to describe the feelings embedded in the problem. Deeply, Shepherd wanted to trust Svana as he always had. But the little black-haired Omega curled up at his side… one look at her, and Shepherd was at a loss.

Never would he trust Svana anywhere near Claire. That fact gave him pain.

And that, at its essence, was why Svana remained with the Enforcer. She knew Shepherd's abiding loyalty had been shaken, and she taunted him by fostering a new champion, lightly touching the Beta at every turn, keeping herself beautiful and engaging.

Was she trying to seduce Corday, to flaunt her conquest?

Never before in his life had Shepherd struggled with so many questions. Answers had always been obvious, his course steadfast.

Now he knew he had to greatly alter the plan. He had to find the contagion and make sure it was beyond Svana's control. Stripped of her greatest advantage, he could reason with his beloved, maybe find her an Omega male so she, too, could be enlightened.

Their partnership, their rich history, need not be tarnished by his natural devotion to such a pleasing mate.

Reassured, Shepherd read the latest update again. There was something in the transcript that was intriguing. Just as Claire had explained, the once disposable minion, Maryanne Cauley, *was* fond of his mate.

In Shepherd's experience, Maryanne Cauley was very easy to control, a creature inundated in self-preservation. Shepherd could use her again, augment Jules' initial plan to win more than just Claire's complacence. She could be a valuable tool, and the selfish Alpha female would even be willing for the right price.

As Shepherd's plot developed, Claire grew restless in her dreams. Absently, Shepherd began purring, lightly tracing the furrow between the Omega's brows until it softened.

Before all could be made right, there was a list of issues that had to be remedied. The Omega was not showing any of signs of the affection she had displayed before their recent… complication. In her waking hours, there were no activities of nesting, not like before. Normal habits of a pregnant Omega must be encouraged, but she no longer touched her belly like she should—never acknowledged the child he'd placed in her womb, even though it was the cause of her almost constant nausea. Only in her sleep would her hand rest above the baby, and even then she looked… troubled.

Claire also was incredibly disinterested in being touched, yet if he initiated, highly responsive to sex.

They were at square one.

Shepherd kept her in a constant state of the mating high, took her so many times her eyes remained half-dilated, almost as if in the first stages of estrous. It was necessary to keep her mending, to keep the bond fresh and unchallenged, and it soothed her. But she no longer whispered or called out his name, seemed half involved but eager for pleasure.

Pure escapism…

When the sleeping woman quieted, Shepherd went back to the latest reports. With only eight weeks before transport would carry those who'd chosen loyalty to his cause to seize Greth Dome, his new life was soon to begin. Svana's lineage and title would place her as the savior queen of what all intel confirmed was a highly repressed population. Transition would be relatively seamless. Of course, there would be turmoil and battles in those first weeks as the usurper regime was decimated, but Shepherd had a worthy supply of Followers to raise his standard, and the Greth government had no indication a nightmare would soon be crashing down upon them.

Best of all, as Shepherd thrived, as he gave Claire the things that would bring her happiness, nothing but corpses and rot would be left in a place he hated with all his heart.

Everyone left in Thólos would succumb to plague.

Toying with a strand of Claire's hair, Shepherd grinned—vindicated, in perfect alignment with the universe, until he heard her call out.

It had been only a little noise in the dark, a voice laced with fear… a call for him to help her.

Mechanically he moved, swift to gather her close. "I am here, little one."

Shepherd could see she was not quite awake when, instead of

tensing up at his touch, she gripped the fabric of his shirt and pulled him closer, urging him to surround her in his heat and strength.

Swallowing, trying to catch her breath, Claire tried not to think of the sound of screaming convicts and lingering echoed flashes of men lining up to hurt her in her dream. It had been another horrible nightmare of the Undercroft Shepherd had described from his childhood; a prison that gave birth to monsters, inhabited by demons even Maryanne had once warned still lurked down below.

Brushing the hair from her face, Shepherd encouraged her to calm. "You are allowing your brooding to affect your dreams."

Claire released her grip on the nightmare-inducing monster at once. "I'm fine."

"You would not call out for your mate if something had not frightened you."

Shepherd rolled them, holding her to his chest so Claire might rest atop him as she had slept before the complications of the last few weeks. In that position his vibrations would pass far more noticeably into her, and the hatred in her eyes would go back to the faraway stare of complacence.

"What time is it?"

Shepherd did not let her budge, but answered the question. "A little after 16:00."

God, she was so tired even after all that sleep. Too tired to protest the thick arms that came to embrace and stroke, feeling guilt she was experiencing comfort from such a thing, she complained, "I hate the hours down here… everything is backwards."

"If you had slept during the evening instead of fighting the rest you require, then you would have settled into regular rhythms."

Claire gave an annoyed groan at his pointless lecture. It was his fault she could not sleep, his fault her mind was *unstable*, his fault she'd had the nightmare, his fault she could feel again and that everything felt horrible. Unsure if she spoke simply to annoy him, or to test him, or because it was what she actually needed, Claire muttered against the fabric of his shirt, "I want to go outside."

The purring stopped.

A moment of time hung between them, the air tangible with mutual dissatisfaction. Trilling her fingers on his chest, she made it clear she was waiting for an answer and that there was only one right one.

Everything about his reply was displeased and growled with great annoyance. "You will eat and bathe first. After we have mated… I will escort you to see your sky."

How fucking romantic.

In the mood to continue being difficult, Claire said, "I want to eat fried potatoes with mayonnaise."

He threaded his fingers in her hair. "No."

"And a chocolate shake."

"No." Shepherd stroked her spine in an attempt to urge her to fall back asleep and forget her expectation of the sky.

"Raspberries, lots of raspberries."

"That you may have."

Aware he was trying to make her melt until she forgot her request, and conscious Shepherd was about to achieve his goal, Claire began to wriggle away, stretching like a cat and cracking her spine. He made her work for her escape. Even with his arm just lying across her, the damn thing weighed a ton, and he seemed far more interested in groping her ass than letting her up. In the end, she bit him and slipped out of reach.

Shepherd found it funny.

She moved into the bathroom, ignoring the light laughter coming from the giant splayed on the bed. A long shower that was blissfully alone helped to clear away the remnants of her nightmare. It was not the first time she'd dreamed she was locked in a cell, her upper body pressed to a stinking cot while a devil rutted her painfully. Beyond the bars, masses of Alphas watched and waited. Their faces contorted, they snarled and snapped, reaching through the metal bars, stretching inhumanly until they could almost touch her.

Claire did not want to think of the Undercroft, of the things that were locked in it, but the feelings of the dream seemed to linger like a stain even a scalding shower could not wash off.

She turned off the water, combed her hair before the foggy glass, and felt the woman in the blurred reflection was a ghost.

Shutting off the light, she went back into the main room of her cage and found Shepherd had created daytime by switching on every light. Once she was clothed, he left to retrieve her food. Her paints had been cleaned up days ago, his ejaculate from the floor as well, but the portrait remained on the table. She was not exactly sure why he had left it there, and she had tried to ignore it as she ignored him, but it seemed the incorrect eyes were always watching her.

Studying the thing, the rugged face of the man who hurt so many people, she could not find what about the painting had seemed to please him. Of course, she may have completely misread his reaction—the Alpha was layered in half-truths, and had no qualms about deceit if it meant he would attain his goal. But something in the cord, something on his end, had been so very satisfied at what she'd done.

Claire had wanted a reaction, she had got one. Now she had no idea what it meant or how to use it.

Absorbed in the flawed eyes, she listed the mistakes in her rendition. They were not hard enough; the silver did not hold back a tidal wave of twisted history. Shepherd just looked like a man. And how would she look if someone were to paint her? Would it be the ghostly blurred image from the mirror, or somebody completely different? Had her eyes become infected with the same thing that lingered in his?

How much time would it take for her to wake up and no longer care about the forty-three lives he held over her head, or the millions in Thólos she had to find a way to fight for? Why had she not just stomped her foot against the ice and cracked it so powerfully that they both were sucked under?

Her slender hold on composure began to slip just as the bolt on the door hissed its metallic warning. Shepherd had returned. Quickly scrubbing her face of tears, Claire sat straight and prepared for the next round.

The man came in with a tray and set it down before her, noticing the redness around the eyes of the woman sitting ramrod straight.

When she saw what he had brought her, Claire began to sniff. She reached for a steaming fried potato wedge, dipped it in mayo, then dunked it again in the chocolate shake. Shoving it in her mouth, tears began to fall, her acknowledgment pathetic. "They're really good."

"There are no raspberries on premises. They will be acquired shortly," Shepherd explained, assuming she was, at last, having some sort of pregnancy moment.

Sniveling, Claire dumped the chocolate shake over the hot fries, smearing into the mess. She gorged, sniffing and frowning, devouring what to Shepherd looked absolutely disgusting as if it were manna from the heavens. By the time she had finished what had to be the unhealthiest thing on the planet, her brief blubbering was over and she felt much better.

Wiping her mouth, Claire looked to the man who'd observed her meal. It was obvious Shepherd wanted her to thank him—he had done something *nice* for her, something apparent and obvious that she had requested specifically. All those other months, she had defiantly used none of his things outside of mere necessity, never made requests aside from demands of freedom… simply to make the point that she was refusing his *hospitality*. But this meal she had blatantly stated she desired, and he had delivered it, though it was clearly something he had not thought was best for her. In his strange language it was almost as if, again, he was affirming there was a new precedent and that he was making an effort.

Looking down at the remaining melted mess on her plate, Claire took a deep breath and breathed it out. "Thank you."

The tray was scooted aside before a large hand came to her face and turned it up. His thumb rubbed away a missed smear of chocolate, Shepherd very pleased. "You are welcome."

She did not want to look into those impossible eyes, but he held her in thrall. Claire was lost as she measured how many deaths stuck to him, how many appalling things he'd done of which she hoped never to learn. Why did he have to have a tragic history that haunted her sleep, and how had he become so distorted he'd developed into the harbinger of Thólos' apocalypse?

Why was she even thinking of all that shit?

Shepherd gave her time, taking in her confused expression as she confessed, "I dreamed of your Undercroft, and I was trapped with the prisoners reaching for me through the bars… while I was being raped like you said."

Elbow resting on the table, he cupped her cheek and purred, "It was only a dream. You are safe here and will never endure the Undercroft."

She sniffed, lost in the quicksilver changefulness of those damn eyes. "What's it like?"

Unsure exactly how much he should disclose, Shepherd said, "Dark, cold. The prisoners eat the mold on the walls. There is no sewage system. In the tunnels it is easy to get lost… many go missing. As a child, an inmate told me those tunnels span the entire continent of Antarctica. They go on for ages; you walk and walk, and never find a way out. But you do find the bones of others who've gone mad searching the paths only to die from lack of water or starvation."

"I dislike that I feel pity," Claire breathed, eyes full of sorrow, "for you."

The way he watched her, the slow move of his analyzing gaze, it was if he already knew everything she confessed. "Little one, it is merely an indication of your nature to feel compassion—even for me."

Her brows lowered, that little line forming between them. "Is this where you call me a coward or a fool?"

Shepherd smirked. "You are somewhat foolish, but you are not a coward—simply naïve. What you are is innocent."

But that was not true. Disappointed in his answer, she rose from her chair, hands tugging the straps of her dress so the fabric could whisper down her body. Eager to finish the final requirement to leave the room, she moved, naked and expressionless, to stand before the Alpha.

He took in the secret places of her body, but did not touch.

Voice harsh, Claire felt the guilt, the anger, the fear eat her up. "What do you see now?"

Slowly, Shepherd met her indignant expression, softly purring, "My mate."

The thrum was deep in her chest, something it took a great deal of focus to recall was unwelcome. Confused, she watched him, unsure why he wasn't touching her. Unsure why they were not already on the bed, or table, or floor?

The moment was growing into something it was not meant to be.

Just as she was about to turn, to just walk away from him, the growl was made. It was loud, expectant, and brought with it a small pleasurable cramp as her body instinctively responded.

Slick came thick and copious at such a call, dripping down her leg. Shepherd watched the little trickle, captivated.

Rising slowly, he pulled his clothing over his head, stripping down to only flesh until he stood before her in an equal state. He was beautiful and grand, all the glorious epitome of Alpha physique in the control of a man who used such strength ruthlessly. Claire had to crane her neck to look up, to keep her eyes off his marked body where she could focus on his face and those hated eyes.

"What do you see when you look at me, little one?"

A monster, the man who had ruined her life, the little boy raised in hell whose mother had performed unspeakable acts just to secure him a knife, a former prisoner who had dedicated his love to Svana, a man with twisted faith, the male who had betrayed their pair-bond and caused her great pain, her jailor, the father of the life growing inside her, a creature she could not trust… Claire drew a deep breath and said the only thing she could. "I see the Alpha pair-bonded to me."

"Can you not see more?" Shepherd hinted, trying to draw out the proper words.

Her reply twisted in the thread and tore out her heart, but Claire stood still, her face a mask, and spoke the hated truth, "I see my mate."

"You are doing exceptionally well today," the Alpha claimed, but still he did not move.

And Claire understood. Shepherd wanted her to initiate sex, he was pushing her boundaries, seeing how much she was willing to exchange for what she wanted.

She let out in a low whisper. "I can't."

"You can." Shepherd was confident, nodding for her to try.

Already half-high, drugged in scent and the call, Claire knew in truth she wanted it. She wanted him to fuck her so hard that she forgot herself, that *Claire* disappeared. It had been her only respite since their deal had been struck, her only succor the distraction of sex. In a sick way she almost longed for a heat cycle, a mindless source of existence that shut off her thinking until all that mattered was physical gratification. But she could not allow herself such a thing if Shepherd didn't force it or take it. It would make the act of mating something she could not bear.

Clenching her fists, she glanced to the side and shook her head belligerently. "I. Can't."

Another of those powerful growls, so loud it was almost a roar, and her pussy clenched, more of that damn slick spilling down her leg.

Shepherd persisted. "You can."

She knew how very easy it could be, how falsely fulfilling his arms would feel—the decadence of fornicating with such a creature, to hear his whispered words at her ear… the culmination of the moment when her world burst apart and everything bad was forgotten. Had she not felt it a hundred times? But Shepherd had to inflict it, if she took that fateful step and admitted that she desired such a thing, it would ruin her.

Crumbling, she closed her eyes and rested her forehead on his chest, doing nothing more than pulling in deep breaths of what nature told her was hers, but what experience had taught her was far from the case. Lightly, her fingertips came to his torso, running upward, delicately tracing over his nipples in their journey to reach around his neck.

Claire froze. She could not sell herself for the sky or oblivion.

"What more do you want from me, Shepherd?" Frustrated, desperate, she whined, "Just fuck me already!"

She felt him bend to reach her ear, knew the press of scarred lips. "I want everything."

The massive male tugged her towards the bed. Claire was spun about and pressed down on her belly, her legs left dangling towards the floor. A hand raked almost too hard down her spine, the pulsing head of his cock positioned at her folds. He did not press in. Instead, Shepherd slapped her; his palm met the full roundness of her ass and left it red and stinging as she cried out in surprise. His hips surged, and in the midst of her yelp he speared her with the entirety of his girth.

"You are so fucking wet, yet still dare to pretend that you don't want this? That you need to be forced?" he roared, gripping her hips even as she presented, arching her back in instinctual invitation. Roughly, he pulled her back to meet each thrust, Claire mewling into the covers, falling into the drugged delirium where she could fade away and forget.

The second her mind grew free of petty feeling and thought, Shepherd took his cock away, flipping her over.

Blazing silver eyes met hers. "Do you want me to continue to fuck you?"

Her eyes glued to the shining, throbbing thickness that he should be burying inside her again and again and again, she snarled, "Yes!"

The man stood there, panting, eyes blazing, with her slick all over his groin… and simply did nothing.

Claire pounded her fist against the mattress and looked up with furious, half-dilated eyes. There was a snarl, her own version of the growl, and she launched herself at him to take back the only thing she had left to ease the pain. The sound of her demand inspired the man manipulating the situation to his liking. Shepherd took her in his arms, plunging his cock slow and deep where she ached, and watched Claire's silent pleas for more.

Kept just at the border of the insensibility she craved, like he knew her game, Shepherd moved with decided cunning in the dissection of her avoidance of what they were and why he mated her—forcing Claire to recognize who offered her carnal satisfaction, what he felt like against her, and how much she loved it.

Without the frenzy, there was no void, there was no loss of self. Claire knew in her bones that he was knowingly denying her the only escape she had left by making love when she only wanted to fuck.

Shepherd smiled like a man standing in the bliss of heaven, whispered to her so she had to recognize his voice, and controlled every thrust no matter how she squirmed or rocked her hips. There was no escaping him or the pleasure.

Her mind grasped the irony with each tender stroke that the one thing she'd fought to preserve when Shepherd first took her had been her sense of self… until he broke her. Now all she wanted, now that her world was so dark, was to forget that identity and waste away.

"Faster," she breathed on a lengthy moan.

There was such pleasure in his voice, Shepherd gently rocking his hips to fill her cunt in slow measure. "No, little one."

It went on for hours, until she was shuddering and cooing small sounds of pleasure. This was how it had been in those first weeks, but the underlying distress was different. She was no longer afraid of what he could do to her; she was far more afraid of her mutilated sense of self and what she very much wanted from him.

A warm hand stroked from hip to breast, over and over, leaving a trail of soft tingles and ending with a little squeeze of her tight nipple until she whimpered for more and spread wider in invitation.

"Open your eyes."

How many times had he already commanded her to do so? Why did he have to make her look? Complying, her green eyes met beautiful silver. She saw her palm cradle his cheek, she saw him kiss the tip of her thumb.

A catch of breath and a long shuddering sigh came from the Omega. "I can't… I need…"

The purr built from deep within Shepherd's chest, the Alpha observing each minute reaction of pleasure on her face. "Soften, little one. Let it happen this way. There is no more need to fight what we are."

He wove his fingers into hers, his sweat-slicked muscles moving over her entire body. Each time he had her stuffed full, he'd grind his groin in a tight circle to tease at her clit, drawing sounds from the Omega that made his balls tighten.

Shepherd's name came to her lips when she felt that first fluttering of the hour's long building climax, a name she never wanted to call out in passion again.

There was not even a hint of a veiling fog in her mind when she felt tears leak from her eyes and her cunt squeezed like a fist around his swelling knot. Claire orgasmed completely, powerfully aware of Shepherd, her insides vigorously milking his cock, drawing out every last drop of his come as the man groaned in his own ecstasy.

Boneless, vibrating from the humming thread, Claire didn't know what to do. The feeling of his cheek slipped past her palm, the Omega wilting against the mattress.

"That was perfect." He kissed her slack lips, nuzzled her cheek. "You, Claire, are superior to any sky."

Her contentment shattered. With a growl guttural and vicious, Claire threatened the man still deeply knotted. "Do not *ever* call me that name!"

# 11

The knot was fresh, the male's cock still filling her with a steady trickle of semen, his fingers still warmly enfolded with hers. Yet whatever tenderness the Omega had displayed as he led her down the path to orgasm had evaporated. Her small body was stiff, Claire's hips moving just enough to communicate her desire to reject his knot, even if trapped by it.

If Shepherd was angry, he hid it well. Looking at her with deceptive calm he spoke her name again. "Claire."

Her building rage blended with disgust, yet she mirrored his move on the board. In a tone so calm it was chilling, she explained, "Every time I hear you speak that name, I feel your Alpha *beloved's* hand crushing my throat. I feel her fingers scratching my insides. I see you, a monster who has the audacity to call himself my mate, stand by and watch. I hear you order me into the bathroom saying *Claire*… a name you refused to acknowledge up until that enlightening moment."

Shepherd had to make use of this opportunity; he had to reason with her. “I did not witness her touching you sexually and only learned of it later. It will *never* happen again.”

Incredulous, Claire’s eyes went wide at his nerve. “And that makes it okay?”

The man tried again. “I am aware you harbor great anger towards me, hatred even, for what was done.”

“I do hate you. I hate her. But most of all I hate myself.”

Rocking his hips, pressing the knot deeper, he insisted, “Tell me the reason you hate yourself.”

She held his eyes, hers violently raging. “We both know why.”

But it needed to be said aloud. “Claire, your self-hatred stems from the fact that you recognized you had affection for me before circumstances caused you pain.”

“Circumstances?” Claire laughed meanly, not at all impressed. “She has a name. It’s Svana. What you did to me has a name. It’s called betrayal.”

Odd remorse burning in his consternation, Shepherd pressed his forehead to hers. “You have my fidelity now. I gave you my word. We could be content in one another if you would forget, and try again.”

Claire saturated her reply with every ounce of disgust she could muster. “You are a very smart man with the skill to inspire others to follow you into evil, Shepherd, but your understanding of people is so primordial. You claim to love me, so answer this: had I fucked Corday while you were watching me in the warehouse, would it be something you would ever forget?”

The man’s entire body went rigid. “No.”

“So you see, it is impossible.”

His eyes were full of a hundred things. “You will forgive me.”

Her black brow arched. “Forgive what you can only call the *circumstances* that caused me pain?”

He knew what she wanted. Growling like a beast, Shepherd gave it. "I mated with Svana and dishonored you."

"You did."

"I did it to save your life."

Claire arched beneath him, wanting to get away. "You are lying."

His hands squeezed her fingers so hard it hurt. "I did it because I could not harm her. She is my only family... Because I was concerned she would take you from me. I gave her the attention she came for to distract her, so you would not be considered a threat." Almost frantically he admitted, "The whole time, I was thinking of you."

"That is disgusting."

Shepherd did not know how to answer such a thing, so he chose silence. While the knot persisted, he held her unwilling hands, he purred and nuzzled, but Claire had lost all traces of softness... In fact, she only looked sad.

When at last his knot diminished enough for him to pull out, he did. "Get dressed." Shepherd stood with grace a man of his size did not deserve. "I will take you to see your sky now."

Claire had lost interest in going outside. She wanted nothing but sleep. "You don't need to waste the effort. I no longer want to see it."

Shepherd gripped her arm and pulled her to stand when she began to roll over. "You will put on a dress at once."

After cleaning up the expected river of semen that came from her womb, Claire grabbed her dress from the floor and pulled it over her head. The giant clothed himself and returned to her, holding out a blanket, waiting for her so that he could wrap her shoulders with it in place of a coat. There were still no shoes.

"Give me your hand," he grunted.

Claire complied and his massive paw closed over her small wrist, leaving cold metal and a grating sound of cuffs being fitted. The opposite end he fixed to his own wrist, Shepherd warning, "You will behave."

"I don't take forty-three lives lightly."

He lifted her into his arms. "Your recent effort has not gone unnoticed."

Once she was settled against his chest, they left the room.

Shepherd took her down an alternate path that ended at a service elevator stinking of his men. The door closed, the contraption jerked, and the long ride began.

He was taking her to the upper levels, a region she had only ever visited once a year as a girl. Or at least that's what she thought. When the door opened, a decadently decorated hall appeared. The walls were well-appointed, clean, and filled with soft crystal lights. There were no windows, and when Shepherd began to approach a sinister looking door, Claire began to think the male had tricked her.

He was going to punish her again.

He tapped a code into the door's console, the hiss of decompression letting them know it had unlocked. Shouldering it open, Shepherd took her inside. The vault closed, bolted, its click exceedingly final.

He set her down. Claire's feet were touching plush carpet that looked like it was out of an old-world picture book. There was golden wallpaper, paneling made from actual wood.

Mostly, there was glowing light.

Eager to reach the window, she stepped forward only to find her arm still chained to the man behind her. Claire was confused. "This is not outside."

Shepherd escorted her forward, his torso warm on her back. "I never agreed to allow you outside. I believe the arrangement was that I would allow for you to see your sky."

Technically he was right, and Claire knew there was absolutely no point in arguing.

The prospect the small room afforded was unlike anything she'd seen in a house: a vast display of rugged tundra. The window was an actual part of the Dome; if she touched the glass, she would be touching the only thing between her and hundreds of miles of snow—a thing forbidden.

Reaching forward, ignoring the uncomfortable handcuff and arm that followed to allow her movement, Claire put her hand to the glass and felt its chill. Wild nature was her view, in a warm room, where she was chained to an Alpha to ensure good behavior.

The room's furnishings had been removed, leaving only that beautiful rug and a single large chair. It was angled at the window, filled with a man who drew Claire into his lap. With the lights on, Shepherd's looming presence at her back was reflected in the glass, his attention acute.

Meeting his stare in the reflection, Claire admitted, "Men have been put to death for touching the Dome."

Shepherd answered, "Or they are thrown in the Undercroft for daring to look outside."

Why would they look, there was nothing but snow outside. Yet Claire found herself taken with the view, all that white, of distant mountains and jutting ice. The land beyond the Dome was glorious.

Shepherd's body was warm, the purr soft and continuous, the perfect recipe for her to ignore him, relax, and just saturate herself in something other than four concrete walls.

The man did not ruin her comfort by speaking or making demands, and Claire was grateful for it. He was deep in thought, staring at the setting sun, his Omega held hostage on his lap.

The dark came, bright moonlight on glittering snow, and Claire fell into a dreamless slumber—the first she'd had in many weeks.

The whole night passed before intruding light set the backs of her eyelids glowing red. She woke comfortable with only beauty before her. It was almost as if Thólos did not exist. She could sit there and pretend. She could forget the man cuddling her was evil through and through.

But the truth could not be ignored. Though she was warm and safe, her people were waking up with nothing to eat, with no power, with no heat. Outside of that beautiful room, behind that grand view, the world was falling to pieces.

Shepherd stretched, his large hand cupped over the place where his child grew. "You enjoy this room and the view. You are comfortable here."

Looking away from the window, she surveyed the empty room. "Why did you have the furniture removed?"

"I did not want you to wrongly cultivate hope that I might allow you to remain."

There was logic to his rationale. Had there been a bed and other objects for comfort, she would have longed for more than just his lap on that oversized chair. She may have even grown upset when he'd demanded that they leave. "I see…"

"As I promised, I will bring you here." He took a breath of her hair, kissed a trail down her neck. "And as you promised, you will live as my willing mate."

WHEN THEY CAME BACK from her sky, Shepherd set her hand free. The handcuff had not been tight, but once he removed it, she felt an ache in its wake. He took her wrist and used his big thumbs to rub the skin, as if he understood the feeling and why she had cradled the offended limb in her hand.

Claire watched his caress, finding it peculiar that with paws that could crush her, Shepherd seemed to know just how much pressure was appropriate. As the odd touching continued, she worried her lip and found him once again watching her carefully. When the silence stretched and his big thumb continued to rub, she grew nervous.

Unwilling to act without specific orders, unwilling to be tricked or manipulated, she thought to withdraw her hand.

Shepherd trapped her wrist in circling fingers that seemed far more binding than the handcuff had been. "How will you fill your hours while I am gone today?"

"Are you mocking me?"

"What did you do with your free time before I claimed you as my mate?"

That was easy to answer. "I spent every waking hour trying to find food for the Omegas."

The giant smirked, using his grip on her wrist to pull her nearer. "Before Thólos became mine."

"Thólos is not yours."

The bastard smiled at her. "Answer me, little one."

With a huff, she began to list off activities. "Aside from painting, I played my mom's old piano. I spent time with my friends… read stories, took cooking classes when I could afford to."

Her response satisfied the man. Shepherd released her arm, the drag of his callused hands against her fingers extended.

Claire used the opportunity to put distance between them, heading towards the bathroom, a place where he generally left her in peace.

When she emerged from her shower, she found Shepherd had brought her tray of breakfast. Scrunching up her face at the offering, she made a noise that displayed her reluctance to eat it. Apparently the junk food of her last meal was off the menu. In its place was some kind of green fluid that smelled heavily of bitter ginger. She drank it, hating it, and then sat in stupefaction when after twenty minutes, nothing seemed eager to come back up.

The Alpha seemed pleased, then he left.

Alone, Claire chewed her lip and found again that the painting of Shepherd was watching her. It was still there, left out in such an obvious position, still waiting for someone to do something with it. Wiping her hands, she reached for it, aware that even in the hours she had been free of him, his face still plagued her.

It struck her then that the Alpha had hardly left her side in her waking hours, or even physically left her touch in days. Whatever had happened between her arrival and the night spent in slumber on his lap must have left him content that she was established back in his power completely.

He was right.

Claire would remain a slave—for Corday, for Nona, the Omegas… for Maryanne. She would do as he wished to give them all a chance, and she would continue to engage, stomach the bond, and play the good captive as she looked for a way to help Thólos by the singularity of her situation.

But it was strange to be alone in that cell, wide awake, and alone for more than just a fleeting hour. Looking back at that damn portrait, at the face of the man on the page, the hard set of his jaw, even the beauty of his lips, she grew uneasy at the apparent change in him. She had verbally attacked him when he could not use his normal recourse—already knotted, he could not fuck her, and had seemed astonished at the amount of malice he felt burning through the thread. Yet Shepherd had not yelled, or punished. Instead he had admitted his wrongdoing, and when their bodies were untied, the man had even supplied what she had demanded before she'd lost her temper—he took her to see her sky, let her wake in the sunshine… then asked her personal questions.

The thread hummed: *Is your mate not trying? Are you not pleased?*

She was not pleased, she was suspicious.

The wave of instant soothing reassurance was immediate from that warm, worming cord. It sang to her that there was no need to panic. Even Claire had to agree. The nightmare would end with his regime's demise before the baby was born, or she would go back on a hunger strike. Or she could break the mirror in the bathroom and slit her wrists. She could just refuse to breathe.

She still got to choose.

A wave of apathy broke, all good feelings from the view swept into ennui. Claire needed to think objectively, she needed to not feel. A finger began to trace the outline of the portrait's jaw. She made herself remember.

Svana… Shepherd's beloved.

Claire had accused him on the ice of being twisted by Svana, but that could not be completely accurate. They had twisted each other in their sick, unbalanced relationship. The man Svana sought out in the Undercroft had earned her attention because he already had darkness in him.

Shepherd had suffered; his mother had been raped until she died. How many children suffered, how many people had been raped in this siege? What did he really expect to accomplish here?

Furthermore, why had he captured her if he had a lover who had been his for ages? It was more than the legacy he claimed to desire from his mate. Otherwise Shepherd would have reproduced with Svana. Why not couple with his beloved?

There was some upheaval, some key beyond simply wanting a child that Shepherd had been unwilling to share. Recreating the timeline in her head, Claire worked through his actions, her reactions, and the consequences of her escape attempts. He had impregnated her as a result of her first escape, injected his fertility drugs into her before she had even regained consciousness. It was such an extreme response, and the more she allowed herself to think about it objectively, to see past her feelings, the clearer it became. It wasn't just the baby; he wanted her devotion, was willing to force it by any means he could. Shepherd had done everything in his power to keep her just for himself, obsessed over it, and hid her away to the point of paranoia. He even thought he loved her.

Shepherd didn't even know her, his love was based off something she could not put her finger on.

*What more do you want from me, Shepherd?*

*I want everything.*

The image of Svana, of the expression on her face and the subtle flaring of her frightening blue eyes… The Alpha female had been displeased with her existence, Claire was certain of that. The woman had also been surprised to find her pregnant. Yet to his face, Svana had numbly accepted that Shepherd would have a toy… one the crazy Alpha female thought should have looked like her, as if every Omega she claimed they shared had been facsimiles of her exotic beauty.

Why would his consort, one Shepherd admitted he loved, not know he'd taken a mate, or that he had created a baby? Why had those eyes looked at Claire almost as if she were a mere nuisance, an aggravating rebound?

Rebound…

*Svana was my lover and I thought she was also equivalently my mate. I learned I was wrong.*

Holy shit. Svana had been unfaithful to Shepherd's devotion.

Understanding dawned and Claire's jaw dropped; she *was* a rebound. Her skin began to buzz as if overstimulated, her mind flew into a thousand directions at once. Shepherd's whole world had been shaken and his mutilated reaction had been to take an Omega—to continue his dedication to the woman who'd freed him from the Undercroft, but ease his own troubled heartache by forcing another to love him as he longed for Svana to love him.

"Why are you crying?"

Startled, Claire looked up to see the blue-eyed Beta had come with a new tray. Turning the paper pinched in her fingers towards the intruder, she ignored his question and just showed him the rendition of Shepherd in watercolor.

With brows drawn low, Jules looked at her painting, then looked away immediately. "You do not lack talent."

"So I've been told," wiping tears off her face, Claire conceded. "Does he know that you talk to me?"

"No."

"I'm glad that you do."

Such startling eyes in such an expressionless face, it was an odd sort of imbalance. "I know."

With a sorry smile, Claire pushed the painting of Shepherd aside. "You asked why I was crying. I was crying because I just sorted out… why he took me. I am not sure if I feel worse for my own ruined life, or for a man who is so fucking clueless. Shepherd may think brushing aside his pain over Svana's infidelity will make it go away, that by taking a mate he might fill that void… but love does not work that way."

Jules stiffened. "Your assessment is incorrect; do not think of it again. Such thoughts are unhealthy for your son."

"Why do you say son? How do you know it's not a girl?"

He sniffed the air but did not alter his expression. "I had two sons once… the subtlety of the scent is specific."

She echoed, "Had two sons?"

His voice never wavered. "My children were murdered when my wife was taken from me."

Everything in his statement was exactly what was wrong with

this whole damn situation. “Children are dying in Thólos now, others’ sons and daughters!”

Jules answered blandly, “It is unfortunate your people prey on the weak, but what we allow is necessary.”

Claire stood, she railed at the Beta. “Necessary? Explain it to me, then! Explain yourself to the woman your master has ruined because he didn’t know how to handle his hurt feelings!”

“Discuss it with Shepherd.” Face blank, Jules left, locking her back in her cage.

Discuss what part with Shepherd? The part about how she was superfluous and he just had not figured it out yet, or the dead babies part? Lying back on her space of concrete, Claire stared at the ceiling and felt like she was drowning in all the fucked up mess of things, the twisted histories, and the pathetic chain that was forged by a man with the emotional intelligence of an adolescent.

She would talk to him all right. She would make him look straight at what a hypocrite he was. She would show Shepherd what she’d discovered, the truth of what he was doing through her eyes… not his distorted vision. The Gods had even directed her to the sign-post of what a sad joke everything seemed to be. That boy. That curled up child she had rested on, the corpse with no name and nothing in his pockets. He would be her mascot, and Shepherd would have to look at him and answer to her.

Claire mixed her paints and began to recreate that lonely moment in the alley. There were hours to spend on the work, hours wherein she detailed the brick, the cold, the withered child, and herself… fast asleep against the cadaver’s stiffness.

She had never painted herself before, used the memory of her black hair on her cheek to mask most of her face, but it was her. The same curled up slender form, the bone structure that screamed Omega, all in the clothes she’d stolen from Maryanne.

Mindless tears were falling on the painting as she worked,

mixing the colors as her hand moved in a frenzy. Shepherd was sitting across from her, she blithely recognized the fact that he had arrived, but ignored him in her fervor to remember her boy perfectly —to not miss a detail of the grotesqueness of his withered face and milky, shriveled eyes. It was not until the hand holding the brush started to shake that he reached forward and stilled her. The brush was taken from her fingers, the painting turned so Shepherd could see. With his hand encasing hers, he viewed what had eaten up the hours of her day.

His rich voice stated fact. "This is you."

Stuck in the artist's haze, that blurry moment where one knows they are creating something monstrous but still mentally indistinct, she muttered, "I was tired and alone. I had been wandering Thólos for hours because I needed to see what had happened, what had been taken when you locked me in this room. I found this boy who'd died alone and sat at his side, feeling as dead as he was… I couldn't go any further so I leaned against him and fell asleep."

Shepherd tightened his grip on her hand, growling, "You could have frozen to death."

Claire nodded. "As that child did. That boy died with no one to care for him… alone and frightened in a trash strewn alley."

The hand on hers suddenly withdrew. The behemoth stood from the chair and moved something new into her line of sight. "You did not eat your lunch."

Claire looked at the cold plate of fish and knew better than to argue. Reaching for the fork, she started to push trout past her lips. After shoveling down half the meal without tasting what was probably a divine recipe, she looked at the looming Alpha. "I carried that boy's corpse on my back all the way to Lower Reaches… So I could bury him with the Omegas. So he would not have to be alone."

Shepherd sighed, fisted his hands at his sides. "You are upset over the child you carried back to the others."

With an open expression, Claire admitted, "I am confused as to how you went from a boy dedicated to a mother who loved you no matter the circumstances, to a terrorist who is the cause of the death of thousands of innocent children in Thólos. Why did you change? What justified this, Shepherd?"

He pulled her to stand, and moved them both towards the bed. "You are tired and I suspect you did not nap as your body requires. We will lie down."

Her words were not slung in cruelty, but curiosity. "Do you not have an answer? No long-winded explanation of legends and greatness to make up for the death of that nameless boy?"

He took her dress, put her in the bed, and followed as soon as his own clothing was shed. Pulling Claire above him, to the place she could feel the purr the strongest, a place that was minorly dominant for the Omega, Shepherd arranged her for sleep. "There is no answer I could give that you would find satisfactory."

But that in itself was an answer.

When her eyes were falling closed and the purr was moving her to stillness, the male shared his frustration. "Did you never wonder that I may have kept you segregated so that you would not have to be exposed to what is taking place outside these walls?"

Half asleep, Claire hummed. "I am a grown woman, pregnant with your son… a baby no different than that little boy who died because of what you inspired here."

Fingers rubbed her scalp and he reminded her, "A baby you almost murdered by attempting suicide. A baby you no longer nest for or touch."

Putting her chin to his chest, knowing the words were true, she did not balk. "After what I witnessed and learned of your nature… the things she said you've done… did *you* never wonder that I would rather kill myself and the unborn child than allow the likes of you and Svana to ruin him as you ruined one another?"

Shepherd's chest swelled, and it was clear from his expression that the man was incredibly pissed off. Rolling her onto her back, looming over her, his large hand closed over her lower belly. "I am not at all happy with your current mindset or accusations."

Placing her hand atop his, Claire held his angry gaze and asked, "Do you suppose you are some paragon worthy of this child? You fucked Svana—"

His anger was growing dangerous. "I was trying to keep you safe."

"Stop lying to yourself. Have you ever told her no, or do you do anything she wants just to please her? You enable her… and she thinks of herself as beyond reproach… because you worship her. I saw it myself! And for that perversion, she crafted you into what you are. A thing she owns: her unquestioning disciple."

The villain roared right in her face. "Svana loves me!"

Claire was on some sort of high, past caring for the consequences of her words. "The same way you claim you love me… the kind of *love* that justifies infidelity and cruelty."

The pain did not register, not at first, and considering the size of the Alpha it could have been a thousand times worse. The grip he had on her arm, the way he bent it back to remove it from his body, Claire ignored, reaching for his shoulder again, wanting him to hurt her.

The room moved, and a great crushing weight made it difficult to draw breath. His grip on her forearms left her hands almost purple, but green eyes held silver as she fought for the short stuttering breaths his mass would allow.

Whatever possessed him was cold in its rage, calculating in speech. "You will never speak of such things again."

There was not enough breath to answer fully so she nodded her head and hissed the words, "It's the truth."

Shifting enough so she might breathe, Shepherd snarled, "You will be punished. Corday will die."

There was no anger or fear in her expression, simply unfathomable disappointment. "Look at me. Look at what you are doing."

Shepherd stared down at the woman he was hurting. When she brought her other hand up to cup his face, ignoring the black marks already blooming on her skin, he did not stop her, but neither did he enjoy her touch.

"I am only trying to help you see, to understand the point you are missing," Claire whispered, seeing that she had shaken him badly, hurt him.

He was unmoved. "You hate me."

*Success in warfare is gained by carefully accommodating ourselves to the enemy's purpose. - Sun Tzu*

"I am trying to be your mate. A woman you only took because Svana was unfaithful and you were in pain."

The furious ache in her other arm abated, Shepherd lessened his grip. "I took you because you were meant to be mine. I could smell it on you."

The warmth of her small hand slipped to his neck, to the ridge of muscles he once claimed hurt him, and she rubbed. "Had she remained faithful, would you have saved me from the mob?"

"What do you think you are doing?" Shepherd's nostrils flared, and though he was furious, his cock lay hard as a rock against her thigh.

Claire stopped her touch. "I was only trying to soothe you as you do for me when I'm upset. When your emotions are calm, you will see that I am right."

Growling, he jammed himself inside her in one sharp thrust. Claire grimaced, and braced herself. Shepherd, heavy inside her, cupped her face, snarling as he touched his forehead to hers. "This is how you may soothe me."

He jerked and rocked her again, making her breath catch as she brought her aching arms up to embrace the raging Alpha. Overly rough, he snapped his hips, pounding away, practically howling when her slick eased his passage. "And you will scream my name every time I make you come!"

# 12

Her entire body ached, even with warm water pouring over the fresh bruises. Overly attentive, Shepherd washed away the dried semen that made her sticky, which matted her hair, holding her to him as he bathed his mate.

They had both slept, tangled and sweaty from hours of fucking like animals. Even as she was now, her eyes were half-dilated as if still in a mating high, which was probably the only thing keeping the Omega from hissing at the touch of his hands on tender skin his zealous possession had rubbed raw.

Shepherd took her chin, drawing her sleepy eyes to his face. "I will not harm Corday."

Flatly, Claire answered, "I knew you wouldn't."

The giant hesitated, the creases by his eyes betraying a smirk. "Did you?"

"If you hurt him, I would punish you as severely as I could."

Shepherd's amusement faded. "You would kill yourself."

"Yes."

Each word was perfectly enunciated and lacked the bitterness the man felt sour his stomach. "His value to you is higher than the rest of your forty-three."

Claire licked her wet lips and thought about how best to answer, or if she should even answer at all. "I owe him."

Shepherd felt the rush of blood behind his eyes, fought to be gentle as he rinsed her hair. "It is more than that. I saw you together. You bear fondness for the Beta."

Inspiring any type of excessive hatred in Shepherd for Corday could be dangerous to her friend, and would serve no purpose except to pointlessly agitate the Alpha. "I do not love Corday, not in the way you imagine. But I owe him, as I said. I have lied to him, and drugged him. I deceived him…"

"To keep him safe," Shepherd purred, finishing her statement, somewhat mollified at the truth of her words and their echo in the bond. "Does that not sound familiar?"

"No." Her answer was harsh.

"Do not lie to me, little one. His situation mirrors yours."

"I said no because I meant no," Claire argued, grimacing at the stiffness in her hips when he began to rub. "You didn't drug me to keep me safe. You drugged me to create a baby."

He took her chin and turned her face up to force her full attention. "And that baby justifies your value to my men. It is keeping you alive."

Scowling, feeling cold even in the heat and steam of the shower, apprehension crept over Claire. "What do you mean?"

Seeing his words had unsettled her, Shepherd spoke in a hard tone. "If you are not careful, if you do not begin to nest again and ensure that our offspring grows, should you miscarry… I would have to replace it immediately."

A look of horror twisted her face. "I don't understand."

"You don't need to. You simply need to be a mother." Shifting his mass, he pressed her back to the tiles. "You are mine, and I will do anything to ensure your continued survival. I would kill millions, I would lie to you, and I would rape you if I had to and fill you with child again should you lose this one."

How had she felt even a moment of power over this man? "You're scaring me."

"Good." He turned off the water and pulled her out. "It seems to be the only way to get through to you."

"What about your legacy?"

He smiled, a nasty thing, and pawed her belly. "It will be unparalleled."

Wilting, Claire muttered, "I have no urge to nest. Not in that bed. Not anymore."

As if the idea had not occurred to the Alpha, he narrowed his eyes and seemed to consider. "You wish for a new bed?"

"I do not wish for anything," Claire sighed, feeling again as if she was talking to a wall.

Shepherd continued, speaking to himself. "If I procured this new bed, you would nest."

Desperately uneasy, she growled. "You are not listening to me, Shepherd."

"And you would desire new materials, in that color you like…" He was running a towel over her skin as if insensible to her bruised skin.

She snarled and batted his hands away. "You're hurting me, you deaf jackass."

Snapped out of his tirade, he froze and looked at the small thing that had just barked at him. Snorting a caustic laugh, he grunted, "You have grown far more outspoken with pregnancy."

"I have grown far more outspoken because I no longer care if you kill me! I don't want a new bed. I want you to explain what the fuck you are talking about!"

Shepherd took her arm and gently turned her so that he might pat her hair dry. “You are only being difficult… you need a new bed.”

“Okay, fine! Since you don’t listen to a goddamn thing I say anyway, here goes. I want a new bed in a big room with carpet instead of concrete. A room with a wall of windows that overlook a garden I planted full of flowers—which would be a miracle, as every houseplant I ever had died. I want to move without restriction through this grand house I will be nesting in, and be free to go outside and sit on grass… And I want a pony too, Shepherd. No, forget that. I want a fucking unicorn.”

Pulling her hair so that she had to look back at him, he scowled. “You may not have a pony, and unicorns don’t exist.”

She really didn’t mean to, was so in knots inside she could not even begin to fathom where it came from, but just for a second, she giggled. Slapping a hand over her mouth, still stuck with her head leaning back at an unnatural angle, she forced her face into neutrality and continued to make her point. “What color is it that you are so certain I like?”

“You prefer green, the same shade as your eyes.”

Was that why almost every single dress he’d provided was green? “What gave you that idea?”

He looked as if such a miscalculation was not possible. “That is not the color you favor?”

“Sure, it’s a pretty color… but it’s not my favorite color.” Understanding, Claire narrowed her eyes and leveled a disapproving gaze at the man. “Let me guess, you got this information from your interrogations of the Omegas.”

“Red, like your picture?” he tried again, letting go of her hair so she might turn and he could see her fully.

“No. Why didn’t you just ask me if you wanted to know something so mundane?” But then it dawned on her. He wanted to provide things she was supposed to like without prompting… as a tactic of sorts because that was the only way he knew how to be.

Shepherd grew aggravated, standing naked and demanding rudely, "What is your favorite color?"

"Bird's egg blue." Mocking him, Claire cocked her head to the side and batted her lashes. "And, Shepherd, since we are being so congenial, what is yours?"

"Expressly, the exact color of your eyes." He wasn't flirting, he was annoyed, but even so the words were… something. They made her blush and he noticed it, his intense gaze losing its edge and gaining that unnerving calculation instead. "I also find the rich black of your hair to be incredibly fetching."

She was positively scarlet and clearly wanted him to look away. It had been months since she had tried to cover her nakedness and she did not know what led her to do it, but her arm came up to hide her flushed breasts.

Shepherd looked only amused, or fascinated might have been a better description. "And now you are shy…" he cooed, evilly. "This is nothing I have not said before."

But she had purposefully never listened… she had ignored it and hated the sound of his distorted raspy voice.

"You know I find you to be very beautiful," the monster continued, proudly prowling, trapping her against the sink. "You are, in fact, the most comely female I have ever seen."

Claire was sorely tempted to snap something nasty at him, to bring up Svana, or the Omegas, or anything to get him to stop looking at her that way. Instead she just stammered, "I… am cold."

"Well then, by all means, pretty little one"—Shepherd's thick arms encircled her—"let me warm you."

A stifled noise sputtered passed her lips as bulging muscle pulled her flush.

His lips came to her ear and the man growled in the most licentious voice she had ever heard, "And you have the most beautiful pussy I have ever known. It is *perfection*. Anytime you should ask, I would lick it, taste you until you screamed my name like you did four times last night."

"STOP!"

Stroking his touch up her body until Claire's jaw rested in his hand, he pulled the Omega from where she tried to hide her face against his chest. Their eyes mere inches apart, his hand delved between her legs to lightly swipe the gathering slick at her folds. Pulling slippery fingers away, he made a satisfied male noise and left her standing, panting, flushed, and aroused, while muttering, "Bird's egg blue," as he left.

THOSE MOMENTS… when one has a black bag over their head, when a body is being jostled, and you know, you just fucking know, your number is up… those moments just plain suck.

Feeling hands shove her back until her rear end made an uncomfortable connection with a hard chair, Maryanne prepared for her greatest performance. Or she did until the bag came off in a swoop and she was face to face again… with Shepherd.

The words caught in her throat, the typical sensual quality she knew how to use to manipulate failed, and all Maryanne could do was stare.

That man had decimated Thólos… ruined her city. That man stank of Claire's cooch. Ewww…

"Well," Maryanne let out a breath, "turns out I was right about just where Claire disappeared to. Guess that means I'm off limits, huh?"

The looming male leaned closer. "Shall we discuss the nuances of the agreement between my mate and myself? I only offered to spare your life. There was no mention of what I would do with said life. Technically, I could break every bone in your body, subject you to torture, take what little freedom you have left. So long as you continue breathing I will have fulfilled my end of the bargain." Shepherd's finger lightly tapped the table between them. "And Claire would never know…"

But he wanted something, otherwise she would not be there. He wanted something for Claire.

The terror was there, the slow rising panic that tainted her sweat and signaled to the much stronger Alpha that she was afraid. "You have a use for me."

"You will be coming back into my employ."

"What do you need me to steal?"

His mouth did not move in the slightest, but Maryanne was certain his expression displayed just how stupid he thought she was. "Your duty will be to bring information about the circumstances of the Omegas and the Beta, Enforcer Corday, to Claire. In these conversations, I advise that you make her happy, or you will be very unhappy when they conclude."

The thought of seeing Claire chased away a fraction of the dread. "Sure thing. I know exactly how to make her smile."

"You will not share detailed information, just the general well-being of the individuals I send you to photograph. You will not interact with these people or be seen. All images will be checked before Claire views them, and should I find anything unsettling, it would not bode well for you. You will speak of absolutely no one else."

Nodding, Maryanne signaled that she understood.

The last warning held the threat of great pain should she fail him. "And if she tries to pass you a note or does anything subversive, you will tell me privately. She will not be punished."

Claire might try, Maryanne knew it in her bones, and she

already hated knowing full well she would hand anything over to Shepherd rather than face the consequences of being the go between in correspondences with Claire's little boyfriend. "She doesn't trust me."

"Let's not play games, Ms. Cauley."

"When do I begin?"

IT TOOK a few hours and another breakfast of the horrible green smoothie before her stomach settled from Shepherd's odd adoring behavior in the shower. He was gone again, a thing Claire was supremely grateful for so she could stretch and pace and formulate her next move.

Looking at the nasty bruising on her arm, Claire flexed the limb, certain it would ache for quite some time. *It was worth it.* Shepherd may have cornered her that morning, made her uncomfortable and bashful, but she'd had him with his back against the wall the night before, just long enough to expose that she had been correct. Pieces of it were coming together, Shepherd's mental need to keep her all to himself, using her to ease the grief Svana caused whether he recognized that fact or not, confirmed.

That was something; it was a place to start.

Shepherd's initial reaction had been violent, even the sex, but when they woke, he was only indulgent. It was as if the rage from the previous night, the force that had compelled him to fuck her so roughly and so long she'd become boneless, was just gone.

The man had exorcised a demon.

Even at his most dangerous, he had never looked from her face, kept much of his skin pressed to hers, ordered her to call out his name, his burning eyes almost rolling back in his skull each time she did. He communicated to her with his driving need, with the force in which he urged her climax. His fiery expressions used to frighten her, the set of his jaw, the glares… now she was beginning to understand. It was longing.

Shepherd was always watching her reaction, looking for something, some small hint as he coaxed out her sordid urges. He had some need that had been neglected. When coupled, she was tender and would stroke him, draw in his scent and smile. Perhaps that was why he mated her so often. He had a base craving for such affection. Shepherd wanted her to love him and was confused as to how to foster such a thing when she did not automatically fall into what he assumed was proper Omega behavior.

Claire did not love him, but she had offered him comfort when his side of the cord displayed the turmoil her words had stirred up. That had been instinctive, and even though she despised Shepherd, it was the right thing to do in the war she was waging. Progress would require her to serve her position as mate if she was to stand even a chance of edifying him, and petty tactics such as seduction or dishonesty would never serve her.

Claire was not foolish enough to believe she could fix him. After all, Shepherd's thinking was warped far beyond anything she could untwist. But she could chip away at the wrongness; she could expose weakness in a man who seemed to have none.

Claire was going to bare him to himself piece by piece if it killed her.

It probably would.

The door opened and the dead-eyed, dangerous Beta entered. He ran a quick appraisal over her and then went to switch the trays. "Your arm," Jules grunted, "do you require pain relief?"

The absolute disinterest in the man's expression made the question completely strange. Edging nearer, circling around to face the male, Claire tucked her hair behind her ear. "That would bely the effects of the punishment."

Aware of what the Omega had done to earn such bruises, Jules mocked, "You believe that to be a punishment? I thought you were supposed to be clever."

Cocking her head, Claire felt something odd in their exchange but could not put her finger on it. "You find Shepherd's actions intriguing?"

"He was gentle with you."

Looking down at her arm, at the black marring blotches, she frowned. "And here I thought *you* were supposed to be clever, Jules."

The male was not interested in further communication and gave her his back.

Slipping the straps of her dress off her arms, she asked in a voice devoid of feeling, "Does this look gentle to you?"

Glancing over his shoulder at the woman decorated in the bruises of rough sex, Jules turned quickly to the wall and barked, "Put your dress back on!"

"This is what confuses me about the lot of you." Claire continued, unmoved by his *morality*. "You won't look because you find my nudity inappropriate, yet you created a city full of rape that you do not even blink an eye at. You are all walking contradictions."

"You are my leader's mate. PUT ON YOUR DRESS."

It was strange to see the man who always appeared unaffected grow agitated. Smirking, Claire pulled the fabric over tender skin. "I think we both made our point."

Once certain she was decent, the man leveled her with a glare that almost held the same power as Shepherd's. "You are playing a very dangerous game."

Standing her ground, Claire said, "Not everyone is playing a game. I am simply trying to communicate, and I do not speak your language."

"You speak it better than you know."

Was that actual praise? "Then speak to me. How old were your sons when you lost them?"

The man was not thrown by her sudden shift in the conversation. "Bertrand was four; Joseph just under a year."

Claire smoothed her skirt, felt sadness. "Why were they killed?"

"My wife was Omega." The sharpness of his gaze was frightening. "An Alpha wanted her. Before I even learned of what had happened, she had been pair-bonded to a friend of Premier Callas'. The same Alpha who'd murdered our boys."

"What was her name?"

"Rebecca."

Somehow she just knew, Claire whispering, "And you killed her when Shepherd led you from the Undercroft."

"Yes, almost a decade ago—at her request."

Claire understood. Even after the man had found her and taken her back, his Rebecca would have been gutted by the power of a pair-bond she must have hated more than Claire hated her own. Her lip began to tremble. "I am very sorry for what happened to your family, but I don't understand how it led you here to do what you are doing now."

"Every member of this army is here for the same reason I am."

It felt like Shepherd had told her a thousand times. "Revenge."

"Call it cultural enlightenment."

Her green eyes, wide and eager, sat in a face bearing an urgent expression. "How do you not see the flaws in your own argument? Do you want the human race to end?"

"How do you continue to deny yourself the truth? I overheard your conversation with Enforcer Corday. You admitted freely that Thólos has done this to itself." Jules approached her, unblinking. "Even before the breach, this very degradation infected all life under the Dome… Do not waste our time by pretending that you did not live a lie just to feel safe."

It wasn't that simple. "Shepherd took me. I had a life before. I had a career. I could have had a future if I'd met the right Alpha."

"Shepherd choosing you as a mate was the best possible outcome for you, though you are incapable of accepting that fact in your ignorance and resentment."

Before she could offer a cutting retort, Jules opened the door and left.

Glaring at the door as if the man were still standing before it, Claire clenched her jaw so hard it hurt. In a few moments and a few carefully selected phrases, the Beta had shared more than Shepherd had in the first five weeks she had known him. Jules was a villain, of that she was certain, but a part of Claire could understand his rage.

Rage, it seemed, was all she was made of most days.

These men were not simply the psychopaths Claire had assumed. They were all on a mission. Jules claimed every member of Shepherd's army carried the burden of a painful past. If that was what it took to distort the psyche, to perpetuate evil in an attempt to do good, how far behind could she be?

Picking at her food, focusing again on the painting of Shepherd that served as companion during meals, Claire did not register the opening of the door.

The giant was pleased to find her admiring his portrait again, rounding the table to brush back her hair.

"I have brought you medicine to dull any pain," Shepherd explained once he had her attention. "Open your mouth."

Between her parted lips, two tablets were placed on her tongue, Claire sitting stupidly as Shepherd held her glass, pouring carefully so she could swallow. She obeyed, and his large thumb wiped away a small drip of milk.

Soaking in her surprised expression, he asked, "Have you been ill today?"

"No. Whatever is in that disgusting green drink seems to settle my stomach."

"But you are in pain and I was notified that you required relief," the male grunted, his concern obvious. "You also look tired."

"I didn't ask him for medicine and you already knew I was sore. You are physically demanding and my body is not always up to the challenge." Claire *was* tired. Very tired. "Besides, wasn't that the point of your punishment?"

Crouching to be nearer her eye level, Shepherd burrowed his hands in her hair and cradled her skull. "There was no punishment." The male began to work his fingers over her scalp. "These bruises… You should know that I was incredibly restrained. Antagonizing your mate to such a point is dangerous, as you are fragile, little one, and I am very strong. Yet in the anger you purposefully fostered, I fought myself. I did not strike you. I could have easily damaged you beyond repair."

The purr was so loud and his fingers felt incredibly comforting tugging her hair… even if his words were disturbing. "It was worth it," she muttered.

The man was oozing patience, still in that seeming calm he'd woken with. "Explain such a statement."

This version of Shepherd was never quite what it seemed. Cautiously, Claire answered, "It is the only way I know of to communicate with you."

He seemed intrigued, eyes shining as Shepherd dissected her stratagem. "You long for more conversation?"

*If you know the enemy and know yourself, you need not fear the result of a hundred battles. If you know yourself but not the enemy, for every victory gained you will also suffer a defeat. If you know neither the enemy nor yourself, you will succumb in every battle. - Sun Tzu*

Claire needed to know Shepherd. She could no longer afford to ignore him as she had done before. She needed to know his Followers. More so, she needed to make sure she knew herself, and did not lose sight of what she was should he hurt her again.

Thinking over how best to answer, she sighed. "It would be normal to feel that I could trust you to simply sit down and talk with me. But you seem incapable of the restraint of listening to what you might not like—and feeling unheard makes me frustrated and unhappy."

"Do you not place some of the blame on yourself, little one? Your effort to ignore my presence is apparent."

"Why would I pay any attention to a man who doesn't listen to me or respect how I feel?"

"Because I am older and wiser. I know what is best."

Claire snorted, a small twitch in her lip. "What you are is a fanatic and a despot. And I don't really think you know me at all, *Mr. green is your favorite color*."

He made no answer. Instead, Shepherd reached forward and the arms he slid around her felt… reassuring. Yawning, wanting to lie down, Claire did not fuss when he carried her to bed.

The Alpha sat on the edge of the mattress, played with her hair, and commanded she close her eyes. "You will sleep now. If I find you in an acceptable state when I return, we will converse."

WHEN SHE WOKE in the dim room, it was the best Claire had felt in some weeks. It wasn't just the nap or the painkillers, it was a small sense of purpose, a deeper feeling that her progress was positive. Good feelings were dangerous and easy to lose in her prison, so she carefully cherished it alone in the dark before putting it away—burying it deep so Shepherd could not take it from her.

The male had claimed he would talk to her. Tthat gave her an arena she could prepare.

It had been fruitful to start a dialogue with him over her painting the day prior, so she would begin simply and try what she knew. Claire mixed up her paints and began detailing the image she had seen through the security feed before she broke the Omegas out of prison. She painted little sixteen-year-old Shanice being rutted by one of Shepherd's Followers.

Everything was as she remembered: nothing embellished, nothing altered.

Shepherd ripped it out from under her brush the second he returned and saw it. Balling it up, his eyes flared in fury, as he breathed so deep it stretched his chest like a dragon about to spit flames.

Claire did not react; she just let out a sigh and set her brush aside.

Speaking inoffensively about a very offensive subject, Claire began. "Her name is Shanice. She is sixteen years old. That was her first heat and I can guarantee that she was not willing. She's cried herself to sleep each night since estrous ended."

"Had my officer been able to pair-bond, she would have been as content as all the others!" Shepherd leaned his weight on the table, aggressively irritated to find what was not the ideal he expected to return to. "You are the only one unsettled."

Claire put her hand over his, not to comfort, but to make it clear she understood the consequences. "That man could not be a day younger than forty-five. That girl is still in school."

"I am much older than you," Shepherd countered hotly.

"Maybe by a decade, perhaps a little more. Not old enough to be my father. I am also a fully grown woman, Shepherd. I am not a child."

Flexing the fist under her small hand, Shepherd growled, "I am aware of what you are doing."

"I am trying to communicate with you about things I don't understand," Claire countered. Small fingers squeezed his hand again, and she let her feelings show on her face. "Considering your mother… explain to me where the line blurs and this becomes acceptable?"

Shepherd took the seat across from her, agitated but growing forcedly composed. "Arranged Alpha-Omega pairings are common throughout history, and are statistically successful."

"If the baby I am carrying were an Omega, would you want that for your child?"

"Under these circumstances, yes. The bonded Omegas are sheltered and protected by worthy Alphas. All are fed; they are safe… they are not mistreated. You are the one who would expose them to Thólos in your foolish misunderstanding of freedom." Twisting his hand, Shepherd captured her fingers, toyed with them, even though his words were harsh. "You never had it, Claire. You were never once free in this city… You have never once been free a day in your life."

She truly hated the sound of him speaking her name, knew that the unpleasant feelings it stirred up showed on her face, and felt her fortification slipping. Furthermore, she hated how Shepherd was holding her hand as if they were lovers, as if he had a right to—even if she had initiated contact. "*You* mistreated *me*. And I do not know what I hate more: your assumptions, or the fact that you just spoke my name simply because you know I dislike it."

A large thumb circled the flat of her palm. "Which makes this discourse the perfect time to begin adjusting you to the sound of it on my lips, little one."

Holding his gaze, forcing herself not to snatch back her hand, Claire admitted, "So we both have an agenda."

Pulling her arm nearer, Shepherd purred, "We will not have a repeat of yesterday's argument."

"That topic was already addressed. I know my feelings, I know what was done, and I know why… even if you will not admit it. It is up to you whether or not you face what is fact." After a breath, Claire looked up from where their hands were joined and tried a different approach. "Are the mated Omegas really settled?"

The word was hard and judgmental. "Yes."

She stared blankly. "You must wish you had chosen with less impulsiveness."

"I have never once questioned claiming you." Almost musically he explained his truth, "And in answer to your question yesterday; yes, I would have still fought the mob and claimed you had Svana not diverted. You were born to be mine."

Sarcastic, Claire cocked a brow and grumbled at the obtuse fool. "And were you always meant to be mine?"

He took her jaw and leaned forward. "Yes."

"Then I must admit I see the irony that, like my father, I received a mate who really wishes to be with someone else. That certainly is cruel of the Gods."

Shepherd did not hesitate to counter, "I only want you, Claire."

She let out a breath. "The first time I saw you at the Citadel, the first time I smelled you, I did not see you as my mate. All I felt was fear. It was very hard to stand my ground and not run."

Running his thumb over her frowning lips, Shepherd forced a question that tightened his mouth and squared his shoulders. "Because of my Da'rin Markings?"

Claire shook her head, her brows drawing together. "No. Because of what you'd done, where you were, how big you are… the violence. My father was a very nice man—funny and kind. That is the epitome of Alpha to me. That is a suiting mate. You are none of those things. Since you forced the bond, I feel controlled, manipulated, you have caused me grief, I cannot trust you, and you only treat me nicely to get your way."

"I will take responsibility for the grief, but as for the rest, much of it is your own fault. You have made little effort to be a contented mate. Your resistance and continued subversion requires a firm hand to ensure your safety. I would be cruel to you to keep you safe, and I freely manipulate you as there is no other recourse to draw you nearer. Had you settled as the other Omegas had settled, your life would be happy. *And I am careful of your wellbeing.* I bring you things you never thank me for. I offer you the best foods. I stroke and purr and please you physically for hours."

Claire had intended the conversation to highlight her concerns with Thólos, not nitpick at the major issues as to why, aside from his many transgressions, their pair-bond was madness. Gritting her teeth at his list of ridiculous accusations, she took a deep breath and tried to control her temper. "When you were in the Undercroft, did you thank your jailors for what they brought you?"

Shepherd's eyes went fractionally wider, the man incredibly insulted. "Thank me for the paints."

Claire snarled, "Thank me for all the hours I have spent cleaning this room."

"Little one." The shift in him was unsettling. The male purred and squeezed her hand gently. "Your domestic behavior in our shared den is nothing but pleasing to me. Thank you."

Scowling, Claire lost ground. "I am concerned that if I thank you for the paints, you will know how much I like them and take them away."

"I will not take your paints. I understand that you need them and that there is little outlet for you when I am not here."

She did not believe him, but it didn't matter. Her lower lip trembled. Feeling her eyes grow damp she whispered, "Thank you for the paints."

"Do you wish to continue talking, or would you prefer to go see the sky now?"

She had made no ground in her agenda, had wasted the opportunity and learned little. The whole fucking conversation had been imperceptibly moved to the tension between them by a man far more gifted in discourse. That was not her goal; that was not her purpose.

Taking a mental step back, needing to reformulate, Claire nodded, disengaged from the ordeal. "The sky."

# 13

Entering the room with her window, Claire was wary the second her feet touched the floor. The setup had changed; a small table held two trays of food… as if Shepherd were going to eat with her—which would not only be odd, but a domestic act she was in no mood to engage in with him.

Like an iron bar around her waist, Shepherd's arm held her flush to his body, the uncomfortable handcuff still in place. They were not moving deeper into the room, just standing awkwardly as he leaned down to possessively sniff her.

"I would have preferred to mate you before this, yet forewent the experience because you desired to converse. I am also going to allow you a short time without the handcuffs," Shepherd said, unlocking the metal at her wrist while still maintaining a stiff hold on her body. "Should you disappoint my trust, this coming moment will not happen again. It would be in your best interest to behave."

Before Claire could reply, the numerous locks on the door began to hiss and her body was shifted so there was no view but that of

Shepherd's chest. The door was opened and closed, and only then did Shepherd turn them so that she might see.

Instantly panicked, Claire eyeballed the stunning blonde and rushed to throw her body between Maryanne and Shepherd. "What the fuck is she doing here? You promised me!"

"Claire, calm down before you give yourself an aneurism," Maryanne teased, throwing an arm around her shoulders. "I was invited for dinner."

Bull-Fucking-Shit. There was a catch, there was always a catch, and cold dread settled over the Omega. Her attention darted towards the folding table, back to her massive mate, then over her shoulder towards Maryanne.

Claire was scared.

The Alpha female herded her forward, smiling and bouncing her eyebrows as if possessing no care in the world. "It was impossible to say no once he told me steak was on the menu… Don't think for a moment that I came to see you."

Claire's nervous laugh did not sound the least bit reassured. The women sat, Shepherd moved towards a third chair in the corner to watch like a warden observing a convict's last meal.

Enthusiastic, Maryanne dug into the food, made pointless inane chatter, smiling as Claire worked through the knot in her stomach and prayed the food would stay down. With the passing of half an hour, the tense situation calmed. Shepherd's soft purr from the corner, and the approving look in his eye every time Claire looked over at him, helped to settle her.

Just having Maryanne near was extraordinary, and for a moment, Claire felt… comfortable.

"Maryanne," swallowing the last bite of steak, Claire looked at her pretty friend and teased, "I think you may be the only woman in Thólos who's still wearing lipstick."

Full red lips curved up in a decedent smirk, Maryanne was

proud as a peacock. “I have standards.” The woman eyeballed Claire’s hair, frowning. “And you have been slack in yours. You need a haircut.”

“As you must have noticed from the pre-cut steak, I’m not allowed access to sharp objects. I am also pretty certain salon services are not part of Shepherd’s philosophy.”

Maryanne cocked a snarky eyebrow and purred, “But gourmet food is?”

Claire looked down at their finished plates, frowning.

Maryanne ran a pet down Claire’s hair so she might show her the ragged ends. “You know, Claire, if it comes to girly things, you’re going to have to outright tell him if you need something. Your Alpha seems dense as a boulder in regards to women.”

Before she could stop it, the Omega burst into uproarious laughter. Hand pressed to her mouth, she imagined Shepherd’s expression behind her, and laughed even harder.

It took a minute before she could chide her cocky, smirking friend. “For fuck’s sake, Maryanne. He’s never going to let you come back now.”

“Oh.” Maryanne lounged back in her chair like a well-fed cat. “I think he will.”

While Claire composed herself, Maryanne began her duty. “I have visited your Omegas. They are blissfully unaware of your situation.”

And that was why Maryanne had come. Claire ran a hand through her hair, worried. “Do they think I killed myself?”

“Yes.”

“That’s good. They would fret if they thought I was still alive.”

“Only because they’d fear you might cause them trouble.”

“Maryanne…” Claire warned, “that is not fair.”

With an arrogant smirk, Maryanne waggled a finger. “Life ain’t fair, sugar pie.”

"Life is what we make it."

"Says the woman with scraggly hair and chapped lips. You clearly have not been making yours that great."

Irritated that Maryanne thought to scold, Claire leaned forward and snarled, "And what the fuck is your point?"

"That after one good look at you, I can see you've been playing the victim instead of trying *to live*." There was no more frisky tone in Maryanne's voice, no more playful looks. "Yeah your situation sucks; yeah it's not what you wanted. But it is what it is. And I know you… I can just see you stagnating instead of adapting, all stubborn to the point it hurts. He might not be Prince Charming, but it's safe here. He feeds you. You have it better than almost everyone else under the Dome."

Looking to be near the brink of ripping off her guest's head, Claire hissed, "Did he tell you to say that?"

"Do I look like I'd do anything he tells me to?"

"Of course you do." Narrowing her eyes, Claire mouthed, "You needed friends once… that's your *friend* sitting in the corner now."

For a second Maryanne looked stricken, and then grew coldly composed. "You don't know what it was like down there, Claire. Even you would have done *anything* to get out. And no, he didn't tell me to say that. It's my own opinion."

"Well, from your life decisions, it's clear your judgment isn't always the best."

"That look in your eye"—the blonde settled back, just as unhappy as her friend—"I know what it means. You know I'm right. And yeah, I've fucked up. I am what I am. But you still love me."

"I do, you cunt."

Sudden heavy warmth settled on Claire's nape. She tensed, unaware Shepherd had silently come up behind her. His thumb stroking her spine, he spoke, "That will be enough for today."

Claire stood to say goodbye, Shepherd maintaining his hold on her neck. "I'm sorry I snapped at you, Maryanne."

"You shouldn't be." Maryanne smiled softly. "You're allowed to be bitchy; you're pregnant. Before you know it, you'll also be fat."

And just like that, Claire was chuckling again, stepping out from under Shepherd's shadow to embrace her friend. Standing on tiptoe, Claire pecked Maryanne's lips, the close friends' customary goodbye.

And it had been a mistake.

Shepherd snarled, Claire darting back against him, begging, "Don't hurt her!"

"She's like my sister, Shepherd," Maryanne tried to pacify, failing to hide the fear in her voice. "Get your mind out of the gutter."

"You will not kiss her again." An arm came around Claire's waist, keeping her locked to his side as Shepherd shouted a stream of foreign words towards the door.

The bolts were thrown and the door opened so Ms. Cauley could be escorted out by a parade of armed Followers. Even as the door was closing, Shepherd pressed Claire to the wall. She heard his zipper, the impatience of Shepherd's growl as he lifted her skirt, and he was inside her in a quick thrust.

It was nothing but an animal claiming, both of them still dressed, but his grunts were loud, and Claire knew that Maryanne, anyone, in the halls could hear them. And that, of course, was his point. Shepherd was loudly broadcasting that she was his. She wanted to be shamed, but found her body glorying in it, her mind already slipping into the haze. It was a quick pairing, especially satisfying when he spun her about just before she came. Face to face, the knot formed, her legs around his waist, his strength supporting her fully when so much pleasure bloomed.

"You didn't say my name," he panted, eyes like molten iron.

She said it, just so he would shut up and let her enjoy the after-effects. "Shepherd."

There was a smear of red lipstick on Claire's mouth. Holding her still, Shepherd went to rub it off. His finger hesitated, changed course, and instead spread it around until her lips took on a rosy hue. "Was Ms. Cauley's assessment correct? Are cosmetics something that you require?"

The man had just knotted, was still spilling, and he was asking stupid questions. Looking at him as if he were nuts, Claire scowled. "Nobody requires cosmetics."

"I see no problem with the length of your hair, nor is it ragged," he grumbled next, stroking in the exact same place Maryanne had, as if erasing the other Alpha's touch.

Claire rolled her eyes to the heavens and leaned her head back to the wall.

His lips went to her cheek, her ear, her neck. "I have never heard you laugh in that manner."

There was nothing she could say that would not be inflammatory, but it was clear he expected some sort of answer. "She's funny. Always has been."

Shepherd understood that it was less Maryanne's comment, and more the fact that Claire absolutely agreed with her friend's assessment. Svana had never found him wanting when it came to understanding her or her needs. She was easy to please, loved the gifts he brought her, and always thanked him profusely. Claire was disinterested in almost everything he had provided, never glanced twice at new clothing, jewels tucked into her drawer, or fine things he put in the room. He knew she enjoyed the food, though her pride kept her from expressing it… and she found pleasure in her paints. Nothing else had ever drawn a reaction.

He had hated every moment of the women's conversation, save

Maryanne's wise reprimand to her friend. It was the only thing that might induce him to allow such a meeting again.

Stranger still, Claire had grown hostile, they had argued, and then it was over. No hard feelings on either side.

The Omega was growing limp, falling asleep in his arms. Still knotted, Shepherd carried her to the lounge chair and arranged them both while he waited for his member to soften. When her nose went to his neck and she began to draw in his scent, the Alpha encouraged her behavior, played with her hair, and listened to her strange musical hum—an Omega noise she had not made since… since Svana.

He had pleased his mate. She was even smiling against the flesh of his neck, Shepherd certain she was unaware he could enjoy such a sight by their reflection in the window. The purr deepened, her eyelashes fluttered, her fingers toying with the fabric of his shirt.

"I would provide female things if you asked for them," the man grumbled, oddly relaxed considering how annoyed he'd been only minutes earlier.

She took a deep breath, and pushed up to look him in the eye. After their conversation downstairs, she knew what was in order. "I don't know why you did it, and can only assume there was some ulterior, self-serving purpose, but at this moment I appreciate it. Thank you for arranging for me to spend time with Maryanne."

He could be so gentle, so different. Cupping her face, he looked at her with a soft expression. "My motive was simply to show you that I am keeping my end of the bargain and for you to enjoy yourself."

Shepherd was behaving properly, he was making concessions… and he wanted her to acknowledge it. Sucking her lower lip into her mouth, she allowed herself a moment to study him up close; raised up so that his softening member slipped out, they were eye to eye. Claire touched where his neck swirled with Da'rin parasites, the arch of his eyebrows, the various scars over his face, collected over decades of brawls.

This man was her enemy.

Shepherd sought to encourage her. “You’re curious…”

Having the male speak snapped her from her abstract regard. What had been a subject became a person, and Claire shrank back. “Senator Kantor told me your Da’rin marks symbolize the men you killed.”

“It is a common thing underground, to threaten potential adversaries.”

“He said they hurt…”

“In sunlight, yes.”

They were sitting in a pool of sunlight, and though he wore long sleeves, the marks on his neck were exposed. He seemed so calm, his eyes focused but soft, that Claire doubted. “But you don’t cover them.”

Shepherd smirked, tried to kiss her unresponsive lips. “I can bear the pain.”

Crooking a finger under his chin, eager to distract the man’s more amorous intentions, Claire urged him to stretch so she could see his neck in the light. Nail scraping over the branching marks, she explored, she counted lives. “How many?”

The male began to purr, stretching, luxuriating, when Claire traced over the patterns. “Many.”

Eyes sad, she confessed, “I have tried to tally them, over and over. I always lose count…”

He wanted her cuddly and content, not frightened and eager to quarrel. “This is tradition underground. You have traditions, too. Most men are in the Undercroft for a few years, maybe a decade if they are strong. I was born there. Before I gave prisoners purpose and will to survive, few lived long enough for Da’rin to spread as extensively as mine. My marks were hope to many that they, too, might endure."

For men who had been thrown into darkness in innocence, for men who had been cast down there for small infractions… for Maryanne… Claire could let herself understand. "The Dome is not what I thought it was, but it's not what you think it is, either."

Running his fingers through her hair, he teased, "You know so little, yet talk so big."

"Don't minimize my life." She ran a hand over her eyes. "An Alpha cannot imagine what it's like growing up Omega. Of course, dynamic is not confirmed until twelve or thirteen, but that fear, to know all your childhood prayers to be Beta went unanswered. To know you would never amount to more than an Alpha's prized possession. I had broken that circle. I'd taken such care."

The man slid his arms around her, as if they were sharing a tender moment. He even kissed her forehead. "Someday, you will thank me—surrounded by our children, happy in the life I've provided."

"You want my thanks? Well, there is something I want."

Wary, pinching down her spine vertebrae by vertebrae, he made the question a warning. "Yes?"

Hand to his chest, her warm breath at his neck, she sighed. "When I wandered Thólos, I saw Lilian and the other Omegas dangling outside the Citadel. Would you bury them properly if I asked you to?"

The tilt of his head let her know he was intrigued, that he was weighing the pros of performing such a thing for her. Turning her chin, Shepherd's eyes glittered, his strategy to get the upper hand developing. "I would be willing to grant your concession, if one was made for me in return."

Claire had been disillusioned by this man long ago. Of course he'd want something. "What do you want?"

His gaze grew liquid, like molten iron. "I think we both know what I want."

"I am not going to be tricked into something. Either be exact, or forget my request."

A soft chuckle and Shepherd said, "You have grown even clev-erer, my little Omega. Kiss me and I will give you what you want."

"You would have to offer something far greater to entice me to kiss you. Instead, I will offer," Claire pursed her lips and tried to consider, ignoring the way he was moving his warm hand in small circles against her lower back, encouraging negotiation. "I will offer…" She did not really have anything to offer. "I will sing for you."

"No."

"I will paint you whatever you wish."

"No."

She had failed so many; she could at least do one thing for the dead women. Moving her hand to hover over his exposed dick, she faked resolve but her unsteady voice betrayed her. "I will initiate sex at a time of your choosing."

Shepherd looked down between them where her hand was so close, but not near enough. Enticed, he purred, eyes ready to devour her. "That is a far more interesting offer. I choose all three."

Fine, then that was what he would get. "I want proof it was done."

The Alpha grinned, thoroughly smug. "Sing something now, in good faith."

She could do this. "What song would you like to hear?"

Moving her hair behind her ears, Shepherd ensured his view would be unobstructed. "The song you first sang, but no crying this time. You must also look me in the eye as you sing to me."

The ballad began and she sang it the whole way through, Shepherd caressing, purring, seemingly well-satisfied with the arrangement. Claire did not cry, far too eager to have her way.

When she had finished, he was tame… looking at her as he'd looked at Svana. "It could be like this all the time, little one."

She put a hand to his cheek and said softly with a heart hard as stone, "No, Shepherd, it couldn't."

"You will see…" Placid, Shepherd drew her back down to rest. "I will show you."

Everything was soft and warm and fluffy. Claire had no interest in shifting, even for the smell of coffee and the warm hand reaching into her burrow. Shepherd hooked her around the waist and pulled until her messy hair cleared the blue duvet and a bleary-eyed Omega emerged.

The new bed had arrived during her dinner with Maryanne—everything in her favorite shade of blue, everything fresh. Even with the effort the Alpha had made, Claire had not felt an urge to nest for many days. But he kept putting her back in it, taking her from whatever she was doing and burying them both under the covers, caressing her belly to encourage his Omega's thoughts of the baby, until at last it just clicked and she subconsciously began to sniff at him, began to press nearer.

Rubbing sleep from her eyes, Claire sulked, unhappy Shepherd had woken her. A wise man, he gave her a cappuccino and waited for her new morning ritual, his little one peeking, trying to hide her interest in discovering what picture lay in the foam that day before she sipped and the art was spoiled.

In her cup bloomed an intricate poppy. Claire begrudgingly loved it. "Does the person who makes these have any idea who they're for?"

Shepherd answered with a question. “You ask because of the flower shape?”

“You have to admit, it’s a little ridiculous they would give *you* a drink with flowers in it.”

“It is a courtship ritual of Dome culture for the male to offer flowers to the female. I ordered it to be prepared this way.”

Internally cringing, Claire sipped the drink and hated that she blushed at his attempted romantic gesture, that he was going to mistake her embarrassment for coyness, that he was already looking at her with an arrogant glow in his eyes.

There was more. “Our agreement has been fulfilled.”

Claire set the cup and saucer on the bedside table, bracing herself. “And the proof?”

Shepherd brought forth his COMscreen. “May only upset you, so I am asking you to trust me and not look at the photographs.”

There was no chance in hell Claire would trust such a man. “It could not be any worse than other things I have seen in this city.”

She took the COMscreen, snatching it from his hands. The first image had been taken from a distance, all three bodies shown dangling, but not near enough to be graphic. The second was from the same vantage, Shepherd’s Followers taking them down. Claire was tempted to stop there, to accept that as good enough, but to do so would be to show weakness in the face of her adversary. Her finger slid across the screen. Bodies side by side in an open grave, rotted faces on display, only pits remaining where eyes had once been. Each corpse was still gagged, shrunken lips exposing teeth, hanging ropes embedded in their necks.

Claire could not look away.

Shepherd gently pried the COMscreen from her hands. “Are you satisfied?”

What she *was* was incredibly ill. Nodding, her mouth grew sour,

Claire sank deeper into her bed in hopes he'd leave so she could run to the bathroom and puke.

Shepherd knew her every tick, knew she was unwell. Claire could either walk to the bathroom and be sick with dignity, or he was going to get involved, his scowl said as much.

Slipping out of bed, she moved past him, closing the door for privacy, and threw up everything she'd just swallowed, pretty certain it would be some time before she enjoyed a cappuccino again.

He left her in peace, waited for her to wash her face and brush her teeth, and when she came back, Claire began to dress as if nothing had happened.

Brushing her tangled hair, she turned to the man still sitting at the end of the bed. "What would you like me to paint for you?"

He took a contemplative breath, voice almost jovial when he spoke. "A portrait of yourself, little one. One I will appreciate."

With the brush mid-way through a tangle, Claire mused, unsure if Shepherd comprehended how difficult self-portraits would be. "That's out of my scope. It might not be any good."

He flicked his fingers, beckoning her closer. Apprehensive that she would be expected to perform the other requirement of their agreement at that very moment, Claire stiffened, but went to him.

Taking the brush from her hands, he set it aside and pulled her to rest on his knee. "I want you to sing for me now."

"I already sang for you."

The man smirked, sly as he spoke, "Our agreement did not stipulate a number of times. You simply said you would sing for me, and I desire you to do so again."

Claire suspected it was far more for her benefit than his, a distraction that would shift her thinking in a more settling direction. "If you set this precedent and begin bending the rules, it's only going to backfire eventually."

He touched a finger to her nose. Shepherd squinted, and the man cooed, "Please."

She sang the first thing that came to mind, a relic anthem about war… a song that was poignant, sad, and far too expressive of the plight of Thólos.

"Do you still feel ill?" Shepherd asked, aware of her little musical mutiny as he gently touched her belly.

Claire did not usually feel well upon waking, especially after being dragged out of bed to see pictures of victims Shepherd had murdered, and she told him so.

"The punishment meted out to those women was earned." The man was unmoved by her declaration. "If your death would have brought them gain, they would not have hesitated to kill you. You were kind enough to see them buried. Do not mourn them further."

"Do you not wish to be mourned when you die?" Claire asked, non-threatening, only interested in his answer.

Stroking over the baby, the tiny thing that had yet to distort her figure, Shepherd asked, "Would you not mourn me, little one? Or would you relish the death of your mate?"

Claire was not inhuman. She had natural feelings and felt a discord in the link, the sudden uneasy throb in her chest that seemed saddened by the mere thought of the bearer of the bond's death. Deeper still, she suspected his death would not equate to her freedom—too much had been done. She would languish as she had when the bond had been damaged. She would die. Unsure how to answer his question, she rubbed her hand over her face and refused to respond.

"The thought upsets you." Again it was the gentle, manipulative voice and the soft touches of a man she knew pretended to be something he was not. "You need not fear. You would always be cared for."

Sometimes it seemed as if Shepherd could read her very

thoughts. Other times it seemed he was so far off base it was as if they lived on separate planets.

Claire had to get off his lap, she needed to think. Shepherd allowed it.

Smoothing back her hair, she thought to press on another subject. "I cannot make myself understand. What is it you want from Thólos? You are king with a list of ambitions, but you let your lands decay. You rule everything under the Dome, but hate your subjects."

Shepherd put his elbows on his knees, spoke with acumen as the Omega paced. "My number of loyal Followers have swelled beyond even what I imagined. Hardship distills the soul."

The things she had seen in the streets of Thólos, the depravity—it made the truth of his words sting. "Those who joined since the breach are traitors who chose your doctrine out of a misguided sense of survival."

"True, but the majority of the terrorism in Thólos was perpetrated by its own citizens. I did not get involved."

Swallowing, Claire wrung her hands, looking for something she could use. "I know. I asked for help… remember? You didn't help me."

The shine of approval lit Shepherd's eyes. "But I did."

Claire thought she might lose her cool. "I will not have this fight with you."

"Think of your assault of the Undercroft," the giant reminded her. "Think of what you accomplished for the Omegas. What occurs in Thólos defines character. You are exceptional."

That was far from true. Ashamed, Claire turned her eyes to the floor and confessed, "Did Maryanne tell you what I had to do to convince her to help me?"

"I have not discussed such things with Ms. Cauley. What was done is forgiven and your motivation understood."

"I threatened her," Claire admitted, certain he must see how his occupation had affected even her. "I threatened her with you."

Shepherd could not help but laugh outright. "How charming you are. Do not trouble yourself. You would never have followed through on the threat. We both know that."

But she had still done wrong to her friend. "I hated doing it, Shepherd."

The man nodded, entirely self-satisfied. "But it was necessary."

He was twisting her words, using the opportunity to influence. He remained unreactive, patient, and Claire wondered why he seemed pleased at her question of, "Where will it end?"

Shepherd answered like a father educating a child. "In a cultivated Utopia."

Fighting not to grit her teeth, Claire went back to the topic at hand. "Full of damaged people? How will Shanice enjoy the world that inspired her rape?"

"Had you not interfered, she would have been safe, separated from the dangers of Thólos, and cared for by her mate—who would have provided all she needed. Charles was a good man, one deserving of the gift of an Omega's love."

She was not going to beat a dead horse. "In this utopia, where is justice for my dead boy? The children suffering and dying are innocent…"

"Children are being neglected and destroyed by their own people. My Followers do not harm them."

"But they don't help them. They perpetuate the suffering. I don't understand how you cannot see what I see," Claire, green eyes wide and beseeching, said. "Shepherd, you set convicts free. You inspired brutality. You are more dangerous an infection than the Red Consumption."

"Less than twenty-thousand men were set free in a city of millions… a city of people who chose to embrace violence rather than stand honorably—a people who are easily corrupted. I never told them to pillage, rape, or murder. Thólos is responsible for its actions."

"You manipulate us all with a skill that is terrible, yet could be redirected." Stamping her foot in frustration, Claire demanded, "Why not inspire goodness, why not try to change the world through nonviolence?"

"It would be pointless in a place so immoral and corrupt. You cannot reason with these types of people, little one. You cannot explain or educate. They are absolutely aware of what they do. They don't care about you, your goodness, or anything beyond their own insatiable desires. After all, what do you know of Senator Kantor, the champion of the people? That man would do anything for power, manipulate anyone for wealth. He knows secrets that, were he to divulge them to the resistance, they would slit his throat."

Fighting not to lose ground or be distracted, Claire growled, "You are bitter because he is still free, because he fights."

Crossing his great arms over his chest, Shepherd said, "What makes you think I don't know where he is at this very moment?"

She took a deep breath, she made herself look passive. "There is no resistance."

"There never will be." Creased skin around his eyes exaggerated Shepherd's smile. "Thólossens will never rise up at the cost of their dwindling comfort."

Knowing the question would irritate him, Claire asked bluntly, "Has my flyer had an effect?"

"Yes." Silver eyes lost their mirth, their shifty furtiveness, and narrowed in disapproval.

That was something, that inspired hope. "So you're wrong."

Shepherd developed a hooded expression, answered as if reluctant. "Your picture has led to a rash of violent murders of black-haired women who look like you. My men find more every day."

Claire's voice hitched, the sliver of hope she'd had shattered. "You're lying!" But she was already crumbling, because it was just too fucking believable.

Gently, Shepherd asked, "Now do you understand just what the citizens of this city are?"

Head in her hands, Claire began to weep, the responsibility for each unknown woman's death carved into her forever.

He had outmaneuvered her again; he had won.

Even scooped into circling arms, wracked with sobs, hating herself for what her flyer had inspired and how utterly stupid she was for not recognizing what it could lead to, Claire sagged to the floor. He was inside her in seconds, purring and petting, holding her tightly so she would not hurt herself by fighting back. She cried the entire time, tears running even as she climaxed, even as he told her sweet, soothing things. When that didn't work, Shepherd proclaimed it was not her fault, that she was good, and even he knew that she could not have suspected such an outcome—she was free of guilt, she was pure, her ideals were noble… the city did not deserve her.

He told her he loved her.

She quieted a little.

The following twenty-four hours, Claire could hardly bear to leave the nest. Shepherd left her in peace so long as she ate everything he brought her, including fried potato wedges with mayonnaise and a chocolate shake.

## 14

When Claire woke the following day, Shepherd bathed her, dressed her, and brought out the handcuffs so that he could take her to see the sky. Deep down, she knew self-pity would get her nowhere. She wanted to rally, to get back to forging progress, because she owed it to those murdered black-haired women, but lost faith was a slippery slope, and she had nothing to hold on to.

Shepherd tried to give her that something.

He carried her to the room with the window. He locked the door and showed her his latest gift. Her mother's piano rested against the wallpaper, his Followers having dragged it all the way from Claire's ransacked apartment.

There was no bench, only a small stool he took himself, leaving her on his lap where she might frown at the scratched keys. As they were still chained, Shepherd followed where her fingers flexed, his body surrounding her like a blanket.

One aching breath and Claire closed her eyes. In a stupor, she began to play Bach just as her mother had taught her. The pedals were tricky to reach with the male serving as her seat—a man with his hand over her womb, who moved as she moved, never once hindering. They were a single creature. Even the bulky arm chained to hers followed smoothly, Shepherd never tugging the metal links, never interfering.

Breathing in time, crying softly, Claire purged. It was all there in the melody: sorrow, shame, guilt. But as the music went on, as rumbling purrs filled the air in concert, despair changed into something that hurt a little less.

Claire was no virtuoso, her fingers hit sour notes, but performing gave her pleasure. It was pleasure she allowed, that she sucked in as if starved for it. Wet eyes opened, more tears fell. Precious sound, the feeling of keys, of warmth, drowned out the pain.

But even so beautiful a distraction could not last. "I would never have made that flyer if I'd thought others would suffer."

Shepherd embraced her tighter. "I am aware."

It was only a whisper. "Thólos needed to know. They needed to see. But they have done nothing. They are doing… nothing."

Shepherd breathed at her ear. "You cannot save Thólos, little one."

Banging the keys in a mishmash of off-putting noise, Claire ended the concert. "I shouldn't have to! You should not have done this!"

Hand on her belly, scarred lips at her ear, Shepherd murmured, "If I had not come, what kind of life would you have had, Claire?"

What she'd always pictured. "I would have found a husband, had kids, painted… I wouldn't be afraid for my friends, mourning more people than I can remember. My beautiful city would not be in ruins or my home destroyed."

Shepherd used her reasoning against her. "The people you care for are safe because of you. My men watch over them. You still paint. You have a mate who would see to any need you expressed to him, so long as it did not endanger you—one who requires your patience. Beyond that, will you not find pleasure in the child I have given you?"

Hot tears falling free, Claire looked to where a very little life would be snuffed out when she ended herself—a little life that was growing daily and becoming more real, which affected her and increased her dependence on the Alpha purring at her ear.

As if he knew she refused to embrace the thought of her son, Shepherd cooed in her ear, "You will love our baby and sing for him, paint him pictures… and he will have dark hair like yours, and maybe your eyes."

Never once had she allowed herself to picture the child. Hearing so tempting a description, Claire could not stop the image from invading her mind, hating the male who whispered so sweetly for the cruelty of what he was doing in making her son real.

Insistence invaded Shepherd's attempt at gentle speech. "You don't have to fight it, Claire. You could forgive me, forgive yourself, and your pain would end. You could do it for your son, so that he need not suffer a disengaged mother as you did."

Her breath caught, she automatically pressed the keys to hide in her music. Gently, Shepherd took her hands, preventing her attempted distraction until his point was made.

"Have things not improved in these last weeks?" He stroked the trembling Omega; he kissed her neck. "I know it has been painful for you to accept what you have faced between us, what you experienced in Thólos. I also know that you understand my purpose to a point, and though you may not want to admit it, you see how wrong this place is."

"Please stop…"

"If you wish."

His acquiescence was unexpected. Claire uncurled, tried to

move her arms, and found Shepherd no longer held her from her goal. She began to play again, the melody slow and wretched. As her fingers roamed the keys, she thought of her mother, the woman who'd sat by her side for hours, patiently teaching her child the one thing she'd taken true joy in. It was an act of love Claire had always wanted to share with her own children, part of the fantasy the Omega had envisioned in her perfect future.

Thoughts of her dead mother led to thoughts of her dead father—to the scent of orange blossoms and remembrance of warm sunshine. Her daddy's laughter had been Claire's favorite sound in the world.

Another male vaguely reminded her of the man: Corday, with his silly boyish grin, his kindness, his patience.

As if Shepherd knew, as if he could tempt her thoughts back to him, he lifted Claire's skirt and caressed her thigh. It felt good, the way Shepherd touched. It felt perfectly nice as the music stirred and her attention relaxed to alter tempo in time with the Alpha's long warm strokes. He grew more daring, and her breath caught when his large fingers explored, teasing in exactly the right spot.

The way he could play her body, the ease with which he parted her folds, how simply her legs spread of their own volition to offer access so he might please her… sometimes it seemed pure. "That's right, little one."

And that voice, the heat of masculine rasps, why could it have not belonged to someone else?

A dexterous thumb exposed her clit, circled it as she mewed and stumbled badly through a musical phrase. When thick fingers penetrated languorous and deep, Claire whined, her breath caught, and it was the Alpha's name she panted.

*"Shepherd."*

The bliss of his fingers slipped away, but in their place he set his member free and gently lifted his mate. He sheathed himself in a slow, deliberate entry. Cock engulfed, the Alpha remained still, set no pace—he only groaned at her ear while Claire instinctively gyrated for her own pleasure.

The heat of his hand returned, plucking at her swollen nub, drawing out whimpers and little stifled cries. Claire no longer knew what she was playing or if it made any sense musically, everything was focused on the building pressure and the comfort of a familiar body. Whatever her hips did, Shepherd's fingers followed. Though his breath was labored and he badly craved to rear up into that tight, little passage, he let her take what she needed.

It was not long before Claire's movements grew erratic. At the sound of the Alpha's desperate moan, she jerked and ground down hard, climaxing so beautifully the world went white.

Shepherd followed on command, drenching her insides in warmth and her favorite scent—something that had become far more gorgeous than the smell of orange blossoms.

Claire didn't cry. For once she did not chastise herself. She simply sat on his lap with the knot fusing their bodies, felt him still spurting in the lingering minutes of his own release, and began to play Bach again—because she had to survive herself, she had to survive to give Corday his chance no matter how badly the odds were stacked against him. And she would not survive if she could not take the comfort Shepherd offered when she was so close to breaking apart again.

The Alpha growled, contented with each exhale. Nestling closer, he held her tight, and enjoyed Claire's pseudo-serenity.

He had won. His mate was allowing their bond to soothe her.

"GIMME YOUR FOOT," Maryanne barked, shaking a little bottle in her hand with quick jerks of her wrist.

Stuffed full of cake—a huge tiered thing, frosted bird's egg blue and beautifully decorated, a cake that could feed half of Shepherd's army… that even after their brutal attack on it could still feed half of Shepherd's army—the friends lounged and played at girly things.

Smiling, sitting slumped in her chair, Claire picked up one bare foot and stretched it over to set in her friend's lap. "Why am I not surprised the color you brought is vampy red?"

Maryanne brushed a careful line of paint over Claire's big toe, smirking. "Too sexy for prudish little Claire?"

"Says the girl who slept with every boy we knew…"

"After I left, did you ever cave in and date that that Seymour guy? He had such a crush on you."

Claire groaned and rolled her eyes. "Gods no. I had my dad chase him off when he started sniffing around the house."

Playful eyes glanced up, Maryanne motioning for the other foot. "What about boys in higher academy?"

Claire shook her head. "I was focused on my studies."

"After academy?"

"Geez, you make me sound so boring!"

"So only Shepherd, huh?" Maryanne pretended to focus on her work, spreading the crimson paint carefully. "That's kinda too bad. I mean, think about it. If you have only slept with Shepherd you have nothing to compare it to. He could be awful and you would never know. I bet you wish you'd experimented now…"

Laughing so hard it hurt, Claire struggled to say, "Stop antagonizing him!"

"That's what he gets for eavesdropping on girl talk. There are reasons why women congregate without men… so we can make fun of them."

Claire was still laughing, green eyes dancing while *innocent* Maryanne blew on her toes. "What other interesting things do you have in your pockets?"

"Look who wants presents?" the blonde sang, reaching into her coat for a tube of lipstick.

Unscrewing the lid, Maryanne made a face like an artist creating a masterpiece. Claire leaned forward, puckered, and let her stain her lips a rich berry red.

"Well, I'm not going to lie," Maryanne shrugged, unimpressed. "It's a little trampy on you, but Shepherd might like it."

"It's the same color you're wearing!" Claire snorted, snatching the tube from Maryanne's hands. "I had a lipstick like this once, never had a place to wear it."

"What do you mean place to wear it? You just wear it," her friend replied, settling back in her chair.

Claire's soft smile was gently reprimanding. "That's easy for you to say, Alpha. If you draw attention, being as pretty as you are, you don't have to worry about potential complications."

Yawning, Maryanne shrugged. "That is just silly, Claire—and paranoid. It's just lipstick. And I guess you don't have to worry about that anymore. Ain't no one gonna to be messing with Shepherd's old lady."

Green eyes grew sad. "That's not what I hear is going on outside…"

"What do you mean?"

A guilt-ridden voice confessed, "Women who look like me… because of my flyer."

"You *told* her about that?" Maryanne snarled at the hostile male watching from the corner. "What is wrong with you?"

Claire could not see his reaction to her friend's outburst, but knew it couldn't be good. She interjected, "I am not a child, Maryanne. I asked, and he told me the truth."

Maryanne had her own harsh take on things. "None of that was your fault, you know. I thought the flyer was pretty ballsy, but you've got to get it through your thick skull, girl. Thólos is a bad place full of bad people."

"People can change," Claire breathed, knowing it had to be true.

Maryanne cocked a brow and made a hard point. "Do you think Shepherd can change?"

The Omega tilted her head, thinking about it before looking over her shoulder. Her eyes met Shepherd's.

He glanced down at her stained lips, seemingly intrigued.

Standing, she walked, careless of her newly lacquered toes, and went to stand before the male. So many contradictory thoughts were running through her head. His behavior towards her had changed, was far more palatable, but all of that could easily be summed up as an insincere strategy to gain her affection. After all, she was certain there had been no change in him outside their den or in his dealings with Thólos.

When her small hand reached up and the female cupped his cheek, Shepherd allowed it, unmoving as she stood between his spread legs. His silver eyes shone, focused and pleased with her attention in front of the Alpha female.

Claire pulled in a breath as if to speak, then hesitated, pouting her red lips until he purred and the back of his warm fingers stroked over her belly.

The question was for herself. "Could Shepherd change?"

It was all there in her expression—how badly she wished he could change. How hard she had tried to affect something in him. Whispering, her voice as soft as the fingertips that touched the flesh of his cheek, Claire asked, "Could you change?"

A warm, large hand enclosed hers, gently removing her touch from his face, Shepherd admonished, "You are neglecting your guest, little one." Breathing, blinking out of her trance, Claire took a step back as the male pressed some small scissors into her hand. "I have given her permission to cut your hair, should you wish it."

Looking down at the little instrument, Claire teased Maryanne. “I don’t trust her with these. Everything will come out cockeyed.”

From across the room, the woman blurted, “How hard could it be?”

Claire smirked, thinking of Maryanne’s godawful attempt ten years prior. “That’s what you said last time, and may I remind you, those terrible bangs took over two years to grow out.”

She moved back to Maryanne and let the blonde trim her hair, fairly certain it would be terrible, and honestly not caring at all if it was. The only thing about the interlude Claire cared about was the COMscreen Maryanne produced, full of photos of the Omegas, and even one of Corday, who was smiling his dimpled grin as he spoke to whoever was just outside the frame. On the smallest finger of his hand sat her gold ring, diminutive, but there.

Corday still had faith in her.

Making sure not to look at him too long, Claire set the COMscreen down and remained still as Maryanne snipped.

When the cut was over, dark hair tousled, Maryanne assured in a playfully thick accent, “Very beautiful.”

Handing her a pocket mirror, she frowned when Claire pressed it back, stating, “I don’t need to see.”

Maryanne shoved it back. “It’s not bad, Claire. Take a look.”

“I’m sure you did fine.”

Maryanne knew what was going on, could see through the cracks in her old friend’s mask.

Holding the mirror up, making a point, she snarled once the Omega turned her head away. “What is wrong with you?”

Moving the mirror to Claire’s new line of sight produced the same outcome. Claire looked away. Enough was enough. Maryanne grabbed a fistful of hair and held Claire’s head still, forcing the mirror before the Omega’s face. “Open your eyes and look in the mirror, Claire!”

She did. Claire looked at a hated face, one with full lips that had been painted to be pretty and black hair that had been cut to frame her face. A face with green eyes and pale skin; a face she had been unable to look at for the last week without seeing dead women who looked like her. Women she had killed.

With a voice that could no long bear inflection, Claire said, "You're right. The lipstick is trampy."

"You don't need to do this to yourself, you idiot." Maryanne gave Claire's hair a little yank. "There is nothing wrong with that woman in the mirror. Their deaths are not your fault."

"Step away from her, Ms. Cauley. Go stand near the door and do not move." There was nothing but the threat of murder in Shepherd's voice, every word enunciated with chilling precision.

Maryanne darted back, the behemoth stalking forward. Watching with awe, the Alpha female saw the mountain kneel to his mate. His purr was aggressive, his hands already petting an Omega who seemed composed and patient, but was anything but.

"She didn't do anything wrong," Claire explained. "Everything is fine."

Shepherd spoke in that other language, loud enough that the Followers on the other side began to unlock the door. In a flash, Maryanne was gone. Once the door was bolted, Shepherd pulled Claire to stand and drew her to the room's luxurious bathroom.

A large mirror hung over the fine sink, and with a flick of the lights there they were, standing side by side, framed in filigreed gold.

"Your skills at deception are abysmal," Shepherd explained, gesturing at her reflection. "So let's not waste time, shall we? Why are you only looking at me in the mirror and not at yourself?"

Humiliated that she had allowed this situation, that she had not performed better, Claire looked straight at her reflection. "My stomach was upset."

"You are lying," the male roared, hating the strange feeling that was coming through the cord. "What is wrong?"

There were no tears, only a blank stare. "I just can't look at them."

A great hand lifted as if to grip her skull. Instead Shepherd clawed through her hair, the nearest thing to a pet an angry Alpha could manage. "Continue."

In the mirror Claire was dwarfed next to the massive man, small and useless. "I am angry that I cannot do anything for anyone, that everything I tried only made things worse. I feel powerless, ashamed of myself for my failure and the horrible effect I had on women who look like me." Beseeching eyes darted to his reflection. "And I'm frustrated that no matter what I say to you, to a man I am pair-bonded to, that it would change nothing—even if I had the power to redeem you—because Thólos did horrible things when the people could have rallied and brought you down."

"The price you are exacting from yourself is not yours to pay. It is Thólos'."

She was getting angry. "I *am* Thólos, Shepherd. Born and raised here. I grew up here. My parents are buried here."

"Look at yourself in the mirror, Claire O'Donnell." The male reared up as he spoke. "You are an Omega, physically small and weak, yet incredibly intelligent. That said, however shrewd you may be, you are also foolish enough to think you must bear the burden of others' sins… That is your true flaw. The psychological trauma you are causing yourself is both immature and pointless. It does nothing to change the scenario. And though I am honored you would consider the thought of my redemption as worthy, it is your own peace you need to focus on now. Self-pity and playing the martyr help no one."

The woman gave a caustic snort. "Well, I failed at playing the hero."

In a voice that was hard and assertive, Shepherd snarled, “But you didn’t, and you know it. Forty-three people are alive because you had the nerve to stand up to me. You won, Claire. No single adversary has ever beaten me before. Ever. Take your victory.”

It was not that simple, not when the world and her mind were in a constant state of turmoil. Not when she was only breathing to buy time.

*In the midst of chaos, there is also opportunity. - Sun Tzu*

Rubbing her lips together, she felt the unfamiliar slide of lipstick and met Shepherd’s eyes again. “The lipstick *is* trampy.”

“And your hair?”

“Looks nice.”

“And the dress?”

“Is something I would never have chosen for myself in a thousand years. I look like the poster girl for a pre-plague Omega housewife—which I suppose is fitting, as I am barefoot and pregnant.”

“Are you attempting comedy?” For once the man actually sounded unsure.

Claire smirked and shook her head in the negative.

FOR DAYS she wasted paper while the Alpha stared, watching her paint her promised portrait for him. Claire was beginning to suspect that Shepherd was trying to drive her crazy with the constant appraisal of her work. But there was a method to his madness, even Claire understood that. He was forcing her to look at herself over and over, until it was no longer quite so nausea inspiring, until it was her face on the paper and not some unknown woman Claire had conjured up.

A deep breath, the type that preceded some grand speech the bastard was going to make, passed Shepherd’s lips. Claire’s eyes shot up, blazing warning as she snarled, “I swear to the Gods, Shepherd, if you say one thing about this painting, I am going to scream.”

Undaunted, he cocked an eyebrow and stated, “I want you to paint yourself smiling more.”

Pounding her fist on the table, biting back the rising noise in her throat, Claire let out a stream of obscenities so vulgar the man began to laugh. Paint-stained hands balled up the picture, Claire throwing it right in his face. Then it was her turn to laugh at the absolute look of murder in his eyes.

Popping her lips, grinning impishly, she reached for another piece of paper and ignored the swelling, angry male. Innocently, she dipped the brush and began the outline again, painting the same smug grin she was wearing at that moment. When the basic form was drawn, she arrogantly held it up, and watched him narrow his eyes and appraise.

Before he could speak, a knock came to the door and a man whose voice Claire didn’t recognize spouted off something in their language. Shepherd’s attention focused on what he was hearing, the Alpha already standing as he replied in kind.

Shepherd immediately began pulling on his armor.

A strange anxiety twisted in her stomach, this situation not having arisen before. Watching him dress for battle at a summons and not simply because he was leaving for the day, meant something was going on—something that could be dangerous to him, to Thólos, to anyone.

“You do not need to be concerned, little one.” There was a smile in his voice.

When Claire’s eyes darted up to meet his, she found him collected and calm. But *she* felt incredibly uneasy, all humor from only a few moments ago evaporating. “What’s going on?”

The purr began. Shepherd pulled on his coat and came to where she sat, alarmed and stiff. Stroking the line of her jaw, he explained, "There is nothing. I simply lost the hour playing your game with the paints."

He was lying. The man always knew what time it was without the presence of a clock. "I don't believe you."

Ignoring her accusation, he cracked his neck and looked down at his worried mate. "I will be back shortly, and when I return, I expect to receive the remaining portion of our agreement."

She fought to maintain an impassive expression while Shepherd traced her lips with his thumb and leveled upon her a liquid gaze brimming with lust and ravenous expectation. He dipped his thumb between her lips, growled richly as if he was about to fuck her, and left her sitting in a little pool of slick.

Dazed, Claire stared at the closing door. She knew what he was calling due, what he had left sitting between them for weeks—in order to fulfill their bargain, Claire was expected to initiate sex.

Unsure whether he had chosen that moment as a means to distract her from her worry, or if it was some sort of victory celebration for whatever he was doing, she shifted uncomfortably at being left in such a state.

It was not as if she'd forgotten what she'd offered for Lilian and the others to be laid to rest, but she'd had other far more pressing things to center her thoughts upon. Besides, physical intimacy with Shepherd had taken place countless times. She knew what he liked, where to touch him to draw out a reaction… so how hard could it be to initiate it?

Hard.

Looking for a distraction, Claire showered and cleaned up the paints, expecting him back at any second. But hours passed and she began to grow anxious, worried about what might or might not be going on in Thólos.

Was it an insurrection? Corday—had he found a way to end this?

Claire was on the edge of full-blown panic when the lock finally shifted. Gritty metal whined and the door swung inwards. She stopped her customary pacing, turning with tangled relief to face the largeness of her mate.

# 15

The severed head of Senator Kantor still lay on the table, wrecked and unmoved from the place it had been dropped once Jules had pulled it from the pike outside the Citadel and brought the repugnant thing to Shepherd. There was no clean cut where neck had been severed from shoulders, just a torn stump of muscle and tendon. Around it lay a splatter of blood, leaking fluids, and the fingers of a man gripping the table so tightly his knuckles had gone white.

Before Shepherd had left, they'd argued, the Alpha's bulging arms crossed over his chest while he'd stared down his second-in-command. "You went against my orders and killed him while he was still useful to us?"

"No…"

Svana.

She had done this. She had murdered her uncle. Who else could move with the stealth to slip right under the noses of trained Followers? Who else would stick the head on a pike outside the

Citadel as if to taunt not only Shepherd but the city she sought to destroy? Who else would gain by this?

It was a delicate thing, tormenting a population just enough to keep them miserable, Shepherd having exercised caution not to press millions past the point of desperation. Hanging a traitor as part of a public trial and execution spread the blame on all who watched. It made the population impotent and held Thólos responsible. This… the Champion of the People and leader of the resistance's head had been mutilated for show, loudly broadcasting the wrong sentiment.

That was what had earned Shepherd's anger, not Jules' accusations that Svana had done this to undermine them all.

Riots had already begun to bloom, Followers acting in mercenary fashion.

Even faced with this kind of proof of Svana's treachery, Shepherd did not see an imprudent mistake—yes, Svana could be difficult, but she would not break rank, not when she stood to gain the most from their great plan's success. If she had done this, it had been for good reason.

Jules had lost his temper. He'd smashed his fist against the table and roared.

Shepherd had only put a hand on his friend's shoulder, both as comfort and as warning. "Do not allow this complication to cloud your thinking. Patrols must be immediately increased to counter potential uprising, rioters dealt with quietly. We cannot continue shooting citizens in broad daylight, to do so would only encourage more unrest. I need you in the field."

Jules swallowed, lips tight. "She seeks to control the rebellion."

Squeezing the smaller man's shoulder, Shepherd growled, "Brother, if what you believe is true, it would only benefit our cause to have Svana at the helm of our enemy's forces."

There was some stinging truth in his leader's words. Had the woman in question been anyone but Svana, Jules may have even agreed. The Beta would not allow her to stir up animosity, having seen years of her manipulations and spite. He would not give her the pleasure. The best course was to follow orders. "Understood."

Shepherd had left him to oversee the sedation of potential riots, to be seen in the Citadel.

Alone, for an hour, Jules crouched, eye level with the severed head of Senator Kantor.

Up close, Kantor's eyes displayed the hazy film of developing cataracts. Between lids half drooping, retinas mismatched in the direction they pointed, and the gaping mouth, the Alpha finally looked as monstrous on the outside as Jules knew he'd been on the inside.

The Champion of the People… had been the vilest of men.

Jules' lips parted and from his mouth flowed malice. "You murdered my children. You took my Rebecca from me."

He spat fully across the corpse's bloodied face.

"And I have watched you be lauded and adored for a decade. I have watched you lie and pollute, and I have bided my time so that you might know true suffering." Raw fury twisted through Jules' hiss. "Your death was *mine*, and I will make her pay for stealing my vengeance. Svana will bleed for this."

# REBORN

ALPHA'S CLAIM, BOOK THREE

**ADDISON CAIN**

# 1

Collar of his coat flipped up to protect his neck from the growing cold of the halls, Shepherd returned at last from being called away by his soldiers. He found his mate nervous, the acrid scent of Omega fear spoiling the air. But, mostly she was expectant and blissfully unaware of just what was going on above ground.

And he would never tell her.

Shepherd made no move to approach the panicky woman, he simply stood as Claire looked him over from boots to skull. The Omega searched out any hint of what had called him from her, looking for blood splatter, or the swelling of his knuckles, relieved when she found nothing out of the ordinary.

His Claire was angry, but far more reassured that he'd returned seemingly *normal*.

When the Omega stepped forward to touch him, to initiate what had to be done to seal their bargain, Shepherd spoke. "You are hungry, little one. We will eat first."

*We* will eat first?

Shepherd did not go to the door to fetch food. Instead, he went to where he stored his clothing and began pulling off his coat, armor, and boots. Bunched muscles flexing, he pulled his shirt over his head, handing it to her. Unthinkingly, Claire took it and put it, as he expected, in her nest.

Distracted by the task, the Omega chewed her lip, taking time to arrange the scented fabric and remove something old to be washed.

A knock sounded, Shepherd barking for the visitor to enter.

Jules came in with their food, set it down and left in seconds—the trivial familiarity he shared with Claire completely concealed by his indifference. She found it minorly amusing, especially the way Shepherd shifted to put his body between her and the Beta.

When the door closed, Claire found it very difficult to suppress a snort.

"What is funny?" the male growled, narrowing his eyes.

"*You* are funny, Shepherd." Claire arranged herself at the table. "That man has brought me meals dozens of times when you are not here—so you must trust him. Yet there you are, glaring at him as if he were not your friend. You have serious issues..."

Shepherd only grunted in answer. Dressed only in trousers, he came to the table. "It is a natural reaction for an Alpha to guard his Omega from dangerous men."

But not dangerous women...

Glancing at the food, Claire felt wholly disillusioned. She began to comprehend what was going on, what he had arranged for himself. This, the meal, was a show—a show where she was not spectator, but entertainer. She was expected to perform for the man lowering himself into the seat across from her. Reminding herself their agreement only required she initiate sex, nothing more, she picked up her fork and chose not to argue. Instead, Claire focused on the beautiful dinner, the male mirroring her movements and tasting the food.

It seemed awkward, the silence, and out of habit and good manners, Claire found herself wanting to make small talk, knowing it would be both pointless and something Shepherd would not respond to.

Except, he began it. "I have been told this is one of your chef's most famous dishes."

Cocking a brow, Claire looked up from the steamed fish and nodded, momentarily confused. "My chef? You do not eat his cooking?"

"Her cooking, and no."

That seemed strange. "What do you normally eat?"

"What my men eat. Communal food amongst those who've endured the Undercroft bears an importance I do not expect you to understand or submit to."

There were a great many things about the man she didn't understand.

Seeing that the woman was puzzled and still tense, Shepherd offered a modicum of explanation. "After years subsisting off mold, our digestive tracts have altered. *Followers'* diets must be bland, and the required nutritional additives have an unpleasant taste and smell. The bulk of my meal was consumed before I returned to you. This is… supplementary."

Was that why he never ate in her presence? She looked at the beautifully arranged plate. "Well, considering all your other physical attributes, I think it's only fair you have one restriction."

The male smirked, gratified. "Physical attributes?"

"You are very tall," Claire quipped flatly, taking another bite, not at all interested in padding the Alpha's ego.

His foot bumped hers under the table. "List another attribute."

Dodging Alpha pride was something Claire had years of experience with. "You are bald. It must save time not combing your hair."

Narrowed eyes matched his agitated reply. "I shave my head."

Claire sneered, pleased her slight had pricked him, and took another bite of dinner.

"You are playing with me, little one," he added, intrigued, once he saw her mischievous expression.

Gesturing with her fork, Claire explained. "You're arrogant enough. I am not going to feed that beast."

Shepherd countered, his own evil smirk appearing. "You will later. When I move inside you tonight, you will hum about my prowess and strength… You will want to say all those things and more."

The self-satisfied expression, the fact she knew what was coming—worse still, the fact he could inspire such a declaration—made Claire's cheeks flame. She would cry out for him, admire him physically with her hands and tongue, but she would keep her words to herself. "We shall see."

The grin that spread his scarred lips, the absolute hunger in his expression, only added to the Alpha's excitement. "A challenge from the coy, little Omega..."

For a second, Claire believed he might reach across the table and devour her. Even the way Shepherd breathed as he watched her eat implied his exercise of control warred with his impulse to mount her.

"You seem like you are in an awfully good mood." Claire thought back to how he had left her earlier, lingering anxiety matching the disapproval in her voice. "What did you do today?"

"Nothing of importance, aside from wondering what would be waiting for me in this room when I returned," Shepherd purred, charmed by her attempted interrogation. "I think of you often when we are parted."

Gods, even his scent was dripping sex.

*The whole secret lies in confusing the enemy, so that he cannot fathom our real intent. -Sun Tzu*

Sucking her lower lip into her mouth, Claire tried to figure out if he was trying to distract her, or mislead her. Looking at him, at the exposed musculature of his chest and arms, she found Shepherd sat with arrogance and authority, as if her regard were his due. Claire cocked her head, she tested. "If you were so eager for the remainder of our bargain, then why are we eating together?"

"Out of respect for my mate. I had fine food prepared and we are engaging in conversation, as you stated you desired... and as Dome culture dictates."

Claire understood at once, this was not just a shared meal. It was Shepherd's attempt at another courtship custom—like the foam flowers in her coffee. Pushing her hair behind her ear, her nervous blush deepened.

He exercised the softer expression he saved for the kill. Claire saw it, and knew at once her assessment was correct. Shepherd was, in his way, trying to woo her.

Unsure, Claire murmured, "This is to relax me."

"Yes."

"So I perform better for you?"

He gave her a long look that said yes, no, and a thousand other things. Unsmiling, his head just a tick to the side, Shepherd grunted. "You do not appreciate the effort?"

There was definitely a wrong answer, and that was the only one she wanted to blurt out. Biting her tongue, she looked at the shirt-less man and said, "You are courting me."

"According to your customs, yes."

She was not sure what made her curious, but Claire had to ask, "Wouldn't they also be your courtship customs?"

The man seemed momentarily at a loss for an easy answer. "There was no concept of courtship in the Undercroft. Men just took what they wanted. Violently."

All too familiar anger bubbled under her skin, Claire aware that was exactly what he had done to her. "So that is the culture you choose to identify with?"

It seemed like such a simple question, but Shepherd took his time measuring his reply, as if tailoring it in his head first. "I choose to identify with military culture."

The corner of her lips curled, Claire took another bite, wondering how on earth the crazy man across the table existed.

Shepherd disliked her reaction. "You find my answer unsatisfactory."

Waving her fork, she stated blandly, "I find it unique. Very Shepherd-like."

"Explain."

Claire leaned forward and met his eyes with a harsh look in her own. "You have strong opinions on *my* culture, have made several claims of our failings and vices... but you do not have a culture of your own. Considering the aspersions you cast, it seems your personal experience with real society is negligible."

The male straightened in his chair. "I have extensively studied Dome life for many years. I lived above ground and below. I watched, learned, followed, and remembered."

The man was completely missing her point, or he was redirecting her on purpose. "Have you participated in *my* society before you tried to ruin it? Only watching doesn't count. Your military culture, the ethos you created for your Followers, is just Undercroft society tailored to conveniently meet your manifesto."

Shepherd warned, "We have our own traditions and an honorable philosophy, little one."

"That's right, a whole army of honorable monsters who probably roast humans on a spit for fun."

The man answered with a very droll, "We only do that on high holidays."

Claire almost choked when Shepherd actually made a joke.

Coughing into her hand, chuckling despite herself, she found the male very pleased with himself for rousing her amusement.

She could feel the wheels in his mind turning, understood he had tried to banter in the same manner he'd witnessed between her and Maryanne. It was very strange to witness the way Shepherd's mind processed and adapted. He was like a sponge that absorbed interaction but didn't quite know how to apply it. So he practiced, usually falling short. Except that time... that time had been perfect.

Taking another bite so she could hide her smirk, Claire asked, "Enlighten me, Shepherd. Where do Omegas fit into military culture?"

Shepherd began to consider. It seemed like such a human gesture, the way he sucked his plump lower lip into his mouth, so totally normal, Claire could not look away. A moment later, Shepherd offered, "Napoleon was an Omega."

Claire blinked, cocked her head, and argued. "No he wasn't."

Shepherd grinned, leaning closer. "It is a well-documented fact, little one. A fact pointedly removed from the Dome's retained version of history. Unlike you, I am not afraid to read forbidden books."

If such a thing were true, then why was it considered dangerous to know?

Claire did not believe him. "Are you telling me an Omega pillaged through Europe's monarchies and created an empire?"

Self-righteous to the core, Shepherd nodded. "That is exactly what I am telling you."

The idea he might be right, made Claire doubt herself. "Why would that knowledge be forbidden?"

"Because it did not fall into line with the Callas family's crafted society all those living under the Dome are slave to."

"Or maybe it was because that man was a megalomaniac and a monster. Napoleon was insane and not the best role model for

Omegas." Even as Claire disagreed, she didn't support her own bad argument. It was obvious in her uncertain tone and disappointed expression.

"Napoleon's rule, even his ultimate defeat, led to enlightenment, art, and the emancipation of the slaves in Britain. Napoleon changed the world through his violent actions and commitment. He was a very clever tactician devoted to his cause." Shepherd offered what he perceived as a compliment. "Would such an outcome not please you, *little Napoleon*?"

Her soft breath conveyed trepidation. "Is this where you try to convince me he was a good man despite all the terrible things he did? That you are a good man?"

"No."

Claire ran a hand through her hair, a nervous habit, and offered, "You could be a good man, Shepherd."

He leaned towards her, expression soft and voice natural. "We are not so different in the absoluteness of our dedication to change the world for the better. You gave up your very sense of self to the mob, reprimanding the city with your flyer—exposing who you were, trying to inspire. I do what must be done, because I am strong enough to do it, and I understand truly evil men in a way I pray you will never know. So you must grasp that I cannot be, in my duty, what *you* define as good—just as you could never safely live amongst Thólos society as Claire O'Donnell ever again. We both sacrificed our lives for the greater good."

She didn't know why she felt compelled to ask, but the question came before she could stop herself. "What was your reaction to my flyer?"

His entire expression darkened. "I was afraid for you, little one."

A cold chill, a creeping icy thing, scratched down Claire's spine. She was wise enough to grasp that for the Alpha, fear was something long ago conquered and not at all welcome. To know she'd inspired it was unnerving.

His grim honesty continued. "I desired very intensely to alleviate the pain displayed in your photograph. I was even impressed with how unfailingly brave you were to do such a thing, though I abhorred it."

Claire's attention went to her plate; she felt like weeping and didn't know why.

Her lack of words did not alter the undeniable tone in the thread. The connection was normalizing, vibrating, and creeping deeper. Before there might be anymore *courtship rituals*, before there might be a greater consequence, Claire stacked their cleared plates, ready to get her duty over with.

"Did you enjoy our meal?"

She nodded, even thanked him politely, hearing his instant purr when Shepherd's eyes flashed at her praise. The feel of his hand on her arm, the long stroke of light fingers, stopped her movement. She watched, stunned, as the man lifted her hand to his lips and tenderly kissed it.

Slightly hoarse, Claire admitted, "I am not entirely sure where I should begin."

He held her gaze, lightly flicked his tongue against her sensitive palm. "You could touch me."

*The worst calamities that befall an army arise from hesitation. -Sun Tzu*

Her entire strategy centered on action, on pushing boundaries between them, on growing stronger as she sought out his weaknesses. There could be no room for hesitation if she wanted to gain ground.

Resting a hip on the table, Claire did as he suggested. He wanted to be touched, so that's what she did. She traced his jaw and nose, ran her fingertips over his lips as he had done so often to her.

Next, she stroked down the back of his neck, kneading the flesh he'd once claimed caused him pain.

Shepherd turned his head up to her, his mercurial eyes watching with such intensity Claire found her gaze rested far more comfortably on the Alpha's broad shoulders.

Keeping her mind separate from how familiar his body had become, Claire tried to approach it clinically, unsure if she was doing well. When a large hand came to rest on her hip, she took his touch as encouragement to continue. Her palms flowed over his arms from shoulder to wrist and back again, forming to the contours of honed muscle and absolute strength. She reached around his back to lightly scratch her nails over the broad expanse of flesh.

He liked that. His breath hitched, and Shepherd made little grunts and groans as she traced his spine.

When his purr grew husky, she rose from her perch and took his hand so he could stand from the chair and she could continue. With his great height, there was a shift in power, Shepherd suddenly so much taller.

Her uncertainty returned.

Timid, Claire's hands went to his belt.

Shepherd took her lowered chin, brought her face up so she might see the contented expression on his. "You are doing well."

His voice was gently encouraging, those expressive silver eyes liquid. Claire assumed he wanted her to continue, and licked her lips, trying to seek out the fastening of his pants. Fumbling, she pulled down his zipper and eased the fabric from his hips. Shepherd stepped out of his remaining clothes and stood naked under her touch.

When the Alpha made no move, Claire understood she was expected to continue.

Her hands found a path from his thighs, near his groin, and across the hard planes of his stomach. She nosed his chest, and pulled in his scent exactly as she once imagined she would do with the husband she'd hoped for all her life. Holding on to the comfort of that fantasy, she put the conjured image in Shepherd's place, and pressed closer, breathing in the smell of his excitement.

The fabricated man in her mind loved her, he honored her; he believed she was more than just an Omega.

It was so much easier to stroke and hum as her imagination unraveled, Claire didn't even hesitate to tease. Pretending he was hers, the mate she had dreamed of, she let it all go. Biting his chest, she playfully scratched near enough his groin that his cock twitched in expectation of attention—attention she denied, to instead reach around and caress his buttocks, relishing his groan of pleasured frustration.

By the time she closed her fist around his cock, touching it for the first time only to please him, Shepherd was already dripping, pulsing in her hand, and arching into her grip.

He wanted more. Hands settling on her shoulders, he began to press her to her knees.

Claire knew he wanted her to take him in her mouth, a thing she'd only ever done in the heat of estrous. At first she resisted, a hiccup in her uncertain seduction. Eyes closed tight, hesitant, Claire counted to five before she could make herself obey.

Drawing in a deep breath, she acquiesced, kneeling to suck Shepherd's swollen crown between her lips.

The Alpha answered with a deep, rumbling groan.

Claire's hooded eyes dilated further at one taste, a dreamy hum expressing pleasure when more moisture dripped onto her tongue. Tangling his hands in her hair, gathering it from her face so he might watch, Shepherd relished her hollowed cheeks and the beauty of her pursed lips stretched beautifully around his cock.

Directing her movements, guiding her skull, with each bob of Claire's head, the male knew bliss.

She seemed so absolutely willing that he grew exceedingly excited, thrusting deeper between her lips, pulling her hair when that wicked little tongue swirled. Almost as soon as it began, he was on the brink of spilling into her pretty mouth.

His thrusts growing forceful, Claire gagged when he pressed too far, but did not fight back... she let him use her. When the Alpha reached down to cup his tightening sack, when he roared, Claire obediently swallowed around his girth and sucked harder for her prize.

Watching her little hands wrap around the forming knot to squeeze so it might feel like he was inside her, Shepherd spurt the first gush of semen down her throat, the male careful not to choke her on the copious fluid.

Claire gulped as much as she could, one stunned Alpha watching her effort, mesmerized by a stream of his seed oozing from the corners of her mouth.

Lost in the mating high, in her fantasy, Claire licked him clean, nuzzling into the broad palm settled on her cheek.

Shepherd's great thumb wiped up the spilled trickle running down her chin and pressed it back between her lips, the man groaning in approval when she eagerly lapped every last drop. "Look at me."

Claire, eyes black, hardly a trace of green surrounding the pupils, obeyed. She was so far gone, never had he seen her give in so completely. Seizing the opportunity, he pulled her to a stand, Shepherd taking her lips, kissing her and tasting himself in her mouth.

Even consumed as she was, Claire did not return the pressure.

Growling in frustration, he kissed her harder... but was penalized by the loss of her touch on his body.

Panting, aroused by the challenge and annoyed she continued to deny him her kiss, Shepherd changed tactics. The straps of her dress were flicked from her shoulders and the fabric tugged down. Breathing in her sweetness, biting and licking the valley between her breasts, Shepherd growled and offered in a voice rich with need, "Will you spread your legs for my mouth?"

Lost on another plane, Claire breathed, "Yes."

The Alpha reared and stalked forward, backing the little Omega towards the bed. "Do you desire my tongue?"

"I do."

He lightly shoved her down and fell upon his prey, his mouth everywhere but where she was wet and eager. Claire arched and writhed, exasperated to receive, but no touch came to ease the growing throb between her legs. Shepherd made her wait until he had marked her in featherlike bites, tasted every inch, until she was dripping slick from her enjoyment of his lips—the Alpha never having growled to call forth such a sweet scent.

Lifting her flushed body in the exact position to perfectly display her cunt, he pinned her. Her pussy was pink and throbbing, her hips wriggling against his hold, all the while her little hole twitching like a tiny sucking mouth.

Slick trickled out to tempt him, Shepherd flicking his tongue in the river of fluid, lost at only one taste. While he lapped up every drop, Claire moaned like a whore, rolling her hips to each flick of his tongue, grinding against his face when he burrowed that writhing muscle deep in her pussy.

With her mind still in that place she'd always imagined for herself, with her body in the hands of an expert Alpha she pretended might be the husband she once longed for, the feeling of a powerful climax swelled—something mindlessly perfect almost in her grasp.

Then Shepherd stopped, he stopped at the pivotal moment, and held her spread to watch her pink little pussy flutter as she tried to buck up to the mouth hovering warm above her. When she whined, his tongue stretched out and gave the lightest of licks, taunting her.

Fighting to move, to find relief from the coil of need he engorged with each darted swipe of his tongue, Claire's agitation turned to anger.

She had given him pleasure, and now her mate was contorting the vision, denying her the perfection of the dream by toying with her. Looking down between her spread thighs to glare at her tormentor, Claire aggressively growled.

The mass of muscle, the thing that was supposed to be fucking her with his tongue, prowled possessively over her body, negating her hips' movement each time Claire tried to rub against him for relief.

Brushing his wet lips over hers, Shepherd purred deeply. "Kiss me, little one, and I will give you great pleasure in any and every way you wish."

Wound up tight, instant wrath drove away all reason. Eager to punish for his attempt to claim something that was not his, to discipline for destroying the perfection of her dream, Claire pulled her lips back from her teeth. Nails scraped the hardness of sinew, her mouth attacking the bulging muscles between his shoulder and neck. In a rush, she pressed her teeth to his flesh and bit down with all the strength of her jaw, heard him catch his breath in surprise, and sunk her bite even deeper.

She wounded Shepherd with all the power of her indignation, all of the rage building up since she'd first looked at the behemoth, and the unfulfilled lust he had taught her body to crave and thought to use against her.

She didn't even want to fuck anymore; she just wanted him to bleed.

When the head of his cock skimmed between her folds, she dug in her claws and refused to let go. Shepherd penetrated her anyway, his warm lips at her ear where she could hear every gasped groan as he invaded her sopping cunt in erratic, desperate thrusts of his hips.

Shepherd began to speak. She refused to listen. He moaned out his name for her. She only growled like a rabid animal. He hit the place where her nerves were raw and need was everything, and that horribly powerful internal itch grew again, blossomed and divided her—blasting her into a sideways place where she had no name or purpose but to fuck and be fucked by her mate.

It was all there inside her, the raging storm that took away reason, it crashed and tore, and finally blissful expansion arrived.

Her teeth left the flesh she had deeply punctured. She swallowed the pooling blood in her mouth, and came as wildly as she'd grown feral. One more hard thrust, and the size of Shepherd's building knot grew impressive. It elongated her climax and tied the twitching thing to him where he could keep her still while his cock pumped her full of spurting streams, bathing her womb with soothing liquid heat.

The taste of blood was thick in her mouth, the red stuff under her fingernails, all ignored as her mind flew away in the intensity of her orgasm. Time seemed irrelevant, an endless field of grey... until a face distorted her vision. The beast whose heartbeat hammered against her red stained breasts asserted himself. Iron shaded eyes full of history and greatness, the silver of deceit and lust... those gunmetal disks looked at her with the devil's version of tenderness.

Full lips panted words, a rich musical voice undistorted by the rasp his scarred lips imposed, distracting her between kisses over her cheeks. "Little one, that was very pleasing. I am very, very pleased."

His mouth brushed her blood smeared lips, Shepherd looked deeply into hers, as if waiting for some act the female was supposed to offer. Claire lay there with his blood pooling on her chest and vague realization began to dawn. In horror, she grasped the consequences of her self-indulgent lack of control.

The depth of the bite... the placement...

In her fervor, she had ripped claiming marks deeply into Shepherd's flesh, almost as savagely as he'd marked her.

The purring brute's forefinger traced over the blood on her lips, the trail that had leaked from the corner of her mouth, sniffing and panting and still deeply knotted. The warm heat of his tongue began to lick her clean of the red, bathing her mouth and neck, tending to a thing half in shock. The second his knot began to abate, the smooth plunge of his cock began again, Shepherd knowing to fuck her immediately before her pupils contracted and his unexpected victory became her sorrow.

Making love to her until the Omega's exhaustion pulled her past consciousness, Shepherd did not allow her a moment of regret—not when everything was so perfect. Not when she was finally responding as the Gods intended.

CORDAY'S HEAD was in his hands, every last testament of violence he'd found stirring up a more horrible thirst than his worn out, simple desire for revenge. What he longed for in that moment, what he craved, were the whims of a violent psychopath.

He wanted to see Shepherd suffer. He wanted to watch him bleed.

Corday wanted to torment his rival himself until the sounds of the monster's screams might drown out the noise of the madness knocking about in his skull.

It was hard to swallow, even harder to admit there was no way to balance what he was with what a darker corner of his mind tempted him to become.

It was the room. It was the broken furniture. It was the blood.

The safe house where the Omegas recovered from the drug pushers' brothel, the place they had been promised, protection was ransacked. The two Beta enforcers set to watch the women lay dead on the ground, wracked with bullet wounds.

Nailed to the wall, his hand raised in a wave, drooped a headless body hung like a sick banner. The clothes Corday recognized, the stature, the smell not quite ruined by the stink of carnage.

Senator Kantor.

The leader of the resistance had been taken, tortured, and murdered, and it had been done right under their noses.

Shepherd was toying with all of them–laughing at them.

There was no sign of the few Omegas who'd called this place home. Though before they had been stolen, based on the stink of terror in the air, Corday imagined they had been forced to watch whatever had been done to a man he looked up to like a father.

"Are you going to say nothing?" Leslie stood at his side, staring forward, her lips bloodless, her expression dazed.

The safe house had failed the women it was set up to protect. The few remaining Enforcers, the stunted resistance, were failing the city they'd sworn to save. The one man unifying the flagging population had been butchered.

What was there to say?

Corday was crumbling no matter the stern look he kept locked on his face. There was nothing left.

Staring at the stump of mutilated neck, at the blood, and the open cavity of the man's torso, stepping over the entrails piled and stinking on the floor, Corday could find no worthy words for the corpse's niece. "We should take him down."

Leslie shook her head as if she couldn't bring herself to touch the abomination. "What do you suppose they've done with his head?"

He had no intention of answering a question they both, deep down, must know the answer to. Instead, he turned his attention to prying the body as gently as he could from the wall.

When it was done, what could be gathered was collected into the only receptacle they might find–garbage bags. Corday stood covered in his mentor's blood. "I am very sorry, Leslie, for agreeing to bring you here. He told me to keep you hidden. Had I listened, I might have spared you this."

"You needed help carrying supplies. *I* needed to do something useful, for once. The months of my seclusion have shown us one truth, over and over. My uncle was wrong... I was wrong. My access to Shepherd's communications did nothing to further the resistance's cause." Leslie let the Beta see her need for vengeance. "The proof is on the wall before you."

Corday's response was automatic. "You have interpreted messages that have saved the lives of many of our brothers and sisters."

"How did they find him? How did no one know he was missing until this morning?" Face pinched, she whispered, "What if Shepherd... what if he only let us think we operated out of his influence?"

An ironic, painful chuckle escaped the Beta.

Rubbing her skull as if it ached, Leslie sighed. "Your visitor, that Maryanne woman, may have been right. If they found Senator Kantor, they know where the resistance gathers. Shepherd knows where you live. He knows about me and my access to this commutations network."

Exactly Corday's unspoken point; the resistance was in ruins.

Leslie had more to say. "What if your Omega Claire had made a deal with her mate? He may have been watching us this whole time." A question wracked with doubt trailed off, "How else could this..."

He didn't want to hear it. Corday didn't even want to think it. "We must get back to headquarters. Brigadier Dane needs to be told what was done here."

Leslie Kantor grew vehement. “This has to end.”

The word left him in a breath, he was at a loss. “How?”

“I have been to your meetings. I’ve spoken with my uncle! Brigadier Dane, Senator Kantor, refused to engage Shepherd’s army. All they did, *all she will do*, is police the population and bribe potential recruits with food and false hope, while our enemy grows more powerful.”

Everything Leslie was saying was true. Corday agreed with her, but the resistance was too undermanned. Weaponry was scarce, bullet stores diminishing by the day. Had they attacked months ago as Claire had suggested, a rebellion might have stood a chance. Now... the only prayer they had was to find the contagion and wait for the city to implode.

Senator Kantor had been trying to prevent such an outcome. He’d been trying to save as many lives as possible. He had tried to outthink a man far smarter than him.

Corday repeated himself, robotic and unable to even hint at what was going through his mind. “We need to take this body to headquarters.”

Leslie softened her eyes and offered a sad smile. “No, darling Corday. There is no more time to hide away. I will not hand our city over to the inept hands of Brigadier Dane’s failing leadership. There is another place we can go, a place my uncle refused to consider. Inside there might be food, supplies, guns, ammunition... everything we need to take a stand and end this.”

Eyes bone dry in their sockets, feeling as if all life had been sucked from him, Corday made himself engage. He knew the very place she suggested and understood why it was off-limits. “During the breach, while my fellow Enforcers were trapped in the Judicial Sector, dying from plague, Callas’ home went into lockdown. For all we know, the contagion was let loose behind that steel barricade. To force the gate could expose the population and kill us all.”

She turned her back on the blood in the room, moving to the dwelling's small window and its slice of sunlight marking the ground. "There is another way inside, Corday, a small, secret entrance. Like my uncle, I know where it is."

The information did not surprise him. In fact, he, others in the resistance, had suspected there must be secondary access—an escape hatch in case of emergency. It had been Senator Kantor who fervently refused to risk the lives of millions to find out what might lie within the Premier's home.

Leslie answered his silence, turning her head to see him motionless, the corpse of her uncle wrapped in plastic and cradled in his arms. "If nothing is done, we are going to die. The proof is in this room. Salvation might wait beyond Callas' door, and Shepherd would never suspect the resistance would gather there. Let him think he's won, that we've disbanded while we rally behind walls he cannot penetrate. This is our only chance, Corday."

There was another roadblock, the woman the resistance would look to for leadership. "Brigadier Dane will stand against you on this."

"That's why we are going to open it, you and I, before we go to her. When we come to the resistance, we come bearing hope, or we die as we should for our ineptness." She sounded so much like her uncle in that moment: imperious, confident. "Now, put him down. Leave my uncle here. He would not want us to waste time or endanger ourselves simply to cart his body to be gawked at by the people he loved."

He put the remains down on the room's only table, took a step back. Spinning the golden ring on his finger, twisting it around and around, Corday turned his furious attention to Leslie Kantor. "If you are wrong, we will unleash the virus."

"That was my uncle's argument as well. Well, here is mine: consider where Shepherd is from, how he thinks. The man created an army, still recruits to swell his numbers. He wants to rule. He has total control." Leslie's passionate words put a stop to Corday's endless spinning of the ring. "An animal like him would rather die fighting than submit to death by infection. Do you really think he would leave the virus lying around where it might be set loose to ruin all he has built? Even Judicial Sector, once exposed, was purified by incineration protocol. What virus infected those charred halls was destroyed the instant Shepherd's point was made. The people of Thólos saw the suffering, they saw the flames. But, we have not seen what happened in the Premier's Sector. Why? Why keep the population in the dark?"

She was as good an orator as her surname implied. Even shaken as he was, Corday could feel a small spark of lost hope threaten to chase away his despair. He wanted to believe she might be right.

"We can end this, Corday." The Alpha female edged closer, offering her hand. "Come with me. Help me."

Possibility warred with the chance that obliteration might lie down the road Leslie would lead him. Something felt wrong, but life was wrong, the resistance had been wrong, and it was time to put his faith in something new.

The Beta took her offered palm and sealed the fate of the Dome.

## 2

Shepherd ignored the blood drying on his skin, possessed no eagerness to clean the wound Claire's teeth had created. He left her claiming marks to crust and drip sluggishly, far more intrigued with discovering each crimson drop smeared on his mate—making a game of tracing them once she was spent and exhausted, tangled up in him and slumbering.

When they woke, reeking of sex, Shepherd made no move to bathe before he dressed, proudly displaying the scent of his injury and the smell of his mate on his body. Claire watched from the mess of the nest, a part of her itching to clean away the bloodied sheets and rebuild her burrow. Instead, she sat like a lightning struck tree, reeling from what she had done, awake and aware, and completely confused.

Her determination had backfired. Every part of her had wanted to bite him... no questions asked... even the parts poisoned with resentment for her mate.

Watching him dress, watching him watch her, it was clear whatever she had done in marking him came with consequences more severe than a beating or subjugation. It came with his apparent joy and her budding fear of herself.

How could she have let this happen?

Shepherd knelt before her, startling her from scattered thoughts when a warm, damp cloth was used to wipe her body clean. The complacent male purred for her. "There is no need to be upset by what you've done."

Unsettled, her voice moderate and full of lies, she agreed, "Of course not. I was angry and wanted to hurt you. That was the nearest place I could bite."

As if she had not spoken such an obvious fallacy, Shepherd continued. "Omegas rarely mark their mates. I am honored you did so."

The cloth was already stained, hardly doing more than smearing the mess on her chest into little swirls of pink. Aware Shepherd was focusing right over the bond, Claire could not determine if he was trying to soothe or gloat. A massive part of her wanted to slap his hands away and rage, to undo all her hard work with a monumental meltdown.

*He who wishes to fight must first count the cost. –Sun Tzu*

She suppressed the rage, the disgust and self-loathing, and embraced the fact that backsliding would be both stupid and pointless. Rubbing her eyes, giving herself a moment, Claire tried to come to terms with the new nature of the bond, unsure why she felt so vulnerable when nothing but reassurance was flowing through it.

Testing herself, Claire put her hand on his arm, cupping the bulge of muscle. Shepherd stilled and waited to see what the woman would do.

"I, um," a wave of burning anxiety made her stammer, "I didn't mean to bite you... I don't know what happened."

Setting the stained cloth aside, Shepherd's fingers burrowed against her scalp. He tugged gently and purred, did all the things which normally calmed her. "It was possessiveness, little one. I felt what was in you—the longing for devotion and happiness. You feel insecure in my affection, so you placed your mark where others will see."

Pulling the neck of his shirt aside, Claire inspected skin swollen and scabbed from her bite. "My motivation was not affection when I did this. I was angry, Shepherd. Furious."

"Yes, an assertive Omega disciplining her mate—reminding him of his place and duty... as I did when I bit you after you fled."

Unsure what to say, feeling uprooted, Claire grumbled. "If I wanted to discipline you, as you so rightfully deserve, I would have bit something else."

Reacting with no anger to her taunt, Shepherd urged her chin up. "You are nesting properly now, no longer ill, even content on occasion when you forget your self-imposed and unnecessary penitence. My attentive presence and our mutual effort has been the cause. You cannot tell me, little one, you have not noticed the adaptations I've made in my behavior towards your keeping. I will even admit many things are foreign and difficult for me to understand, but I do them to please you."

Verbal acknowledgment of his effort was odd, even more so, the man's admission he'd struggled. "Why make an effort now? Why not still treat me like your pet?"

Shepherd tensed, muscles flexing as if he'd been insulted. "I never treated you as a pet. I treated you as a mate, approaching the situation of our bond instinctually—as all Alphas do."

There was that word again. Looking back at the mark her teeth had left in his skin, she said, "Your *instincts* and my *instincts* say very different things."

His counter was so quick, it was clear he'd thought through the issue beforehand. "You do not follow your instincts, little one. You live entirely in your ideals. Therefore, I have researched the subject of pairings under the Dome and tried to adapt to what you anticipate as much as I can allow. I want you to be happy even if the circumstances are unfavorable and the goal requires massive effort."

There was something between the words, something she could not put her finger on. "You dislike the changes?"

"Many things suggested are unsafe for you."

Claire could not help but imagine a long list of horribly cheesy romantic interludes the man had probably read as if studying for war. Utterly sarcastic, Claire muttered under her breath, "Such as walks in moonlit gardens and dates to watch old films? Yes, those are indeed incredibly dangerous moments in life."

He didn't answer.

Claire looked at him as if he were something totally alien, seeing the man raised underground. Even crouched he was so damn big, looming, and too close. The male was playing the part of the attentive, well-meaning mate. That was not Shepherd, not the Shepherd she'd known—no matter the alterations, or the bite… or the suddenly wide-open connection between them he was waiting for her to acknowledge.

Before she just started crying in confusion, Claire dared an honest question. "Can I ask you something?"

Shepherd took her hand, enfolding their fingers—another thing he had recognized was important when communicating with his female. "You may."

Unsure where to begin, she blurted, "I cannot imagine you were so possessive..." She looked away for a moment in consideration. "That might not be the right word. *Obsessive* maybe." Starting again, making herself look him in the eye, Claire said, "I cannot imagine you were so obsessive with Svana. Her autonomy must have been respected. I also assume, and I am admitting this is an assumption, that you disregarded her negative behavior within the confines of your relationship quite easily. I saw how you looked at her..."

"What is the question?" Shepherd growled, not hiding his distaste for the direction of their conversation.

Claire rubbed her lips together and tried again. "Aside from the fact I am an Omega and you consider my dynamic inferior, why are we regarded so differently?"

Though muscles of his neck bunched, the man remained quiet, thinking. Speaking abstractly, Shepherd began, "I do not believe Omegas are inferior. I believe they are precious and delicate. Your purpose and roles are different, and thus your treatment must reflect that."

"Precious?" Claire's voice dropped dangerously low. Considering how he'd used Omegas in the past, she could hardly believe his gall.

Irritation flashed in Shepherd's narrowing eyes in instant reaction to her challenging tone. "You are very rare. Alphas vastly outnumber you."

Indignant, Claire pressed. "So you are telling me that because of your archaic view of social strata, you expected your Omega mate would respond well to a lifetime of imprisonment... based on instincts and your concept of preciousness?"

He took her chin, less a sweet gesture and more an act of dominance. "Your scent intoxicates all who breathe it. My Followers are well-trained and loyal... but animal impulse can cloud rational judgment. I will not risk your exposure to harm or tempt their lack of focus."

Claire knew better. "There are pills and soaps I am well acquainted with that mask Omega scent. Your argument is illogical. Intoxicates is also a very strong word that implies those around an Omega no longer need to claim personal responsibility for their actions. It reduces Alphas and Betas to animals."

"You should embrace your dynamic."

"No matter my feelings on my dynamic, you would still lock me in this room."

Shepherd countered. "You are my mate. It is my duty to protect you—even from yourself."

"Can you not see your behavior is extreme and unhealthy for us both?" Claire made herself hold his gaze, made herself still. "It is unreasonable and unnatural. So back to my original question you are so skillfully trying to evade. Why didn't you treat Svana in the same manner in which you treat me?"

"Svana is an Alpha."

Leading him to the words Claire knew he was avoiding, feeling there might be some small victory in this for her, she hounded further. "But you held her as your mate."

"It is different." Shepherd grew agitated, the male's breath coming faster, swelling his great chest. "I will not risk you—"

"Me what?" One black brow arched. "Betraying you?"

"I regret allowing conversation!" Shepherd quickly reared to stand over her. "My answers will not please you, and you only seek to put tension between us because you are disappointed in yourself for marking me. I am fully aware of your motivation, Claire."

Her point had been made—goading him further, even though she was very tempted, would be purposeless.

*There is no instance of a country having benefited from prolonged warfare. –Sun Tzu*

Claire had to agree. She and Shepherd had reached a point where fighting was not going to get them anywhere.

"I'm sorry… I just…" Claire let out a sigh, confessing something that cost her dearly in an effort to gain a stronger position. "I will admit I don't really know how to process my marking you, and I am overwhelmed right now. Causing a quarrel was not my goal.

You've made an effort. I know you have. I have questions. That is all."

Shepherd exercised a chilling tone. "Your questions are incendiary."

Claire used Shepherd's favorite argument against him. "Considering the history between us, that is inescapable, but *necessary* if you want to move forward."

"Fine. Then answer this." Shepherd's massive hand gripped her shoulder, assuring she could not scoot away. "What is it you found so appealing in the Beta? You touched him freely and were open with him. You were absolutely different with him than you are with me."

The question was an unexpected one. "You mean Corday?"

Shepherd's eyes narrowed dangerously. "Enforcer Samuel Corday, yes."

"First off, I did not even know his full name. Secondly, you are hurting my shoulder." Claire glanced down to where he grasped, Shepherd's hold lessening considerably at her complaint. "Thirdly, I hardly know him."

"Do not play games with me, little one."

Exasperated it needed to be spelled out, Claire blurted, "He's nice. The man had no agenda. He never tried to touch me or was sexually inappropriate. Corday respected my thoughts and wishes. He made me feel safe and unthreatened when I was very frightened and alone. He put himself at great risk and *actually helped* the Omegas..." Claire's voice dropped, the thread whirled, and something long unsaid slipped from her mouth. "The reason I originally came to you, if you had forgotten. Imagine how different our connection would be had you done the same—instead of weaving your mind games and constant manipulations. Instead of infidelity and threats!"

An animal roar, a thing of great violence ripped past the Alpha's lips. "Every last thing I have done, EVERYTHING, has been for your benefit—even knowing my actions cost me your favor. THAT IS WHAT A WORTHY ALPHA DOES FOR HIS MATE!"

Claire was struck speechless by the echo at his end of the link. Shepherd was not lying or hiding facts in justifications or outright deception. Whether or not she agreed with him, he believed every last word—passionately. In his mind, he offered repeated sacrifice for her and had gained nothing by it but the burden of her unhappiness and disdain. But there was so much more to his uncustomary outburst, layers of suppressed feeling that had to be difficult for a man like Shepherd to process—all there in the link, exposed where she could see.

Jaw dropped, Claire felt *everything* inside him.

Shepherd looked lost for a moment, the same expression he'd worn when he came to her in the bathroom after fucking Svana... when she had laughed at him.

His name came softly to her lips, Claire calling to him for a reason she did not understand. "Shepherd..."

His great paw seemed to hesitate, a resigned movement in lifting from her shoulder and moving to cup her face. Old habits die hard. He was already reaching for the zipper of his pants, but Claire's small hands stopped him, and for once he did not brush them aside. She tugged on his arms, urging Shepherd down to the wreck of their nest.

Watching her with unconvinced wariness, Shepherd stiffly complied.

Arranging the male with gentle prodding, Claire placed herself on his chest, pulling the blankets over them both so they could lay still in the burrow and have the mutual solitude of the dark. He did not purr, not at first, instead she hummed her strange music for him.

HE'D SEEN it with his own eyes. Leslie Kantor was right.

Access to the Premier's Sector had not been a straightforward turn of a knob or a shifting bookcase hidden in the library of some neighboring house. In order to reach the second entrance, there was a series of tunnels, ladders—an ant farm sandwiched above the Undercroft and below the city's foundation. From the look of them, those dusty, unused crawlspaces had been untouched for years.

Shepherd's men had not left boot prints in the dirt; they had not unsettled the cobwebs.

Was that because they knew the virus lay at the end of the path? Or, could it be that the tyrant did not know of this secret passage?

If Leslie was right, if what they hoped lay in wait, it almost seemed too good to be true.

The woman knew her way, though once or twice she'd paused and listened to the dark. Both of them had crouched silent as the grave, but noise could be heard: the whining of buried pipes, the distant clank of metal. Not once did she seem unsure, but she was extremely cautious.

The crawl took less than an hour, though every passing minute felt like a lifetime.

One final turn in the path, and a pressurized door adorned with a crank wheel waited. The design was clever, one that would not be affected by electricity, or a lack thereof. The Callas family had exercised caution in the design of their home.

Not that it had saved them...

Between the two of them, the Beta straining and an Alpha small for her dynamic, they barely had the strength to turn the rusted crank. One would think it had been decades since a soul had used this passage by the way the gears stuck. It took the pair longer to unhinge that door than it had to manage the difficult path to it.

On the other side, once the portal swung in, waited more darkness, more dust, and stale air. When they stepped over that threshold, Leslie suggested they seal their entrance, whispering that should she be wrong, the airborne virus would have little chance to escape and potentially infect the population.

It seemed even darker on the other side of that terrifying door.

A shoddy flashlight between them, Leslie and Corday were forced to press themselves together in the confined space; both inhaled and exhaled air that might kill them. After ten ordinary minutes, Corday actually smiled.

Leslie smiled right back, reaching forward to embrace him in their triumph.

His clothing was still stained from his encounter with Senator Kantor's corpse, he smelled vile and was laden with dust, but she didn't seem to care. Leslie pressed closer, thanked him in repeated sweet whispers at his ear.

He could not help but hug her back. "Let's remain vigilant. We still don't know what waits inside."

Enthusiastically, she pressed a kiss to his cheek, a happy tear running through the dirt on her own. "But there is no virus here. We'd both be coughing by now if there were."

It was a victory Corday sorely needed.

The deeper they got into the mansion, with its private gardens and warmth, the more they realized this segment of the Dome was still intact. There were no cracks, no ice. Trees in the atriums bore fruit in the environment's false summer.

Surrounded by thriving plant life, Corday reached for an orange, stared at the overripe fruit's dimpled peel. At his feet were its rotting brothers, each one having been wasted with no one to tend the garden or gather the produce. In those fallen fruit, he saw a parody of the resistance, the waste of lost souls, and the foolishness of almost a year of inaction.

How many good men and women had died while Senator Kantor had been extolling caution?

They had only grown weaker...

Leslie claimed he'd known of this place. Why had the old man been so afraid of a door he must have recognized would not have led to the infection of civilians... not when it was underground and difficult to approach. Teams could have been sent, communication via radio established, and a cave-in organized should the volunteers fall ill with infection.

Walking through those silent, elegantly appointed rooms, Corday begin to feel the stirrings of anger towards the old man. Why had he been so afraid of this place?

Claire was also there in his thoughts, her timid smile and faith. How much more had she suffered because Senator Kantor had refused to open a single door?

Room by room, hall by hall, Corday and Leslie found more than fruit.

There were decomposed bodies that had sat so long in the heat, they had putrefied, then mummified. The elite Enforcer guard of the Premier, every last one of them lay dead. But, it was the way they had died that was most unnerving.

No virus had been there.

Not a single guard had drawn their weapons. Yet, many had broken necks, their heads completely turned around—as if one by one, a shadow had crept up upon them and laid them to waste.

Corday did not see one gunshot victim. This carnage had been done with bare hands.

The deeper they moved, the more obvious it became. Something very wrong had taken place here.

Shepherd, his Followers, had done this, and then they had shut it up.

Why?

Why seal up the Premier's Sector? Why not make use of the

arms, the food, the space, the warmth? Under the Dome, even Shepherd's soldiers were suffering from the cold.

They found what might be an answer in the most prominent room in the mansion. With a view overlooking the icy mountains in the distance, sat a desk, a flag every citizen of Thólos had seen via COMscreen during Premier Callas' mandatory weekly address to the population behind it. There was not a wall, a piece of furniture, or even a window that was not grimy with old, crusted blood spatter. What was left of Callas' body was in pieces scattered all over the floor. Fingers, parts of an arm, segments of leg... his limbs had been splintered, ripped from his torso, and flung about. Even the ceiling held traces of mushed organs stuck to it.

Shriveled up innards coated the floor, lay tossed aside in the corners, the broken, splintered edges of exposed bone a testament to the rage of his killer.

Not two hours prior, Corday had imagined committing this very type of violence against Shepherd. Seeing it in person was extremely sobering.

He could not do this to another person... not even the man who'd murdered his people.

Leslie went to her knees near the fragmented and crushed skull of the man she claimed was preparing to make her his bride. "I knew he was dead, but this..."

Corday had watched her when her eyes roved over the scene in the safe house, seen how she'd looked at the lifeless body of her uncle... as if she didn't understand what she saw. Her face had been blank, her eyes blinking slowly. Never had she cried.

It had been the shock, he was sure.

Now, there were tears on her face.

Corday watched Leslie grieve over a man who had been one of the first true casualties of the breach, and wondered at the difference between her impassive, determined reaction to her uncle's body and her silent tears seeing the old remains of the man she'd loved, ripped to shreds.

Something seemed strange in the behavior.

A loving uncle who had secreted her away so that even the resistance might not harm her, and Leslie Kantor would not even help in removing his body from the wall it was nailed to. Now this, her open weeping over a man she admittedly accepted as long dead, her fingertips tracing the sharp edges of his cracked skull.

"You must have loved him very much." Corday took a deep breath and let a sigh past his lips. "After you left your parents' safe room, why did you not come here first?"

Open apology in her wide china blue eyes, Leslie admitted, "I tried to. I could not turn the crank on the door with my strength alone."

There had not been a single set of footprints in the corridor's dust. If she had tried a few months ago, then the accumulating grime would have shown some trace of her tracks. She was lying.

Corday was unsure if it mattered, so he nodded as if he understood. "Of course."

Hand to her knee, Leslie abandoned the bones of Premier Callas, and pressed her body to stand. "We found what we came for. Now, you and I must draw the resistance here."

It was not going to be quite that simple. If they had been infiltrated, then Corday understood it would be an easy thing for Shepherd to learn of this new place. "If your plan is going to work, Shepherd cannot be allowed to believe the resistance perseveres. We have to let him believe we've given up."

"Agreed." Wiping her hands on her pants, Leslie offered a sad smile. "We must make him think we've failed. Let Shepherd believe the murder of my uncle broke our lines. The resistance as it is today will fade away. A new rebellion will rise up in the shadows where our oppressor cannot see. He'll never even know we were here."

Looking out her window, Claire tried to focus on distant snow-covered peaks. But there was a much brighter, far more tempting view sitting behind her. Fingertips cold on the glass, thread warm in her chest, she felt pulled in two directions.

The familiar rasp purred, "You are thinking of my shoulder. You wonder if I am in pain. Would you like to see it?"

She always wanted to see the place where she'd bit him, could hardly suppress the need to touch her fresh mark when he was near. But Claire didn't answer, aware he was trying to tempt her from the view.

Her anxiety spiked with the understanding of how easily he could do it. Shepherd's purr heightened, she calmed.

Rolling her neck, letting out a sigh, Claire gazed at nature. How ironic considering nature was twisting up her insides.

Drumming her fingers against the glass, debating available courses of action, Claire kept her eyes off the male.

*When the enemy is relaxed, make them toil. When full, starve them. When settled, make them move. –Sun Tzu*

The directive seemed simple enough, but over the last week, Claire kept catching herself enacting the opposite effect on Shepherd.

He was already toiling and weary; her presence relaxed him. The Alpha was starved for affection, so hungry for it he soaked it up like a man who had never known such a thing—greedy for any scrap at all. A soft pet here—Claire looking down to find her hand on him, unsure when or how it got there. A gentle smile there—her expression relaxed without her knowledge or intent. And all it seemed the Alpha wanted was to settle and be still with her.

She was slipping, failing, her resistance having been crushed by her own strategy to know him… or offered up to advance it. She was not sure which.

Perspective, to seek out her enemy's weaknesses, that had been her goal. Having marked him and the subsequent blossoming of the link left Claire with a view so undiluted, no other person would ever see her Alpha as she could. Mission achieved.

She *knew* Shepherd.

What she found inside the man was so inundated in his makeup, she wondered if he even understood what it was—loneliness, emptiness calling for her to fill it.

When she mustered the courage to look, Claire could see his perceived selflessness. Shepherd wanted the world to be good because he had never known good, he had never lived it, and he could not fathom it outside of books and study. All Shepherd knew was that *good* was the opposite of the Undercroft, and that *bad* had to suffer in order for change to bloom.

He purred behind her. "Do not frown, little one."

Seeing him past the hubris made it so very hard to resist giving him exactly what he wanted, especially when faced with the eagerness in which he offered himself and openly admired what he saw in her. Unless she stopped and drew back, unless she gave up her mission to open his eyes, she was going to feel... more than empathy or compassion.

Maybe she already did.

Claire had worried over it, fallen into brooding silences, and found herself more than once asking for the room with the window where she could seek distraction. Shepherd tended to comply with her vocalized desires, would sit with her as Claire did as she pleased —played the piano, stared out over her vast snowy landscape, painted in the sunlight—whatever she wanted. And he would remain attentive and watchful, his side of the bond wide open,

Shepherd practically yanking on the link to draw her emotionally nearer.

He was the one making her toil, making her starve, and making her move. And all he had to do was sit there and wait as her own nature worked on her.

It wasn't fair.

"Shepherd," Claire said, turning mournful eyes away from the glass to glance at him over her shoulder. "I am tired."

He knew she was not referring to physical exhaustion. "I know you are."

"I'm not very good at this."

"You are improving daily."

She sighed, partially unconcerned they were discussing their long running personal war as if it were openly acknowledged between them. "Are you tired, Shepherd?"

Lounging back in the comfortable chair like a king on his throne, he shook his head. "No. I am the opposite."

Narrowing her eyes, Claire fought the overwhelming urge to kick him in the shin. Feeling the need to knock him down a peg, she coolly reminded, "On the ice, I told you an apology would not make any difference." Squaring to face him, feeling something unpleasant surge in her gut, she tried to make him toil, starve, and move. "I want one now."

He was somewhat surprised, slowly standing from his chair, towering over her.

When it seemed he was only going to loom, Claire chose to walk away, but Shepherd began to lower and the anger all but fell off her face.

He got on his knees.

They were almost eye to eye when Shepherd said, "Claire O'Donnell, I am sorry."

"Gods dammit," Clare snarled under her breath, moving past

him to flop back into the oversized chair, confident she'd lost another battle.

Swiveling, he faced her and leaned over, caging her with his arms. "Did I not grovel properly?"

A slight tick came to the corner of her lips. "Would you have knelt on the ice?"

He shifted enough that his torso parted her knees. Shepherd smiled at her while he warned wickedly, "Little one, you are in my chair."

"What happened to the whole Shepherd philosophy of take what you want? I wanted it, I took it. It's my chair now," Claire quipped. A second later, she realized she was practically flirting.

Confusion weakened her smirk.

Shepherd started purring, his big hands kneading the muscles atop her thighs.

Closing her eyes and leaning back, Claire let out a shaky breath. "Maryanne was right. I have it better than everyone else in Thólos. I am kept warm. I eat great food. You have created an alternate reality for me filled with distractions, including time with my friend whom I know you dislike, and pictures of the people I care about so I won't worry over them."

Shepherd grunted. "You did not make a point in your statement."

Dark lashes lifted and Claire looked at the man whose face hovered so near her own. "Do you have any idea how hard it is for an Omega to ignore the call of her Alpha? It's torture. It physically makes one feel as if their skin is peeling off. Then there is the fear, not only of the searching mate but of oneself. You hear things... there are tactile hallucinations. Your mind rebels against your wishes. You become powerless."

Heartbreak lay in her eyes. "The first time I escaped I would have sworn you were watching me from every shadow. I woke screaming each night. Every time you weren't there, I felt betrayed, even though I had run from you. My second lapse of freedom, I wandered Thólos and felt nothing. There was no pain, there were no dreams. I was empty—that in its own way was hell. But, day in and day out, I was searching for something, and every day I would get a little closer to the Citadel." Claire shook her head as the truth had only just dawned on her. "I did not even realize that until now."

Shepherd's eyes were glowing as he soaked in every word like it was vital, so still it would have frightened her in the early days.

Claire touched a slightly puckered scar on his cheek. "I cannot paint this expression. That right there is the enigma, isn't it?"

Shepherd wrapped his arms around her waist, pulling her to the end of the seat so their bodies could be flush. "Tell me more, little one. I want to hear more."

There was one more thing she could say that would affect him.

"I can't live like this." She studied his eyes, trying to capture the image in her mind. "I need to go outside. I need to taste fresh air."

"No." Shepherd let her go, stood, and moved away, dismissing the conversation, leaving her disappointed and awkward.

Already pulling out the handcuff, he waited near the door, silently signaling their time in the room was at an end.

"I give you my word I won't try to escape," she offered softly, seeing his head fractionally turn her way at the confession. "There are too many lives at stake."

Cocking his head, he asked, "Is that the only reason you would stay?"

*All warfare is based on deception. –Sun Tzu*

Fisting her hands in her skirt, Claire stood and went to him so he might chain her. "No, it's not the only reason."

Shepherd watched her hold out her wrist for him, the man reaching out a hand to ever so softly run the back of his fingers over her delicate skin.

While she stood obediently, he spoke again, pocketing the handcuff and leaving her arm free. "You are asking for my trust when you have not earned it."

Claire did not so much as blink an eye. "You ask me for the same thing daily."

# 3

His Omega's cheeks were pink and lovely from her exertion trying to match his larger steps, but it was the flatness of her eyes Shepherd did not like. They turned another corner, walking down the hall that led to his quarters, no soul in sight, as he had ordered all his men to vacate the halls so his Omega would be left alone.

There was no handcuff between them, an act Shepherd felt deserved a great reward, but Claire seemed to not recognize his generosity on the topic. She'd hardly even looked around, not that there was much to see.

She was so unhappy...

His mate reminded him of a fish in a bowl, staring vacantly at a world she would never be able to breathe in. It was clear from her end of the link that there was no pleasure in it for her, that the walk was unwelcome—that she felt more trapped without the chain than she had felt for weeks locked away in his den.

He wondered if she was punishing herself again, if that was what made her cling to his arm when she was miserable. Or, if it was some test. Shepherd did not ask. Instead he stayed close, looking over his domain, measuring what might be a threat, what waited around every corner, observing those stark halls in a tactical way she never could.

But this walk was not working. He pulled her another direction, and punched a code into a steel door. It opened, and though there was no sky or view, icy wind blasted their way.

The armed soldiers at the portal kept their heads forward once they realized who'd come. Claire went to step out, to pass through the tunnel to see where the breeze was coming from.

Shepherd did not allow her move. "I cannot guarantee your safety outside right now, little one. Breathe your air, feel the cold, enjoy what you can before I must return you to our nest."

She had not expected him to even partially concede to her request, not after feeling the swell of unease that rolled through the male when she'd told him she needed to go outside. Shepherd was too determined to keep her quarantined underground.

Leaning as far forward as his great arm would allow, Claire had a slender glimpse of a city blown away on the wind, all of her ideals made into some mockery with the stink of dead bodies, of smoke wafting her way. Thólos had grown so much harder to comprehend. A part of her had begun to resent it, and at moments like those—moments when Shepherd's feelings somehow mingled with hers—Claire struggled to remind herself that she loved the city she could barely glimpse down the passageway.

Abiding disgust for what she'd seen, run from, feared... not all of it was Shepherd's influence. It came from her.

It shamed her.

Her memories of happier times were growing tarnished. She was finding flaws in them—almost as if Shepherd were whispering in her ear the darker things she'd endured and refused to acknowledge. Thólos had been dangerous her whole life. She'd hardly felt safe walking the street alone, even in broad daylight... because the city had teeth and claws.

No one had talked about it, but Omegas out in the open had always been snatched up by predators. Thólos' rich and powerful… the ones who made the rules… taking without permission, pretending it was all civilized, all acceptable. After all, who on earth had the power to stand up to the Senators, the Enforcers, the Judges?

Shepherd was right. She had never once been free.

Even in civilized Thólos, her life had been one of perpetually hiding what she was. And what of the Betas? Had they felt the pinch? Had they been tired of proletarian toil? Had they suffered oppression?

Alphas too had fallen victim. Claire's own father had lost all social standing with the suicide of his wife. Before the body was even cold in the ground, the government had ordered them to leave her childhood home and move to a neighborhood just above the Lower Reaches—Claire's father publically condemned as failure undeserving of midlevel life.

That new home had been damp and cramped. On the rare warm days, the air outside had stunk of garbage. Her father had weathered it with a smile and constant jokes. He had done everything for her, as if he'd suspected she was Omega long before puberty confirmed it—and was trying to atone.

Never once had he told her not to use the soaps that made his daughter smell like a Beta. He'd paid for her pills without asking her what they were for, made sure she had all the time she wanted with Nona.

Based on his personal experience, her father had known the world was unsafe for her, and he had done his best.

He'd known Thólos was miserable and bad, and shielded her

from all of it long before Shepherd's targeted campaign had turned the city against itself.

Her mate said what no other Alpha would dare. He'd called the leadership deceivers, the citizens swallowing every word…

It made them worse still. Thólosens chose to bow and cede to his will out of fear, not because they took his words as gospel. It was because they were bad. Why else would they use the new paradigm to riot, rape, murder, indulging in the darkest parts of the human experience?

Shepherd had once said that it was not his Followers responsible for the violence. If Claire was willing to admit the truth, even she had never seen them do evil on the streets. No, their evil had been openly conducted at the Citadel. It had been her neighbors —like Mr. Nelson who she'd seen stealing from her apartment. It had been her mentors like Senator Kantor, in charge of the resistance but doing nothing.

It had been Premier Callas throwing women into the Undercroft.

Claire's free hand absently slipped to rest atop her belly, a poor shield over her son as if to protect him from her personal agenda, the wasteland, and her darker thoughts.

Everything was going to get worse.

"You're just one man." Troubled, Claire looked up and met Shepherd's eyes. "There are millions under the Dome. Desperate people transform. Soon they won't be afraid of your virus. It's only a matter of time before they come for you."

Shepherd took in her hand on their child, the blankness of her expression, and knew what she was thinking.

He scowled deeply.

Internally the Omega was a jangled mess, yet outside Claire remained placid, her face emotionless, and Shepherd greatly disliked it. He'd rather she cry and purge, than remain blank… reinforcing her misgivings. His mouthy, strong Omega was poisoning herself.

Shepherd called an end to their stroll. He swept her into his arms. She didn't complain. She didn't notice. Even marching her back into their room, where Claire was safe in a familiar place did not alter the flatness.

Food was brought. She didn't want to eat.

He purred. She stared into space.

Where was his thank you? Where was his reward? She should have been content, praising him… humming! Why was she being difficult again?

Instead, the Omega began pacing like she used to, fretting and wringing her hands. And then she did something that pushed him beyond the pale. Claire lay down on the floor, nonverbally refusing their bed, frowning as her eyes traced the cracks in the ceiling.

The seething mountain had had enough. Standing over her, Shepherd ordered, "If you wish for rest, you will rest in our nest." He then pulled off his shirt, holding it out so she might get up and place it accordingly, giving her one last chance to act on her own.

Claire waved a hand at him and made a snorting sound.

He nudged her with his toe, eyes narrowed, growl deep. "Get up."

Claire shook her head and spread out further on the floor.

He'd drag her to the nest if he had to, break her of such behavior. Leaning down, preparing to tug her up, Shepherd put his face in her line of sight. "Get. Up."

Claire planted her foot right on his chest and pressed him away, hissing, "Piss. Off."

The male froze, eyes flared in furious disbelief she'd had the audacity to physically challenge him, to look at him with such eyes... to hum out of tune on her end of their bond even though he'd given her what she wanted.

A meaty fist wrapped around her ankle. Claire showed her teeth, and that was all it took to push the monster to react. She yipped when he yanked her leg, the Alpha falling upon her so fucking fast the Omega never stood a chance of escape. Twisting until he contained her, he *toyed with his food.* Allowing Claire to wiggle and slip, Shepherd made a mockery of her strength, so that she might find how utterly useless such resistance was.

Claire wrestled with every ounce of old anger. Grunting and hissing, freeing an arm only to lose its mobility a second later, kicking a leg that was pinned in a heartbeat. Hardly aware, her nose went to his neck. Out of nowhere she groaned lowly, the strange burning thing inside her growing more satisfied by the struggle. When he moved again, when the rippling bunching flesh shifted, Claire got her arm free and instead of clawing her way out, she found her fingertips running from the hollow of Shepherd's throat down his defined torso, the Alpha arching immediately into her touch, his ribcage expanding in a great breath.

When Claire stretched just enough to mouth the mark she had made on his shoulder, Shepherd growled in absolutely violent bliss.

Nails raking harshly down the male's hard stomach, she made an impatient squeak, her voice thick with frustration, and the one thing he always craved from her, need.

"Shepherd." Arching up so her mouth rested against his ear, Claire's voice thick and filthy, animalistic and dark, growled in a maddeningly filthy lure, "Help me."

With a roar, one huge hand roughly rolled her under him face down upon the concrete, and yanked her body until her saturated sex was flush with the massive erection confined painfully in his pants.

Breathing hard under a vibrating mountain of muscle, Claire could hardly register the feeling of her skirt being tugged up, or the sound of a zipper breaking before a punishingly hard thrust filled her to the brim. Shepherd snaked his arm under her torso, gripped her by the front of the throat, and understanding dawned. His Omega felt weak from her loss of the war. She needed him to prove he was stronger—strong enough for both of them. That was their way... a relic from the Undercroft he'd taught her.

"Scream all you want. Fight me." Shepherd licked his lips and eyed her jerking body each time he forcefully fucked into her slippery pussy. "You won't win." A thumb swiped over her pulsing carotid artery. "You want to be conquered by your mate. Constrained submission calms you when you rage—when you feel lost and confused."

Compressed as she was, slippery and scented, Shepherd shoved in hard when she snarled, relishing the ooze of more Omega fluid and the wet music he created over the sounds of her purging anger. He began to describe the tight feeling of her cunt, how it was his to satisfy, how he would fill her and she would relish every last drop of his come, even if she fought—because he knew what she needed, and as her mate, he would give it to her.

The Alpha's voice was so saturated in guttural possessiveness, in greed, in the arrogant confidence that she was his to dominate, it sickeningly only made her want more. Each pounding thrust was angled to mercilessly bring friction at that raw craving inside her. The rapid smack of his balls against her, the slight burn from such a stretch, the intoxicating sounds of his loud, vicious grunts, and the almost too tight pressure of his fingers gripping her throat, fueled her urge to clench around him.

She shuddered, felt the walls of her cunt tighten like a fist, all the while ranting out a long list of venomous nastiness. Claire blamed him for her torment, for the deaths of her friends, for all the darkness in the world. It only made him more animal, dangerously savage as he constrained her and conquered, doing exactly what he threatened to do—jamming himself deeper, filling her to the point it scraped her warring emotions blank—transforming her insides to the point that Claire began sobbing out his name over and over, begging him to stop, begging him to fuck her harder, begging for something she could not name. Her pussy seized in an overburdened release. The knot was shoved deep, she screamed into the floor, and the male roared so loud at her ear it added an edge of fear to her bursting relief, extending Claire's frenzy and making her squeal.

It was not until his meaty hand on her throat loosened its grip that Claire began to feel the end of her wild, shattering climax. Soothing fluid was pumped so perfectly inside her, her body greedily taking it all while her Alpha whined low in his throat with each extended gush.

He was crushing her, her face mashed into the ground, his panting form seemingly content to continue to hold her trapped. Claire could not move, she could hardly breathe, yet his loud labored gasps were music, pressing calm to replace exorcised rage.

She began to hum brokenly between pants. Shepherd stretched, rubbing his sweaty skin against her as he began to purr in praise to her perfect response to his domination.

Knowing to offer comfort after such a savage mating, his weight shifted so he might turn them side by side. Locked deep in his mate, knotted, and supporting the exhausted woman in his arms, Shepherd began to pleasure her gently with his hand—rubbing the labia stretched around his shaft, circling her clitoris, enjoying her twitching with each soft pluck.

Claire did not understand what he was doing, Shepherd never having fingered her in such a way when they were fused. Melting, still so sensitive, she tried to push his hand away, but he hushed her and continued to give soft pleasure that built up into an easy cresting wave of warmth. Still full of him, stretched and possessed by the knot, she gave herself over, drowning in what he offered.

He felt her internal reaction around his girth, the new pull that drank in the last drops of his lingering come, even though he could not climax with her. It was still very pleasing, each ripple and milking compression, the fact he had offered his mate the comfort she needed—something tender after so much necessary savagery.

All of it for her.

When he had drawn out every last ounce of her second orgasm, his hand left her pussy and began to trace the various angles of the exposed side of her face. Ghosting over her cheekbone, her lowered lashes, swirling around the shell of her ear, Shepherd asked, "Did I hurt you, little one?"

All Claire could offer in response was an exhausted, unintelligible whimper.

Shepherd pressed his lips right to her ear and purred richly. "Did I *please* you?"

A grunt, almost inaudible, came out on her breath.

Shepherd chuckled, relishing the pulse of his knot and the feel of her tight cunt still fluttering, her body speaking for her. "You pleased me, would-be Napoleon." He stroked her from shoulder to hip. "Your submission was beautiful."

Petulant, Claire reached down and smacked Shepherd's bent knee. "I am sure I will be feeling very beautiful later when I see all the bruises."

The nature of his growl lost all traces of tameness. "You chose the playing field. Had you not fought so savagely, I would not have restrained you while I claimed my prize."

She wanted to turn over, to look him in the eye, but the knot prevented more than a cursory glance over her shoulder. "Your prize?"

The male's deep chuckle shook her, Shepherd's fingers dipping into the top of her dress to pull at her nipples. "All of this is mine. You offered it to me when you began to stroke my body and placed your teeth on my mark. You promised it to me when you called out my name and begged. I gave you pleasure because I am yours. And feeling you come all over my cock, knowing your body takes satisfaction from mine, it is something I love to give you." Holding her a little tighter, Shepherd growled into the purr, lecherously fondling her breasts. "Confess that I fulfilled what you wanted. There will be no pouting or allegations."

Stroking upward, his big hand enclosed over her throat again, but did not squeeze, only encircled the smooth column, a possessive gesture that made her flutter down below.

Warm words were purred at her ear. "Confess, little one."

*Disorder came from order, fear came from courage, weakness came from strength. –Sun Tzu*

Disorder, fear, and weakness were all she'd seen wandering Thólos.

"You're my mate," Claire whispered. "You wanted instincts… and I'm all out of ideals."

He stroked her again, Shepherd's voice low and sincere. "I realize you are struggling to accept that everything was not as you originally believed. Growing wiser does not mean you failed. You should be proud that you possess the strength to face the truth."

It felt far more like losing her faith.

Shepherd caressed her body, teasing further arousal until the knot subsided enough that he could take her to the nest and begin again—eager for his reward and her attention.

Arms full of Omega, Shepherd lay back on the mattress, pulling Claire to straddle him. Voice velvet, he teased. "This time I will be your prize, and you can take me anyway you desire. I will even put up a fight if you want me to," a rich heady voice flowed, a smile thick in his voice. "And I'll let you win, little Napoleon."

Since they had opened the Premier's Sector, the rebellion's progress had been gaining almost alarming momentum. It had been too easy for the one now addressed as *Lady Kantor* to usurp Brigadier Dane. The resistance wanted a savior to make everything better after the Senator's death, and it looked as if one had appeared. None of the surviving Enforcers knew Leslie Kantor. She had no reputation, no fame or infamy. But she had a name—the same name as their newly dead hero.

All it took for the group to fall under her power was the name Kantor, her stunning smile, and promises of freedom from Shepherd's tyranny.

One by one, the resistance bowed willingly—all but Brigadier Dane, who seemed vastly unsettled by what she was witnessing.

It was not that Corday doubted Leslie; it was that he trusted Dane. Even if he didn't like his superior officer, after watching her tirelessly fight for the suffering people of their city, seen the look in her eye each time one of their family had been reported dead, he'd come to trust her instincts implicitly.

Brigadier Dane never openly spoke against Lady Kantor, not once she'd seen the Premier's Sector with her own eyes. She obeyed every order, but it was her lack of communication that Corday noticed most. He knew her well enough to see the older woman discerned what was important. She knew what was at stake, and she understood the importance of unity... and the danger of what even Corday could see was a developing demagogue.

People went missing under the Dome every day. It made Lady Kantor's ability to swell her hidden militia simpler as the weeks passed. A small portion of those missing people, those with no surviving family, who had lost everything—those hand selected by Leslie—joined the ranks of an organized and dedicated rebellion.

To join her cause, was to offer your life, literally.

Leslie Kantor spoke a great deal, her speeches fiery, the flagging men and women under their banner once again alive with faith. She said there was no need to fear infiltration again; they were untouchable now, simply because those recruited to join their crusade and enter the Premier's Sector were not permitted to leave until the day they would take back the city.

The only souls who could pass through that secret underground door, were those charged with maintaining a charade. Brigadier Dane, Corday, a few key members of the original resistance, were ordered away to continue their lives outside the rebellion's inner workings, to meet regularly, Leslie Kantor occasionally amongst them. In the same house where Senator Kantor had once laid out his plans, Brigadier Dane now laid out the sham of hers.

She had been ordered to serve as head of this puppet resistance, a great many of those who followed her having no idea a shadow organization had sprung up within their numbers.

Day in and day out, Corday did his duty, and day in and day out the *resistance* grew weaker while the rebellion grew stronger.

Unlike Brigadier Dane, Corday had been back inside the Premier's Sector more than once to confer with Lady Kantor. Each time he'd returned, those who had been chosen, seemed more like Followers and less like citizens. There was a fire in their eyes when they looked to their leader, a zealotry that made Corday nervous.

All in the name of progress...

Leslie had taken to the dead Premier's desk. His office had become hers, even though not all the bloodstains could be removed from the wallpaper or carpet. She always smiled when he entered. She always stood from her chair, circled the desk, and greeted him with a kiss on the cheek.

"I am so glad to see you, Corday. What news have you brought?"

"Fifteen of our men died last night trying to procure a shipment of food." He wasn't talking about the soldiers she had gathered around her. He was talking about the original supporters of the resistance who were still in the dark about what was going on here. "Shepherd's men defended their cache. Every case of fresh produce made it into the Citadel."

"They didn't die for nothing, dear Corday." Leslie put a hand to his cheek, offering an expression of deep sadness. "They served as a distraction so my team might acquire a great deal of fertilizer left forgotten on the farm levels. Our first mission was successful. Those men and women's sacrifice will be remembered."

No one had discussed this with him. How could she knowingly have let him lead his men to their deaths? "A team left here on your orders?"

Smiling, Leslie nodded. "Yes, a small squad, hand-selected by me. I trust them implicitly. Last night each one of them proved they were worthy of that faith. Soon, we will have everything we need to craft military-grade explosives."

There was one major impediment to Lady Kantor's grand scheme, one Corday could not be quiet about. "We still do not know the location of the virus."

"Your men have scoured the city with nothing to show for it for almost a year. Shepherd must keep it in the Citadel. We burn that building to ash, set off enough explosives to incinerate everything inside, the virus will be destroyed. Wasting time searching, as my uncle did, got us nowhere." She took his hand, squeezing his fingers as she led him to sit so she might serve him a drink. "The true rebellion is about action."

Watching her pour coffee from a china pot into a decorative cup, Corday wondered if she knew how ridiculous such an act of congenial etiquette was when they were talking of inciting a massacre.

If the plan was successful, several city structures would collapse, burn, bury people alive. Tens of thousands could die. But, if Shepherd's regime fell, millions more would live.

Corday didn't want the coffee, he didn't want to sit in a lavish bloodstained room. He wanted his people to be free. "Claire is in the Citadel. You gave me your word that no attack would commence until she was rescued."

Nodding, Leslie considered, offering an alternative. "The classified data cubes housed here have blueprints of the Citadel, the underground, even the Undercroft. Take them, study them, chose the most likely locations she might be held. On the day of the attack, I'll send teams ahead of the blast. It will be a coordinated effort."

Spinning the golden ring on his finger, twisting it around and around, Corday turned his furious attention to facts. Should the plan succeed, when Claire learned what Corday had agreed to be a part of, she would never forgive him. But if it worked... she would be free. The survivors in the city would be free.

Whispering, aware what she offered was a monstrosity, the beauty urged, "Asking our men to divert their attention from freeing their families to rescue a woman many here see as a traitor would undermine our mission. This is the best I can offer you. Sacrifices must be made, Corday. I think even your Claire would understand that."

Taking her seat behind the desk, Lady Kantor became nothing but business. "Now, I will be honest with you. You may find things on this data cube you'd rather not know. Don't dig too deep. Keep to the maps."

CLAIRE LAY FAST ASLEEP WHEN JULES' voice sounded beyond Shepherd's door. The Alpha had worn her out as he was wont to do. Knowing she was unconscious when he was called away was a small relief in the storming sea of Shepherd's growing agitation at the interruption.

Jules had not tried to contact him via COMscreen. There was only one reason the Beta would have dared approach and physically knock on the door: Svana.

Slipping silently from the room to see Jules waiting in the hall, Shepherd scowled. His second-in-command stood with many soldiers, ordering them to take up guard outside Shepherd's door as if war threatened from above.

There was also something very disturbing about the set of Jules' mouth when he spoke. "Svana is on the premises. She waits to *parlay* with you."

The Beta's word choice was utterly unamusing. As if Claire might hear through the reinforced steel vault she was locked inside, Shepherd spoke lowly in their shared language. "She has been off the grid, out of range of your trackers for weeks. Describe her approach, was it elusive? Apparent?"

"I have yet to decipher her point of origin, but I can tell you, she was first spotted in the GW94 tunnel walking from east quadrant. She wanted to be seen."

Considering how long she had been *punishing* them with her absence, Shepherd had some choice words to share with the Alpha female. "Did she bring the virus?"

Jules fell into step with his leader, blank and focused. "If it's on her person, it remains unseen."

Looking to the COMscreen offered by his second-in-command, Shepherd watched a feed of Svana fingering through schematics spread on the main table of the Followers' Command Center.

"It's unorthodox. Spying on your men will lead them to believe you don't trust them." Shepherd wanted to be angry. More so, he wanted to not feel relief his second had acted in such a subversive manner.

Jules didn't trust Svana and it was no secret. He was thoroughly unapologetic. "There is nothing in that room I have not anticipated she might see."

Shepherd grunted, the noise deep in his throat. It was neither an affirmation nor a negation.

The way the Alpha female had crept down there with no fanfare, spoke volumes. There was a reason Svana had breached the underground, and it wasn't to speak with him. She wanted something. "You will wait outside while I speak to her."

Jules turned down the corners of his mouth. "Understood, sir."

Shepherd was not finished. "But you will watch and listen through the COMscreen. I doubt she would suspect you would plant surveillance equipment in your own Command Center, especially since we know the resistance has partial access to our communications network."

"When I heard she was in our halls, surveillance equipment was not the only thing I planted in the room. I placed a micro-tracker on her person."

Shepherd had suspected what the Beta had done before Jules had confessed. "We will discuss what you've done later. For now, don't make me feel my faith in you has been misplaced."

Buried deep in his expression, was a small sliver of hurt. "Brother, I am loyal to you, always. Which is why I am telling you now, do not allow her to leave that room."

Shepherd made his final point before reaching for the door to his Command Center and leaving the Beta in the hall. "Svana killed Kantor. It's done and cannot be changed. So remember, without her compliance, we cannot subvert the population of Greth Dome. Without her, not one of your brothers will know freedom. You, we all, need her."

The hinges moved smoothly, even for a door of such size. As he had been ordered, Jules remained in the hall, cut off from his leader, glaring down at a dissatisfying exchange on his COMscreen.

Door sealed tightly behind him, Shepherd took a deep breath, and looked over his statuesque *beloved*. Glowing with health was such a cliché term, but it fit Svana well.

"Svana, you have been missed."

Her dark hair was loose, glossy, and clean. She pulled it over her shoulder as if to display its beauty, offering a soft smile. "I knew you'd be angry I was gone for so long."

Cocking a brow, Shepherd asked, "Was it your intention for me to worry?"

"No." She shook her head, contrite, her usual imperiousness waning. "Beloved, we quarreled. It was my fault. I know that now. Once I had some time to think, I realized a verbal apology would not be enough. So I have crafted something valuable to offer you."

Shepherd thought to lecture. "The murder of Senator Kantor was unwise."

Her laughter trilled, china blue eyes aglow. "On that point, I disagree with you. His death was necessary, though I won't pretend I didn't enjoy it."

There was no immediate rebuttal or argument, not from the Alpha male. Shepherd kept his silence until even Svana began to grow uncomfortable in the lengthening quiet. Not once did he move his eyes from her face, not once did he blink, he only waited for the inevitable.

When she began to look uneasy, he said, "Your actions prove redundant and provocative. You now owe Jules a debt you will never be able to repay him." Shepherd, fisted the collar of his coat.

He measured his words. "We had already infiltrated the resistance. How does removing an advantageous pawn help our goal?"

"How does it not?" Svana walked closer, as if she expected to be praised. "His murder coupled with my manipulation of those fools, has caused our only opposition to disintegrate. As of now, they are powerless, scattered, and dying. I did that for you."

Shepherd crossed his great arms over his chest and scowled. "Svana, your role in our coup was to hold the virus and keep it safe. Furthermore, endangering yourself in an attempt to dismantle an organization *I allowed* to exist is, in fact, subversive to our cause. The resistance offered a rabid population just enough hope to keep them lazy and waiting to be saved. If they have no souls fighting for them, they will begin to fight for themselves."

Svana was done playing, done trying to smooth over their dispute. Her voice grew hard. "They already have begun *to fight for themselves*. Your Omega stirred up the city with her flyer. Rebel recruitment increased, as did guerrilla attacks. Thousands of people keep her image in their pockets."

Cocking a single brow, Shepherd warned. "I caution you. Desperate Thólosens are nothing more than a pack of ravenous dogs. Remember, we are outnumbered and cannot leave until satellite imaging shows a storm-free environment over the Drake Passage. Considering the season, our exodus could be months away. Do not stir up trouble."

Svana threw up her hands, half in defeat, half in exasperation. "I did not come here to argue with you. I came here to warn you." Reaching into her coat, the woman produced a packet of hand written notes. "You need to protect yourself."

Shepherd took the offered papers, and found the photograph of a man he despised. Shepherd hesitated, his eyes drawn to the circle of red marker around Corday's hand.

"Enforcer Corday wears a woman's gold band on his smallest

finger." Svana's nonchalance slipped, her voice hinged on desperate. "Every time he hears the name Claire, or talks about her, he touches it, toys with it. When I asked him about the ring, he confessed. Has your Omega told you she's betrothed to him? Has she told you he promised her he'd end your life? Remember that while you are enraptured by your pair-bond, she has appointed another man to kill you."

Seeing her china blue eyes looking over him with pity and disappointment burned. Shepherd swallowed, squared his shoulders, pretended he did not feel a knife slice straight through his heart, and lied. "She told me. The confession was... cathartic."

"I see..." Svana braved placing a hand on Shepherd's chest, stroking up to touch the bare skin of his neck. "I am begging for you to forgive me, my love. Look through the information I have brought, do what you will with it. Please remember what we are to one another."

His voice came out worn and sad. "I never forgot, Svana."

"I know you are going to ask me where the virus is, and you expect I have been keeping it from you—that I will continue to keep it from you, as if we are in opposition and not partners looking to build a great future together." Heartache was open in her voice, in her expression, and falling in liquid testament from her eyes. "In order to reaffirm what we are, I've brought it. It's yours."

Reaching into the layers of her clothing, Svana produced a biohazard banded cylinder, the thing so small and unassuming, it was hard to believe what that little device was truly capable of. Inside something smaller than Svana's fist lurked a nightmare, the very disease that almost eradicated the entire human race.

She offered it freely, her one bargaining chip gone. "Take it, my love. I don't want you to have reason to doubt me."

The cylinder was placed in his hand. Closing his fist around it,

Shepherd sighed. “When you act on your own without talking with me, I fear for you. It was not a question of doubt.”

Voice dropping to a whisper, Svana’s eyes shifted to the man’s scarred lips. “I wish I could kiss you.”

The tension softened in Shepherd’s face as he smirked. “I will kiss you the day you take your throne and free our people.”

“Yes, that will do.” A warm smile on her mouth, Svana slipped away and eased towards the door. “Goodbye, Shepherd.”

The virus now in his power, he let her go. “Goodbye, Svana.”

It was three minutes before Jules dared enter. “She’s gone, spotted above ground moving east.”

Once the door was sealed, Shepherd looked to his second-in-command and saw that the Beta fully understood what had just happened. The Alpha cracked his neck, the man miserable under a stone-faced façade. “Have this analyzed to confirm the virus is inside and the containment untampered with.”

Jules displayed the depth of his feelings in one infinitesimal hitch of his brow. “You lied to her.”

Yes, Shepherd had lied to her, because Svana had lied to him first. “Have this room swept for surveillance equipment *you did not plant*. The guard stays outside my room, even when I am there.”

“Yes, sir.”

# 4

While folding laundry, Claire sensed the link chime like soft bells. The sensation was a fair deal calmer than the inferno she'd felt over the last hour. Shepherd had been exceptionally angry, Claire was relieved he'd gone and that the rage was not directed towards her.

And then she'd worried something was terribly wrong. Misgivings came with the manipulation of the pair-bond. Worse was the doubt. Claire never did know just what stirred him up, and they both knew he'd remain mute to her questions. He never told her anything about how his time was spent tormenting Thólos… as if she'd forget what he was.

A warm hand slid down her flank. "You are thinking of me."

Claire jumped under the unexpected contact, yelping as her heart leapt into her throat. Since she'd bitten him, he had taken to sneaking up on her, lingering in the shadows... watching her. It was always unsettling, Claire unsure if he'd been doing so all along.

Now, the link was *open*—he could not hide from her.

"If your plan is to murder me by scaring me to death, you're on the right track!" Claire glared over her shoulder, barking, "I should sneak up on you and see how much you like it..."

His lips were against her crown, the beast all grumbly and soothing. "You would never be successful in such an endeavor."

One hand cupping the subtle bump of her belly, Shepherd enfolded her in his embrace, offering a treat on the palm of his other hand.

She snatched it at once, shoving a chocolate in her mouth, all the while arguing, "I might not be as sneaky as you, but I am a lot faster."

"Yes." Shepherd grew marginally annoyed at the reminder. "You are very fast. A good trait for an Omega. Gloating, however, is less desirable. Eat your chocolate."

And there was that other new thing, the smirk he was learning to inspire. Claire popped another truffle between her lips, slaked and impish. "So you are trying to feed me candy until I'm fat and slow?"

Shepherd purred, enticing the Omega when he rolled his groin against her. "My mate is a glutton, but I exercise her often."

Mouth full, Claire argued. "Sex is not exercise."

Shepherd nestled closer, thoroughly pleased she'd engaged in a playful back and forth, and very eager to reward her. Or he was, until Claire backed away, her scent suddenly laced with sharp anxiety.

Shepherd watched her fidget and dart her eyes to every corner, he watched her waver between anger and alarm.

Distraction typically realigned his mate, and he was perfectly comfortable with manipulation when the outcome would make her calm. Maintaining the distance she'd put between them, Shepherd cocked his head. "What have you painted today?"

Claire waved towards the table so that he might look for himself before she began to sniff at the air.

Keeping his eye on the woman, Shepherd approached her work. A cursory glance went over what was splashed on the paper. He saw her point of view of the very afternoon he'd first laid eyes on her. She'd painted him to be monstrously large, herself small, draped in rags, holding a bottle of pills. Jules stood sentry, his cool-eyed disdain captured perfectly. Every detail was beautifully done. He would have told her so, but in his heart, Shepherd knew his appreciation of that moment was not what she'd hoped to encourage.

His pleasure would inspire her pain. Claire only ever wanted him to see more and be moved to change. He already was more—a great deal more.

He waited for Claire to make her speech, to offer her insight and whatever lesson she'd cooked up all the hours he was away. Instead, she ignored him, nervously toying with the bedding.

Shepherd cleared his throat. She didn't look. He chose a neutral comment of their shared memory. "You pulled down your scarf to swallow one of those pills. You exhaled. That was the moment I first caught your scent."

Claire stilled. Her eyes didn't leave the nest, but she did speak. "How many hours did I stand there?"

"Six." Shepherd set aside Claire's painting, leaning a hip on the table. "You stood in the Citadel for approximately six hours."

A line formed between her brows. "It felt like much longer. I'd been so sick, but I could not leave... because you would not acknowledge me."

"Women come to the Citadel daily to offer themselves to me or my men. All are ignored."

"I'm not sure what to make of that statement..." The idea made her skin crawl. Claire worried her lip. "You could be wrong. They might only wish to speak with you."

Shepherd's offering was gentle, the man crossing the room so that while he spoke, he might trace her claiming marks. "You were different, little one."

She didn't mean to cringe. Claire knew he had not intended to insult her, but she did feel something. It was not a good feeling. Truth was, Claire understood the motivation of such women. After all, had she not done the same thing, trading her body to Shepherd? "Not in the long run."

He absorbed her reaction, her poorly veiled shame, her misconception of injustice. Fingers burrowing into her hair, he purred all the louder. "You are my mate, Claire. Not a whore. You carry my child... There is no correlation to what those women offer and what you share with me."

Claire looked back at the table, thinking to edge around him. "I can understand why they would offer themselves. I do not appreciate that you call them whores. They are just trying to survive."

He could have made a snatch for her, he could have pinned his mate to the bed to show her his displeasure with her hesitation to be near him, but Shepherd let her be. It was more than her abnormal scent. She was acting very strangely.

Again he gave her space when she walked away.

When she got to the table, out of nowhere she set her fist to the wood and snapped at him, "Why did you not bring a tray?"

Because he had spent the last hour in conference with Jules, furious to find that Svana had indeed stripped off every stitch of clothing she'd worn underground and stashed them in an abandoned home. "Your meal is being prepared as we speak."

"Oh..." Recognizing her rudeness, the blush in Claire's cheeks, the tone of her voice, was self-conscious. The flush deepened an instant later, embarrassment replaced with growing agitation.

She circled back to the bed, brushing past Shepherd and began to sniff the air again. Turning on him, eyes narrowed, the hiss came back to her voice. "Something is wrong with this room. Did you change something while I was sleeping? Move something?" Her attention darted all over, Claire growing breathless. "Fix whatever you did."

Shepherd narrowed his eyes, unamused with the strangeness of her behavior. "I have changed nothing."

"No. no." She looked at him, had the nerve to point and blame. "Something is different; something is not right in here."

"There has been no alteration, little one."

She growled and fisted her hands. Right before it seemed she might start shouting, she seemed to snap out of it. Confused, Claire forced a softer tone, stammering, "Of course not... Everything looks the same."

"Is there something that you desire for the room?" Shepherd cocked his head, measuring her every breath. "Something you think is missing from our nest?"

"No." She tugged her hair, once again looking around and very uncomfortable. "Yes."

"You are behaving as if your nest were threatened." As if that explained everything, the man crossed his arms over his chest and waited for her to confirm that he was correct.

The weight of the glare she leveled at him was monumental. Rationality fled and Claire shrieked, "It is, you jackass. The room is wrong. FIX IT!"

"In what way?"

Was the man an idiot? Beyond caring, she threw up her arms. "I DON'T KNOW! If I knew what you had done to the room, I would fix it myself."

"Do you want me to leave?" This was not normal. Shepherd needed her normal. "To retrieve your meal at once?"

"Yes." She spun around, changing her mind, "No. You have to stay. This is your fault. You don't get to leave until you fix whatever you did."

Shepherd stood taller, commanding, "On the bookshelf, top far right, is a book with a white cover. Bring it to me."

Claire huffed, shuffling her bare feet over to do what he demanded. She grabbed the only white book and threw it right at the man. It bounced off his chest, landing on the concrete with a thud.

The Alpha growled—it was not the guttural call to mate, it was a warning, a threat, and something that would have sent grown men white as a sheet. Claire ignored it, choosing instead to wring her hands and pace.

He came upon her so quickly that when a great arm slipped around her middle and hoisted her up, she shrieked in surprise. Once seated at his desk, Shepherd pulled her to his lap, held the squirming Omega still, and opened the book. The giant flipped through the pages, stopping when he found a marker, and raised the book to the female's eye level. "This is what our baby looks like in his current week of development."

Claire stiffened, staring at the glossy page.

He tapped an underlined paragraph. "And here it says that at this stage in pregnancy, hormone fluctuations will occasionally make you exhibit irrational behaviors." The arm about her middle tightened, the greatly irritated male growling, "Take note, little one, that I am being extremely indulgent of you at this moment."

She felt his nose at the back of her head, heard his deep intake of breath, and read the book's offered list of tips for the father. He was right, she was acting crazy. Nodding, she admitted, "I think you may have followed 'how to handle pregnancy mood swings' to the letter: 'Do not argue, offer food...'"

A small gleam in his eye, Shepherd agreed. "I did."

She was a little embarrassed. "Considering your temper, I suppose I should be impressed."

With the mood seeming to have passed, Shepherd sought out the trigger. "Articulate what brought on your distress."

"I have no idea."

The Alpha had the audacity to chuckle, the skin at the corner of his eyes creasing.

Still annoyed, Claire muttered, "You're a bastard."

He gave her hip a light smack. "Watch your mouth."

She began to protest, wanting up. "But the room is wrong, I can feel it. And I *need* more chocolate, and I hate the grey walls, and I have this weird urge to eat charcoal, and you stink of Svana." Her mouth snapped shut, green eyes beginning to burn once she recognized the truth in her words. He did reek of Svana! Growling like she might rip out his throat, a haze of fury clouded her every thought. "That is what is wrong with the room!"

Dashing the book against the wall, Claire inhaled deeply, her nose to his chest.

Wisely, Shepherd held still, let her crawl over him so she might find the limits of where the scent might linger. He'd caused this discord by unthinkingly not considering such an outcome, but he would not allow Claire to believe the worst. She smelled him everywhere, clawed her small hands into his clothes, finding every last trace. The stink was so subtle, she was surprised she'd even noticed. The man did not smell of sex or slick or a recent shower. In fact, he mostly smelled of her.

Cautiously, Shepherd offered a remedy to the issue. "Shall we bathe?"

*We?*

Claire pulled away as far as his hold on her would allow. She repeated what he'd crowed only moments before, the phrase much more menacing coming from her lips. "Take note, I am being *extremely indulgent* of you at this moment."

Shepherd drew breath as if to speak, but Claire held up a finger, and cut him off. "You stink of the Alpha you fucked in my nest a minute after you found her trying to murder me and your baby! Speak and I might just have to kill you."

The Alpha kept his mouth shut—but it was not her tone or threat that stopped his lips, it was the smell of his mate's arousal already seeping, hot and thick, into the fabric of his trousers. He watched her small hand hike up her skirt, saw her reach under to cup her sex. Once her fingers were covered in slick, she met his eyes, smearing her hand down his neck, directly over the spot where he stank of his *beloved.*

Gathering more of her wetness, Claire soaked the patch of his shirt until she could only smell herself.

It was not good enough.

Unable to comprehend anything beyond black rage, Claire clawed the fabric and ripped Shepherd's shirt to threads.

Her nose went back to his exposed chest and she let out the most threatening growl an Omega could make.

If he was hushing her, or reprimanding, touching, or in shock, Claire was absolutely oblivious. Every fiber of her being demanded she stake claim, that she scratch her marks all over his body, that she leave a sign all other females would see.

She left him bloody.

Breathing hard, she reared up until eye level with the man. "Now you will fuck me, hard, in every way that pleases me. And when it is done, you will get me food, because I'm fucking hungry!"

He was on her with such force the breath was knocked from her body. Shepherd did exactly as his mate demanded, pounding into her with a fury that set her howling amidst their shredded clothing. In Shepherd's experience, there had never been a coupling like it. She was beyond estrous, beyond fiery passion. Her angry possessiveness blended so beautifully with the lustful need to claim what was hers—but it was so much more than that. What began as violent evolved until they were more than physically joined. He had what he wanted, her covetous emotion honest and pure in the bond. Shepherd gluttonously reveled in it.

She wanted *him*.

THEY HAD NEVER OPENLY DISCUSSED it, or even furtively shared whispers after the sham meetings they pantomimed week after week for Shepherd's surveillance team. Both Brigadier Dane and Enforcer Corday had played their parts, openly quarreling at the old location, hosting meetings where nothing of value was accomplished. It was all a performance, but the continuous suffering of their people was very real.

The old resistance was dying. Their friends were dying—not just from violence, but from crushed hope. In the eyes of the Dome, Brigadier Dane and Enforcer Corday were two great failures.

The title did not disturb either of them. Both clung to what really mattered: survival.

Not their survival, both of them could see the writing on the wall. They needed their people to live. They needed to give Leslie Kantor and her growing band of rebels a chance.

At least that's what they told themselves.

More people died, more disappeared.

Since the day Lady Kantor told him in secret exactly how she was going to take back the Dome, Corday could do nothing but nod dumbly. It sat there, that horrible knowledge, like a rock on his chest, but he could not see any other options.

Brigadier Dane had needed to know what her actions would be consigning, what the two of them were a part of.

That's why they found their way to one another the first time they'd met in secret, how they found their way to the ruined safe house where the headless remains of Senator Kantor still lay wrapped in garbage bags on the table.

The causeways were empty, the city hollow, and cold, the two standing in a room that reeked of decay.

There was no one there to watch. Lady Kantor and her minions, Shepherd and his Followers... no soul knew who met and why.

No one ever visited the corpse. It was more than the smell. After all, the entirety of the Dome stank of unburied dead. People didn't come here because only three people knew whose body was decomposing in that room.

They stood with the table between them, eyeing one another with open animosity and desperation.

Lady Kantor, her misused leadership, what it was costing those who'd valiantly served, had grown out of hand. Too many people were dying, 'necessary sacrifices' she would say, so her growing band of handpicked revolutionaries might build bombs from garbage. Bombs they planned to strap to their bodies on the day the *chosen* would free the city.

As usual, Brigadier Dane's voice was filled with disdain when she addressed the younger man. "You have never been a good Enforcer, and that is because you questioned everything. Insubordination, anything but blind obedience, was not allowed to flourish under this Dome. The wise ambitious do as they are told until they reach a position where they give the orders. Then there is no need to question, because everyone else must obey. It seems you've finally learned this lesson."

And that right there was the reason it had been so easy for Shepherd to seize the city, and so easy for Lady Kantor to wrestle control of the resistance into her hands with only the Kantor name to validate her. "And what part of yourself was sacrificed to attain the rank of Brigadier?"

Brigadier Dane did something unimaginable—she lifted an eyebrow and actually smirked. It was such an unusual expression to see on the hard woman's face, that it was vulgar. "I have seen enough of the workings of this city. I have done what I could, knowing more could only be accomplished if I rose higher. Sacrifices? You become numb to them. You hang on to an ideal, and you strive not to forget it."

The sickness that had brewed in Corday's belly for weeks, churned. "If you are trying to justify the things we saw on Callas' data cube—"

"Me?" the smirk became a sneer, Brigadier Dane cutting off Corday's quick-tempered complaint. "Boy, what you have done, your imprudence… can you even begin to grasp the consequences?"

There was a reason they came to this place, where the pair of failures might whisper in the dark, because there was no safe place to question amidst the fanatics rising to Lady Kantor's secret cause. Corday was not afraid of Brigadier Dane's disapproval, or in admitting he'd made a grave mistake. "Leslie Kantor..."

"Men like you are so easy to influence—you know everything, feel too greatly without questioning *yourself.* She pegged you for what you were the moment she took that first whiff. As Brigadier, I've seen veiled ruthlessness, the rise and fall of those who would attain the title of Senator. She is nothing new, a politician through and through, who hid in a room for the first months of this occupation thinking only of herself. When she was forced to leave or starve, she ran straight to her powerful uncle, saw an opportunity, and is using us all to achieve the highest goal a person like her might attain. The amount of people who will die when those bombs go off, the chance we might bring down the Dome, she is willing to risk all that and more to become the new Premier."

"The enemy is Shepherd."

The woman let out an extremely agitated breath. "How blind

you are. The enemy has never been Shepherd. The enemy is us. We are fighting ourselves!"

"What you are saying is treason."

Brigadier Dane didn't give a fuck. "There is no government left to judge me. All that is left is Leslie Kantor, her ambition, and those so desperate for reprieve they will believe anything she proclaims as if the Goddess herself speaks."

The words passed almost tonelessly, from Corday's mouth. "If I move against this mission, I won't stand a chance of saving Claire."

"If you believe Leslie Kantor gives a single fuck about your Claire, then you're even stupider than I thought." Brigadier Dane ran her hand through her short, clipped hair, shaking her head at the man's foolishness. "Have you never noticed how often she mentions your Claire? Why do you suppose she does that? Does she mention her often in front of her *rebels*? Do they hate her?"

Corday shook his head, unsure how to answer.

"The Omega is lost, we all know it. The only thing Claire exists as now is the strings Leslie pulls to make you dance as her puppet."

The temptation to strike what had once been his commanding officer, was so strong, Corday forced himself to take a step back. "I don't trust Leslie Kantor's motivation any more than you do, but she has lit the spark Senator Kantor failed to ignite. She might be our only chance."

"Yes," Brigadier Dane nodded. "She has set the wheels in motion and there is no stopping them now. But two people can *question*, they can alter the future if both of them are ready to pay the price."

"I promised Claire," Corday hissed, disgusted and tired. "I have maps of the Citadel. Leslie gave them to me."

"Leslie Kantor did not give you the Premier's data cube so you could save Claire. She gave it to you so you would grow to hate the man whose corpse lies between us... She gave it to you so you would grow to love her in his place."

Leslie had warned him not to look into the files, and of course it was the first thing Corday had done. Every Senator had a secret, some of them monstrous.

"What he did to Rebecca..." Leslie's ploy had worked. Once Corday had read the file, seen horrific video footage, he had begun to despise the old man. "His dead wife was the reason Senator Kantor would not let us enter the Premier's Sector. Knowledge of his crime would have been uncovered, he would have been exposed."

"Boy, Premier Callas had something on everyone, and everyone had something to hide. But when Rebecca died, I saw the change in Kantor myself." The hard woman looked down at the wrapped corpse; she frowned. "For the first time in his life, when he spoke of *the people* under the Dome, when he spoke of bettering ourselves, he meant it."

"I cannot forgive him for what he did to that poor woman, her husband, and their children. The footage of those boys' murder burns me every time I close my eyes."

"Leslie was shrewd in her dissection of your"—Brigadier Dane smirked again—"ethics."

Grinding his teeth, caught in the riptide of all the bullshit around them, Corday hissed, "How else do we stop Shepherd?"

"We don't."

"What?" His patience, his understanding of the woman before him, was worn out.

"You've left us with no options. Lady Kantor's attack on the Citadel will take place. You will be at her side as it burns."

Corday knew what she was driving at. "You want me to kill her..."

"After the bombs go off, right as the citizens rally." Brigadier Dane, nodded.

"I'll be busy searching for Claire!"

"No, you won't. The only member of *our* resistance who can truly search for the Omega is myself. If this is what it takes, I will give you my word I will find her or die in the flames trying. So accept the fact that Leslie is not going to spare you, a known figurehead of the old rebellion, when she might have you at her side to inspire our troops to follow her into war. You have value, and unlike me, she trusts you. You'll be in position. One bullet to the head will take only seconds, then you can kill Shepherd, or you can waste your life searching for Claire while the Citadel crumbles around you."

Absolutely not. "I would be killed the second I pulled the trigger. You are asking me to risk my life, to fail my friend? For what?"

"Don't tell me you don't see it. I know you do. There is something wrong with that woman. There would have to be for her to do what she did to her uncle."

"No..." Corday had never fathomed that Leslie might have done such a thing. "She didn't."

Crossing strong arms over her chest, Brigadier Dane asked, "Since when has Shepherd not advertised his exploits? When he infected our brothers and sisters in the Judicial Sector, their deaths were broadcast over every working COMscreen under the Dome. When he hung the Senators, it was done before jeering crowds. Why make a secret of Senator Kantor's demise? Why take the head off the pike?"

It was too convenient to be conceivable. "One woman would not have been able to accomplish all that was done in that night. The body parts, the missing Omegas, it isn't possible!"

Dane nodded. "And doesn't that frighten you all the more?"

# 5

*Conceal your dispositions, and your condition will remain secret, which leads to victory; show your dispositions, and your condition will become patent, which leads to defeat. –Sun Tzu*

Well, she had failed that one. Miserably...

Claire had no idea what had come over her, but the sign of her lapse into madness was a visual Shepherd took much pleasure in displaying. His chest and back were covered in lines of scratches artfully done: her own little pattern that made it clear they were not marks gained in a fight, but adornment of a sort. More so, they were mesmerizing and she had trouble keeping her eyes from them every time he entered the room and removed his shirt for her nest.

And he was doing it on purpose.

Shepherd wanted to show them to her, he wore them proudly. Hell, she would not be surprised if he had made a point of displaying them to his entire army. A situation that was infinitely humiliating for her, was nothing but delightful for him.

Whether it was the pregnancy or the pair-bond, Claire didn't know. All she knew was that she had not been in her right mind. Maybe the book had been right. She'd been absolutely irrational and could not stop the furious blush that came to her cheeks every time she found him looking at her with those eyes.

It was that same damn expression he'd favored her with after she had painted his portrait.

Catching his eye again, glancing away as she felt the color rise to her face, Claire heard the memory of her voice demanding that he fuck her, explaining in filthy detail the exact position she desired, how fast he was to move…

Shepherd enjoyed calling her coy in the past, and gods if she didn't feel that way now.

There was no scolding on his end for her demure behavior in the aftermath, or how she tried to keep her distance and her eyes to herself since. Shepherd was simply patient, sitting with her as she ate, offering her a piece of chocolate every time he'd seen her since —as she'd belligerently vocalized a *need* for it.

When he did reach for her, a thing that was as inevitable as breathing, there were ages of purrs and long caresses until she was sedate and melting, even smiling softly as she arched and hummed. It was in those moments she would distantly recognize her fingers were tracing the marks she'd placed on his body, having memorized them, enjoying the feel of the slightly raised wounds.

He had just taken her again, employing the exact same position she had twisted him into that day, only having moved far more luxuriously so that she might feel it all with her legs folded between their shoulders, bent in half so that he could plunge in as deep as possible. When it was finished and she was tame, Claire lay on his chest, green eyes following the path of her hand as she asked, "How many weeks have I been back?"

A rumble deep in the sedated Alpha's rib cage answered, "You have been back home with me for eight weeks."

Home?

"This is not a home, Shepherd." There was no rancor in her voice, just soft words as she stilled her fingers and woke a little from the stupor. "It's a bunker underground in a city full of evil."

A palm came to her cheek, pulling her attention from his flesh to see the hungry smile in his eyes. "That is correct, little one. Thólos is evil."

The warmth of the cord deflated and her voice fell flat, "We both know it's not that simple."

He answered her with a long slow stroke down her naked spine. "That is not the reply you would have made six months ago."

"Six months ago many good women I knew still lived; the city was not totally in shambles." Her calm began to evaporate and sadness took its place. "Six months ago I had not met you."

"And you were starving to death... hunted and tormented by your fellow citizens."

"And blissfully ignorant of just how ugly the world could be." Claire sighed, feeling his thumb pass softly over her cheek.

"Look at me, little one," Shepherd ordered in a soft voice. When her gaze came back to his, her expression just a little challenging, he promised, "All that was done here, it will only inspire a better world."

Fanning her hair over his chest, Claire pressed her ear to Shepherd's heart. Tracing the muscles over his ribs, she sighed. "The very idea what you have done, what the people of Thólos have done, might improve the world, makes it a world I don't want to live in."

He hushed her and played with her hair, knowing that she meant every word. A moment later Shepherd's great body shifted, pouring her off of him so that he might ease down above the pouting Omega. Pressing his scarred lips to where his son grew stronger daily, Shepherd inhaled. One large hand came to feel her there, to seek out signs of new life in the subtle swell of her skin.

Eyes almost dangerous, Shepherd spoke in a voice one uses on children, explaining to his baby, "Your mother is speaking nonsense." The expression he leveled at her even as he traced patterns on her belly would wither grown men. "She thinks I do not know what is in her thoughts—that I have not recognized her avoidance of any mention of you, my son." The palm of his hand closed over her little belly and he gripped it as if to reassure the life inside. "But I know she would never follow through on her plan. Claire O'Donnell would never harm her child nor would she suicide and abandon you like her mother abandoned her."

The blood drained from her face, her heart seemed to drop out of her chest, and Claire gaped. He had exposed her; he had upended her lie.

Rearing up, looming his bulging mass over her, Shepherd held her guilty stare and stated harshly, "Because you love him." Unsure if he moved out of compassion or if he was trying to draw out some type of confession, Shepherd moved back to where he had been and gathered her up so that she might rest on his chest again in her preferred position. "You would never hurt your son."

It was an underhanded tactic, but underhanded was Shepherd's specialty. The male was making a point he knew she had yet to address: Thólos, or her baby. It was a complicated position for Claire that only led to denial of the issue. Taking her survival day by day, pretending there was no child, was all she could do without going mad.

Thólos had to be free.

And then what?

Shepherd's reign might fall and she would be without the Alpha who fathered the small thing inside her. Corday's resistance might fail, and the remainder of her days would be spent underground in a life unworthy of her child while Thólos still suffered.

Either way, she could not endure.

A corner of her mind spoke over the mental chatter, whispering incessantly that her baby could never stay there—that Thólos was not good enough, and it scratched and scratched, infesting, and reminding her that she had a duty to her unborn son, that he was more important than any other life.

It was getting harder to silence that voice every day.

*So in war, the way is to avoid what is strong, and strike at what is weak. –Sun Tzu*

That is exactly what he was doing to her, even if he was holding her comfortably as he jammed in the knife.

Talk of the baby was acutely painful.

As if he knew, warm, reassuring arms wound around her, Shepherd held her with love and murmured that she need not fret, that she need only remain patient.

What she needed was so far beyond patience. She needed to strike back.

"You are the strongest Alpha I have ever seen," Claire began, compelled to make her point. "You have limitless potential. But, just like this unborn child, you are trapped in the dark. The acts of bad men shaped and distracted you. Serving your mission, even after you climbed from the Undercroft, you were never given a chance to be part of the world, Shepherd. Like me, you have never been free." Her eyes went to where his hand had frozen in a caress over the life they had created. "So what of him? Will he live a mimic of your life? Will he wield murder and pain against those he's taught to hate?"

Shepherd began a slow languid stroke that ended at the scruff of her neck. Gripping Claire's nape as if she were a kitten, he held her immobile. "You do not know of what you speak, and that is no fault of your own. So listen when I tell you that our son will be raised to greatness... nurtured and educated. Loved." His voice dropped, grew chilling, and he growled, "But far more importantly, how could you imagine I would inflict upon my child what was done to me?"

Face impassive, Claire spread her hands on his chest. She had one weapon, the truth. "Svana was in your company days ago. What have the two of you planned for this baby? Will your schemes, your examples, make him the next Premier Callas?"

It was like watching a storm gather in his eyes. The silver went dark, the rage began to build, and the man's expression grew almost violent. She wanted a strong response, and she got one... she got even more than she anticipated. At last, she had struck him where he was weak. It was not her accusations that had burned him, it was that forbidden name: Premier Callas.

Leaning on the link, she felt Shepherd's boiling animosity. But there was more, Shepherd was seething with disgust.

Widening her eyes, she grasped the secret; Claire knew exactly what inspired the hostile feelings buzzing on Shepherd's end of their bond. There was only one reason to harbor such hatred. She knew it because Shepherd had given her cause to feel the same way.

Claire said it again, just to be sure. "Premier Callas."

The Alpha's end of the link turned rancid, old anger crashing down between them like a wave of acid.

It was more than what that monster had done to his mother, it was jealousy.

Jealousy...

Claire could hardly believe it, couldn't even begin to fathom why, but she knew—It was Premier Callas, Shepherd's enemy, who Svana had been unfaithful with. It had to be for him to feel such betrayal.

Looking away from the feral mate who was silently raging, Claire fell into her thoughts, shaking her head like it could not be true. Premier Callas was responsible for the torment and death of Shepherd's mother... why would Svana harm her lover in that way? Resting her head on Shepherd's chest, she stared at nothing, shared in his pain through the link, and felt as if the floor had fallen from under them both.

Like thoughts of the child growing in her belly, Claire had pushed memories of the exotic beauty away each time they'd cropped up. It had felt essential to maintain her sanity and her composure when faced with the man who had defiled their bond by fucking the Alpha female. But she had to look, had to face the discomfort and sadness that squirmed in her insides when homicidal china blue eyes flashed to the forefront of her mind.

She had to, or she would turn into Shepherd—a man who had buried such anger as if it might just disappear. The link was slowly assuring that such a demise would be inevitable... his personality was just too strong.

Svana's was a face Claire could never forget. That beautiful, frightful image carved into her.

It was as if someone had shattered a window, light pierced the darkness in her mind. The wide eyes and soft lips... she'd seen them before. Claire had never paid much attention to high society or politics. Of course she, like everyone under the Dome, recognized the key players: Premier Callas, Senator Kantor...

But Claire had seen her somewhere before.

The woman had been dressed differently underground, less glamor, less makeup, but still radiant—incredibly beautiful.

The magazine...

Claire had had it on her coffee table for months. The woman on the cover of *The Thólosite* was dressed in a gown and smiling like the princess of the city. Claire had bought it for an article on cooking, but the woman on the cover had also inspired the purchase, Claire thinking the softly waved hairstyle was something she might try herself.

What was her name? Why was Claire suddenly sick to her stomach?

It had been printed in big block letters.

There was a soft intake of breath when Claire came to terms with her blindness. How could she have not recognized such a thing when the knowledge might have been useful to Corday?

Her voice shook, her veins turning to ice. "Her name is Leslie Kantor..."

"You will not think of her, Claire."

"She was important enough to be on the cover of the *The Thólosite.* I cut my hair to look like hers... I am a little copy of your beloved, just like she said."

Shepherd narrowed his eyes. "You are nothing like Svana."

A rough snap came from Shepherd's end of the thread, as if the male demanded she stop the direction of her thoughts. Claire ignored it and opened her mind to stutter though everything that flooded in.

Leslie Kantor, Svana, had been underground only a few days ago. She had touched Shepherd, communicated with Shepherd... and she was out there, in Thólos working to destroy the city. That was why, that horrible day months ago, the woman implied she saw Shepherd rarely.

Muttering under her breath, impatient and equally horrified, Claire said, "Kantor is a very powerful name."

Shepherd removed his hand from her nape, laying his arms

stiffly at his sides, where the mountain's fists clenched until his knuckles became white. Idly hushing him, petting his flank, Claire hummed, deep in thought, her actions merely instinctive as she stroked the angry Alpha sweetly. Shutting her eyes, turning her face to nestle in the musculature of his chest, she shut out everything but what she saw in her mate. Her mind fought to piece it together, feeling as if she was on a precipice, that the moment held a great value that she needed, that Thólos needed, that Shepherd needed.

She felt physically ill, plagued by all the anger bearing down on her from the male. The link was aflame, her eyes pricking. When she could bear no more, Claire leaned up, her humming ended, and she put her fingers to Shepherd's chin. His face was turned away, the man pointedly looking elsewhere. Silver eyes were boring a hole into the wall instead, and even Shepherd's scent was full of the warning musk of imminent violence. So Claire sat up and began to sing to him, a soft song in a pre-Dome language she suspected he would find pleasure in.

The fire of his eyes jerked in his skull and settled on the little thing straddling his chest. He growled at her, not sexually, but with immense threat. Her voice did not waver, the song continued, and with strength of purpose she lured him. The beast continued to watch, to follow the movement of her mouth, and Claire saw his neck twitch, saw him swallow and fractionally relax.

The last refrain passed her lips, the music ended, and she did not start again.

With a voice grainy and dark, Shepherd demanded lowly, "Do you know the meaning of those words?"

"I have a general idea."

"You sang that you loved me, that I was the one you longed for —that you would grow old in my arms."

"It was just a song, Shepherd, sung for a man who was angry and needed to take a breath."

Bitter eyes watched so very carefully. "And so you are offering your mate comfort."

Claire had touched him, she had petted him, she had done it all for that very reason. "You once told me that bruised emotions would not serve me. They will not serve you either."

One hand unfisted, meaty fingers reaching up to twist around a strand of midnight hair hanging over her breast. "You are far too clever, little one."

Not clever enough to have failed to notice something so important sooner. "I want to know about Svana."

"And you wish to offer some trade with me for knowledge?" he growled derisively, angry, because he could see plainly what his mate thought to bargain with.

"You could just tell me," Claire added, absolutely serious.

"I could." A malicious light turned his expression to evil, the pad of his thumb ghosting over her lips. "But I won't."

He was expecting her to deny him, pushing her so she would drop the subject and he could win with minimal effort. But she couldn't. The very fact he was reluctant to discuss what he sensed in her thoughts made it clear it was something she needed to know.

Her purpose had not been forgotten.

Thinking back on the conversation with Maryanne, the idea of redemption, Claire frowned and asked him softly, "Could Shepherd change?"

"No, little one. In this I could not."

And it was so heartbreakingly sad. Feeling her eyes well, looking into the face of her captor and her Alpha, Claire met mercurial eyes harboring an expression caught between insult and reassurance.

She drew a deep breath and offered the only thing she had left. "If you answer all my questions, I will give you your kiss."

Voice cold as death, Shepherd spoke. "It is not so simple, Claire.

If you wish to speak of our history, to know of my Followers' inner workings, then you must prove you are dedicated to me in every way. I will need much more than a kiss."

But she had nothing else to give him.

Shepherd stated plainly, "You will tell me every detail of this plot you've thought to carry out against me."

She shook her head, scowling slightly. "What plot? You know what I want."

"You are lying, little one. You think you have been cunning in the war you wage. But I have decades of experience and have outmaneuvered your every move. There will be no negotiation. Either you give me what I want, or I tell you nothing."

Claire did not even hesitate to lay out exactly what she desired. "I want you to fail in Thólos, Shepherd. That is not a secret. Even pair bonded to you, even carrying your child, I would stand against you in this matter for as long as I could. I also won't pretend I don't partially understand your motivation, that what I saw out there didn't sicken me. But a cause that uses the suffering of many, innocent or not, to make your point, is something I could never condone. I have to believe in redemption or all I have done has been for nothing."

"I already told you the resistance was fully infiltrated months ago," Shepherd explained, his voice was riddled with disgust. "You were not duly upset. The reason you accepted my words was because you hope, you believe your Corday might overcome the invisible prison he's trapped within."

"My Corday?" The pit of her stomach dropped out, Claire understanding just who Corday had been smiling at out of frame of the pictures Maryanne had brought her: Svana. "Are the pair of you really so insidious?"

"The reason I was called away before our first dinner together, was because Senator Kantor had been beheaded. Since that day, the resistance has crumbled into dust."

Claire blinked twice, her face impassive, and felt that flicker of guilt knowing the resistance had been infiltrated because of her, because Corday had been seen with her. Green eyes looked to his chest, to where they were chained forever, and she tried to convince herself that Shepherd was lying, that he was trying to trick her.

He was not.

She'd been the one lying... lying to herself. And she could have stopped all of this if she'd only ignored her pain and focused on fact. If only she had let herself recognize the woman sooner and warned her friends.

Shepherd always flipped the table on her in these battles, outfoxed her with cutting information he could wield like a weapon. Not today. Today she would make her stand and she would not back down.

Claire shared her story. "I was warned by Senator Kantor himself, that should the city be made aware of who I was and what I was to you, that the resistance would hand me over. I was told I had to be hidden. I begged him to reconsider, argued that his best chance would be to use me and the baby as a hostage—inciting a rebellion at once in hopes you would not unleash the virus. He declined. In that moment, I knew any operation that mirrored yours, that counted one life as insignificant, would fail. The truth is, I have had no faith in the resistance. My faith is in the few unruined by you. My faith is in the few who survived your worst and came out better."

He took her jaw, held it gently but strong enough to make a point. "Do you really think you're going to win?"

Her repulsion was obvious. "We both know that I am not going to win."

"Did you give him your ring?"

Black lashes lowered and a pair of tears ran over pale cheeks.

"It was my mother's. He found it in my house while I was trapped here. Corday returned it to me after I jumped off the roof. The morning I decided to kill myself, I slid it on his finger, so he would have something to remember me by."

"Did you ask him to kill me?"

"No."

Shepherd's chest expanded in a great breath, as if relief might have found a way inside a heart so black.

Claire chose to correct his moment of emotional reprieve. "I did not ask him to kill you, I didn't encourage it. His oath was offered without my prompting."

Shepherd looked at her as if she were the most deceitful thing he had ever beheld. "Do you love him?"

Her hand came to where Shepherd cupped her face, her move on the game board not yet finished. He had made specific demands, and she would see them through, she would show him that she was stronger. Turning her face into his palm, into the heat of a hand that had crushed throats, beaten the weak, that knew every curve of her body, she held his eyes, her own laced with worry for them both, and pressed her lips to his palm and kissed. "I have given you what you demanded."

"Not everything," Shepherd answered, absolutely unashamed. A large thumb traced the lips that had just kissed his palm. "Love me."

That worming thread was so needy, so invasive and searing, and his wants were so remarkably simple, animalistic even, but she could not give in to him. Claire swallowed, and leaned into his hand.

Shepherd spoke first, as if he knew the very Sun Tzu quote and intention she had in her mind, "It is easy to love your friend, but sometimes the hardest lesson to learn is to love your enemy."

Seeing her eyes widen, hearing her soft inhale, Shepherd explained, "I watched you read *The Art of War* at the Omegas' hiding place. You have used its lessons well, little Napoleon." He pulled her closer, drew her near until their lips brushed. "The night you marked me, when you touched me, I did feel your affection. Other times as well. I know you care for me. I also know that you don't want to, just as you don't want to care for the baby you adore who grows in your womb."

Claire was walking thin ice and she knew it. "The night I marked you I pretended you were the husband I had waited for, the one who loved only me as I loved him... that there was no sticky evil permeating our link. No ruination. No disappointment. No Svana I had to share you with." Those words had cost her and it was written all over her face. Claire pressed, saying that hated name again, "Svana, the woman who pretends to be Leslie Kantor. She is the one who overtook the resistance."

Shepherd nodded, his eyes taking in every facet of her expression, tracing parts of it with his fingertips.

Steeling herself, drawing in a breath to face a greater opponent, Claire fought the demands of the link and outlined the little she knew. "Before the breach, it was Leslie Kantor who set this nightmare in motion. You told me she came to the Undercroft, discovered you. She whispered in your ear, in Senator Kantor's ear... in Premier Callas' ear." His hand on her cheek slipped down to her shoulder, gripping her claiming marks as Claire added, "And because I can feel how strongly you loved her, I believe that you were unaware of Svana's intentions towards your enemy. You did not know of her affair with the Premier, not at first."

Shepherd did not nod or agree, he remained silent which was answer enough.

Claire took a breath, and spoke what the link whispered to her, "She seduced him, you destroyed him, and your Followers took over Thólos. But there is something very important that you have failed to mention during our talks in the past. I suspect the reason, the real reason that motivated this madness, has been hidden from me."

The Alpha was stiff, his eyes smoldering as he corrected, "I was honest with you in regards to our purpose. Thólos must be cleansed of evil. It is why the Followers exist."

"Your beloved, she laid with the man you hate most," Claire put her fingers over Shepherd's heart, "and put grave pain here, pain worse than any torment you'd survived in the Undercroft. And still you follow her."

"Claire..."

Looking him directly in the eye, Claire risked pushing him past the point of no return. "We are too different in our ideals for love to ever be easy—especially given... what happened, what still happens." Her voice caught, unsure if it was his suffering or hers that threatened to drown her. She took a moment, and then gave the last fraction of herself. "And that gives me pain, because I would like the dream, more than you could ever know. Affection is natural, I see that now. But love..." she shook her head, "If I was to allow myself to love you the way things are now, it would destroy me."

"You will kiss me again." He demanded, something strange in the recesses of his gaze.

"For the rest of the night if you wish," Claire countered, unwilling to bend until he broke. "But the cost was the truth. You have not given me that. Tell me, admit to me what she did."

Breath labored, Shepherd continued toying with a strand of her hair as if it might bring him comfort. "Svana fornicated with Premier Callas to create a child that might carry the Callas bloodline's superior immunities. It was her belief that future generations would be enriched, that the resource, no matter the man, should not have been wasted."

"That is a lie—one you don't believe anymore than I do." She leaned over him, looked him dead in the eye. "The probability of an

Alpha female conceiving with an Alpha male is slim to none—even with the help of pharmaceuticals. She is not pregnant. If she wanted his baby, a woman as calculating as Svana, the woman responsible for the fall of our government, would have covered all bases—had him use a condom so she could collect his semen and tried in-vitro —kept him alive and imprisoned, where she could harvest what she needed from him, like you did to me." Claire sat straighter, glaring at the male who was linked to her forever, feeling her anger and personal outrage mingle and surpass his. "That's not why she slept with him, Shepherd. Svana did it because she is a sick emotional predator, shameless and self-absorbed; because her agenda is flawed; because she..." her voice faded away and she stopped herself before she went too far.

Vehement, Shepherd bellowed, "Say it!"

Deep panting breaths stretched the Alpha's ribcage. Claire knew when she spoke he would strike her, but it was another brick she could take from his delusion, a price she would pay. This was the very reason she waged the war.

Looking into his eyes, her own soft with pity, Claire cupped the cheek and spoke with certainty. "Because Svana never loved you. She never could have to have done such a thing."

The blow never came, instead something strange happened. Shepherd's eyes welled, and the monster Claire could hardly think of as a man did something utterly human. He spilled a tear.

It was only one silent drop of salt water, yet it must have cost him greatly. Claire brushed it away in the kiss he wanted, soothing him as he had done for her each time he'd brought her to tears—only she did something he never did, she felt remorse at another's suffering and offered with trembling lips, "I am so sorry, Shepherd."

Her words made the man screw his eyes shut. When Claire tried to shift, to move away and leave him in peace, his arms snapped around her, squeezing, holding as if she might vanish to a place he might never reach her.

Claire settled closer and asked softly, "Would you like me to sing you another song?"

He nodded once.

# 6

When her song had finished, Shepherd held her where he could look at her, the man staring for hours. It made her uncomfortable, the intensity of his scrutiny, but each time she turned her head away he would gently bring it back so that the green of her eyes was not denied to him.

Their cards were on the table. Claire had proclaimed Svana did not love him, and in doing so proclaimed he was a self-deluded pawn. The revelation cutting him deeply, though she suspected it was something he already knew and laboriously struggled to accept. Shepherd had accused her of harboring thoughts of killing their child before Svana or Shepherd might ruin him. She did, and it made her hate herself for all the doubt that flourished inside her, how every day her resolve weakened.

Neither was at peace, each of them raw from battle. But Shepherd was still bigger and he would not let her move.

Between them the thread was... a nameless sort of discord. And it kept changing, evolving. A part of Claire wanted to continue the assault, to demand that Shepherd stop this madness in Thólos now that he must accept Svana for what she was. The wiser part kept her silent.

*When you surround an army, leave an outlet free. Do not press a desperate foe too hard. –Sun Tzu*

Confronting him about Svana, it may have been Claire's greatest victory against Shepherd yet, but she took no joy in the deep-set anguish she sensed in the Alpha. Nor did she feel content in the confessions she'd made to get what she wanted. She may have brought him to his knees for a moment, she may have bluntly torn at his delusion, but for some reason, she wondered if she had not given him, an unscrupulous man, more reason to fight.

Thólos was a plaything for Svana, an entertainment and ploy for some endgame Claire could not grasp. Thólos was a mission to Shepherd, a man who had been a lifelong inmate in one sense or another—a man who truly believed in the cause. Following through on the mission, Shepherd wanted to do it to save them all, to even save Claire from herself.

Maybe that's why Shepherd was looking at her; maybe he was afraid for her. Or maybe he had finally seen the purity he seemed to adore was gone. Perhaps now that he knew everything, now that he realized the truth, he would kill her. A part of her wanted him to. Watching his eyes, the unending stare, the hardness and calculation, Claire felt her bottom lip tremble just enough to give her wretchedness away.

Flexing her muscles, sick of his game, Claire found again he would not allow her to retreat. Just like with each other time she fussed, Shepherd's answer was to place the weight of his palm on her chest and increase the incessant purr only long enough for her to still again. All the while those eyes were moderately narrowed, heavy upon her, communicating something she could not even begin to fathom.

It seemed like hours passed before the mass of the Alpha finally lifted and set her free. At once, she left the nest, locked herself in the bathroom, and tried to find solace in the solitude. There was no comfort there, not in the haunted face of the green-eyed woman staring back at her from the mirror.

She bathed and attended to the needs of her body, stretching out the time, hoping that when she left the steam filled room, Shepherd would be gone.

Claire was not so lucky.

He was there waiting for her, still naked, standing proudly near the nest.

Stern, his brows drawn low into a scowl, a large hand came forward. He flicked his fingers, still silent after so many hours, and beckoned her forward.

Claire shook her head in the negative, feeling exposed and awkward. The man did not hesitate to approach, to take her by the shoulders, but it was not with a harsh, punishing grip. Shepherd was holding softly, rubbing her chilled skin with his thumbs.

When he leaned over, when their faces were only an inch apart, Shepherd let one hand slide down her arm to take her fingers in his and bring them up to touch his face, placing her palm over his scar spattered stubble.

Shepherd was calling forth the debt.

The timing could not have been worse. Claire did not want to kiss him. She didn't want to touch him. All she wanted was to hide from those eyes and burrow in her nest. Her cowardice made her feel weak, and she was tired of feeling weak. That was why she forced herself to draw his head down the final distance so she could touch her mouth to his and be done with it.

The sensation was strange. Shepherd's plump lips were not foreign to her, he'd pressed them uninvited to hers many times, but something about applying pressure back... about actually kissing him... it made the experience completely different.

The slow extended moment of a simple kiss, Claire still heart-sick over their conversation, knowing he was too, the almost cautious fusing of their lips felt... it made her feel a little better.

In the past, living as a Beta, there had always been an issue of growing aroused. Slick was an aroma no soap or pill could cover. That was the reason she'd never really kissed a boy, not even after the end of a date. Just a quick peck if anything... similar to the platonic way she kissed Maryanne. Yet standing with him at that moment, hardly moving, hardly touching, Shepherd's kiss was utterly different. It was decadent and soft, the feather light slide of his mouth on hers pleasurable.

And he seemed so patient.

Claire suspected that he was giving her time to feel it out, as if he knew she was a novice. When it seemed the natural time to stop, she let her heels hit the floor, and looked at his mouth, rubbing her lips together as she wondered if it had been done right.

"Yes." Shepherd said it softly.

Claire hardly had time to address the fact that he had answered her thoughts before a low rumbling throat noise came from the Alpha. He backed her against the wall, and with a breathy groan, retook her mouth.

Shepherd feasted, grunting the second she hesitated—a damn bully, until she followed his lead and ended up breathless and dizzy.

Where there had been silence, an aggressive purr filled the air. Where there had been discomfiture, there was loss of sadness. Claire had never known kissing could be so consuming, so fulfilling, that the act could be so very intimate.

Between the assertive purr, the strength of his hands roving all over her body, and the long forbidden enjoyment of his mouth and tongue, Claire felt the transformation from ragged to something reconciled. Everything was different, but it wasn't, but it was. Every breath in her lungs came from him, air they shared, and when he made the growl, it was not because he needed to call forth the slick, for she was pooling with it. It was simply because he was an Alpha calling to his Omega mate.

Reaching down he hooked her legs over his arms, lifted her against the wall. He opened her up, without ever breaking the contact of their mouths. The first spearing thrust of possession was almost enough to draw out her climax. Claire felt him smile against her lips, and whined when he pressed biting kisses down her jaw, her mouth tingling and hungry for more attention.

Brimming with Shepherd heavy and thick inside her, the Alpha tasting every inch he could reach, Claire found herself mirroring his movement. She kissed his neck, bit his ear as he often had done to her, lapping at the shell. When her actions brought the man to slam his fist against the wall, it didn't frighten her. Deep, under layers of complications, worry faded, because she felt safe. Fear disappeared, because she felt loved. And the link sang that so long as she remained in that room, so long as she was bound to the Alpha adoring her with his mouth and body, she could be both those things.

Her arms were wrapped tightly around his neck, the Omega climbing a thrusting mountain, until she claimed his lips again. He seemed almost surprised, the flash of silver between his lashes only thrilling to her. The rut turned far more aggressive, a part of Claire wondering if he even realized how desperately he moaned as he jerked against her body.

She could almost hear his thoughts: *Take your victory...*

That's what this was. She'd made him vulnerable, she had the power, and that was why he had stared... gauging if she knew. It was rare for him to be the one to lose control, yet there he was, mumbling something against her skin, something soft and breathy, a sound very much like, "love me," over and over.

And god help her, she wanted to.

Shepherd's hips rocked, angled so he could hit that fleshy spot inside her, groaning when Claire keened appreciatively from his effort.

"Love me," he said it again, demanding and loud, absolutely unashamed.

The sensitive flesh of her swelling breast was fondled, a nipple toyed with as he surged. He smelled so perfect, tasted even better, Claire's tongue dancing with his, relishing Shepherd, mimicking the penetration of his cock. The feeling of him smiling against her mouth again was all it took in the end, a taste of his joy so much more exquisite than any sexual gratification. The swell of pleasure crested, broke through her as she held him tighter, Shepherd's name passing from her lips.

The saturation of the groan he made once the rippling strangle on his cock began, it wrecked her. She shivered, feeling him grind deeply to knot. They were both panting when their mouths broke apart, each gazing at the other, expressions opposite of the distrust and suspicion from before.

Watching his kiss-swollen lips form his declaration, "I love you, little one," was captivating.

Glancing from his mouth to his liquid silver eyes, Claire gave him the only olive branch she could. She took a deep breath, and claimed, "Your son is making me hungry."

Shepherd laughed, the rich sound that came out was beautiful when suspicion did not alter the tone. For just a moment, she was struck by the splendor of his smile. He kissed her long and deep. "Then I shall feed you. I will care for my mate and our child."

"I want raspberries."

The nature of his arms around her grew gentle. "I always make sure there are raspberries on the premises for you."

"I know you do."

WALKING through the door with a scowl and bruised jaw was not exactly the picture Corday wanted to present to Leslie Kantor. She did not respond with favor to perceived weakness, and he needed her to keep him in her counsel. Brigadier Dane had been right. Leslie's talk of saving Claire had diminished. But, there had been a spark in her the second Corday handed over his analyzed maps of the Citadel, his notes, and tested her. "You might be right. Claire may have betrayed us. If your rebels can find her, there should be a trial."

He did this because he loved Claire. He did it because he knew Brigadier Dane was the only soldier who might actually care if the Omega lived.

Leslie's subtle hints had done their work. Around the Premier's Sector, the name Claire O'Donnell had become a whispered curse. He'd seen their contempt when the few rebels chosen for the rescue mission absorbed their orders. He felt it every time Leslie spoke of Shepherd's mate.

Day by day, he trusted Lady Kantor less. Day by day, he silently prayed for Claire.

Today, his prayers were answered. The morning had started simply enough. Scrounging for supplies was second nature at this point. Corday knew what to watch for, who not to look in the eye while he scuttled through the causeways.

Armed with Callas' data cubes, the rebels now knew exactly how to craft explosives, where certain chemicals were stored, and likely locations of other supplies the rebellion's growing numbers might use.

Once Leslie's list of necessities had been acquired, Corday began the journey back to the Premier's Sector, aware he was a target the second his hands were full of anything that could be deemed useful to another.

When the thugs came, Corday simply offered the box of random items to the three unwashed men, unable to reach his gun with his hands full. Before his supplies had even hit the ground, a boney fist connected with his jaw. He'd hit the snow, somewhat surprised a man so skinny packed such a punch. Another got him with a cheap shot to the kidney just as Corday saw the third pull a knife.

A shot was fired… but not from Corday's gun.

A woman old enough to be his grandmother stood on a stoop with a haggard face, aimed, and fired again. Two of the thugs had been hit—one dead, the other howling from a bullet to the leg. Asshole number three grabbed Corday's box and ran off, abandoning his bleeding cohort to whatever fate awaited him.

The woman shot one final time, the bleeding man took one to the chest, and she lowered her weapon.

Visibly shaken, far more frightened than he was, the lady offered, "Why don't you step inside for a minute. I'll make you a cup of tea."

She'd just saved his life. It was the best damn tea he'd ever drunk.

He learned her name was Margery, that all her family had died or gone missing as the occupation continued. She and several of her friends had taken refuge together in that apartment—safety in numbers—until those numbers started diminishing too. Being over sixty and a single woman in Thólos was a death sentence... she'd begun to despair, until she found faith in herself.

The woman reached into a pocket of her coat and pulled out something Corday had seen before, something almost everyone in the city still whispered about: Claire's flyer.

"If she can stand up, so can I." The way her gnarled fingers brushed the photo spoke of reverence. It spoke of pity and compassion—something Corday had not seen amongst the mustering rebel forces. No, they were hard. They had to be to have chosen to make themselves living weapons to serve the *greater good.*

Looking at Claire's picture was like a knife in the heart. Brown eyes shining with pain, he glanced away from the paper. "Claire was my friend."

"She's my friend too." Margery said, that same trembling hand reaching forward to pat Corday's hand. "Though I have never met her."

It seemed Claire had gotten her last wish. Some part of Thólos had become inspired. And because of it, one old woman had just saved his life.

Claire O'Donnell was right.

Corday sat there like a dunce, worrying the ring on his finger as he talked about his time with the missing Omega. He let Margery fuss over him until the adrenaline wore off and her hands stopped shaking. He told her everything he could remember about his friend.

His supplies were gone, hers were meager, yet she packed him a bag of food anyway.

"There are more of us, you know," Margery offered, "passing around the flyer. We help each other." She gave him a fresh copy of Claire's picture, held out the food, as if she could draw him to the cause." Rheumy eyes shone bright as she smiled. "We have to help each other."

Reluctantly, he took her scant offering, certain it would do harm to the woman's morale if he did not let her do her part.

He was hours late by the time he returned to base, hours Corday had spent regathering the supplies Leslie Kantor needed, but he was not going to skulk in.

"Leslie," Corday called to the woman walking down the polished marble lobby of the Premier's mansion.

Her head was bent over a COMscreen, the Alpha female busy

passing a litany of orders to the men following at her heels. Hearing someone use her name, glancing up to see one of the few who would presume to address Lady Kantor familiarly, she smiled.

Stopping in her tracks, she asked those circling to give her a minute. “Dear Corday, I have been worried.”

China blue eyes got one glimpse of his face and she reached out cold fingers to trace the growing bruise. Despite the others nearby, Leslie took his hand, led him to a place where they both might sit. “What happened?”

“I was jumped by some thugs. They are all dead.”

Her agitation was replaced with an expression of approval. “Well done. And to cheer you up, let me share fresh news of your Claire.”

That was the last thing Corday had anticipated to hear. He forgot the pain in his jaw, far too focused on listening to anything relevant Leslie might know.

“The maps you analyzed, I have looked them over, as have the team chosen to free her. Based on food delivery locations, we don’t believe she is in the Citadel proper,” Leslie brought forward her COMscreen, pointing to a far corner of a schematic, “but here.”

The place she pointed to was the top floor accommodations of a neighboring structure suspected to serve as barracks and training rooms to several of Shepherd’s newer recruits.

“The food Shepherd has delivered here is of a finer quality than the rations sent to his Followers.” The brunette was beautiful, she was charming, and she smiled at him as if the world were wonderful only because he existed. “Women’s clothing was also seen being delivered. There is a room near the top, a window overlooking the land outside the Dome. This is where he keeps her.”

Shepherd kept her underground, in his den where none could see her, not in some lavish apartment with sunshine and views. Claire had told Corday those facts herself. Leslie was wrong, or lying.

That didn't stop him from vocally taking her side. "I knew you'd find her."

"In five days, you'll have your Omega back."

There was something in between her wonderful news that sent a chill down Corday's spine. He said what he knew Leslie wanted to hear. "If she is not in the Citadel, then in five days, I won't be breaking my oath to her. She can be collected later. The freedom of our people is paramount. Your uncle tasked me with your protection. Only you can save us. I choose to follow you into battle."

Lady Kantor threw her arms around Corday, hugging him hard. It all felt so staged, nothing like the warmth that he'd found in Claire's embrace.

It felt as cold as the air outside the Dome.

Five days were left before Shepherd would face the fire. The Citadel would be burned to ash, a great many citizens' lives lost while they huddled in homes crushed by falling debris. Buildings would collapse, panic would ensue. The survivors would have to take responsibility for rebuilding their future together or they would freeze and starve.

The woman standing elegantly before him, the way she spoke of sacrifice, saw in herself only a hero. The surviving masses would cheer her, a savior who led them out of the dark. Little would they understand, Leslie's plan may very well doom the Dome. The culpability was his, as were the lies, the desperation.

Enforcer Samuel Corday would be remembered as a monster, and he knew it. He was going to assassinate the woman he smiled at; he was going to allow her to carry out her plan.

There were no other options.

Lady Kantor's rebels remained on a tight schedule, the last bombs being assembled that very morning. In forty-eight hours they would be strapped to the bodies of twelve of the *chosen*, and then an attack organized to exacting detail would be unleashed in the midst of the afternoon—right when the Citadel was most crowded, when the causeways were full, when the highest probability of casualties would be likely.

Shepherd was going to die in those first fiery seconds, a great deal of his men were going to die.

Anyone within the blast radius was going to die.

There were not enough medics under the Dome to save even a portion of the civilians who would be wounded. And while their people suffered, armed rebels would be climbing over their charred bodies, bringing war upon all Followers yet unclaimed by the flames.

When their embrace ended, Corday took Lady Kantor's hand, made a point of doing so before the rebels gathered in the halls. He smiled his lopsided grin and thanked her. "To your victory."

Leslie placed her other hand atop his, wrapping his fingers in her hold. "To *our* victory, dear friend."

"FOR A MAN who is supposed to be some kind of scary soldier, you certainly fidget a lot when posing," Claire complained, dipping the brush in blue.

"I have better things to do, Miss O'Donnell, than stand around so that I can amuse you."

She could not stop her snicker at Jules' petulance. He hated every moment of her painting him, yet submitted to having her do it when asked... which meant the Beta had his own agenda. Looking up from the half-finished work, Claire looked to those unfeeling, but vibrantly colored, blue eyes.

Lifeless was easy to paint.

She translated what she saw, the scruffy quality of the man, the air of danger. “Are you going to tell me why you are allowing this? Or am I supposed to guess?”

The man had always been painfully blunt with her. “I wanted to observe the change in you.”

“And measure it?” Claire asked, cocking a brow just to be bitchy. “Do you find me lacking?”

“I always do.”

She chuckled again, peeking up to meet his eye. “I take that as a compliment.”

The Beta stood a distance away, at attention, stiff yet twitchy... and glaring at her in that way he did. “You need to progress more. You need to accept what’s in front of you.”

The painting’s final touches were rendered, Claire squinting at her project, looking for flaws. “If I was to tell you how much I hate your enigmatic bullshit, would you believe me?”

“Thólos, Miss O’Donnell.” The man grunted. “You can’t save Thólos.”

“I don’t want to save Thólos.” Setting the brush aside, she gave him a long look. “I want Thólos to save itself.”

“And there is that clever brain I keep hearing about,” the man snorted, rolling his eyes.

“For my only friend down in this prison, you’re kind of an ass.”

“I am not your friend.”

“Yes, you are.” She turned the painting towards him and watched his eyes flick down momentarily to appraise it. “I doubt you intended to be, but you are.”

Jules always sounded so unamused, leveling that dead-eyed gaze at her. “You made me look different.”

At his words, Claire burst out laughing.

Pushing the painting towards him, she mused, “I wonder if all of you see yourselves in some distorted way. This is what you look like, Jules.”

Pinching the parchment between his fingers as if he found it distasteful, Jules lifted the painting and frowned at it. "I want to see your other work."

"Even the paintings of Shepherd?"

"There are more than one?" It almost seemed as if he cocked a brow, but there was no movement on his face.

For some reason the question embarrassed her and color flamed in her cheeks. Claire didn't answer. She reached for her stack of paintings and leafed through them, removing several and setting them aside before placing the bunch before the Beta.

Unsmiling, he set his wet portrait down and began working through her collection: her images of Thólos, the nightmares she'd seen all there for him to examine as he flipped through the pages. Some paintings she could see were meaningless, boring to him. Some he stared at a little longer. There was no comment made until he reached the picture of Corday making eggs in his kitchen. "You should not have painted his rival."

"Corday is not Shepherd's rival. Corday is my friend."

Flatly, Jules claimed, "Not anymore. Svana has him now. She's turned him against you." Those demonic blue eyes gauged her reaction. "It wasn't hard."

Of course she had. Leslie Kantor would have locked right on to him.

"You already knew..." For just a flicker of a second, Jules appeared intrigued.

Claire still had something to hold on to—something important the Follower discounted. In every photo she had seen, Corday still wore her ring. Whatever Jules, Svana, or Shepherd believed was not the total truth. So long as Corday wore that ring, he still had faith in their shared belief.

That was all that mattered...

A curve came to the corner of the man's mouth. "Do you still think I am your friend?"

Face bloodless, Claire looked up from where her eyes had been boring a hole in the table. Leaning back in her chair, crossing her arms over her chest, Claire countered, "And the Omegas? How have they been corrupted?"

"Do not worry on their account." He set down her paintings. "They are still cossetted and well-fed."

"And Maryanne?"

The jerk took a grape from the lunch tray Claire had yet to touch, popping it in his mouth. "Will get herself killed eventually. Nothing anyone can do about that."

Claire growled, menacing and angry. "If you eat one more grape off that tray, I will stab you in the eye with this paintbrush."

Jules actually laughed, every aspect of his face coming alive. But the burst was hoarse and almost unnatural, a long unused reaction that ended almost before it began. But a smirk remained. "During training I have seen the scratches and the claiming mark on Shepherd. You are quite a possessive little Omega."

"Be careful about who you call little, Beta."

Whatever false playfulness he had been enacting faded, but he was not offended, not even in the slightest. Putting his hands on the table Jules leaned over and asked, "When she tries to kill you, what are you going to do?"

The answer was simple. "I'm going to die."

The way his thin lips stiffened, Claire could see he was disappointed in her answer. "Your dramatics do not impress me."

"I think you comprehend a lot more about what's going on than even your leader. Shepherd knows she does not love him, she has used him, yet still he, like you, believes in something incomprehensible and obeys." Claire tapped her finger on the table. "With all this knowledge, you both follow the psychopath we know wishes

Shepherd's mate and his unborn child dead. The situation as it is, with men like you, how long do you really think I will survive? You and all your unsolicited guidance, friend, do not impress me."

Jules straightened and snorted. "You know what I see when I look at your pictures? All of them are finished. All but one." he tugged out the smirking self-portrait she had made for Shepherd weeks ago. "Tell me, Miss O'Donnell, why the portrait of yourself is only an outline?"

"Why don't you tell me, Jules." Her voice was as unfriendly as her expression.

"I once thought it was cowardice that held you back." The man shook his head. "I was incorrect. You are no coward. And yes, you are clever... just as clever as you are stupid."

Claire quirked her lips, fighting a smile at his lecture.

Jules ignored her and continued. "But I know what it is. I see you now." The painting of her was pulled from the others and turned so that it faced the artist. "You're willfully incomplete."

"It sounds like I fit perfectly into Shepherd's army of psychos."

"You lack unbiased perspective and throw so much motivation at the wrong problem... and you know it. Had you met Shepherd under different circumstances, this painting would have color. You are very lucky Shepherd fights for what he wants."

Gritting her teeth, she snarled, "I fight. I fight every goddamn day."

The man shook his head of unkempt hair. "Not for him."

Looking away, sullen she grunted, "I fight for Thólos."

"Stop fighting for Thólos. Fight for your family."

With narrowed eyes, Claire leaned forward in her chair to confront the standing male. "And just who would I be fighting against? To me it looks as if the enemy is the same."

Jules put his hands on the table and leaned down menacingly. "You cannot have both and you know it. Thólos or your son—a city full of murderers and rapists, of people who have turned their backs on you—or your own innocent flesh and blood."

Frowning, ready to throw the barb back in Jules' face, Claire asked, "What would Rebecca have done? Would she have sacrificed her ideals?"

"In every way. My Rebecca willingly gave herself to Senator Kantor to save the lives of our children." The man spoke as if it was nothing, taking on his mask of lifelessness. "Yet he mounted her and made her watch as his soldiers executed our boys the very moment he made the claiming marks. He wanted a *free* Omega."

There were very few things in life that cut as deep as what Claire had just heard. It trumped everything she had seen in Thólos and pained her greatly. Slack-jawed, it took her a minute to speak. "I am sorry."

A flash of something dark came to Jules' expression. "No you're not. If you were sorry, you would want to make certain such a thing never happened again, no matter the cost."

Claire echoed his words. "No matter the cost."

And then he knew. "You still think your death would make any difference? You would throw away your life for nothing, destroy the child growing in your womb for nothing. Do you understand me? It would change *nothing*. Remove those thoughts from your mind."

Spine ramrod, Claire made no reply.

Cocking his head, Jules came to a decision. "Shepherd needs to be told that you are struggling in this manner."

"There is no need," Claire offered, her own voice laced with weariness. "Shepherd is standing right behind you."

Jules was still. There was no look of disbelief on his face or even a trace of fear, simply placid acceptance. At the first obvious sound of another man's breathing, the Beta turned and nodded at his leader. "Sir."

Looking at Claire, the Alpha barked at his subordinate, "You're dismissed." Jules moved at once towards the door. Once the sound of the locks was thrown, Shepherd took the seat across from her. "You know his name and history... he has freely told you these things." Shepherd seemed amazed and equally unsettled.

"You should not be angry with him. He is your greatest advocate, and I was the one who initiated all conversation." Urging him to not react negatively to what she'd revealed, Claire admitted, "There were times I needed someone to talk to, and he only did it for you. I know he doesn't like me."

There was a look in Shepherd's eye, buried under heaps of disapproval was a large dose of envy. "He has spoken on your behalf more than once. Jules *likes* you a great deal." Something was going on inside the Alpha, a stiff calculation of odds. "Do you always argue with him?"

"Always." She fought back the tick at the corner of her lips. "Your friend greatly enjoys reprimanding me."

Hooking a finger on the tray, Shepherd pulled it before his mate and gestured for her to eat. "You are behaving as if you feel playful, but you are upset. I am willing to discuss Svana and Corday."

"I don't doubt that for an instant." She knew he was trying to maneuver, and offered him a sullen smirk at his attempt. Claire picked at the fresh fruit. "I, however, do not want to hear you gloat about how my friend has been manipulated by your beloved."

"Little one." Shepherd leaned back in his chair and leveled her with those eyes. "You need not be threatened by her. I love only you."

After swallowing a bite of melon, Claire put down the fork. She let out a sigh, her expression falling flat. "If I say please, can we drop the topic? You have taken my world from me. I don't need to hear about how I have lost him too."

The purr began the second it was clear she was upset. "You have Maryanne."

"But for how much longer?" It was a pointed question that matched the sinking feeling in her stomach. "I feel like everything is slipping through my fingers and I don't know why."

"We will lie down now." Shepherd purred louder, standing and moving towards her. "Come, little one."

Frustrated, she complained at his course, feeling he did not understand what she was saying. "No amount of fucking is going to make me feel better about what I just heard."

He was already pulling her dress over her head, kneading the tension in her shoulders. "Time will soothe you and so will I. This is just one bad day. It will pass."

## 7

"We are running out of time. Decide. Where is Shepherd keeping Claire?"

They were back in Senator Kantor's tomb, arguing over his body as they always did. "I DON'T KNOW where she is, Dane. That's the point. All I know is that she is in the Citadel."

Brigadier Dane, leaned closer to their shared COMscreen. "Show me a projection of the building's layout again."

"Claire jumped off the roof near the back," Corday explained, squinting at the image. "He keeps her locked out of sight, and would not have taken her far from his den, especially knowing her penchant for escape. She has to be near this location."

The older woman nodded in agreement. "And there are no windows in her cell. She told you it was grey, so no decorations either, only concrete. There must be running water for her use." Pointing to a segment embossed in the middle of the building's foundation, Brigadier Dane said. "She is here, somewhere on one of these two underground levels. Or she's here—another branch of the building in a completely different quadrant was highlighted —"tucked between the loading docks and the ventilation systems. Both locations are fortified, few entrances. Once I am inside, there will be even fewer exits."

Brown eyes hard with intention, he warned, "Bombs will be going off above you. The only plausible way to get her clear of the blast is to go underground."

"The Undercroft?" Brigadier Dane hummed, scowling over her thoughts. "There must be tunnels spanning the building, the very tunnels Shepherd used the day of the breech. Show me the maps of the prison. We need to estimate which locations he would have found strategic for invasion."

"These are outdated, originals from when the Undercroft was built. Shepherd's Followers may have designed a whole network of shafts not on these maps. If you get lost..."

"I don't get lost." Irritated, Dane's eyes flashed away from the screen. "So tell me, Enforcer, which one of these locations am I going to infiltrate?"

Sighing, knowing if he picked the wrong place to look for Claire, that she, that Brigadier Dane, would die, Corday said, "We need a second team."

"That is not possible." Dane had explained this before. "You know that is not possible. Not with two days. Not without Leslie learning what we plan to do. You have to choose one of these potential locations. You have to commit."

How on earth was he to do that without more definitive information? What if she was in neither spot? What then?

Brigadier Dane had seen him question himself over Claire's position time and time again. "Don't even consider going after her yourself. You would be noticed by the rebels, shot for a traitor before you got within ten paces of the Citadel. Think of what Claire would want. She wants our people to be free more than she wants her life. You have a duty to her. When Shepherd has been deposed, there must be elections, real democracy. Leslie Kantor will not offer those things. She will declare martial law... nothing under the Dome will change except the name of our dictator."

His superior officer was right, of course. Anyone who had seen how Leslie, *Lady Kantor*, comported herself, how she fed zealotry to her rebels in the name of her uncle, would grasp that any power she had at the end of this mess would be amplified by her desires.

She wanted to be a queen, was going to massacre tens of thousands of people to achieve her goals.

Seeing that the Beta grasped where they stood, Brigadier Dane got back to the subject at hand. "Now, tell me Enforcer Corday, is Claire in the east corridor or the basement?"

He didn't know, but he was desperate enough to approach someone who might. "Give me one more day."

Brigadier Dane frowned. "Fine. One more day to make your choice, or I choose for you."

Corday left the woman with his precious data cube so she might study and memorize every last pathway. Hands shoved into his pockets, he walked the streets, squinting from sunlight glaring off dirty frost. Light snow invaded the Dome, crusting everything, the white flakes a sign the glass above them had cracked further.

It was going to be a long walk to the place where Maryanne Cauley hid.

Almost three months had passed since the first time he'd found out just who Claire's old buddy really was.

During a standard reconnaissance mission, he'd seen a familiar face climb the Citadel steps. Blonde braid tied at her back, red lips smirking as if she were the true villain behind it all—the bitch who'd once burst into his apartment looking for Claire had walked right into Shepherd's seat of power.

She was dressed in Follower's blacks.

Corday had waited, sneaking closer. It was hours before she'd left, but when the scamp dared walk down those steps, he shadowed her home. It was easy to track her—so easy he suspected she was *letting* him follow her.

Seeing that woman, one who'd claimed to be Claire's best friend, had stirred up the most sickening hope. After all, it was the Alpha female who'd come to his home looking for their shared acquaintance, who'd had the clothes Claire had last been wearing, who'd claimed that their mutual friend would have traded her life for theirs. Why else would that sneak visit the Citadel, smirking as if bearing a gold embossed invitation to tea?

Everything was about Claire.

He had not approached her then, could not risk the mission by engaging with the female wild-card. All Corday had done was watch her. Now, Maryanne Cauley might be Claire's only hope.

Desperate to uncover any information about his friend's prison, the back of his knuckles banged out three staccato knocks against a traitor's door. A few seconds later Maryanne was there, smirking like a cat about to lick up cream.

The bitch had the audacity to purr at him. "I was wondering when you were gonna come crawling to me. The men always do, you know."

Ignoring the female Alpha's rich vibrations, Corday elbowed past her and barged inside.

Just as he'd hoped, there was a trace of Claire's scent in the cluttered room... one that emanated from the pile of dirty clothes in the corner.

Moving deeper, tracing his finger over lines of furniture, Corday said, "You have been frequenting the Citadel. Why?"

Brushing against him as she moved to the couch, full red lips held a naughty smirk. "I'm a Follower, Corday."

"Do you always lie? You know I'm an Enforcer. You know where I live... no one has come for me."

"I survive. You do your thing, I'll do mine."

The very tone of her voice revolted him. "Knock off the whole temptress game. That shit is never going to work."

"That's too bad," she chuckled, taking a seat on her couch. "I like pretty Beta boys."

"I'm sure you hate me as much as I hate you."

"That would only make the sex more interesting, don't you think?"

Corday snorted.

"It's okay," Maryanne teased. "I can smell Leslie Kantor all over you. Going after the Premier's leftovers..." She tutted. "You must have a thing for entangled women."

"I want to talk about Claire."

The Alpha's shark smile withered, Maryanne grew deadly serious. "Talking about my dead best friend is the last thing that is going to happen here."

"When you go to the Citadel, does Shepherd let you see her?"

"Claire is dead, Corday. Move on."

"I know he has her." God, it was hard to admit that out loud. "I have to get her out. If you love her, you need to help her."

There was a look of honest emotion, a deep sadness in Maryanne's lovely eyes. She took a tired breath and sighed. "Claire is gone, Corday. She killed herself. You need to stop whatever madness you're cooking up."

Voice curt, Corday admitted, "If I can't get her out in the next forty-eight hours, she's going to die. Do you understand what I'm saying?"

Maryanne shrugged. "Keep on dreaming lover boy."

He took a seat at the far end of her couch. Elbows on his knees, forehead resting against his clasped hands, he whispered the greatest secret under the Dome. "Leslie Kantor has convinced the rebels to blow up the Citadel. The bombs have already been built. There is nothing I can do to stop it."

There was no reaction from the blonde; it seemed she didn't care.

Corday's scowl deepened. He looked her dead in the eye. "There are only two days left before they strike. Please, just tell me where he keeps her. Tell me so I can save her."

"You're kinda cute when you're delusional. Now, if you'd like to fuck I'm still game." Her sultry voice was back, Maryanne crawling towards him like a playful kitten. "Otherwise, go pester someone else."

Disgusted with the woman and her malice, Corday told her to go fuck herself before storming out of her home.

When he was gone, Maryanne let out a long breath and let her head fall back against the couch. For a second there, she'd been so certain Claire's other lovesick puppy could see right through her act. But she'd done well. Even Shepherd would have to agree, and she was certain he'd seen every last moment of the conversation from the surveillance equipment she knew he'd stashed all over her home.

Now she needed to brace for Shepherd's reaction, because it was clear the psychopath had it bad for Claire and possessed no clue how to properly handle such feelings. Shit, he'd almost ripped her head off when Claire only kissed her goodbye once.

Did anyone appreciate how much she was actually doing to help these resistance assholes? And Enforcer Corday, Maryanne hated his fucking guts, and was keeping him alive when all she'd have to do to assure his slow death was hint that the Omega lived, or warn him that there was absolutely no plausible way to get to her.

But, if what the Beta claimed were true, Corday may have saved Claire simply by opening his big, fat mouth. Shepherd would not expose his mate to danger. Heck, he wouldn't even expose her to anything but plastic cutlery.

Maryanne raised her head and decided she deserved a medal. After all, what if Corday had actually taken her up on the offer to bang her?

Shuddering at the thought, she stood and went to take a very hot shower.

JULES WATCHED THE SCREEN, having heard every last murmured insult traded between Maryanne Cauley and Enforcer Corday. Rooted, overlooking several monitors mounted on the Command Center's wall, he issued an immediate order. "Summon Shepherd. Code Red."

The Alpha was at the Citadel, less than five minutes away. That was all the time Jules required to initiate command sequence Exodus.

When his commander arrived, Shepherd watched the recorded exchange; he looked to his second-in-command. It wasn't a ruse on the Enforcer's part; Shepherd could read the pathetic resistance fighter too well. Onscreen there was no scheme or subterfuge. The man believed every word he'd spoken, was disturbed by it. Furthermore, Maryanne Cauley had begun to pace once the Beta slammed the door. Both of them had been infected with what would be dangerous intention.

Shepherd knew the cause of the disease.

Love.

Maryanne, Shepherd could control, but the Beta was going to be a problem. He would have to be disposed of, deal with Claire or no.

There was a throat noise, a grumble, as the Alpha absorbed what was slated in the report. There was only one plausible explanation. Leslie Kantor, *Svana*, was planning this terrible thing.

A fire in Shepherd's eyes, a scent of righteous fury emanating from his pores, he said, "You were right, brother."

There was no vindication upon hearing Shepherd's confession. Jules was above such things. "Svana would plan her strike midday, assuring the majority of your Followers were trapped inside. I estimate she would need less than fifty men if her plan is indeed to demolish the Citadel."

Of course she would plan mass causalities, take out as many of her enemies as she could with one blow; Shepherd had taught her that. It was exactly what he had done when he'd unleashed the prisoners from the Undercroft. "Push up launch procedure. I am calling for an immediate exodus."

"The order was already issued." Jules had to state the risks, the chance of failure. "It will take a minimum of twenty-four hours to ready the ships. Your men will be scattered, occupied with loading and prepping transport. The Citadel will be exposed, the guard greatly reduced. The Followers might not be able to find all the bombs."

There would be no bombs to find. Svana had always preferred human cannon fodder. What they had to fear, was regular citizens ready to end their lives. "What are the current weather conditions over the Drake Passage?"

Jules pulled up a new screen. "Not favorable."

Shepherd understood the consequences. An expedited Exodus had been discussed and strategized at length. "We will fly over the storms."

"It would take the twelve ships over three days to collect and deposit every last Follower." The Command Center's screens filled with a manifest of soldiers, battle plans, data logs. Jules pointed to the most relevant information. “If Svana stirs up a true rebellion, we may be under siege the entire time, both here, and while annexing Greth Dome. Projected casualties may more than double.”

Exactly. Shepherd looked his subordinate dead in the eye. “Then it will not take three days... The final wave of our men will not survive to see freedom.”

“Every last one of our brothers understands the sacrifice. All of them would die at your command.”

Knowing all of this, Shepherd calculated. “Mated pairs, those who’d recovered their families after the breech will go first. Those in prime reproductive years will follow. The oldest and wounded will remain to defend their brothers’ future.”

Jules offered, “If we put the Citadel on immediate lockdown, there is a greater chance for our brothers’ survival.”

“No.” Speaking the truth as he knew it, Shepherd warned that Svana was not to be underestimated. “There is a possibility Svana had this planned all along. Our regime removed her every last adversary. She knows the inner workings of our organization. Taking Greth Dome would be more difficult than cutting down our authority. If we let her know before launch that we anticipate attack, she will strike all the sooner. We have to buy our men time.”

Nodding, Jules agreed.

“Svana must be detained immediately. Her capture will not stop true rebels from attacking, but we need her alive.” Though from the look in his eyes, Shepherd was greatly considering killing her himself. “Enforcer Corday is the key.”

“I request that you assign me to track her.” There was a darkness under Jules expression, a bloodlust. “I know Svana very well.”

Shepherd denied the request. “I need you here, leading our men from the Command Center while I defend the Citadel from attack.”

It was very rare for the Beta to question a direct order. "Shepherd, we need her. Without Svana, there is nowhere for our transports to land." Eyes so vibrant a blue they seemed unnatural, Jules asked for something he'd earned over and over again. "Trust me. I will find her. I will hold her accountable to us all."

The future slipping from his fingers, Shepherd conceded. "The instant transports light up the sky, Svana will know her plans were uncovered. You may have less than twelve hours before war begins."

In strategy and war, there was no mental match under the Dome to Shepherd. Jules knew that better than anyone. "You can hold her back, bring the city to its knees. Outmaneuver her men, and save our brothers."

The Dome would have never witnessed such carnage as what Shepherd intended to bring down upon Svana and her rebels. "I swear it to you, Jules."

Jules nodded, wasted no more words, and left Shepherd alone with his guilt and his great obligation.

Thólos was making its death rattle. Shepherd let the fools scrounge up false honor in the eleventh hour, set a shadow perimeter around the Citadel, and ordered his men to prepare for war. If the rebels' own bombs didn't bring the Dome down on their heads, then Shepherd's vengeance would kill them all.

The virus would be set free. Thólos would be wiped away, and nothing would change that.

Had the Followers no forewarning, Svana may have stood a chance at victory. Now all that would ensue was a bloodbath.

Shepherd would stand as victor.

When the battle was over, when his family was established in Greth Dome, he would be legendary. His success, a thing he had obsessed over once upon a time, would be nothing compared to the new world available for his son and the children who would follow.

There would be peace... after an acceptable period for his mate to mourn, of course. Her breakdown was assumed once she learned the truth, especially as hormonal as she had been lately with the pregnancy.

Claire would not take the frenzy of transport, of flight, and of settling in a new den well if she were unaware of what transpired. Shepherd had agreed with Jules in this, and each man had acted on his own to lay a foundation for her to build upon. Every brick had been fitted together, every hint prepared. All that remained was for Claire to let go of her attachments and willingly choose their son.

Shepherd had absolute faith in her.

His clever Omega knew more than she let on. She was also stronger than she realized. Though Shepherd recognized Thólos had been unhealthy for her for quite some time, his hands had been tied on the matter. But her suffering and unknown sacrifice would lead to great reward. All would be well in the end. He would make Claire happy.

There would be no underground den in her future, only her sky and clean air.

He would find orange blossoms for her.

He would give her anything she wanted, anything in his power once this was over. She would be the most spoiled Omega on the planet, because she deserved it—because even if he showered her with jewels and material things it would never change her character. And there would be children, perhaps even a little Omega girl, like her mother... a girl who would probably boss any Alpha brother about.

But first Thólos had to be destroyed. The world had to be set back in balance so that the woman sleeping in his den stood a chance to survive in it.

His loyal Followers would stake claim to Greth Dome. No soul the wiser as they flourished while the contaminated bones in Thólos bleached in the arctic sun.

A year, maybe two, and Claire would be all smiles. She would see all the benefits; she would forgive, because he knew her secret… he could feel it flowing from her even as she slumbered.

Shepherd smiled.

# 8

"Jesus, Claire, I only took one fry off your plate." Maryanne gawked, wide-eyed, and a little stunned.

Recognizing that she had barked at her friend, Claire took a deep breath, looking sheepish. She was tired, having been woken up and dragged upstairs when all she wanted was more rest. Shepherd had insisted she go see her sky, claimed he'd had special food prepared and Maryanne waiting as company. "I'm sorry, Maryanne. But if you touch another piece of my food, I might have to kill you. I can't help it."

Maryanne snickered, tutting, "Sweet little Claire is all knocked up and nuts. Come on now, show me the baby bump."

Since that painful conversation with Shepherd, everything seemed to keep coming back to the pregnancy... as if he were maneuvering her into a position where she had to speak on it over and over and over. Green eyes looked down at her cotton dress and the tiny bulge that had only just begun to show. "There is nothing to see yet."

A deep, rasping voice ordered from the corner, "Show her."

It was the first time Shepherd had interjected during one of her meetings with Maryanne, and it fed Claire's suspicion. Looking over her shoulder with a pouty scowl, she let out a sigh and stood. Turning sideways and holding the fabric of her dress taut, she made her point.

Maryanne cooed, brown eyes settled on her friend's torso. "You do have a little one! Do you feel anything moving around in there?"

Claire snorted, and looked down at her belly, smoothing the fabric in a small caress before she could stop herself. "What I feel is tired all the time and crazy if I'm hungry... I worry a lot."

"That's nothing new." Maryanne smirked as if trying not to laugh.

Looking at the beauty of her friend, Claire muttered, "I was honestly nicer when I was starving to death than I am when I'm hungry now. I mean look at me. I just threatened your life over a fry. I can't even imagine what other pregnant women in Thólos must be going through."

"Before you sit down, can I touch your belly?" The blonde asked, totally ignoring Claire's mention of Thólos and already reaching out a hand.

It felt very strange to have anyone but Shepherd touch over the infant that was going to be a boy. Claire had not meant to voice her misgivings, they just slipped out as she felt her friend rub the little bump. "It's a strange feeling you know. I can do nothing for this baby..."

Maryanne's hand drew away and soft brown eyes looked to hers. "What do you mean?"

Claire snapped out of her darker thoughts. The damage was done, Shepherd had heard her. "I don't know what I'm going to do. I don't know what I'm doing." She wasn't even sure if she was talking about the baby anymore. Something was very wrong with this meeting, with how hard Maryanne was trying. The whole damn world was wrong.

"Well," Maryanne cocked a little smirk back on her lips. "First you're going to sit down, you're going to take a deep breath, and then you're going to eat the rest of those fries."

Feeling manipulated and cagey, Claire did as she was told until her plate was clean. When it was done, her eyes wandered to the window. It was nearing nighttime, the last of the blue sky peeking between the swollen clouds. Beyond the Dome was the real world, a place she no longer understood, no more than she understood her own thoughts as the hours wore on.

It was obvious that Shepherd, Jules, even Maryanne had been especially obliging lately. And of course, because she felt crazy, Claire's paranoia only grew at their unlikely dispositions. Shepherd had brought her to this room almost every time she'd been awake, listened for hours as she played the piano or just sat with her in the chair, always touching her belly, cupping, stroking, changing his patterns of touch so she could not disregard them and focus on whatever she was doing.

Had the circumstances been normal, it would have been cute—the fanatic Alpha father already bursting with pride... just like her dad had been. She'd lost her temper with him twice for no reason. She just could not stand another moment of being touched. The thing about it that had been most unsettling, was that Shepherd had actually acquiesced.

Then what had the bastard done? He'd pulled out one of his forbidden books... and read to her. And she'd actually liked it!

While he was reading, Claire had glanced at the shelves, Shepherd's *windows*, and glared at the spine of the baby book she avoided like the plague, wondering if there had been some suggestion on soothing pregnancy tactile aggravation with story time. She hated that book, hated that its bright white cover did not fit in with the other books, hated that she was always tempted to look inside, but had to fight herself, to keep distant, because she was afraid.

To stop the whirlwind in her thoughts, she had pressed closer to Shepherd in that confusing moment, sniffing and humming, eyes closed as her hand stroked up his thigh straight towards the distraction she wanted. She'd fondled over the fabric of his cargo pants until he was as hard as she was wet.

Claire O'Donnell had initiated sex.

There was absolutely no hesitation on his end to give her what she wanted, Shepherd going so far as to crawl down as she pressed him lower, her body arching up to silently ask for his mouth. Like a greedy, self-serving woman, as soon as she had come all over his tongue she'd fallen asleep. He must have tucked her in, because when she woke she was deep in her burrow and he was gone.

She had not woken happy... Claire had woken in complete distress.

Shepherd was in a terrible mood again, but that was not her worry. It was that dream, that terrible dream of the Undercroft that seemed to come out of nowhere and wreck her mind—the prisoners foaming at the mouth as they watched through the bars as the devil fucked her.

These horrible phantoms were always reaching. Sometimes they touched her and she'd scream.

Sitting up, trying to shake off the chill that followed her out of sleep, her world fell apart. In that moment Claire was certain the gods hated her, that she was cursed. Moving her hand to her belly, she sucked in a breath, and realized there was a sensation she could never ignore or forget. It was the quickening of her baby, the small internal flutter that let her know her son was alive, and that she was a mother, even if she refused to think about him.

When Shepherd found her bawling her eyes out a few minutes later, he had rushed to her, his expression disturbed. Her reaction had been to initiate sex again, and for once he'd responded reluctantly, asking her what was wrong. She'd use her lips to kiss his neck, to mouth the claiming marks, knowing it was manipulative, knowing he would not stop such a thing, but absolutely unwilling to explain what a monster she was.

Since that mating, he'd watched her closely, sniffing her frequently, hyper vigilant. He had a good right to be. He was the father of the baby she had been determined to kill for months, a child who was going to die if she suicided—a baby who existed but did not exist until she'd felt it move.

But now... what was she going to do now?

Claire put away her thoughts and forced herself to focus on the guest waiting patiently for her to speak. Smiling sadly at Maryanne, she asked, "Do you remember the night after my mother was termed a suicide, what the government did?"

"Yeah, why?"

"I'd sat up with my dad that night. He was unusually quiet," the unsmiling Omega began. "We were watching a film when they came banging on the door. Can you imagine how my father reacted?"

Maryanne shook her head in the negative, but watched her friend very closely.

"Our home was comfortable. My mother had flowers flourishing in the windows. I had friends, did well in school, played safely in the causeways. When they came, when orders were given, Dad grabbed me, no questions asked, both of us in our pajamas, and pushed past the Enforcers. His transport had been confiscated, so he dragged me behind him the final distance to the nearest bridge to the next sector. He pulled me so fast I did not even have time to turn around or look back. We went up the elevators, almost all the way to the top of the Dome. The Gallery Gardens... my dad took me to the orange trees before anything bad could touch me. He took me away from the sight of my house being stolen. We stayed in the highest level, for two weeks, some of that time I even forgot to miss my mother. He kept me there until his savings were depleted and we had no choice but to leave."

"That sounds like Collin." Maryanne nodded, unsure what the point of her story was.

"I can't carry my baby someplace where he will be safe. There won't be any orange groves. No playdates in the park, or family vacations." Claire's voice grew darker and slow tears fell down her cheeks. "I cannot even begin to imagine what there will be."

Brown eyes softened and Maryanne said nothing, could think of nothing to offer that would suit. She was not going to lie to Claire and say it would be okay. Her friend was a hunted woman with a mate who had the power to take down the greatest city in the modern world—a man millions of people wanted to see dead. The best she could do was ask, "Have you picked out a name?"

"No."

"Are there any you like?"

"No."

"Well, you better pick one. I can see your Alpha thinking Shepherd Jr. is acceptable, and it just... isn't," Maryanne teased.

Claire offered a tired chuckle, a small twist in her lips before her mouth grew hard. "I tried to kill myself, Maryanne. Shepherd found me preparing to drown in the Thólos water reserve. At this moment, I am only breathing for you. If I had died, you would have died, Corday would have died, the Omegas..." It was the first conversation Claire had attempted of that nature in Shepherd's presence, the man choosing not to interrupt. "I did not walk off the ice for my son. Now here I am, alive, and my child is in the hands of a man who is responsible for the genocide of millions and the…" Claire's voice just stopped before she could add, *the mad woman he still kneels to*. Realizing she would have signed Maryanne's death warrant by sharing knowledge Claire knew Shepherd would never allow her friend to walk out of the room with, Claire swallowed and continued, "…the army who follow him."

Narrowing her eyes, nodding, Maryanne looked a little disturbed at the course of conversation. "What are you thinking?"

Reaching for her glass of water, Claire offered, "I am thinking I will name my son Collin, after my father."

Rubbing her crimson lips together, Maryanne looked over her distressed friend and agreed. "Your dad would like that."

A strange feeling came over her. Claire straightened in her chair and spoke bluntly. "I think you should leave now, Maryanne." Standing she gave her friend a sad onceover, "I love you, but I don't want you to come back." Pale arms reached out before Maryanne could react. Embracing her friend, Claire spoke softly into Maryanne's ear. "Shepherd is using you. We both know it, and we both know I can't keep you alive forever. Whatever he wants, don't do it. Save yourself."

When she pulled back and Maryanne's eyes automatically went to where Shepherd approached behind Claire, the Omega sighed and nodded. "You can tell him what I said."

There was something going on between Claire and Shepherd, and at that moment, Maryanne was not sure which one of them was using her more. Claire was making a statement, but Maryanne could not fathom what it was. What she could fathom was that she wanted to get the fuck out of that room and do as she was told.

Claire was eyeballing her with unsettled, tired eyes. "I want to kiss her, Shepherd."

The man behind his mate slowly turned his head to look down at the Omega as if they held some silent communication between them. He did not look pleased. "I will allow it this last time."

Maryanne hardly knew what was going on. Claire stepped forward, stood on tiptoe, and kissed her friend's slack lips. When the small exchange was over, Claire frowned and admitted with a broken heart, "I'm going to miss you more than I can say."

Stepping back to Shepherd, Claire felt his arms circle her middle, his habit of restraining her each time he called for the door to be opened familiar. Shepherd gave the order, and in a matter of seconds, Maryanne disappeared from Claire's life forever.

The table was pushed aside by a thick leg and the chairs brought nearer. Shepherd sat her down, took the seat across, and waited for his mate to meet his eye. "I want you to consider the consequences of what you are thinking right now."

Claire could see it in the link. Shepherd had no idea what she was thinking; he was simply playing the odds.

*Engage people with what they expect; it is what they are able to discern and confirms their projections. It settles them into predictable patterns of response, occupying their minds while you wait for the extraordinary moment—that which they cannot anticipate. –Sun Tzu*

"I lied to Maryanne when she asked if I could feel the baby," Claire said in a steady, emotionless voice. "I felt him move yesterday... I can feel it even now." Looking back to the window, she parroted what he had said to her weeks ago. "Black hair like mine, maybe my eyes. How many qualities will be paralleled?" The feeling of tears running down her face seemed at odds with her calm tone. "I cannot give him more than an unnatural existence underground. I will not be able to save my son."

Shepherd leaned his mass forward so his elbows rested on his knees and looked pointedly at his mate. "Our son will not be raised in Thólos."

Mirroring his body language, she leaned closer, her voice completely non-reactive, even if she looked like she could kill him. "You will take this child from me over my dead body." Green eyes hardened. "You think you have seen me act out before? What I would do to you if you make one unsatisfactory move against this baby would make you wish you were back in the Undercroft."

"You will never be parted from our children." He answered at once, the Alpha taking immense pleasure in her scathing threat. Shepherd held her hand. "Thólos is not an acceptable place for *either* of you. As such, your departure is imminent."

Claire took a slow breath. "And there is the complication. No one can leave Thólos."

"There is no Thólos. Thólos is gone... it's time to accept that." That big hand moved higher to cup her cheek. "You need to let go and move forward."

"You think I don't know that?" Taking his hand away, running her own over her face to wipe the wetness away, she explained, "I have seen what's happening on the streets no matter the pretty view you provided from this window."

"Then let's embrace the fact our son deserves better. You will live in comfort, be provided for. Paint all day if you wish. I will grant you a piano, teach it to our child." Shepherd was using that earnest tone he employed when speaking of the future, of his plans for the world, all the little promises he had made that she had ignored.

It was making her nervous.

The way his eyebrows lowered at her stubborn expression, the shine of incredulity in his eyes matched the tone of his voice. "Why would you wish to remain here? Why choose the citizens of the city who murder women with dark hair, who are the ones responsible for the deaths of countless innocent children, who turn on each other, climbing like rats on a bloated corpse? How could you possibly be loyal to that over our son? Imagine what they would do to him if they knew who he belonged to."

Squeezing her eyes shut so hard she saw spots, Claire tried to find an answer that made sense. She could not fathom forsaking

Thólos even if she had come to hate what it had become—even if everything about a home that she once loved was gone. It was like clinging to the bones of a long dead friend thinking they might one day wake up and hug you back. Grasping at straws, Claire said, "Being parted from the Alpha is dangerous during gestation."

"I would not be parted from you either, little one," Shepherd interjected, his voice holding the trace of a smile hidden in his eyes. "We will travel to our new home together."

Forcing her eyes open, she looked at the set of Shepherd's eyes, dissected his almost eager expression, and did not trust a word he said. "You will leave Thólos, really?"

Shepherd increased the purr, and noticed at once how the sound made her jump and glare right at him. "I am going to leave Thólos... with you."

Clutching at the hand that held hers, feeling a little shaken, Claire demanded, "What of Nona, Maryanne, Corday? What of them?"

He shook his head before his words hissed passed his scarred lips. "Little one, you have to give them up. Aside from Miss Cauley, they believe you are dead. Make peace with it and move forward." Shifting from the chair, kneeling before her, Shepherd wrapped an arm around her middle and cupped her cheek again, his big thumb swiping away the tears. "There is a home for us in Greth Dome; I will give you something beautiful. The best tutors for our children, plenty of unrestrained culture for our family to enjoy..." He spoke honestly, "But, no, there will never be a future in Thólos, or further time with your friends."

Reading between the lines, Claire saw what Shepherd intended towards the people of Greth Dome. "And what of friends for your son?"

He explained simply. "There will be Follower children, and we will create siblings."

Bitterly, Claire asked, "And will this grand home have windows?"

"Many windows with views of distant mountains, and you will be able to move freely through our den."

Claire nodded, finishing Shepherd's thought aloud, "Because it will be on a base full of armed Followers who do your bidding, where I might live locked away from real civilization while you control a new population."

"I will order for a terrace to be cleared for your use as a garden as well." Gently he tried to coax, "You can ineptly kill all the plant life you like."

She felt his urging through the thread, the heated pulse and forthright reassurance. Her attention ran over every part of the man who was offering her a future. But something was very wrong and she could feel it bubbling up inside her like panic. "I need to go outside."

Liquid iron eyes, hard and serene, sat above a serious mouth. He was not smiling. "No, little one."

The miasma was choking her. Claire leaned closer to his warmth, needing to smell the thing that was supposed to keep her anchored. He pulled her forward, carefully and slow, to let her settle where he knew she wanted to be, purring louder until his mate's breathing grew less labored.

Resting her forehead on Shepherd's shoulder, Claire's thoughts began to tumble. It should have been horrible to feel such comfort from the man who she should hate, who fed her reassurance through the link, who was going to allow an entire city full of people to cough up blood as they suffered horrific death from Red Consumption.

Her eyes went wide at the thought, her breath hitched, and Claire finally grasped the missing piece as if she had lifted it from his very thoughts. "You are going to release the virus!"

Shepherd did not even blink. "There is nothing but evil here, Claire."

Frantic, she offered the first word that came to her mind. "Nona."

"Is a murderer," Shepherd answered. "And it was more than just her husband. Did you know that?"

Eyes welling, she shoved at him. "Do you think I would believe anything you told me?"

He urged her to listen. "Your friend, your mentor, is responsible for the deaths of at least seven Alpha males."

All who probably deserved it, Claire thought. But that was the same argument Shepherd was using towards Thólos. Feeling her expression crumble she tried again. "Maryanne."

Shepherd countered, "You told her to hide. I know what is in her dwelling. If she is wise, she will heed your warning. My men will not interfere."

Claire felt so lost, gripping the front of his armor she knew there was one, one man even Shepherd could not count as evil, one man who had asked her to survive. Heartbroken, Claire whispered, "Corday is a good man."

The Alpha stiffened. "The only civilians who can leave the city are the family of my Followers and newly bonded Omegas."

And she finally understood what he had hinted at for months. "Because the Omegas carry the offspring of your Followers? Because *I am pregnant* with your child..." More tears fell.

"Yes," Shepherd answered softly, kneading the tension where his hands rested on her back. "It was the only way to save you."

The weight of the nightmare fell on her shoulders. Claire slid from her chair. She got down on her knees, mirroring Shepherd's position, but so much smaller, and begged, "Please don't do this. I will do anything you want, bear as many children as you desire. I will love you. *Anything*. Just don't do this."

She had never actually seen the man look desperate. The sound of his breath caught, a quick suck of distorted air preceded his confession, "I cannot stop it. I will not chance an uprising of the scum of this city who may muster, build transport, and threaten our family. Nothing can stop the inevitable." He was already wrapping his arms around her. "Please do not cry."

But she couldn't stop. Nor could she stop how she clung to him as she wept, seeing in the bond the motivation for his deception. It was a pure emotion, acts made from the only good he knew—his absolute love for her. It was the very reason he had inflicted every last horrible thing on his mate, including pulling a syringe out of his pocket and driving a needle into her flesh at that very moment.

# 9

Four precious hours had been wasted in the pursuit and pointless questioning of Maryanne Cauley. Corday had nothing to show for it, no further progress made on his dilemma. On the long walk back to his apartment, outside temperatures grew uncomfortably cold, but the pain of numb fingers was welcome—anything was welcome that might make him feel as wretched as he should.

Hands shaking from the chill, he unlocked his door, his eyes on the spot where Claire had once propped herself up, knocking in the night so he might give her shelter. The smears of blood on her pale skin, the torn flesh, the look of unbearable pain in her eyes, he hated the memory. That's not how he wanted to recall her. Corday wanted to remember her cautious smiles, the spark that would come into her eye on the rare times his jokes chased away the cloud of fear storming inside her.

Had they the fortune of meeting before the breech, Corday was certain they would have been friends, lovers even. Sometimes you just see a person and know... and he'd lost her before she had ever been his.

She'd felt the pull between them too. After all, she had come to him after she'd leapt from the Citadel's roof, ran through the dark and the cold, to reach *him*. He wanted to be there for her, but there was so much she belligerently carried out on her own.

Claire had fought her pair-bond.

Claire had stormed against her mate to free the Omegas.

Through her flyer, Claire made herself a beacon and a movement.

She did it with no support. She did it knowing it would cost her her life.

Releasing a shaking breath, Corday sat back upon his couch, put his head in his hands and, muttered to himself, "Claire..."

Leslie Kantor was a sad shadow in comparison. The Alpha female's fire may have inspired the men and women hidden in the Premier's Sector, she may have successfully reconstructed the resistance into a true rebellion, but she was not eager to sacrifice herself to keep her people safe—not like Claire had been. Instead, she was ready to sacrifice others. Leslie's rebels were fanatical in their adoration of their *gods-sent* leader. Men and women Corday had known before the breech—calm, collected, rational people who'd lost too much, seen too many horrors, had transformed into willing suicide bombers. He hated to even draw the comparison, but his compatriots had begun to behave like disturbing reflections of Shepherd's Followers.

They never questioned, they only obeyed.

They were willing to draw innocent people into the crossfire.

As Lady Kantor would say, that was the price of change.

The sad truth was, no matter the outcome of their attack on the Citadel, unlike Senator Kantor's resistance, the rebels would accomplish something. It might not be the outcome they hoped for. After all, if even one bomb should be incorrectly placed, it could bring down the whole Dome. But revolution would take place. Shepherd and his virus would be eradicated.

New life could be built upon the ashes.

One blast and the stagnation of citizens under the Dome would stop. Riots would ensue; everyone would fight or be killed.

As Leslie loved to say, the people of Thólos were to be reborn.

Corday pressed his palms to his face and tried to rub the nightmare away. Little more than one day was left. Brigadier Dane would carry out her mission: Corday with no ability to know of her success or failure. Instead, he'd be marching with Leslie Kantor.

His former commander expected him to assassinate the leader of the rebels, Dane's reasoning disgustingly sound. Pulling that trigger would most likely cost him his life. He would never see his lovely Claire again. The only thing left he could do for her was to pick the right location of Shepherd's den, so his friend might have a chance to survive.

The words came on a sigh. "The basement or the east corridor?"

From a shadowed corner of the room, an unexpected voice sliced through Corday's concentration. "I'm surprised you would return here, given what you now know. It almost appears as if you want to be captured. Do you, Samuel Corday? Do you want me to take you to Shepherd?"

At the sound of the intruder's taunt, Corday's heart skipped a beat. Breath coming quick, stiff where he sat on his couch, the Beta searched the dark for the source. It was more than fear that churned inside him... it was a strange sense that the intruder was right. Breathless, adrenaline tightening his voice, Corday answered. "I haven't been able to decide."

Again, the toneless voice moved through the dark. "He has a temper. I don't think you would survive a conversation with him.

Fortunately for you, whether you tell me the truth or lie, I have no intention of ending your life tonight."

Eyes wide, Corday looked over his shoulder. With so much shadow, he could barely make out the shape of a man—an outline armed with an assault rifle pointed right at him. "What is it that I *know*?"

"You don't know anything but what we've fed you. There is no single fact squeezed into your brain that is wholly correct... And yes, before you ask, Claire *is* alive. Shepherd has nursed her back to health. Four months from now, she will give birth to a boy."

*Nursed her*? The man in the dark made it sound as if Shepherd were some sweet lover, not the monster who murdered men with his bare hands. Corday did not even try to hide the look of disgust from his face. "After she was captured, Claire exposed the resistance. You've come here to gloat."

"Is that what you believe?" Twisting his smirk with an evil chuckle, Jules took a step out of the dark, exposing his face to enough light that the Enforcer might grasp just who had come. Recognition was instantaneous: Shepherd's second-in-command, the harbinger of death. It was more than the flat expression and lifeless voice. It was the outcast's intention. "She would be so disappointed to hear such a thing from a man she admires as much as you."

The Beta looked heartbroken. "I know she'd never have done it if he hadn't forced her."

"Shepherd's mate has never once offered even a hint of information about you or your pathetic resistance." Face suddenly blank of expression, Jules stared forward with a pair of strangely focused eyes. "It was you who betrayed her."

Confusion darkened Corday's voice. "I would never betray Claire."

Without breaking eye contact, completely aware of how threatening he was, Jules lowered his weapon. "It was you who led me to Claire, you I followed right to the Omegas' hiding place."

Corday knew his eyes were filling, that he could not hide the effect the Follower's words had on him. "Does she know?"

"She's painted a picture of you. You were cooking something in this kitchen, smiling. She left the gold ring you wear on your little finger out of the portrait. I assume she didn't think I'd notice the obvious lack of it." Rifle in one hand, Jules began to stalk from his corner. He walked through the apartment as if the man on the couch was absolutely no threat to him. "She esteems you, Corday. Why else would she have promised her life to Shepherd in exchange for yours? And her infatuated mate has kept his word: his men watch over the Omegas, make it so they have access to supplies and clean water without ever interfering with them. You have been left in peace, your rebellion allowed to exist. Even Maryanne Cauley was not murdered for her part in Claire's attack on the Undercroft."

The Enforcer's voice came out, ragged and worn. "Why are you telling me this?"

Lowering his chin to his chest, allowing a subtle sinister curl in his lip, Jules spun a perfect lie. "Claire has asked me to talk to you."

Corday refused to rise to the bait.

Jules taunted, "You lack complete subtlety in your expressions. Five years of torment in the Undercroft would cure you of that weakness. I spent more than a decade underground. What do you think it did to me?"

Corday said nothing. He said nothing because there was nothing to say.

Jules was more than happy to fill the silence. "Many prisoners are quiet in the beginning. If they don't talk, the nightmare isn't real." Jules cocked his head to the side, running his eyes over the Enforcer. "It doesn't take long for them to learn that the nightmare is all that exists. Unfortunate enlightenment leads to despair. Despair leaches away everything else, until a clean slate is all that's left. We were all like you once—silent prisoners. Soon you will be just like me. Leslie Kantor saw your potential and took advantage, she has done well in conditioning you to fit her needs."

There was a thick oppression in the air, a weight that made Corday's body feel immersed underwater. Grinding his teeth until the muscles in his jaw jumped, Corday barked, "What do you want?"

"I don't like you. You are not a good soldier. You would be an even worse leader." It was conversational, Jules' admission. The man even had the audacity to cross his arms over his chest, his deadly rifle's barrel resting against his shoulder. "The entire city will be caught up in the flames of revolution in a matter of hours, and all you can think about is your selfish need to free one woman instead of trying to protect your people."

"I will tell you nothing."

"Keep your plans and your war. There is only one thing I want to know." Edging closer, Jules let his voice drop to a terrible, grating hiss. "I want to know where Svana is hiding."

Corday knew that name had been planted on purpose, and could not stop his reactive growl.

Jules did not miss a beat. "Do you love Claire?"

The Beta refused to answer, but his face contorted into an image of fury.

"Do you believe Claire loves you?" Jules pressed, growing more menacing with each word.

The air in the small room seemed to thicken, grow dense with the poisonous hate. The stink was coming from Corday

"Tick tock, Enforcer Corday." Jules gestured towards the window, pointing to where a fragment of the Citadel could be seen in the distance. "The answers are there. Claire is in there. Are you going to let them die over one woman's greed?"

Corday shook his head because it could not be true. It was all some trick so he would betray the rebels, too convenient a name to drop. "I have never heard of a Svana."

"But she has been in this room with you. The very woman who hurt Claire, you have been indulging for months. A lovesick fool who pines after Shepherd's mate is the exact kind of toy she would have enjoyed the most. Twisting your mind, your memories of so sweet an Omega to reflect what she desired, is Svana's specialty. I suspect her victory wasn't hard. You doubt your friend. You believed the woman who saved your life betrayed you, even if it was in a small, coerced fashion."

Throat tight, Corday's voice faltered. "Stop."

"Begging already? But we've only just begun."

A great pain growing behind his eyes, Corday said, "You cannot imagine I would believe a word from your mouth."

"I'll confess that you were not under surveillance when Claire must have told you about Svana, so I don't know the details of what the Omega shared. But, I was with her after it happened, I found Claire lying on the floor. What did you call Svana, a sex-offender?"

There was no point in continuing to pretend that name had no effect on him. Jules had noticed it, and Corday was accomplishing nothing playing dumb. He ground out the words, "Enough! Svana is Shepherd's lover."

"Again you are wrong." There was no hesitation on Jules' part to share the secret. "Svana is Shepherd's *partner*... or she was until Shepherd fell in love with an Omega. Now, she is his rival for power."

Corday swallowed the sour taste growing on his tongue, sick with the possibility that the terrible man might be telling the truth. "You make him sound weak."

"Love is an interesting thing." A knowing glow in his eyes, Jules looked pointedly at the Beta who'd made foolish decision after foolish decision all based on his *love* for Claire. "Svana will know we uncovered her betrayal in three hours. Her forces will attack immediately. I am telling you this because I know there is no way to stop them. Even if I kill her, even if you kill her, the slaves she has created will act out her will. Shepherd will be able to mediate a portion of the attack, but bombs will still detonate. How many, I cannot say. So, how will you save Claire?" Unflinching, Jules demanded, "You tell me where Svana is hiding, and I will tell you what Maryanne Cauley would not."

"You have no proof that Leslie Kantor is Svana. I will tell you nothing."

"Perhaps you are right. Sometimes it is best to let storms run their course." Jules smiled, his whole face turned strange with the action. Straightening, he nodded his goodbye. "Claire is kept in the basement: corridor 7, sub-room 3. As the Citadel begins to crumble, she will be crushed to death. Or, if she is really unlucky, she will be trapped under layers of immovable rubble to slowly die from dehydration. Maybe her painting of you will keep her company in the dust and lonely dark."

Once the door was closed and Corday was left alone with his thoughts, he began to shake. It was as if he'd just survived hours of torture, as if just a few soft-spoken words had irreparably damaged him.

~

GROANING, trying to roll away from whatever was shaking her awake, Claire found her body stiff and numb. Head swimming, it all started to come back. Thólos was going to be turned into a pile of corpses; the Red Consumption would be unleashed. A virus the man sitting at her side, the adoring mate holding her eyes, claimed could not be stopped.

"You have been sleeping for many hours, little one." The purr came strong and sweet. "You must eat now."

The last thing on the planet she wanted at that moment was food.

Claire opened her mouth to complain, only to have a spoonful of something pressed between her lips. Swallowing instinctively, still caught in the fog, she tried to focus on the one man who seemed to blur into two and make him listen.

Shepherd forced more food on her tongue.

"When you have finished, I will help you dress for the journey." That raspy voice was commanding, almost stern, as if he were relaying orders to his Followers. "Then you will be sedated again." A warm hand smoothed back the hair on her forehead. "And next time you wake up, we will be in our new home."

"Please..." Claire barely had time to voice the entreaty before more soup was spooned into her mouth.

"It is important that you eat, or the anesthesia may make you ill. Swallow."

He fought her when she seemed willing to be difficult, rubbing and pinching her throat just enough to earn an automatic response until the whole bowl of soup was gone.

When it was finished, her transformation began. There would be no more green dresses in Thólos. Instead Shepherd outfitted her in the clothing of his soldiers, tugging warm layers over limp appendages, lacing her feet into boots, everything dark concealing fabrics, while Claire lay there, dizzy, and half cognizant from the drugs.

Shepherd kept up a constant stream of what to expect, telling her of the team that would escort her to a waiting transport ship, all explained in a matter-of-fact tone as if she would care.

She didn't.

Even under the influence of drugs, Claire tried to force her thoughts to muster. She tried to think of Thólos, but could only imagine the last things she'd seen in the causeways, dreamed up for the thousandth time the faceless dark-haired women whose bodies littered the streets, the dead frozen boy in the alley, all the Omegas who had gone missing, saw the faces of those who had been left in the city to die.

And what of Thólos, what was left now? The dregs? The worst possible offenders? Would they stand up and fight? Would they evaporate in a burst of blood and wash away everything that had happened here?

This place he was determined to take her, would Shepherd force the people of Greth Dome under the yoke of his *philosophy*? A mess was inevitable, all of it based on the horrible evil that had been done in her city. And if she was dragged away, no one would know of the people who had sacrificed and suffered... so many inspiring stories, stories of good men like Corday, would be lost.

The world needed to know that not everything under Thólos Dome had been dishonorable. Who would tell them?

Refusing to even think for a moment that he might win, Claire stopped all her black thoughts and fisted her hand in the fabric of his sleeve.

Shepherd took her fingers in his, watching her, waiting.

Whatever drug he had given her dulled her emotion, made her listless and rag-like, but she still had the power to accuse, "You gave me your word, Shepherd. On the ice you promised me."

"You were trying to kill yourself, little one. I would have promised you anything," he admitted freely, a hand closing around hers like an anchor, "anything, Claire. You cannot fault me for needing to protect my mate and child. I'd made a mistake, it needed to be rectified. You needed to recover your health and wellbeing in a situation where you no longer had to spend your thoughts on worry for those you count as your friends. You would have done the same had the roles been reversed."

"Is that why you drugged me?"

The man nodded once, placing his huge palm on her belly. "You can be very reactive, and you are very upset. I cannot be with you every moment right now, and I cannot allow you to lash out and harm yourself."

Claire felt warm tears seep from the corner of her eyes.

Suicide had been her plan, her only recourse against Shepherd: to punish him, to deny him who he would have as mate, to keep his child from him. Yet time had worked on her just as Shepherd must have intended. The baby was more than a blob of cells that made her constantly ill. It was a little moving sign of life... her son. And the man who had created him was at her side, tending her as if she were a dying woman.

But she wasn't dying and she wasn't going to kill herself. Shepherd was right; she could never harm her child. And so he'd won the war against her. And Claire knew, deep down, he had won weeks ago. That did not change the lingering fear something very bad would be exacted for his sins.

Claire's voice broke. "You're going to lose, Shepherd. I don't know how, but I know you will. You are going to lose everything in this madness. All your good intentions, all your progress, will have been for nothing if you follow this evil agenda."

"Now is not the time for arguments. When this is over, when we are established in our new home, grieve your friends if you will. In time, you will see I was right. We stand on the dawn of a new world. Do not be afraid of it, little one. You never have to be afraid again."

She could hardly see straight, but she did try to fight when another syringe was produced and injected into her arm. Then there was no reason to fight, for the world was nothing but strange noisy dreams.

# 10

Out of breath, Corday burst into Brigadier Dane's sleeping chamber, startling the woman awake. The man was wild, doing nothing to restrain his voice. "They know an attack is coming. They are probably listening to us even now."

There was no time for nonsense, Dane furious the man would speak of resistance matters in a room they both suspected was bugged. "What the hell are you talking about?"

"I had a visitor tonight. Shepherd's second-in-command, the Beta, he was in my house." Corday peeked through the blinds, looking for movement outside. "I'm sure he's followed me."

Shoving the covers from her body, Brigadier Dane rushed to dress. "And you led him here? Have you lost your mind?"

Using the meat of his hand, Corday wiped the sweat dotting his forehead into his hair. "You don't understand. He told me where Shepherd is keeping Claire."

She let out a groan, as if she could not believe the stupidity of the man standing before her. "You idiot!"

"Hear me out. Do you recall the name Svana?"

Dane's brow grew tight with thought. It took her a minute to pin it, but she had heard that name. "Half a year ago you reported Svana was the name of Shepherd's lover... the woman who attacked Claire."

"Yes. Tonight Shepherd's Follower offered Claire's position in exchange for the location of this woman. He claimed she'd gone rogue, said she was looking to unseat Shepherd and take his power for her own."

It sounded like a very scary parallel to a woman neither of them trusted. "Tell me you did not betray Leslie Kantor's position."

"I didn't and I don't have to. The man gave me Claire's location anyway. Basement corridor 7, sub-room 3."

Brigadier Dane shook her head. "He lied to you, Corday."

"No." Vehemently, Corday disagreed. "I don't think he did. Look at it from a broader picture. They know the attack on the Citadel is imminent, he told me so himself. He also told me they understood there was no real way to completely stop it. They know you and I are key figures of the resistance, because they *have* been watching us all this time, but they don't know where Svana is. She outmaneuvered them, manipulated us, and I don't have to go where Leslie Kantor hides for Shepherd's Follower to find her. I only have to show up on the front lines, her soldiers will take me straight to their leader."

There was something massive Corday had missed. Brigadier Dane closed her eyes and let out a weary sigh. "If they know rebels are going to attack, the virus will not remain inside the Citadel. All the casualties and structural damage will be for nothing."

Which is why Corday had run here. There was one, terrible option. "If we tell them what we know, we can minimize both of those factors."

It wouldn't work, and Dane was wise enough not to play right into their hands. "If they thought you had any relevant information, the Follower would have taken you. We know they are not above torture. More importantly, Leslie has been clever in compartmentalizing her forces. Both of us lack details on the attack."

"I know the intended detonation point of at least six of the bombs. We know the names and faces of the men and women chosen to wear them."

After a moment of thought, Dane was solemn. "If you were to do this, to betray the rebellion, *no matter your reasons*, you are condoning Shepherd's rule. As it stands now, the rebellion still has some power."

"He said Svana," Corday shook his head, clarifying. "I mean Leslie would learn that Shepherd had uncovered her plot within three hours. It took me thirty minutes to get here. In two and a half hours, something is going to happen. What?"

"I don't know." Dane looked miserable, as if she'd wished she'd never woken up. "No matter if she's Leslie Kantor or Svana, don't deviate from the plan. Even with Shepherd's knowledge of the attack, this might be our only chance to free Thólos. Let her attack him... *then do your part*."

Corday could not help but ask, "What of Claire?"

"If you swear to me you will do as you promised," Brigadier Dane offered her life, on the miniscule potential Claire might actually be saved, "I will find a way to keep our bargain."

"They will know you're coming."

Dane snorted a laugh. "Thanks to you, they know we're all coming."

Before the two might find comfort in their mutual agreement, the ground shook. It was a slow moving rumble, one that grew louder, almost deafening. It was not the distant boom of detonation that made such a racket, it was the following roar of bending metal and screams of falling glass.

Dane threw back the blinds, her view of the disaster sucking the breath from her lungs. "No!"

The Citadel had not been the source of the blast. Someone had detonated explosives right against the glass of the Dome. The East and West sky were caving in.

"It's too soon..." The words were spoken with such disbelief that shock appeared on Shepherd's face. "Svana has discovered we are prepping to launch."

When the unexpected blast had torn girders and solar power collection plates from their moorings, Shepherd had watched from the Command Center, calculating as damage reports flooded in. There was no denying what they saw. Rebels had purposefully shattered two massive segments of the Dome's protective glass. Shepherd, the Followers gathered in the room, stood there, while the northeast and southwest barrier wall crumbled. The city was turned into one giant wind tunnel.

Svana had altered the battlefield.

Turning to the Followers gathered behind him, Shepherd did not hesitate to counter her move. "Lock down the Citadel. Broadcast a fallback order and shut down communications and power to every segment of the Dome outside this building."

Watching the monitors, an outside change in air pressure was already sucking out huge gusts of debris. A soldier diligent at his post warned, "Shepherd, with catastrophic failure of the Dome, the temperature in the city is rapidly dropping. If we divert power from the Dome's heat generators, our men outside will freeze to death."

Under incredulous brows, Shepherd's eyes burned. "They won't have time to freeze to death."

The soldier didn't understand, "Sir?"

"This was not like an attack against the Citadel, their *enemy*. This was an attack on the population. Panic will ensue... riots. Cutting their power will slow them down."

Typing furiously across the Command Room's console, another soldier interjected, "Sir, I cannot shut down the communications network. The fallback order has not been sent."

"What is preventing it?"

Frustration was palpable in the man's voice. "Someone has taken control of the system."

A message began to roll across the screen: *People of Thólos, the rebel forces are in possession of the virus. Storm the Citadel, destroy our enemy.*

There was a blended murmur of curses offered up once the soldier read the lie. It was brilliant and also painfully devious. Svana had openly just betrayed every last Follower who had sworn an oath to install her as queen of Greth Dome.

Shepherd didn't have time to roar out his anger. Not now. "Get the first wave of transports ready to launch. Ship 7 must remain until Svana has been captured and stowed onboard. Have our men build a fire around it to keep it warm."

A young man who had survived the torment of the Undercroft thanks to Shepherd, looked to his commander and acknowledged that he could not carry out the order. "They need another hour, sir."

Shepherd impatiently detailed the outcome should they not get those ships in the air. "If the transport ships' engines freeze, they will seize. Successful launch will be impossible. Svana is attempting to cut off our exit." He had more orders to give. "Bridges linking the Citadel to the city must be destroyed. That will remove at least seven access points to our gates. That leaves only the promenade before the steps. We will funnel the citizens into that arena, and kill them before they can storm our walls."

"Yes, sir."

"I will return in an hour." Shepherd looked to his COMspecialist and barked, "By that time, I expect you'll have regained control of the communications network and disrupted the rebel's message."

"Yes, sir."

Shepherd looked to leadership gathered in the Control Center and said what they were all thinking. "We fight for our brothers now. If we can hold the rabble back for twelve hours, if we can keep the Citadel and the transport pad intact, they will live the life we've dreamed of."

There was a cheer, a lack of desolation. Every man in that room was more than willing to die for his brother.

Shepherd left them to carry out their orders, the expression of detachment and ruthless focus he had maintained for his men falling away the instant he was running to his mate through the underground catacombs.

Jules had sworn to him he would do his duty and gather Svana. His men would lock down the Citadel and destroy as many access points as time would allow. Now all Shepherd could manage was one hour before he had to send his mate to a future where more and more it seemed he would be unable to follow.

All he could do was buy time.

It would not be enough... not for the seventy-two hours it would take before the third round of Followers might be rescued.

The groaning of their metal door did nothing to stir the beautiful woman sleeping in her nest, and for one minute, Shepherd allowed himself to just look down at her, to pretend he would get to enjoy that vision every day as they grew old together.

Long black hair streamed over pillows in what Shepherd had learned was a shade called bird's egg blue: her favorite color. She looked so peaceful in sleep, the fan of her lashes lowered to pale cheeks, her lips gently parted, and of course, her little hand resting over their son. At the upcoming moment of his death, that was the image he would carry to the grave.

Taking a seat on the bed, he pulled Claire to his lap and cradled her. He held her in the same manner in which she would cradle their child once Collin was born. Shepherd did not miss the parallel, tracing his favorite parts of her face and trying to memorize this last peaceful moment.

There was no other time in Shepherd's life he could recall a handful of minutes as being so precious.

Time in the Undercroft had dragged by, moved at the grating pace of skin slowly scraped over broken glass. There were days it had been almost unbearable, and it drove many prisoners mad within a few years.

Since Svana had guided him from that hell, time had taken on a quality of almost moving too fast. There was never enough of it, always so much to do, hours that needed to be dedicated to training, to planning.

All of that had changed the instant he'd seen Claire.

Time affected him differently in her presence. One soft look from her felt like an eternity—one of joy not tedium. She had breathed life into him, restoring whatever the Undercroft had claimed before Shepherd had even been the wiser he'd been deprived.

In that moment, holding her as she slowly woke from his gentle prodding, an hour was not enough.

Regret was not a sensation he was accustomed to, but as he held her on his lap and called for her to wake, to open her eyes so he might see them one last time, he intensely regretted a great many things.

"Look at me, little one." By the fourth or fifth time he called to her, her lashes parted and glassy green, his favorite shade of green, was there for him to smile at. “I need you to wake up just for a little while.”

Her pupils seemed to focus enough to express he had her attention as she fought the drugs and whispered his name. “Shepherd...”

“Little one,” Shepherd beckoned, “Listen closely. I have to send you away, and I cannot go with you now.” The man felt pressure building behind his eyes when the look of alarm widened hers. “There is a team prepared to escort you to your new home. I will do everything in my power to follow after you, if I can. In case I cannot, an Alpha, his name is Martin, was chosen by me to act as surrogate until our son is born. He is a good man. You will approve of him.”

“NO!”

“I am sorry.” Shepherd heard his voice crack for the first time in his life. His shoulders shook, breath difficult as he tried not to frighten the pleading woman.

Drops of fluid fell from him and landed on her when she grabbed the lapel of his jacket and pulled their faces closer together. “Shepherd,” Claire knew this was not a nightmare no matter how dreamlike the drugs made it feel. She struggled not to slur as she spoke to her grieving mate. “Whatever she has done to force you, just say no. Leave with me now. Chose me, chose your son... and wash your hands of this. It’s not too late.” She sobbed in earnest, kissing him as she begged. “Please.”

“I love you, little one, but I cannot leave. I have a duty—”

“To me!” Claire cried her arms circling his neck, holding onto him with all her strength. “To our son!”

Lips at her ear he tried to explain in a rushed whisper, “Even if I were to leave and abandon my men, I would be a labeled a traitor. Before our ships might even land, you would be slaughtered. You have no idea how powerful this army is, how far each member is willing to go. The only way I can make things right, is fight here so that you and Collin can live."

His armor was between them, dampening the purr he projected as loudly as he could. Even so, Claire kept pressing closer. Her mouth was on his mark, her tongue swiping up the salt of his sweat.

He knew what she wanted. He wanted it to.

Shepherd pulled off one of her boots, tugging her leg free from clothing so that his mate could climb to straddle him. She wrapping around his body as if she might actually possess the strength to reject his verdict and hold him there. As he caressed her bare buttocks, she reached between them to set his member free. Lowering to accept him, she begged him to stay with her, sliding her body down with no urging from his hands, until he was sheathed root to tip.

He told her he loved her so many times he lost count, brushing his lips over hers, feeling her clench as he rolled his hips up to meet her warm internal embrace. With desperation on both sides, far more wrapped up in the press of their lips, in the war of searching tongues and shared breath, than even the act of mating, each of them tried to communicate why things must be their way.

Shepherd's hands were buried in her hair. She never once stopped kissing his face, feeling the wetness on his cheek, unsure if it came from her or him. When she came, it seemed almost too soon, and Claire tried to fight it until he murmured, "Please."

Moaning his name against his lips, calling to her Alpha, climax rolled over her no matter the despair. "*Shepherd...*"

Shepherd held her tighter, his body shaking with the plea. "Please... just tell me once."

Even as the waves of pleasure filled her with warmth in her core, even as she felt sexual gratification, her voice broke, and with hitched breath, she met his eyes and sobbed, "You already know I love you."

His release came, paired with a man pulling in a breath as if it was his first. He looked at her with undying devotion, liquid iron eyes memorizing every last detail of her tender expression, of her heartbreak.

Through the entirety of the knot, Shepherd touched her as if she could not be real, kissing every part of her face. Petting, stroking, as if the memory of her flesh was something he could carry with him if he just caressed a little longer, lingered a little more.

The mating, the purrs, the worshipful touching, blended with the power drugs. Before he could leave her womb, his Claire had fallen back into the slumber of her drug-induced sedation. He embraced her so powerfully she would be bruised, so that when she woke up and he was dead, she would know he had been with her.

Aware time was short, he placed her folded portrait of him into her jacket's inner pocket, the back of the painting covered in a hastily scribbled note. Her clothing was righted, boot returned to her foot and laced. Then there was one final thing he told her, a thing he had never once said in his life to anyone else but her, not even to Svana. He told her again that he was so very sorry. And then he whispered the name Claire had chosen for their son. He called to Collin while palming the small sign of life and said the same to him.

With not even a minute to spare, Shepherd hoisted her up and carried her to the elevator where a hand-selected team waited to escort his mate and heir out of hell. Amongst his brothers stood the Alpha surrogate Jules had suggested weeks ago: Martin, a man who had stood outside his door for months on guard... a surrogate Shepherd had approved, though he hated doing it.

Handing her over to another man, even one as respected as the Follower standing before him, was almost impossible. Not killing that man when Shepherd's red eyes viewed Claire in his arms was even harder. Martin had read her dossier, he knew what to expect and what Shepherd's orders were in regards to how she must be treated—like a queen.

Looking the man dead in the eye, Shepherd snarled, all traces of softness gone, "She is going to be exceptionally difficult when she wakes. If she refuses food, force feed her if you have to. Do not allow her to harm herself in her temper. Should it reach a point where she is out of your control, and it will, explain to her that I told you to call her a little Napoleon. She will be shocked, she will cry, and then she will calm down."

The Follower nodded his understanding. "Yes, sir."

Shepherd cocked his head, signaling that they must close the door and make their way to the Citadel's launch pad.

As the elevator door rolled down between them, Shepherd caught it with one darting hand and leveled the full power of his intimidation on the surrogate, adding, "Under no circumstances are you ever to strike her."

"I understand, brother," Martin answered, stoic yet honored. There was even a spark of compassion in his eyes. "I will treat her as if she were my own."

Shepherd dropped the door and knew it was over. As he walked back to Command, he counted down the seconds like a madman. He knew exactly how long it would be to launch, the exact amount of time before Claire would be airborne.

She'd teased him for that skill time and again.

Back at Command Center, he felt the first building tremors of the launch, video confirmation showing eleven glowing ships lighting up the pre-dawn sky over the broken glass of Thólos Dome.

Stage one of operation Exodus had been a success, and even though the men left behind stood little chance of survival, they cheered for their brothers who thrived.

Shepherd sighed and refocused on the problem at hand, unaware Claire had never made it to the ships.

Svana had made certain of it.

# 11

Maryanne Cauley had everything she needed: generators, enough fuel to last her for years, food, water, clothing, medicine—everything a person might need to survive the apocalypse.

Tucked safely in her sanctuary, she could hear the wind howling like a freight train outside, and chose to ignore it. Huddling next to a heat source, she kept the lights off, so no other soul might realize she had power when they had none. There was no reason to peek out her window or unbolt her door, her COMscreen told the tale of what was going on outside. The Dome had been purposefully ruptured. The networks had gone wild, computer viruses plaguing every last corner.

She knew how to work around them.

The hacks were inexpert, yet so numerous that it took her some time to recognize that Shepherd's men were not responsible for the disaster. In fact, she could see that they had their hands full trying to clean up the communications mess.

One dangerous message continuously rolled across her screen:

*People of Thólos, the rebel forces are in possession of the virus. Storm the Citadel, destroy our enemy.*

Another series of blasts went off in the distance, small little pops that made Maryanne jump.

So, who the hell was attacking the Dome? Who else did she have to contend with?

That prick, Corday, had said the resistance was going to attack the Citadel. That made sense, even if it was pointless. Why bring down the glass encasement that kept them all alive instead?

This would lead to more than a coup. The entire city would panic, there would be riots.

Shepherd would be blamed. Whoever had done this wanted to start a war that no one could win.

Between the icy wind and the unmitigated violence, between the possibility Shepherd would release the virus, everyone would die.

Wrapping her arms around her body, her knees tucked under her chin, there was a strange internal stirring Maryanne wanted to ignore. A smattering of shame knocked about in her breast.

She knew what the panicking city did not. The only thing in store for those who rose up against Shepherd was a bloodbath.

Unless...

No. It was not possible, and she owed this city nothing. The only soul she gave two fucks about was Claire. Her friend had told her to hide. Maryanne was going to listen to her.

But, maybe she could just fiddle around, take down that message, and reopen the communications network. After that, she was done, no more. Screw Thólos.

It took time to unravel the mess, to outthink whoever was responsible for hijacking the networks, the more Maryanne disrupted their work, the more she understood what they were really doing.

It was fucking horrible, sloppy even, as if there was no concern for the consequences. For that reason alone, Maryanne continued to ghost her cyber-attack right against their gates. Sneaking behind their firewall, she found something she could not wrap her head around.

The rebels were the party responsible for ruining the Dome. It was their chatter back and forth that showed units spread all over the city working in unison to stir up riots. They were using the very civilians they claimed to be fighting for as human war fodder.

For all her flaws and selfishness, even Maryanne was disgusted.

Because she felt like a salty bitch, and because she could, Maryanne seized control of the networks completely and shut the whole fucking thing down. She might not be able to save the idiots of Thólos, she didn't even really want to, but she could offer an alternative.

She set up a new message to stream over and over.

*The only safe place is underground.*

Knowing what was down there, what was up here, Maryanne was not sure if she had offered mercy at all.

A NAUSEA INDUCING feeling of vertigo broke through Claire's stupor the instant a hard smack landed against her cheek. Blinking, confused at the circles of lime deposits she saw on an unfamiliar ceiling, she tried to touch her head and found her hands bound together, stretched above her body and fixed to something she could not pull away from. As she struggled, a beautiful face came into view—a beautiful face belonging to an incredibly evil woman.

Even with the drugs in her system, a feeling of terror brought ice to Claire's veins from one simple sight of those psychotic eyes looming over her again. Careful to keep her face blank, to not give the woman the pleasure of feeding off her fear, Claire nodded and said, "Hello again, Svana."

"Hello, pretty one." Svana gave a small, knowing smile, a facsimile of the smile that had played on her lips when her hands had circled Claire's throat months ago. "I see you've been studying Jules' art of expression."

Claire felt a chill creep over her skin, and it was not only brought on by fear. She was cold because all her clothing had been removed, and the cot Svana had put her on was bare of blankets. Instead, it was covered in blood stains and stank of foulness.

"I can't play with you for too long. You see I have plans to visit someone I am very much looking forward to seeing." A long fingernail traced lightly from the valley between Claire's breasts and down her belly, Svana insincerely admiring what was beneath her. "But the gods gave me this time with you, and I will not waste it. Martin, the others, did not even question when the elevator doors parted on the fourth floor. Why would they question their savior? I shot them so quickly, I am surprised there is not more blood on you… but, it won't take long before you are covered in it."

"You do realize you are giving me what I want?" Claire offered a challenging gaze, forcing her body not to tense when that nail scraped over her child. "I could not live without my mate anyway. It is fitting we die together."

Svana purred, lightly tracing a circle over Claire's mound. "Then I will allow you to thank me."

Claire spat full in her face.

The look of disbelief, the instant rage that someone would dare such a thing, was something Claire was only able to enjoy for a moment before Svana reached up to wipe the wetness from her cheek with her sleeve.

"You know what I have learned, little one?" Svana giggled under her breath, her tongue darting out to lick at the spittle nearest her lips. "It's to let the men always underestimate you. Let them think you are flawed, that you need them. Do you have any idea how many times I have stood in your room and watched him fuck you? Neither of you knowing I was near enough to touch. When your eyes were closed, when he buried his face in your neck, sometimes those fingers carding through your hair were mine."

Claire's mask cracked. It was impossible to keep the revulsion from her face. Feeling Svana chip away at the little courage she could manage, the Omega knew in that moment the exact type of wickedness Shepherd spoke of when he spoke of the true evil that had been cast in the Undercroft. It was all there, a conglomeration of vileness in the woman running her nail up and down the slit where Claire was still slippery from Shepherd's last ejaculation.

"It has been unpleasant, the way things have gone," Svana pouted, her mouth heading towards a cold tightened nipple. "But I have done Shepherd a favor in this. You are a whore, desecrated and as disgusting as this city—unworthy of a man like him. But like all men, he is weak." That single finger slipped easily inside Claire, no matter how her muscles clenched to deny her entry. "They all bow to this. Premier Callas, Shepherd, even my dead uncle. It's a pity I was not born Omega. I would have ruled the world ages ago."

Once the initial penetration had passed, Claire did not fight; she lay passive knowing Svana desired her resistance. Drugged as she was, she had no energy to fight, had extreme difficulty even focusing her eyes, and embraced the wave of chemical euphoria over the terror of what was taking place.

Swallowing back a shriek, unwilling to cringe when the hated woman lapped at her nipple, Claire lay still and fixated instead on her son's fluttering movement deep inside her. Everything else was shut off.

"Now," Stroking Claire's black hair affectionately, Svana smiled as if they were old friends, still pumping in and out of the Omega's body, "I won't be able to stay and watch. Far more important things than you require my attention."

With a lingering kiss on Claire's mouth, a little flick of the tongue forced between her lips, Svana pulled her fingers from Claire's body, licked them clean, and made her goodbye.

"I want you to know," Claire called to Svana's back before the woman exited the cell.

Svana turned, eager to hear the Omega beg, "Yes, dear?"

It was not even difficult to say, "I want you to know that I love him. That even after everything, I learned how to do it. And that is something you could never achieve."

Svana laughed as if the very concept were absurd. She stood a moment, taking in the view of her enemy bound and at her mercy, the tip of Svana's tongue licking over the edges of her teeth. One more chuckle, and she opened the barred door, leaving Claire naked and bound on a musty bed, while three men covered in Da'rin markings entered, smiling and eager.

Claire knew what was coming; a monster like Svana would require degradation and horror before death was achieved. Claire could smell the two putrefying corpses piled up in the cramped cell's corner, could see from the withered limbs and small frames that the poor women had been Omega.

Death was coming for her. Death was coming for her baby. And it was all there in the smiles of the Alpha outcasts who circled like sharks.

The instant the first one touched her, Claire knew she would not be able to hold back her screams for long.

BRIGADIER DANE HAD to fight her way through the mob clogging the tunnels. The streets were chaos, having made it hard enough to get close to nearest underground access point, but navigating underground through the confused throngs was almost impossible. Some of the city was wise; a portion of citizens chose not to engage in the war, but to retreat to the Undercroft, away from the bitter cold already leaching the life from the city.

Or they were just plain cowards.

The farther Dane moved underground, the more she believed the latter. From all directions, a cacophony of voices, of screams, wails, and outright shouting was so loud, was amplified so greatly by the tunnels, that Dane could palpably feel the tremors of their fear

She'd only stomached it for less than an hour. This place had once been crammed full of tens of thousands of castoffs. What would five years trapped in the Undercroft do to a mind? It would unhinge a person, that's what it would do.

She wanted out, but the only way out was up. Even with a COMscreen projecting the data cube's maps, often she'd have to guess when she found a newly carved out juncture. The ant farm Shepherd's men had carved was a maddening circle designed to trap the unwelcome. The paths made no sense. Every direction led her back to the same place.

That had to be why so many were screaming; they were lost.

Behind the heavily barred door she'd strained to force open, Brigadier Dane saw the first one. A man little more than bones, his body covered in the repulsive, telling marks of Da'rin. He rushed at her from the dark. Reaching for her weapon, she'd fired without thinking. It was not until after he'd collapsed, she realized her hand was shaking.

The Undercroft was getting to her.

The corpse lay crumpled, gripping a shiv, hardly a rag covering his body.

There were more of his kind, she found them around almost every turn. Most shrank from her, from the light of her screen. They cowered against the walls and wept, as if she had come only to cause them pain. Some tried to stalk her through the twists and turns. Fortunately for Dane, she had more bullets than they had life to spend.

These men were never supposed to be set free. Shepherd had left them here for a reason.

Saturated in the stink of human waste, of things far more rotten than any corpse aboveground, Dane plodded forward. She went North, always North. It took an hour to reach the gate she assumed must block this sector from the city center.

All that metal, all those gears and locks, someone had thrown them open.

Sniffing the air, Brigadier Dane hesitated. Something was not right. The citadel was on the other side of that door, of that she was certain, but the smell of Omega was here.

The sound of screams, the very horrible music she had been subjected to. Dane began to listen.

She heard a sobbed name buried in the noise. Someone was screaming for *Shepherd.*

CORDAY COULD HARDLY BELIEVE what he was a party to. The rebels had done enough damage that outcome of the battle aside, millions would die from exposure. Subsequently, just by coming to this place, he had betrayed the resistance. Everyone was doing harm to everyone else.

There was no *right* path. Not in Thólos.

It was so cold his fingers were losing feeling, the rebels around him buried under layers for warmth—because, unlike him, they had known what to prepare for.

It was as Brigadier Dane had said: Leslie had purposefully

concealed the details of her battle plans from the pair of puppets she used to distract Shepherd's men.

What else had she hidden? Was it as Shepherd's second-in-command claimed? Was she Svana?

Had she been the one who'd assaulted Claire all those months ago?

The seed of doubt had burst and blossomed. It was hard to admit, but Corday *believed* the Beta who'd invaded his house, and he hated himself for it.

He had helped the woman seize power. He had helped her plan, gathered items used to craft the very bombs that had shattered two segments of the Dome. She had used him, and he had come to where the rebels mustered, knowing Shepherd's second-in-command was still out there somewhere, watching him.

"Where is Leslie?" The words came in a rush, Corday pulling his body up the last segment of the ladder. The roof before them held ten men, Leslie's men, all standing atop their perch, watching the city devour itself.

"We were told to hold position." A man grizzled in appearance and unruffled by the situation said, "Lady Kantor will arrive once her mission is complete."

"What mission?"

Jaw covered with a red, bristled beard, the man turned his eyes to Corday, and said nothing.

His reply, it was something Dane would have barked. Mouth in a firm line, Corday chastised a man who'd only recently been recruited, "I will remind you of your rank in our forces. While you were warm and fed, protected in the Premier's Sector, I was running missions, risking my life so this day might come."

There was a brief instant the man's composure slipped. He stood abashed. "Her mission was classified. We don't know where she is.

All communications went down twenty minutes ago, so we wait. Chances are, she moved to another position."

As if it were his place to command, Corday pointed to the youngest in the group. "You, climb down and run to the team at sector G. If she is there, update us immediately."

"I am afraid that man already has his orders, Corday."

Corday rounded, looking for the source of Leslie Kantor's voice. She had snuck up right in the midst of their collective, not one of them having heard her crest the roof. "Leslie?"

She smiled to see him, remaining at a distance. "Our plan is advancing exactly as expected. Every rebel was prepped and knows their duty. The disruption of the communications network changes nothing."

His fingers were so close to the gun holstered at his hip. "Leslie, why didn't you tell me our men were going to blast holes in the Dome?"

From the absolute steadiness of her expression, it was obvious Leslie had been prepared for and unconcerned by the question. "The airstream surrounding the Citadel is a countermeasure in case Shepherd unleashes the virus before our bombs might cleanse it from existence."

The virus was airborne, heavy winds would only spread it faster. Her excuse was so lacking in substance, that Corday could not contain his feelings of despair. "Without protection from the elements, it will grow uninhabitable in the city. You've condemned our people to the Undercroft."

"Really, Corday... you can be so dramatic." Waving him off, Leslie marched to the edge of the roof, assuring the only way Corday might hear her continued explanation was to follow at her heels like a dog. "Yes, it will be difficult at first. Given the state of manufacturing and resources, projections show it will take four years to repair the damage. In the meantime, citizens unnecessary to the immediate reconstruction of the Dome will be *safe* underground. Those key to the effort of restoring our city will find sanctuary in the Premier's Sector."

Some would live in grandeur and luxury while others wasted away in the dark. "I see."

She hesitated, looked him in the eye. "This was the only way to ensure change. Sacrifice must come from all of us."

And what was she going to sacrifice?

He hated her in that moment. Even so, he nodded as if he understood. Staring down at the madness, Corday found that the number of angry citizens circling the Citadel had increased, compacting into a single waving mass working to reach the steps.

Followers were shooting at them like fish in a barrel.

They were dying for nothing, in fact they would all die should Leslie's bombs detonate. Cutting a glance back to the smirking woman at his side, he knew she saw his distrust. It seemed pointless to continue his charade. After all, he'd already condemned them all.

Corday's lip almost shook when he asked. "He told me your name is Svana. Is it true?"

The corners of her mouth curved up from smirk to smile. Impudent, she asked, the question coming out as absolute confirmation, "Who?"

Behind them a rough edged voice rang out. "It's time, Svana. Shepherd has sent me. He wishes to negotiate the terms of his surrender."

Like Leslie, he'd appeared with no sound.

No longer was Shepherd's minion dressed in the blacks of Followers. He looked like any other civilian. Or he would have, if he didn't have such a massive firearm resting in slack arms.

Turning her back to the carnage below, Leslie held up her hand, signaling to her men all was well. Once they had lowered their weapons, she offered a twisted greeting. "Jules, I expected you sooner. Hasn't this gone on long enough?"

Seeing him in the daylight, Corday found the Beta to be only a ghost of a person. There was something wrong with the way his eyes tracked their movement, a lifelessness to his face. When he spoke his voice was not only disinterested, it was dead. "It has."

"Fine." Leslie nodded, crossing her arms over her chest. "Kill these men, and let's make our way."

Before the word *kill* had crossed Svana's lips, the Beta acted. In a blur he'd shouldered his rifle and showered a spray of bullets on Leslie Kantor's bodyguards. As the untried rebels fell, only two had squeezed off return fire before their death—a single bullet embedding in the concrete at Jules' feet.

Lowering his weapon, he scowled at the woman, disgusted by the men's utter lack of skill when it came to actual combat. "You did not train them well."

Leslie ignored the taunt. Instead, her focus was on where Corday lay. The impact of a bullet had knocked him down, a growing bloodstain marking his thigh. Rattled breath twisted his groans. One hand to his wound, he scrambled to lift his weapon.

All it took was Leslie's foot atop his wrist to stop the pathetic attempted attack.

Reaching down to take Corday's gun for her own, she complained. "He's still alive."

Jules' answer was dry. "Shepherd desires that this one suffer."

"Poetic." Pointing his gun at his skull, the woman seemed to debate the benefits of letting Corday meet a cold, lonely death on the roof. Maybe it was the way he cursed her name over and over. Maybe it was because he had been her plaything for so long. Either way, she took a step back. "Fine. I will give Shepherd this one last concession."

On the edge of the roof, standing confident and free, she cut a glance at the Follower and explained her deeper thinking. "He forced my hand, you know. This wasn't how I wanted it to be. Shepherd made me do this. You understand that, Jules."

Jules stared down at the panting man, took a long look at his handiwork, and curled his lip. "I gave you your chance to shoot her. You hesitated."

The smile Svana wore, the self-assured cocky smirk, diminished to the point where her face was blank, chilling. "You would dare insult me now? Not one of you—"

Jules didn't acknowledge a word out of her mouth. Before she could make any grand speeches, he unloaded ten bullets into her chest.

Eyes bugging out of his head, Corday struggled to scoot out from under Svana's collapsing body. "What the fuck?"

Jules ignored the inconsequential Beta, choosing instead to tower over Svana's pretty bleeding corpse. "After some recent thought on the subject, I disagree with Shepherd. I don't believe we need you alive to take Greth Dome. We only need parts of you to bypass scans—a hand, some blood, maybe an eye. The rest of you is garbage that we will harvest at need. Enjoy your legacy."

Reaching down, he hoisted the woman across his shoulders, hesitated when her body brushed his face. He crinkled his nose in a deep sniff, and growled once the trace of fading scent registered. His face contorted and he looked as if an ocean of profanities were rising up to his tongue.

As quickly as the rage began, he shut it off.

Jules swallowed, and once again became an empty, hollow thing. Svana bleeding all over him, he glanced once to where Corday grew pale, slumped against the roof's retaining wall. The Enforcer was dismissed with one derisive glare before Jules climbed down from the roof with his prize.

He left Corday alive.

## 12

The grand doors of the Citadel wide open at his back, the city in shambles at his feet, Shepherd looked over his dying kingdom. Sun sinking over a broken wasteland, aging light stretched shadows atop the sea of Thólosen men and women desperately trying to reach their tormentor. His men had done well disrupting pathways by destroying bridges and hastily constructing barricades. The unwise who approached, had only one plausible path to his doorstep.

To his loyal Followers armed on the overlooking fragmented causeways, he ordered, "Fire at will."

A wave of gunfire erupted, an upsurge of enraged citizens falling under the stampede of their rabid neighbors. More protestors climbed over the growing hill of the dead—like locusts they kept swarming, hour after hour.

All Shepherd could do was clog the path, and keep the masses, and Svana's bombs as far from the Citadel as he could.

He had broken down the odds, added up all known variables. Soon those desperately trying to climb over the dead would be hungry and thirsty. If he were lucky, they would make it until nightfall, where violent winds barreling through the Dome might drive Thólosens to seek shelter in the Undercroft, as every COMscreen under the broken Dome suggested. But the colder it grew, the more arrived in mass to shout and throw things across the divide separating the Citadel from the city.

There was a greater unresolved issue beyond the insects gathering at his doorstep: Svana.

She was yet unaccounted for. The ships that had already launched would be stuck hovering out of range of their intended target until they had their key to Greth Dome in hand. His men, his mate, would be trapped out there just as he was trapped in here, if Jules failed to find her.

Until she was delivered, those same ships would not be able to return and gather the army waiting for freedom. Unless the transport ships returned soon, a second round of evacuations would be impossible.

There was no hope left for those deserted in Thólos. His men knew it.

Should Shepherd have the opportunity to lay eyes on Svana again, he would be hard pressed not to reach out and tear her limb from limb.

Claire had been right; he had created a monster in Svana just as she had harnessed the violence in him. As a team, they had been unstoppable. As adversaries... they knew one another so well, it was like fighting against one's shadow.

Moves and countermoves, and they were still at an impasse. She knew he would not unleash the virus so long as there was even a chance his men might survive. That's why she'd given it to him, a final taunt he'd been too foolish to recognize.

Even armed with the greatest weapon in history, he was powerless.

She held control, her absence aside.

He'd put her on that untouchable pedestal himself. In tormenting Thólos, he'd created for her the perfect fodder to fling at his wall. Svana knew what to look for in the hearts of men, and had used her experience to her ultimate advantage. Worse, she had done it right under his nose.

Jules, Claire, had both tried to warn him.

No matter the roaring ice of the wind, Shepherd stood like a beacon atop the steps of the Citadel and fought for the brothers who'd offered their devotion and the woman whom he loved with every fiber of his being.

He'd felt Claire's panic through the pair-bond for hours, and ached that he could not comfort what he knew must have been frightening for his mate. She was calling for him through their link so loudly that Shepherd was almost certain he could hear her voice caught in the shrieking gale. More than once it had stolen his focus, but he had persevered in his duty.

The hours defending the Citadel were hard fought, but they had survived the siege through almost one day.

Looking at the battle below, Shepherd knew his men would not make it one more. There were millions tearing at the barricades, hastily constructing rudimentary brigades to reach the Follower's sanctuary. Some had even begun attempting climbing the sides of the Citadel with ropes flung over anything that might hold the weight of a man.

There were too many.

His men were outnumbered, and though those who stood by him had superior weapons, the savages below with their kitchen knives and swinging pipes no longer seemed to care if they lived or died.

The herd was slowly breaking through the barricades, using the dead as shields as they crept closer by the minute.

There were not enough bullets, not enough men, to take them all down.

Sooner rather than later, it would all be over.

Shepherd took a deep breath and took his eyes away from the line of filthy citizens rushing his gates, turning his attention to Claire's sky. It was a beautiful sunset, a small flurry of snow falling lightly. His mate would have enjoyed such a glorious view. He would have enjoyed standing next to her while she looked at it.

It pained him greatly that she was so distraught. Longing to feel her comforted, he tried to send her love and reassurance through their bond, a thing he had done for hours.

Shepherd wanted to give her more. But he could not.

All he could do was punish the city for ruining their future and forcing him to leave his mate and child alone in the world. All he could do was take Svana from the city she wished to rule.

He would break any who made it up the steps with his bare hands, watch them bleed, and smile.

Then he would unleash the virus and die for Claire.

The grand doors of the Citadel wide open at his back, Thólos in shambles at his feet, Shepherd tensed at the sound of running feet behind him.

Breathless from running, a Follower rushed towards him. "Svana has been collected."

Shepherd almost closed his eyes when a wave of warm relief ran over his flesh. At last. "Report."

"She's dead. Jules dumped her body on the transport's gangway and told us to pack it on ice immediately. He took a med-kit from the ship, sir, and abandoned his post."

Shepherd had no words to match the look of incredulity that blazed in his eyes. "Where is he now?"

The Follower was grim, shaking his head. "Unaccounted for, sir."

Shepherd's lashes flared, the Alpha glaring. "How long before that ship can be in the air?"

"The engines are cycling now. Five minutes to launch."

They might not have five minutes if the rumbling Shepherd could feel vibrating from the Citadel's dirty marble floors was any indication. Too many raged outside. There was a finite number of bullets available, and it was only a matter of time before one of Svana's bombers crept near enough to detonate. If the building was brought down before the ship was airborne, everything would be lost. "Forgo system checks. Launch immediately."

The order was given just as the building lurched. Segments of the north ramparts began to crumble, one side of the Citadel folding in on itself. Another bomb detonated, Shepherd was thrown, a wall breaking his body's trajectory and breaking his bones.

HOURS HAD PASSED since it had begun, hours in which sedation that had been a blessing dulling her panic and pain began to fade. Now that Claire dimly recognized all that had been done, she was far beyond screaming.

She no longer remembered their faces, only told them apart by the way they made her body jerk when they raped her.

Hard and fast, he was the one inside her when her child began to die, when the real blood began to flow... and he had howled like a wolf as if the gush of red fluid easing his way inside her body had pleased him. Then there was short and twitchy, he was the one who rode her the most violently, clawing his nails into her skin, marking her with little bleeding puncture wounds shaped like crescent moons.

Half aware, reeling from another blow when she refused to part her lips for the filthy cock held to her face, Claire blinked gummily and heard it again—the Undercroft prisoners were screaming for her in the halls.

She'd thrown up three times, vomited all the semen they'd shot down her throat each time one of them fucked her mouth and forced her to swallow as she choked on the gushes. She was still lying in it, face down, and it was cold, and pink. Sometimes she cried for Shepherd, when she grew lucid enough to feel the pain. Mostly she just stared at the cell's only door, watching the feet of monsters shuffle by in their rags, terrified they would turn their attention on her and reach through the bars.

One swollen eye went wide when the third of the Alphas pulled her hair so hard her head was forced back. She heard him grunt savagely, knew him from the others by the way he liked to grope her when he rutted, and felt him knot amidst the bleeding wreckage of her body. There was no sound from her throat, only a strange echo that seemed to seep from a place far away.

"We agreed no knotting!" A growled complaint was flung at the man with his head thrown back, too busy moaning at the ceiling to pay any attention. "It was my turn next, and now you got the cunt stuck on you cock. Pull out!"

The only answer was a low phlegmy moan, the sound more animal than man. A sharp series of tugs shook the knotted pair, one of the men trying to yank the bastard away. It was useless, his knot was locked behind her pubic bone, but it woke Claire from her stupor, encouraged a shrill stab of horrific pain, and though it had been hours since she'd been able to manage it, Claire found another scream. The high-pitched shriek and the sobs that followed were wretched, a thing full of hopelessness and pain.

"Don't kill her yet, cocksucker. I want this piece to last longer than the last ones." It was the one who had laughed when her miscarriage began, the cruelest of her assailants who warned. "You'll just have to wait it out."

"What's that noise?" the man who had been trying to pry short-and-twitchy off let go, and moved to the door. "Get the bitch to stop screaming!"

But they couldn't, she screamed and screamed, no longer human, staring out through the bars as more of those tattered legs came into view, certain the Undercroft demons had come for her.

Claire's arms stretched until her joints began to burn, she fought the binding again when the monster outside paused and grabbed the cell door in an attempt to force it open. A ragged face appeared, but where she had been expecting lips pulled back to show sharp teeth, what looked back at her was outrageous fury and wide eyed concern.

It was just like Shepherd's story, the shadow ripped the bars straight out of the rock to come inside her cell. A demon had come to claim her for itself. The noise of her attackers' panic echoed off the walls. There were grunts and screaming. Like magic, the knot inside her shrunk, and the invading painful thing was pulled out. Another wave of blood gushed from her in its wake.

There was a roar of noise. A great beast stood over her. The rope was cut, gentle hands turned her over in the pool of vileness. She could hardly see, couldn't understand why she was being lifted from the bed.

The three men who had used her lay naked and blood smeared, sprawled on the floor where they'd fallen.

"My name is Brigadier Dane." The Enforcer touching her was female, her eyes determined and shaken as she covered Claire's nakedness with the Omega's discarded coat. "You're safe now, Miss O'Donnell."

# 13

There was so much blood, Claire clung to the woman with the soft eyes, the one who had come to save her from the pool of pain and take her out of that cage. She only had the jacket and her long hair to cover her, but once they were clear of the tunnels, the Enforcer tried to wipe her down with her own shirt, cleaning the wounds as best she could, while Claire leaned against the wall in a stupor and felt more of her insides slip out.

"They killed my son." That was all she could manage, confused and unsure where she was.

"You are miscarrying." The older woman nodded sympathetically. "Yes."

The sounds of a battle raged all through the city, and Claire dimly recognized what it must mean. A revolution had begun. That's why strangers were rushing by. That's why the woman had saved her.

It did not fill Claire with the rush it should have, there was too much pain for that. But somewhere past the shock she knew, though her life was over, at least a few would be redeemed.

Under the support of Brigadier Dane's arms, Claire tried to walk through the heaving crowds. Her savior was shouting over the mob, calling for a medic, a doctor, anyone who might staunch the Omega's wounds.

Claire was bleeding to death—no amount of makeshift bandages and encouraging words from a stranger would change that. Nothing would bring back the son that had been ripped out of her womb. All that was left was to die with her mate.

The instant the woman turned her back to dig though the nearest dwelling for some supplies, Claire found the strength to get up from where she had been placed. On the cusp of unconsciousness, her legs did not want to work, fresh blood was running down her thigh, but Claire forced herself out the door, shuffling through the streets, a trail of red drops speckling the ground behind her.

It was like moving through a dream, climbing upward towards the light. What remained of the Citadel was shockingly close, Svana having arranged her torture near the very place Claire had been forced to call home.

The war, the rebels, they were right in front of her, all around her. Gunfire, explosions, screams, but all she could feel was Shepherd. He'd been right there the whole time.

She walked as steady as she could, but tripped over the mangled body of one of Shepherd's Followers. The cracked marble steps, those same steps she'd walked up the day she met Shepherd, were only across one last barrier. She opened her eyes, realizing she had almost fallen asleep, and knew all she had to do was crawl through the field of corpses and pull herself up to where she felt her mate's great pain.

That was what gave her the strength to move again, to crawl forward even as the ground shook, and huge chunks of the Citadel began to fall off.

None of it mattered. There was only time for Shepherd.

Claire continued forward.

Her love was so close, and there were only a few more stairs to manage. Claire pulled herself up that last step, resting against the nearest pillar to catch her breath.

Her vision swam just as another corner of the Citadel began to crumble.

The great door was before her. Claire shuffled through blood and glass, finding her legs again, ignoring the way her bare feet felt each shard. And there he was, twenty meters, ten, five...

On his back, still as a corpse, Shepherd lay.

Half-dead, she went to him, saw his silver eyes find hers and fill with horror as he took in what she'd become. All her black hair was matted with blood and fluids, the corners of her mouth torn and crusted. There was so much damage, a river of fresh bright red trickling down her battered legs, smeared her thighs.

Falling to her knees at his side, she tried to speak his name, voice hoarse, to call out to the man bleeding and trembling as if trying to move. But he was badly hurt, blood seeping from under his charred armor.

There was a noise in his throat, those silver eyes trying to express love past the panic.

Pawing his face, seeing that her fingers were gnarled and swollen, Claire whimpered in grief as she tried to crawl over him. "Svana took our son from my body. She gave me to three monsters, Shepherd."

One large hand twitched, Claire knew he wanted to hold her, but could not. So she lifted it to rest on her hip, splayed over him, pressed to his side where his armor was black and burnt.

She sought comfort from a dying man who could hardly bend his fingers to grip her hip.

Whatever had damaged him, she did not have the power to see. Claire's fading attention found only the wet, silver eyes pleading with her as they grew dim, heard the wrongness of Shepherd's far too spaced apart breaths.

The last of her life drained from between her legs in a pool of crimson, Claire sagged, her ear above where his heart should have been beating.

Thólos earned its freedom, Shepherd's tyranny ended, and Brigadier Dane wrestled control of the resistance from the few surviving members of Leslie Kantor's rebel contingent.

With no one willing to share the true story behind the uprising, unfitting as it was, it was Dane who was lauded by the public as the hero who'd saved them all.

When a hasty election placed her in the lifetime appointed position as Premier, Corday kept his silence.

What Thólos needed was solidarity, focus. They also needed to come to terms with the fact that despite round the clock cleanup crews picking through the Citadel's rubble, the virus was still unaccounted for.

To survive the cold, the population moved underground, daylight hours barely warm enough to conduct repairs to the Dome's infrastructure and search for necessities.

What happened in the Undercroft, the life of the people forced down there, was not worth speaking of. It was no life at all.

Until the Dome was repaired, there was no other option.

In the months of toil underground, Corday wore the ring, never once slipping the golden band off. He'd developed a nervous habit where he twisted it so hard it bit into the webbing between his fingers. He wanted it to hurt. He would never let himself forget what she'd given, how she'd suffered... how he'd failed her.

Not after the way the masses portrayed Claire O'Donnell as a traitor, not after the government inquest and the amount of times he'd given testimony for the girl on the flyer.

To the public, verbally crucifying a dead Leslie Kantor as a traitor was not enough, confirmation Shepherd had been killed, insufficient. They wanted the culpability of the living. Who better than the dead terrorist's mate, the one found half-dead and draped lovingly over his body.

The Alpha's corpse had been confiscated, she'd been taken away, and each time Corday had fought his way into her sickroom to see her, Claire had been in a coma, surrounded by armed guards, savaged and only breathing by ventilator.

Standing as Premier, Dane extolled Claire's vital role in the resistance, advocating for the woman as much as she reasonably could without inviting riots. As the weeks carried on and survivors began to slowly recover, more stepped forward to speak for her. Strangers holding her flyer testified that she'd been their inspiration, claimed the Omega had offered her strength for the entire city.

That did not stop Premier Dane's soldiers from taking her away.

Dane refused to speak with him on the matter. It took Corday six months to find what they had done with her, petitioning any member of the hastily scraped together government who would listen, demanding to see his friend. He stirred up trouble until the Premier had to assure the torn public that Claire O'Donnell, war criminal, was not being mistreated.

But Corday was about to judge that with his own eyes.

The location of her imprisonment was classified, yet there Corday waited, Dane at his side in the only place under the Dome that was still warm. There were manicured lawns and stunning architecture, a quiet corner of the only functioning region above ground crafted into Claire's new prison.

It was a location Corday knew.

All this time, Dane had kept Claire in the Premier's Sector, out of the grime of the Undercroft, and hidden away where no one could touch her. And not only her, but many Omegas who would never survive the close, dirty quarters trapped with the masses underground.

The North Wing's barred doors were pulled open, and inside Corday saw a place of beauty. There were so many windows that light drenched everything, and though there were armed guards, they seemed employed to keep people out, not force them to stay. Everything was clean, the furniture rich, an Alpha doctor stood waiting to escort the Premier and her guest to the Omega.

The man in the white coat glanced suspiciously at the unwanted visitor.

To Corday, the entire thing was awkward, backward.

Her door was a heavy oak thing, carved and weighty on its hinges, the last barrier Corday would have to cross to get to her. Premier Dane unlocked the panel and pushed it in, the robust Alpha female moving before them to announce her arrival in a jovial voice, nothing at all like the tone in which she'd greeted Corday.

"Good afternoon, Miss O'Donnell. An old friend has come to see you."

And then there she was. Sitting in an upholstered chair, her face turned towards the nearest window, looking out at the surrounding greenery and nearby trees. But she did not move, not even a tick, when Corday stepped nearer.

He knelt at her side, looking over her body for some sign of mistreatment or damage. There was no bruising or sign of neglect, but it was clear from the glassy faraway stare in her eyes she was highly sedated, and that alone was very telling.

Taking her hand, Corday called to her. Green eyes shifted so slowly it seemed unnatural.

"What have you done to her?" Corday growled to Dane, refusing to look away before Claire might recognize him.

"Miss O'Donnell is recovering from severe trauma under the best possible care," Premier Dane replied, tone irritated.

Turning his head towards his old comrade, Corday leveled her with a disbelieving snarl, "She is drugged out of her mind. Afraid she was going to tell me something? What is going on here?"

The Beta's voice had risen louder and Claire seemed to wake, if only for a moment. Her little fingers toyed with his ring and she whispered, "This was my mother's."

Corday forced the anger from his face and gave her an encouraging purr. "Yes, Claire, it was."

"I gave it to Corday."

"You did." The Enforcer nodded.

It was as if she could not register the Beta in question was speaking, continuing as if talking to herself. "So he would not forget me. He saved Thólos."

Lightly taking her chin between his forefinger and thumb, Corday lifted her face so she might find his eyes. "I am Corday, Claire. I am here. I came to visit you."

The woman seemed as if she had no idea what was going on, leaning closer as if to share a secret. "I still hear him you know, purring in the room with me. Sometimes I feel him stroke my hair."

Corday fought not to draw back in disgust, not to let his eyes widen even fractionally. In a gentle voice he explained, squeezing her hand as he smiled, "Shepherd is dead, Claire. You don't have to be afraid of him anymore."

"I want to go outside."

It was the doctor lingering back by the door who spoke. "That can be arranged at once, Miss O'Donnell."

It seemed a small army of nurses appeared from nowhere, and the woman, the inmate, was granted exactly what she asked for. The French doors overlooking the private lawn were unlocked, a small patio table and chairs exposed. Yet the strangeness of the prison was apparent to Corday, the thickness of the glass, the fact the exterior doors were made of dense metal and not wood, that they had been painted white to seem inviting and not vault-like, didn't add up.

Claire was raised from her chair, the soft green of her dress settling around her legs. Her doctor took her into the sun. In the midst of the commotion of white coats and guards, Corday wandered about her room, the natural appearance of it, finding nothing clinical. He would have thought it was all a sham if not for the watercolors littering the blue walls.

Everything was images of Thólos, the horrors she'd seen, the Da'rin marked body of the tyrant in several of them. Between the finished paintings were dozens that were only a study of silver eyes in every possible expression. Corday was amazed they let her keep such things, all those stark images of Shepherd pinned to the wall as if he were lingering in the room. There was even a portrait of the man practically smiling, a thing Corday stood before, intently studying.

The paper was crinkled, you could see where it had been folded over itself. It was also bloodstained.

Corday reached up and plucked it from the wall, knowing it was a memento from the siege. He did not know what possessed him to turn it over, but he found a note scratched on the back as if written frantically by an author with scant time.

*Little one,*

*I know you understand why I am not with you, even though it may take some time for you to accept. Do not forget that I love you. I love you, Claire O'Donnell, and I know you will be a wonderful mother to our son. I would give my life a thousand times over to assure your security and wellbeing. Knowing how much you dislike when I tell you that I am doing this all for you, I am going to hazard your anger when you read this, and say it again anyway. Everything is for you, my love. Everything I must do.*

*Promise me that you will tell Collin daily that his father had pride in him, that I loved him.*

*I will meet death meditating on how I have adored you from the first moment I found your green eyes in the Citadel, redeemed. You were my redeemer. My sky.*

*Forever,*

*Shepherd*

"I would put that back immediately if I were you." There was a brisk agitated warning in Premier Dane's voice. Even her expression was hostile. "She would be very upset should she see you touching it."

Corday held it up, demanding gruffly, "What the fuck is this?"

It was Dane who took it from Corday's hands and returned the portrait to its prime position on the wall. Dane's eyes that lingered over a smaller painting of a little boy with black hair and silver eyes hanging beside it.

"I tried to warn you." The Premier put an arm around the young Enforcer's shoulder, less an offer of comfort and more a physical assurance he would follow her. "But you never listen. Come, she is waiting for you outside."

It was humid again, light rainfall scenting the air with the smell of earthy grass. Claire liked when the windows fogged. Everything smelled better for one, the room glowed, the white windowpanes translucent, heaven-like.

She liked to picture the room that way sometimes, as if all that moisture might form into a single massive wave to wash her clean. If she wasn't careful with those thoughts, sometimes they expanded into dark territory, the city being sucked down into the bottom of an ocean, decimated. The imaginings would be paired with intense anger, a racing heart, and loathing.

Deep down, Claire hated Thólos.

She would dream of it burning, feeling only relief as flames devoured her city, and wake up in tears. Every time it happened, the air would be rich with *his* purr until she was calm again, until she was back in control.

"You have not eaten your lunch, Miss O'Donnell."

Dipping her paintbrush in red, Claire answered without looking away from her work. "I'm not hungry."

Approaching slowly so Claire might not panic, Premier Dane said, "I thought you enjoyed the rain. Yet you are agitated and have not touched your last two meals. Therefore, I do believe now might be the time to discuss what you are afraid of."

Every morning six or seven pills, physical therapy, psychotherapy, group therapy with the other damaged Omegas who dwelled in the house. Then there were the endless injections. Life was always half in a fog, if you could even call what was inside her life. But there was one thing no amount of anti-depressants could alter—the very real fear of the inevitable.

"You have been recovering for eight months and still refuse to participate in group therapy, to share anything with any of your doctors or the staff." The woman lifted a small Chippendale chair from near the dining table and carried it over to where Claire sat at her easel. Sitting back, Dane looked at her painting. "Are you not drowning in the silence?"

Claire turned her face towards the woman, accustomed to her short-cropped silver hair and wire-rimmed glasses. "And what is it you want me to say? I told you, I don't know where the virus is."

"You have been given a dose of heat suppressant daily, but they cannot repress it forever. Estrous is coming, perhaps as soon as the morning, given your current temperature and disposition."

The Omega's lips formed into a line and anger found its way past mind dulling medication—as did a healthy dose of terror.

Premier Dane tried again. "I do believe it would be good for your recovery to engage in sexual activity."

"No."

She had a way with Claire, a skill even her psychiatrist lacked in gentle prompting. "An Alpha could be chosen for you. Or if you prefer, you can choose from any of the existing staff. Should they agree, of course."

"No."

"Your mate is dead, Miss O'Donnell. No matter the hallucinations or dreams. What you think you feel is not a pair-bond. It is only an echo you are afraid to let go of."

Green eyes went back to the painting of poppies and Claire flatly declined to engage. "Who says I feel anything?"

Moving to the edge of her seat, Premier Dane asked, "Do you not wish to move on in your life? To have children?"

"I had a child. He died."

"Your miscarriage was a terrible ordeal." Dane took her paint brush away and set it aside. "You were raped by three of the castoffs your mate had left lingering in the Undercroft. This went on for many hours and left you scarred physically and emotionally."

"Do you know when I woke up in this place," Claire began, sneering and bitter that there was no trace of the purr in the air. "One of the first things the doctor told me was that he had saved my reproductive organs, as if I should be overjoyed. Tell me, what the fuck is wrong with all of you?"

Dane nodded, her face serene. "You believe you should not have been resuscitated."

Claire said nothing.

"You were given a field blood transfusion. Did you know that?" Premier Dane tapped her knee with her finger, "A Follower bleeding out from many severe wounds gave you the last of his life instead of saving himself. He died next to you, assuring your heart would keep beating until help arrived."

Looking away, riding the wave of drug induced apathy, Claire did her best not to picture Jules, knowing it had to have been him and doubting herself all the same—the Beta would not have done such a foolish thing if they were all going to die in a matter of minutes from the virus. Yet, all in all, when had life really made sense anyway?

Scowling, realizing the Premier had been successful again in making her think of things, Claire let out a breath. "There will be no estrous. Inject me with whatever you have to."

"That is dangerous, Claire."

The use of her first name made the Omega's lips quirk and brought a small trace of amusement into the glassy gaze. "Is it Claire now?"

The older Alpha smiled warmly, like a mother, and leaned back. "I do believe we have reached that point in our association."

"I am not going to call you Martin."

A small frown came to the woman's face, her brows drawn down. "You know my name is Lucile Dane, Miss O'Donnell. Who is Martin?"

Out of nowhere Claire's lower lip began to tremble from the flash of memory. Eyes running over with tears at her slip naming the surrogate Shepherd had chosen for her, Claire whispered, "I want to be left alone now."

Dane stood and put a hand on her shoulder, staying with her and purring through the entirety of the Omega's meltdown, watching the woman press her face into her hands and sob as if the world was ending.

It was Corday's habit to surprise her with paper flowers he'd made himself during his infrequent free hours, pulling them from behind his back as if she did not know they were already there. The act was always matched with a charmingly boyish smile. And then brown eyes would take a few seconds to look her over for marks or signs of unspoken trouble.

Setting aside *The Art of War*, Claire left her seat at the window and went to greet her friend. "I am amazed you made it. I have been told there is a blizzard in the Dome."

"Yeah, well." He shrugged sheepishly. "It's only a little snow."

Corday had been furious when he arrived two months prior and had been turned away, told by men with machine guns that no one could see patient 142. He'd assumed the worst, and practically charged the North Wing's gates. Alpha guards had forced him off. Biting down on his temper, he had come back in the night, using the ventilation ducts to break in... and found the real reason he'd been denied entry.

She was in estrous, contained to enforce her desire for celibacy. He distanced himself immediately, already far too close to the scent of her slick. Claire had never known he was there, but Corday stayed nearby for the entire three days it took for her to come through the heat... because she was crying, and scared, and he could not bear to leave her.

Twice a day she was attended by her physician, vitals taken, the Omega injected with something she readily offered her arm for each time. The man never touched her inappropriately; he never responded to her scent. Considering Corday had always found Premier Dane to be an absolute shrew, he had to admit, the amount of care she'd guaranteed his friend seemed almost unbelievable.

"You have a grand piano in your room..." Corday gaped, seeing the hulking thing set up in the corner.

Claire chuckled. "Is that what those are called? I just thought it was a fancy new table." Setting her flowers aside, she moved to the bench and began to play a song that had been popular before the first Dome had been erected.

While she played, he looked over the wall to see what paintings had been removed and replaced. They never discussed it, Corday's appraisal, but he could read her life on that wall. It was one filled with Shepherd. Many of the most offensive paintings had vanished to be replaced with watercolors of flowers, what looked like the foam of a cappuccino, and a sea of silver eyes.

As always, the bloodstained portrait of the man held a position of honor.

"You know," Corday spoke over her music, "you're much more fun to hang out with when you're not drooling on yourself."

He heard her laugh and trill the keys in that comic riff old films added after shitty jokes.

It was one of her better days, so Corday chose to take the initiative and slide onto the bench next to her, pretending he didn't notice when she stiffened at the physical contact and swallowed nervously. When all he did was start to play chopsticks, she loosened up and laughed.

Shoulder to shoulder, they screwed around, banging on her pretty new instrument like misbehaving children until out of the blue, Claire froze. At first, it was as if she was trying to hide that her gaze was darting around to all the shadowed corners. Moments later, she put her hand on his to make him stop with the noise, and closed her eyes.

Scowling, Corday asked, "What are you—"

"Shhhhh," she hushed him, face serene, softly smiling. Over the next few seconds she seemed to melt, all her tension faded as she breathed slowly and kept her eyes closed.

Corday was angry. "He's not there, Claire."

Her dark lashes lifted and she peeked at the man at her side, a little sad, and very lonely. "Yes he is. He *is* there."

It was not the first time she had done this, and it was so fucking frustrating. How do you compete with a ghost?

"Shepherd is not there!" Corday climbed off the bench to glare down at her. "Do you hear me? Shepherd is dead. He was a monster. He hurt you! He hurt a lot of people! What you think you felt for him was forced by the pair-bond and the baby he drugged you to create. Pure manipulation. You didn't love him!"

Corday had figured out a long time ago that she'd need time, having sat in the hearings as the government officials pieced together what they had learned from inspecting her cell, her paintings underground, the nature of her rape. There was a reason so few Follower bodies were found. They had used the ancient transport ships docked atop the Citadel. They had abandoned Thólos... Shepherd had tried to get her out of the city. Even the letter on the wall made that clear. It was the only good thing he'd ever done for her, and Shepherd had failed at it. And in the fucked up half-drugged reality the doctors kept her in, his Claire could not see what was right before her, as if she had shifted the blame to that bitch Svana and didn't remember the truth of her history.

Fighting to control his temper, Corday put a hand on her shoulder and turned her to face him, purring as loud as he could to cut through whatever sound her mind was creating. "Claire, I am a living breathing man, and I do love you. I would never hurt you. And I am willing to wait for you to get your head together, but you have to open your eyes and accept facts."

A little suspicious, the Omega remained silent, her ears pricked as she listened to the Beta purr. Shepherd's was still louder, it was richer, and it was far more beautiful.

That night after Corday left, Claire lay in her bed in the dark and waited for the phantom hand to touch her hair. Sniffing into her pillow, she felt the throb of the link, the twist that came to warm her insides when she was lonely.

It had been almost a year, and though her body had healed, her spirit was adrift.

Corday was deluding himself; the Beta would never understand. Whatever future he had imagined could never exist. She would rather die than mate another man. And though it had never been officially said to her face, she knew there was no leaving the room and walled garden they kept her in... unless she submitted to another Alpha. This was her prison, why else would the guards walk the halls with assault rifles and every door be locked like a vault? Even her windows were inches thick glass, seemingly unbreakable, probably bulletproof.

She never talked about Shepherd. She never talked about Svana. And only once in those horrible group therapy sessions had she been able to speak about the rape. And she'd spoken, and spoken, and spoken until she was screaming and threw up all over the floor. They had kept her sedated for days afterward. Several times Premier Dane had come to speak with her about the event and Claire refused to even look at the woman. All the Omega had wanted was the noise that wasn't supposed to be there and the dreams that occasionally fought through the drugs where Shepherd held her in their nest, whispering that he loved her.

Though Claire knew it was only the rush of the wind against the side of the Dome, it was as if she could hear him, calling to her. And like she always did, she slipped her toes from the covers and left the warmth of her bed to look out the window, hoping that for once she might actually see the man waiting on the horizon.

The nightgown swished around her legs as she crept to the glass doors to look out at the blizzard on the other side of the Dome, and heard him again, louder.

She was done with this place and hollow echoes. If he was calling her to the storm, that's where she would go.

Claire had seen the code enough times to punch in the correct order of numbers until the mechanical hiss of the lock being thrown met her ears. She went outside, clambered to the highest point of the Dome she could reach, needing to stand in the wind, to hear *little one* once more.

The blasting cold on her face as she wandered through the ripping gale, climbing towards the source of that call, rushing through the driving snow, ignoring the sting of her feet.

He was there.

Claire could see him, blurry, standing like a mountain, the golden thread between them singing, chiming with each nearer step. All she had to do was climb over the side of the safety rail and take the hand he offered.

So she did.

Violent wind whipped her hair around, she ignored it. She ignored everything.

He was so close, and the glow of his eyes was full of pleasure to see her. It was so loud in the storm, like thunder and pounding of a beast's heart, but Claire smiled and never wavered in her purpose. Not even when the bitter cold waved around her and began to leach away her strength. So long as she could see those smiling eyes, the fact she was falling was meaningless. Because his arms were around her and the sharp needles of pain seemed to drain away until only black warmth remained.

# EPILOGUE

It was a small service, closed to the public and attended by less than six people. Nona French gave the eulogy, the homilies were lovely, and the people who actually cared about her, devastated.

It had been an absolute nightmare for Corday. He sat there, the Premier in the seat beside him, and glared at the empty coffin while he worked his jaw.

The date of Claire O'Donnell's death had been two weeks prior, but the fucking North Wing doctors would not release the body. He had screamed, railed, threatened to bring the wrath of god down if they did not hand her over. Yet they continued to claim that her plummet off the crossing had left the body in pieces, so they delivered ashes in place of a corpse.

Corday had absolutely lost it.

Omegas were supposed to return to the earth, the death ritual burial... Dane's bastards had desecrated her.

When word traveled between the wretches subsisting underground that the infamous Claire O'Donnell had killed herself, she was suddenly a saint in their eyes. It was sickening. Those same people had treated her name like a curse, had blamed her for their suffering after Thólos' liberation. Now the tragedy of her suicide opened their eyes?

People were disgusting.

On the dank walls underground, pictures of her were pasted everywhere Corday turned.

The Premier even called for a day of mourning, and Thólos had a fucking ten-minute moment of silence.

Corday had gone through her loss once when she'd disappeared from the Omega sanctuary. It was nothing to the pain he was in now. Everything had gone wrong; furthermore, the guilt was killing him.

Why had they not given him the body? Was the fall really so bad she was totally unrecognizable? Thinking back over the last year, obsessing over every last detail, Corday searched for the thread that would explain away his building feeling of foreboding.

How many times had he sat in the softly colored blue room with her when she had hardly been lucid enough to speak? Why were they constantly sedating her?

Claire had never complained about it... and he wondered if she'd had the mental capacity to understand the extent to which they controlled her. She was just one small Omega the Premier kept sequestered like a pampered pet.

Why had they not pulled the plug when she refused to breathe for weeks after she had been found in the Citadel?

And the doctors had been so possessive of not only her, but of the things Claire kept in her room... like she was some specimen, or experiment, and everyone wanted to see what she would do.

Corday began to have a sinking feeling whatever they had been pumping into her was not for her benefit, but for theirs. That was why they would not release her body—they wanted to poke around inside first, to take her apart.

Did they think she knew where the virus was? Had they been using pharmaceuticals to try and pry it out of her?

Corday had slunk around the building that imprisoned her enough times to know the North Wing was exactly what it claimed to be: a refuge for Omegas who could not protect themselves had they been forced to live with the masses in the Undercroft. So why had they kept him away? And then why had they suddenly given him carte blanche to visit her? The doctors were aware he was gently courting her. In hindsight it seemed almost as if they encouraged it, even the less than congenial Premier Dane.

He'd always assumed it had been beneficial to her recovery.

But that went back to the original question. If she was recovering, then why was she constantly sedated?

After the funeral, he returned underground. Sitting on a worn chair, tucked into the small stone grotto where he slept, Corday stared into space, distracted by the injustice of the situation.

Something was very wrong. Why did he feel like everyone, including Dane, was lying to him?

He waited until nightfall before sneaking into the Premier's Sector.

He cornered Dane alone in her office, and put a knife to her throat. "What did you do to her?"

Even as he threatened her life, the Alpha had looked somewhat impressed. "You saw for yourself, we were only trying to help Claire."

In the months he'd had access to the Omega, he'd been blinded by his own joy, had stopped asking questions and stirring up the people underground. He could see it now—that's why Dane had let him near her.

He let the blade dig in until a line of blood dripped along the sharp edge. "You've lied to me enough."

"You were the one who unleashed Svana on us, who pointed Shepherd's men at our resistance." Hissing, trying to pull her neck away from the blade, Premier Dane growled, "You cannot be trusted, Corday. Be glad that I let you live, allowed you to continue work as an Enforcer, and that no one knows what your part really was in the suffering of our people."

The words cut him deeper than his knife pricked her throat. "You know the circumstance, the reasons, for why I did what I did."

"Yes." Dane did not say more.

"I want to see pictures of Claire's body. I want proof she's dead."

Continuing to appear unperturbed by Corday's threat, Dane gestured to her desk's COMscreen. "Patient file 142."

Withdrawing the knife, Corday typed in the file name. There was a year's worth of gathered data on Claire: physician notes, photographs of her paintings, a log of her treatment. At the end of it all was a series of disturbing images. The face of the dark-hair corpse had been crushed on impact. It was just gone. Something had darkened her skin to grey, left it blotchy in the places where bone stuck out."

"It took us three days to find where she'd landed in the Lower Reaches. We don't even know how she got out of the North Wing. The only video we have is of her walking down the hallway, alone."

"Why does her skin look like that?"

"The heat of her body melted the sludge just enough that it encapsulated the corpse. Sewage leeched into her, there was some kind of chemical reaction."

Corday cut her a hateful look. "I know you, Dane."

A frown defined the wrinkles on her cheek. "I know you do."

It's what she wasn't saying, what she'd never say... because unlike him, Premier Dane knew how to keep her mouth shut.

Since the breech, it had been a hard two years for everyone under the Dome, perhaps even hardest for Dane. Now that she was Premier, she had the responsibility of every person above ground and below. Day in and day out she toiled with her cabinet, organizing repair crews, trying to figure out how to keep livestock and crops alive without sun. Her people were starving, several had gone mad.

It didn't matter that she was warm in the Premier's Dome. The weight of the world was grinding her down. Corday knew it, he didn't judge her for it, but he did hold her accountable for everything concerning Claire.

Dane offered him one small hint. "If I could have unhooked Claire from the ventilator, I would have done it. But, so long as the virus is still unaccounted for, it was not a safe risk to take for the people of Thólos."

Eyes narrowed, Corday stood totally confused. "What?"

"I did everything in my power to keep the Omega safe, well fed, and happy." She wasn't defensive, she wasn't explaining herself to Corday, Dane was merely stating facts.

As if the reason was suddenly obvious, Corday's eyes grew wide. Horrified, the man felt the yet unseen nightmare sink in.

There was only one reason a pragmatic woman like Dane would have done such a thing.

The reports were a lie. Shepherd had never died.

That's why Claire had heard him; that's why they sedated her... and every purr she had imagined had been real, sent from his side of the link to comfort his distressed mate as she recovered.

"Did she kill herself?"

Dane shook her head because the truth was not quite so easy.

"She left her room and wandered out into the storm... we found a body."

Heart in his throat, Corday demanded, "WAS IT HERS?"

The greying, exhausted woman only offered a whisper. "All tests were inconclusive. We don't know."

**Thank you for reading Reborn. Shepherd and Claire's story is far from over.**

**Craving More? Please enjoy an extended excerpt of STOLEN…**

## STOLEN

### *Alpha's Claim, Book Four*

Everything had been prepared, extraction flawless.

Huddled on his lap, her body enveloped by his coat, slept an Omega who was his. The risk of the leap into his arms she'd handled well; the way she'd slept once he had her, a sign she felt safe. Not once had his purr faltered, it projected powerfully, so Claire might continue her rest and Shepherd might take the time to examine his mate.

Her head cradled against his shoulder, he moved a light touch over her face. The bridge of her nose, last he'd seen had been badly broken. While she'd convalesced, doctors had set it, but a sharp eye could see the slight bump and hairline scar. Shepherd traced over the flaw, going next to circle the socket of her eye. That too had healed well, no permanent mark remaining from the orbital fracture, no impairment of vision.

She was in perfect physical health.

A small whimper in sleep, and Claire turned her face toward his chest. It was so like her to be fussy whenever he'd inspected her beauty in the past. Shepherd smirked at her unconscious protest, hugging her to him so he might deeply inhale his Omega's scent.

Across from where Shepherd fawned over his female, a woman read through pages of a chart, quick fingers flipping quietly. "Severe PTSD—improvement nominal. Her list of medications has altered since our last update. Claire O'Donnell is on a great deal of sedatives, some of which are highly addictive."

"She will be given whatever she needs," Shepherd, cautious to keep his voice low, answered the unwelcome interruption.

Dr. Osin looked up from the pages. "There is a list of twice daily opiate injections here, doses larger than what I would deem safe. Considering the cocktail of medications, I cannot foresee the side effects of abruptly ending this *treatment*. Inevitable withdrawal may make her very ill. She will have to be carefully monitored."

He didn't care what she may or may not be addicted to. His Claire probably didn't even know what poison they'd been pumping inside her. None of this was her fault.

The only one in the cargo ship who Shepherd found fault with at this moment was Dr. Osin. Shepherd glared, eyes threatening death, certain the woman's voice was disruptive to Claire's rest. "Leave us."

"As she is still fully medicated, I suggest you mate her the moment she wakes. It will be better to have it over with rather than something she ruminates over. Anticipate fear." The woman stood, spine ramrod as she exited the forward cabin of their transport to join the soldiers in the cockpit.

It had been over a year. Clinically mounting his mate in the cargo hold of a transport ship was not exactly the elegant treatment Claire deserved, but there was wisdom in Dr. Osin's suggestion. It was something Shepherd had already considered himself. And it needed to be done.

Transition would be easier if the bandage were ripped off, so to speak.

A quantity of blankets had been prepared, set in a quasi-nest in case she needed such a comfort. Once he laid her upon it, Shepherd woke her with the growl. Dazed, Claire groaned, half aware when her body automatically responded and slick flowed. The instant he parted the jacket covering her damp nightgown, her eyes went wide and the Omega fully awoke.

Her end of the link frayed, buzzing in panic when an Alpha

pressed her down to something soft and held her there under his weight.

"Shhhhhh," Shepherd cooed, trying hard to resonate properly for her so Claire would recognize that he was not going to hurt her. "Spread your legs for me, little one."

It was as Dr. Osin had claimed. Claire was frightened. "Shepherd?"

He placed a kiss on her lips, over her cheeks, moving his mouth to her ear. The Alpha growled again, louder, calling to her to remember what was theirs. More slick dripped, but Claire's breaths were shallow and uneven. Every part of her was tense.

Sex was not going to be pleasant for either of them.

Unzipping his trousers, Shepherd took his member in hand. He was still clothed when his thighs forced hers to open. It wasn't the romantic coupling she deserved, it couldn't be. He lined up. With the initial thrust, looking her right in the eyes, Shepherd found her almost as tight as the first time, and knew without estrous it was uncomfortable for her. For ages he did little more than slowly stretch her, pressing his cock deeper and waiting, stroking and petting, calling her beautiful while she trembled and endured it.

Shepherd knew the secret places of her body, teased and rolled the sensitive nerve bundle atop her sex, all the while speaking to her as one spoke to a frightened animal. It took time, but she grew pliant, the little Omega's pupils blown when she relaxed her pelvic floor and finally let him in.

Bottoming out, Shepherd groaned.

The noise excited her further. The Alpha withdrew, Omega hips followed. It was a gentle rocking, cautious, and only for her pleasure. But pumping into a willing body, feeling her cunt squeeze him so tight—remembering the look on her face as she climbed atop the causeway's safety rail to answer his call—Shepherd could not have loved her more in that moment. He kept her cocooned in his body, brought her to climax, calling out his own long needed release once the knot began to swell and his seed surged deep.

While they were joined, she touched his face as if he could not be real. "They told me you were dead. Why did you make me wait so long?"

He wasn't going to lie to her. "You needed to heal, little one."

Claire began to grow uncomfortable, the knot something she had not borne in ages. He had to catch her hip and hold her still so she wouldn't harm herself by trying to force out his girth with her squirming.

Staring fixedly at her face, Shepherd watched as sadness overtook her expression. Between the war and their separation, the last few years had been unbearable for her; they had changed her and taken from her.

"They wanted me to accept another Alpha."

Murder was written on Shepherd's face. Silver eyes smoldered, his hips snapped, and the knot was pressed even deeper. "You are mine. No other male will ever touch you."

His anger was reassuring. Shepherd's feeling on the matter absolute.

His Claire held on to it, on to every scrap of true emotion in her mate. "Are they going to come looking for me?"

"No one will look for you." Shepherd nuzzled her cheek, stubble lightly scraping over her skin. "And even if they tried, Thólos is an ocean away. You no longer need to worry over such things."

He knew his Claire didn't want to know the details about her city or people. She did not want to know what he'd done to retrieve her. She knew enough horrible things already.

Green eyes full of fear, wet with unshed tears, her voice broke. "I can't ever go back there."

Shepherd understood. The largeness of his palm cupped her

face. He wiped her cheeks as he had done a thousand times before… when she'd been his in the underground den… when he'd kept her safe. "Never."

Encased in the arms of her lost mate, warm, the purr pouring into her, Claire sobbed. "I can't do that again. I can't, Shepherd."

He could hardly bear the torrent of tormented feeling resonating from her end of the link, but he would. He would do it with devout resolution, because he deserved every ounce of pain her sorrow might stir in his breast. "Quiet down, little one. It's over now."

She looked so happy and so heartbroken at once. "I watched you die."

"No, Claire." The tortured look in his eyes was nothing to the sorrow she felt on his end of their link. "I watched you die." Damaged as he was, he'd been able to do nothing *but* watch. He'd watched Jules run toward them, watched his second-in-command administer CPR, the man bleeding from a wound to the torso. He'd laid there as Jules pulled tubing from the med kit hanging from his shoulder and hastily slapped together a direct blood transfusion, the Beta pumping her heart with his fist until he'd passed out.

When the resistance finally found the opportunity to storm into the crumbling Citadel, Claire wasn't breathing, Jules lay pale and unresponsive, and Shepherd… he had to watch as the Thólosen scum dragged his mate away.

If the building had not begun to crumble, they would have finished him. But the ground fiercely rocked, fissures cracking through the marble floors, and they left him there for dead to save themselves.

One or two had even laughed as Shepherd lifted his hand and tried to reach for Claire.

In that moment, he prayed her soul had fled to the Goddess, watching her flop over the shoulder of a man who had no right to touch her.

His vision blurred, death closing in.

*"Debris smashed into my roof, you fucking son of a bitch. Everything I'd prepared was ruined!"*

Bleary eyed, Shepherd had dared to turn his head, and saw his unlikely savior. Gods he hated her. He hated more that he passed out the instant she tried to move him.

The next time he woke, he lay wrapped in bandages, trapped on the last, stuttering transport ship out of Thólos. And Claire, she was parted from him, in a fortress on a ventilator.

All reports claimed she was too damaged, that she would not survive—just as his child had not survived. He had raged before the ragged remnants of his men, broken in that cargo hold. Lost in grief, three of them he had condemned to death for abandoning her and saving him. But he could not carry out his intended punishment. Shepherd had been too wounded to move.

Once alone, he'd wept like a child.

But day by day he could feel that Claire hadn't died, she was too stubborn by half—even if the people wanted her blood. While lying savaged in the Premier's Sector, Thólos, her Thólos, had made her into a villain. The very people she'd fought for spat her name as a curse.

Shepherd wanted to hate them, but he could find no room. His hate for Svana was too consuming.

That lying cunt's quick death at Jules' hands had been a mercy she did not deserve.

Reason returned when Shepherd had learned Claire took her first unassisted breath.

And now he had her back in his arms.

His anger at such a memory grew sharp. He knew Claire found the link too much to bear, made himself stop, made his mind blank, and focused only on her.

In a whisper, she confessed, “I don’t want to know what was done to get me here.”

“All you need to know is that I am taking you home.” Between them, the thread harmonized. Shepherd showed her love. He looked at her as if she were precious, the purr strong.

That was all she needed, that look forever. The knot felt less invasive, the ache in her body bearable. Where her legs shivered from the tension of spreading, she strove to relax them.

Shepherd saw the effort on her end, pleased she was trying. “Sleep, little one. Soon we will be comfortable in our den and our life will begin. You have no need to fear, you’ll see.”

Read **STOLEN** now!

# ADDISON CAIN

USA TODAY bestselling author and Amazon Top 25 bestselling author, Addison Cain's dark romance and smoldering paranormal suspense will leave you breathless.
Obsessed antiheroes, heroines who stand fierce, heart-wrenching forbidden love, and a hint of violence in a kiss awaits.

**For the most current list of exciting titles by Addison Cain, please visit her website: addisoncain.com**


facebook.com/AddisonlCain
bookbub.com/authors/addison-cain
goodreads.com/AddisonCain

## ALSO BY ADDISON CAIN

*Don't miss these exciting titles by Addison Cain!*

**Standalone:**

Swallow it Down

Strangeways

The Golden Line

**The Alpha's Claim Series:**

Born to be Bound

Born To Be Broken

Reborn

Stolen

Corrupted

**Wren's Song Series:**

Branded

Silenced

**The Irdesi Empire Series:**

Sigil

Sovereign

Que (coming soon)

**Cradle of Darkness Series:**

Catacombs

Cathedral

The Relic

**A Trick of the Light Duet:**

A Taste of Shine

A Shot in the Dark

**Historical Romance:**

Dark Side of the Sun

**Horror:**

The White Queen

Immaculate